MURDER
AT PEARL HARBOR

Mysteries in Time Series

A NOVEL BY

JIM WALKER

BROADMAN
& HOLMAN
PUBLISHERS

Nashville, Tennessee

Published by Broadman & Holman Publishers, Nashville, Tennessee

0-8054-2160-2

Dewey Decimal Classification: 813

Subject Heading: WORLD WAR, 1939–1945—HAWAII—PEARL
HARBOR—FICTION / PEARL HARBOR (HAWAII)—FICTION

Library of Congress Card Catalog Number: 00-029776

Published in association with the literary agency of Alive
Communications, Inc., 7680 Goddard Street, Suite 200,
Colorado Springs, CO 80920.

Library of Congress Cataloging-in-Publication Data

Walker, James, 1948–

Murder at Pearl Harbor / Jim Walker.

    p. cm.

    ISBN 0-8054-2160-2

    1. World War, 1939–1945—Hawaii—Pearl Harbor—Fiction. 2. Pearl

Harbor (Hawaii)—Fiction. I. Title. II.

    PS3573.A425334 M865 2000

    813'.54—dc21

00-029776

CIP

1 2 3 4 5 04 03 02 01 00

This book is dedicated to my agent and friend
Greg Johnson. He believes in me and works hard
to keep me writing.

MAIN CHARACTERS

Gwen *Williams*. Gwen is the daughter of missionaries to Japan. Gwen was born in Japan and speaks the language fluently. She is twenty-eight years old and a Ph.D. student in Far Eastern studies at Stanford University. She is currently a language specialist working for the Office of Naval Intelligence in San Francisco.

Aki Kawa. Aki is a woman of twenty-four, a graduate student from the University of Hawaii and a language specialist working for the Office of Naval Intelligence in Pearl Harbor.

Brian Picard. Brian is a lieutenant in the U. S. Navy. He commands a gunnery crew on the battleship *USS Arizona*. He is a graduate from the Naval Academy. Brian is Aki's sweetheart. His father is an admiral in the Navy on active duty.

Sam Diamond. Sam is a thirty-five-year-old reporter for the *Washington Post*. He is a graduate from Yale.

Duskov Popov. Duskov is a double agent from Serbia working for the British and German governments. Duskov Popov is a historical figure.

Pete Allen. Pete is a fifty-five-year-old captain in command of the Office of Naval Intelligence in San Francisco.

Takeo Yoshikawa. Takeo is an attaché working at the Japanese Embassy in Honolulu. He is a former ensign who served in the Japanese navy. Takeo Yoshikawa is a historical figure.

Mitch Krinkle. Mitch is the twenty-six-year-old playboy son of a powerful sugar baron.

Otto Kuen. Otto is a forty-three-year-old resident of Hawaii. He is a Nazi sympathizer and is involved in espionage for the German government. Otto Kuen is a historical figure.

Nick Lowry. Nick is a sergeant with the Honolulu Police Department, Homicide Division.

Yasuo Kawa. Yasuo is Aki's twenty-two-year-old brother. He works for the Krinkle Sugar Company.

Dai Kawa. Dai is Aki's seventy-eight-year-old grandmother.

Quon Eng. Quon is a Chinese radio operator on the British steamer *Nautique*.

Dick Morrow. Dick is a chief petty officer and the noncommissioned officer in charge of the Office of Naval Intelligence in Pearl Harbor.

Jeff Walsh. Jeff is the city editor for the *Washington Post*.

Jack Rorke. Jack is a lieutenant in the Navy. He is in charge of the defense room of the Office of Naval Intelligence in Pearl Harbor.

Hiroki Fujiyama. Hiroki is the twenty-five-year-old friend of Aki's brother, Yasuo. He is in sympathy with the Japanese conquests in the Pacific and works for the Krinkle Sugar Company.

Terry Gardner. Terry is a chief petty officer in Naval Intelligence.

Admiral James Picard. Admiral Picard is Brian's father. He is protective of his son's career and opposed to Brian's romantic involvement with Aki Kawa.

Admiral Husband Kimmel. Admiral Kimmel is the commander of the Pacific Fleet based in Pearl Harbor. Admiral Kimmel is a historical figure.

PART 1
THE GATHERING STORM

LISBON, PORTUGAL
AUGUST 16, 1941

CHAPTER 1

A large drop of black dye splashed into his water glass, spreading a greasy stain around the ice cubes and nudging up against the slice of lemon. Duskov blinked at it and, jerking the napkin from his lap, patted his forehead. He stared at the napkin. The blotch of black dye looked like a storm cloud. He could only hope he had stopped the flow of his hastily arranged disguise. The black shoe polish he had used that morning tended to melt in the hot sun. He had also applied mascara to his pencil-thin mustache, but even now he could feel beads of perspiration melting its dashing appearance.

His wide-lapeled, snow-white suit was crisply creased. The white was supposed to keep him cool. A bold blood-red tie set off the outfit.

Becoming an agent for a foreign power had promised wealth and some degree of excitement. Allowing himself to be turned into a double agent had almost seemed safe. One could play both ends and collect on either side. Now, however, he was having second thoughts. A man could as easily make two powerful enemies instead of just one. Given what he was carrying for the Germans today, he felt like a target in a shooting match. Fortunately what he had was nearly undetectable. It was hiding in plain sight.

He touched the wave of hair he had plastered over his brow, gently sweeping it back into place with his pudgy fingers. Then he wiped the tips of his fingers on the already smeared napkin. There was no way he could disguise the extra forty pounds he was carrying—his cheeks were puffed out, and his small dark eyes looked like two lumps of coal.

Flowering vines covered the patio of the elegant restaurant. Red and yellow tiles set off the white wrought-iron furniture. Large terracotta vases stood at attention with flowers and herbs giving the place a scent of spice mixed with perfume. The walls were whitewashed, and murals of the gentle seacoast were painted on them. Bobbing red fishing boats with fishermen tending their nets set the scene. It was peaceful and not at all like Duskov's stomach. The breeze from the ocean mixed with the aroma of the food to sharpen the appetite. Unfortunately, he had lost his.

Duskov snapped his finger, attracting the attention of the waiter in his white cutaway jacket. Having the man seat him on the patio had been a mistake. The restaurant's cool interior with its spinning overhead fans would have been a better choice.

As the waiter turned in his direction, Duskov noticed an additional set of eyes that had been attracted by his signal. A man in a brown suit and yellow tie was seated directly behind where the waiter had been standing. The man was tall and thin, and Duskov was certain he had seen him before.

The white-coated waiter took long strides and snapped his heels at the edge of the table. "Yes, sir. May I be of assistance to you, sir?"

Duskov blinked up through the bright sunlight filtering through the vines. "Just bring me the check, please."

"But you haven't ordered, sir."

Pushing his hand into his coat pocket, Duskov fished out a few shillings and laid them on the table. "Then this ought to cover your inconvenience."

Once again the waiter snapped his heels, a broad smile forming on his polished face. "Yes, sir." He dipped his head and bowed slightly.

Duskov got to his feet and rushed for the iron-grated doors. He stepped out onto the cobblestone street and made his way past a fishmonger who was barking at passersby from behind a cart.

Moving down the block, Duskov passed women chatting in a doorway. They both glanced up at him, and he flashed them a smile and doffed his cream-colored Panama hat as he strode by. He quickened his pace.

Glancing back, he spotted the man in the brown suit emerging from the restaurant. Whoever it was was after him. No doubt he was a tail.

Duskov dashed into an alley and broke into a run. He made his way past women who were hanging laundry between the buildings, hoping to catch the overhead sun. Duskov ducked his head and then lowered himself into a crouch, the wet sheets and clothing slapping his backside as he wound his way between them. If his tail hadn't seen him dart into the alley, the laundry would make good cover.

His shoes made a clopping sound on the stones. He picked up his feet, dancing over garbage and sliding over grease that had been discarded out the back door of the apartments.

The smell of rancid fish rose to fill his nostrils. He was certain the heat of the day only allowed the fishy grease to coat the stones even more. He spotted what must have been scores of cats lurking in the litter of barrels and broken-down crates. What was an assault to his senses was a delight to theirs.

He rounded a corner in the alley, breaking into a clear view of the busy street up ahead. He would find a taxi there and make his way to the plane. New York would be many hours away, and his belly would be empty, but just then it didn't seem so bad. Long flights always allowed him to collect his thoughts and contemplate his next move. The problem, of course, was that he really didn't know what his next move would be until the coded message he was carrying could be read.

Duskov slowed his pace. His heart was pounding, and the sweat poured off his back, winding its way along his spine and puddling where his belt held his belly to a rolling bounce. He took a deep breath.

Crates were piled high along the alley, empty with hollow black spaces that stared at him as he passed. Several alleys led into where he was walking, and he stepped cautiously, listening for the sound of running feet. He heard nothing, only the beating of his heart. The safety of the plane was close now, yet so far away.

When he made his way past a stack of crates, two hands reached out and took hold of him. Duskov spun, pushing his attacker against the crates and stumbling back into the wall. It was the fishmonger he had seen on the street. The man leaped toward him once again, wrapping his powerful arms around him.

"I got him. Back here. He's back here."

The man slid around Duskov with a viselike grip, pinning his arms to his side. Lifting him slightly off the pavement, the fishmonger dropped his head, laying his chin on Duskov's shoulder. Almost in a whisper he spoke. "Just be still. It will be over soon."

Raising his foot, Duskov drove his heel into the top of the man's shoe, sending a bolt of pain into his attacker and causing him to scream. Duskov swung his foot forward and sent the heel of his shoe backward into the man's shin, rocking him with an agonizing and sharp jar.

When the fishmonger loosened his grip, Duskov spun free.

He reached into his coat pocket and wrapped his fingers around a switchblade knife, springing out a four-inch blade with the touch of a button. Rushing across the alley with the force of a bull, Duskov jammed his forearm into the man's throat, driving him back against the building. Then he planted the tip of the knife under the man's rib cage and pushed hard. He could hear the rush of air and feel the man's breath.

The fishmonger's knees buckled, his widening eyes staring straight into Duskov's soul. "Why?" he asked. It was a breathy whisper.

Duskov turned and ran, leaving the knife in the man's chest. He didn't want to be caught with a murder weapon on him. He couldn't afford charges that would stick. He also didn't want to be anywhere nearby when the help the fishmonger had called for arrived. He had no doubt it would be the man in the brown suit, and no doubt he, too, would have help. They were determined to stop him at any cost. They obviously hadn't been content with just putting a tail on him. They wanted him surrounded. His only question now was whether he could find a taxi and get to his plane before the help arrived.

He glanced back as he neared the light of the open street. The fishmonger had slid to a sitting position on the cobblestones. But no one else was in the alley.

Duskov stepped into the street in front of an oncoming taxicab and put his hand up. The black car skidded to a halt.

Almost two hours later Duskov settled himself into the seat of the Pan Am clipper. He slid the seat forward and pulled his Panama hat down over his eyes. A mother and a small child occupied the seat in front of him. No doubt they were members of the diplomatic corps returning home. The child, a boy of three or four, only made Duskov pull his hat lower. If he didn't make eye contact with the child, there would be no reason to speak. Of course he would still have to hear the caterwauling of the youngster for almost a full day.

The stewardess made her way down the aisle, checking each passenger's ticket and taking orders for drinks. Duskov peeked at her from under his hat. She was shapely and appeared to be in her mid twenties. Dark black hair cascaded over her shoulders and down to the middle of her back. She would be a diversion during the flight. Perhaps it hadn't been wrong to dye his hair.

The flight appeared to be full, and it took her some time to stop, check the tickets, and note the drink selections. She scratched down the orders of the mother and child in front of him, Scotch on the rocks and an orange juice. He smiled. No doubt the woman would need to be rendered unconscious if she was going to have to put up with the child in this confined space

The stewardess stepped forward and smiled at him. It was a knowing smile, and Duskov wondered if she hadn't already spotted his hasty hair dye. "May I see your ticket, sir? I will need to take your order for drinks as well."

Duskov reached into his inside pocket and extracted his ticket. He handed it over to the woman. "I'll be having what the lady in front of me is having." He smiled. "I have a feeling we're both going to need it."

The stewardess looked over his ticket and wrote down the order. "Mr. Duskov Popov, Scotch on the rocks."

Suddenly Duskov's smile disappeared. Getting on the plane was the man in the brown suit he had seen in the restaurant. He evidently knew right where Duskov was going and had followed him aboard. He was tall and lanky with a mustache and chiseled chin. His dark eyes narrowed when he spotted Duskov.

NORTH PACIFIC
AUGUST 17, 1941

CHAPTER 2

The *Nautique* cautiously made her way from Petropavlovsk on the Kamchatka peninsula to the open waters of the North Pacific. Even in August the cold wind blowing out from Siberia could cut through the skin on the back of a man's neck. Lookouts braved the winds with binoculars trained on the white caps, doing their best to spot any periscopes that might be cutting along the surface. England was at war with Germany, and while the waters of the North Pacific were not considered particularly dangerous, every man aboard the *Nautique* knew their ship was an inviting target.

Louis Devries had been first mate on the *Nautique* for five years. It had seemed like a dead-end job before the war, but he had hopes that the hostilities would end that and make him the captain of his own vessel before the war was over. At age forty-one he was a thin man with thinner hair. He pulled the strands he had left over the top of his head and mashed them down with his hat. His uniform was wrinkled. The truth of the matter was that not only did it look like Louis had slept in it, but in fact he had.

He climbed down the stairs and made his way to the galley. A hot cup of tea would go very well just then. He needed something to cut the chill of the morning air. The corridor was dark. It was too bright to turn on the lights and too dark to give much credence to the notion that it was daylight outside. Given the time of year and how far north they were, he knew that most likely they would have twenty hours of daylight. It made it hard for a man to sleep, and he hadn't gotten much in the past two weeks.

The hallway emptied into a galley that had a row of portholes. They didn't offer much in the way of a view, but they did allow some natural light to brighten up an otherwise gray room in the gray belly of the ship.

Louis noticed Quon. The man was hunched over a stack of crossword puzzles that were spread out in front of him on a table. He was licking the tip of a dull pencil, trying his best to make sense of the English words. Quon was a whiz at languages, but mostly Chinese and Japanese. How the man could make any sense at all out of the gibberish of those languages Louis could never tell. But he did. The man was an excellent radio operator, even if he did seem lazy at times.

"Who's tending the store?" Louis asked.

Quon looked up and shrugged his shoulders. "I don't know. I just need me a break."

"You'd better get back at it. We might be picking up radio traffic from the States. We have to be in San Francisco a week from now. It would be nice to know if we're facing some weather."

Quon frowned and swept the pieces of paper together into a pile. Picking them up, he drummed the puzzles on the top of the table to form a neat stack. Quon was given to neatness, which was an unusual thing for a man his age. He was Chinese, born in San Francisco where he had signed on as a radio operator several years earlier. The pay for merchant vessels belonging to a nation at war was much better than the normal rate of pay, and Quon had always been motivated by money. He was also very good with the radio, quick and sharp. He got to his feet and tucked the stack of crossword puzzles under his arm. Picking up his cup, he downed what remained of his tea.

"You looking forward to getting back home?"

Quon grinned, showing a set of perfect teeth. "You betcha."

"I'll come check on you in a bit," Louis said. "I'd like to see if there are any signals you pick up—you know, find out what the news is."

Quon nodded and waddled off in the direction the corridor.

Over an hour later Louis was standing on the bridge, looking over the charts and trying to plot the best course for San Francisco. There were times in the North Pacific when the compass gave off imperfect readings, but he didn't imagine they were having too much trouble where they were now. He laid down his ruler and drew a thin line. Their course didn't concern him. The Germans rarely operated in these waters. There were too many richer target areas in the North Atlantic for the Nazis to waste a submarine in chasing down a ship like the *Nautique*. Then Louis remembered Quon. He put down his pencil and stepped out into the hallway. The radio room was next door, and he could hear music coming out of it, strange tropical music. Opening the door, he stepped inside.

Quon had his feet on the desk and was leaning back with a big smile on his face. The man seemed lost in another world, drifting off to a place where he didn't have to think about the cramped quarters of the *Nautique*.

"Doing some dreaming, are we?" Louis asked.

Quon grinned and dropped his feet to the floor. "That a station in Honolulu. It plays local music. Nice, huh?" He curled his lip when he said it. He then sat up straight in his chair and began to wave his hands back and forth like a hula dancer.

Louis reached over to the dial and turned it slightly, killing the music and following what had been a beautiful, dreamlike state by a series of squawks, squeals, and a blanket of static. Then a set of flash dots and dashes came over the speaker. He moved past the spot where the signals were being transmitted, but Quon reached out and grabbed his hand. "Wait. Hold on." Taking the knob, Quon edged the dial back into position to pick up the transmission.

"What is that?"

Quon grabbed his headset and clamped them to his ears. He leaned over the table and strained to listen to the signals. Taking out a pad of paper and twisting his face into a scowl, he began to furiously write down the words. "That strange."

"What is it?" Louis could tell by the expression on the man's face that he wasn't understanding everything that was being said. "Is it news?"

Quon shook his head. "No, it from Hawaii." He then looked up at Louis. Then he began a search of the papers on his desk. "I know what the weather is like in Hawaii." He shuffled through stacks of papers. "I got a report today."

"From Hawaii?"

Quon nodded. "It is Japanese, but it from Hawaii."

Louis watched Quon write down the message being sent. He was writing it down in Chinese characters, no doubt because it was faster to write in his native language. He gave an occasional glance to his desk while he wrote, probing and scrambling the piles of paper with his other hand. "I know it here."

Finally, he extracted it from a pile of yellow paper. He looked serious as he held it up to read. Then he frowned.

"What's the problem?"

"Weather report in Honolulu today say it warm with occasional afternoon trade winds."

"So?"

Quon twisted his face. "This Japanese radio message from Honolulu say, 'East wind, rain.' That not right."

"You sure it's coming from Hawaii? Maybe it's coming from Tokyo. After all, it is in Japanese."

Quon shook his head. "No, it from Hawaii all right. It being sent out by the American communication station in Honolulu. I pick up signals from there many times. Why would they be sending wrong weather reports in Japanese?"

"Good question. Maybe it's a code of some sort?"

Quon wrote the message down quickly. As Louis looked over his shoulder he could see line after line of Chinese characters. "Can you make out what they're saying?"

Quon shook his head. "No, it does not make sense to me. It might be in some kind of code."

"Bizarre, and coming from Hawaii?"

Quon nodded. "Yes, I have a friend who might know what it mean. I ask him when we get to San Francisco."

AUGUST 17, 1941

CHAPTER 3

T

he Pan Am clipper glided over New York harbor, its engines in a dull whine. For the first six hours of their flight the threat of German fighters had been on everyone's mind. British Spitfires had flown with them out of Gibraltar. The sight of the small English planes had been a comfort to the passengers. After that, the open ocean and an occasional ship had been the only thing to capture the eye.

Boats dotted the water below, and the Statue of Liberty held her torch out in the sultry August sky. Duskov had seen it all before. New York City was fast becoming home away from home. This would be his twenty-fifth time in the city since 1936. His passport was studded with stickers showing New York as his port of entry.

He couldn't relax, though, not with what he was carrying. He also found it hard to close his eyes with the brown-suited man on board the plane. At least the man was seated near the door in the front of the plane. He had seen him get up several times during the flight. The man looked to be in his mid thirties, with dark brown hair pulled straight back and parted down the middle. His mustache was well trimmed and sharply sloped to the corners of his mouth. The man glanced in Duskov's direction when returning to his seat. The man's eyes always made contact with his; he had the deep, penetrating look of a hunter on the prowl. It was plain to see his interest in Duskov hadn't changed.

Duskov took comfort in being in the tail section of the plane. The ride had been bumpy, and the child in front of him had given him no small amount of irritation, but his ordeal was almost over now. He would be in New York in a matter of minutes, and then he would catch a cab to the German embassy.

He was troubled by the prospect of this being his last trip to America, perhaps for some time to come. The United States had settled into an uneasy peace with the Axis, but that would change, and in the not-too-distant future. He knew that. It would make his job all the more difficult. There would be no more coming and going as a tourist.

The giant plane touched down on the water, skimming the surface and wagging its wings. The child seated in front of him squealed and bounced up and down in his seat. The boy's mother reached out a weary hand to steady him. Duskov would have felt sorry for her if he hadn't shared her fatigue so completely.

It took the big clipper some time to glide to the dock and secure itself to the waiting arms of the Pan Am ground crew. He watched the copilot walk back into the cabin and twist the wheel that released the inner door of the big plane.

Moments later the big door sprang open, releasing the air inside and filling the cabin with the hot, sticky air of the New York summer. His white suit would come in handy here.

Duskov shot to his feet and reached into the overhead bin for his Panama hat. He kept his eyes forward, waiting for the man in the brown suit to leave the plane. He could afford to be polite for just a while longer and wait for the woman in front of him to wrestle her child out the door. The two of them would give him some distance. He forced a smile onto his face as she stood up and looked in his direction.

One by one the passengers disembarked from the plane. Duskov waited patiently, thankful he had sent his bags from the hotel. They would be waiting for him; customs agents would already be poring through them before he even got to the terminal. Perhaps they would be satisfied and not ask him any questions. He hoped so.

He took his place at the end of the line and followed the woman with her child to the door. The bright sunlight streamed through the cabin door, bleaching his eyes with the hot New York sun. Drops of sweat were already forming around the brim of his hat. He could only hope his sweat wouldn't send a river of black dye down his face when customs officials questioned him. Even then he could only smile and shrug, trying to protect his playboy image.

A short time later he took his place in line, in front of customs. A man in a hot, sticky, blue uniform was checking passports. Several other men in dark suits and blue ties were watching the people as they filed through the line. Their look seemed to shout "police." Duskov reached into his coat pocket and handed over his passport. The man studied the photograph in the document and then looked at him.

The official was wearing a blue cap. He pushed it back, showing a balding head and a fringe of red and gray hair. "Duskov Popov?"

"Yes, that's correct."

"Your passport says you are from Serbia."

Duskov smiled. "Again, you are correct."

"And what is the nature of your business here in the United States?"

"I am on holiday. I'm a tourist."

The man studied the passport, turning the pages. "It would seem to me that you like our country. You seem to have taken quite a few holidays here."

"As a matter of fact, I do. It's my favorite place in the world, other than Serbia." Duskov smiled. "And as you know, all the war is in Europe. Your country is at peace."

The man studied him, as if trying to read his mind. "And you enjoy England and Germany too, along with other destinations."

Duskov chuckled. "Yes, I do. I'm thinking of opening up a tourist bureau. I might just spread some of this knowledge around. No sense in letting it go to waste now, is there?"

The official frowned, turned, and stepped over to the men in the suits. He flashed Duskov's passport at them.

One of the men in the blue suits glanced in his direction and then followed the customs official back to the table. He was wearing a crushed blue fedora hat. His long nose and thin lips set off a cleanly shaven face with a dimple in his chin. "Excuse me, sir. Would you please follow me?"

"Is there a problem?"

The man reached into his coat pocket and produced a brown badge holder. He flipped it open, showing a rather large and impressive gold shield. "I'm Special Agent Morton of the FBI. We would like to have a word with you."

Pointing at the customs official, he motioned toward a back room. "Bring the man's bags into the interrogation room so we can take a closer look."

Duskov followed the men into the back room and watched as they again started to go through his luggage.

"You say you are a tourist?"

"Yes. I hope to travel to the Hawaiian Islands from here. I understand they are very pretty this time of year."

"They're pretty any time of year."

One of the men going through Duskov's black leather briefcase held up a piece of paper. "I think we found it," he said.

"Found what?" Duskov asked. "All I have there are business papers and some personal effects."

Morton unbuttoned his jacket and put his hands on his hips. "I am afraid you're going to have to stay here with us, Mr. Popov, until my man can return from our lab. If you're right and those are simply business papers, then you have nothing to worry about. We'll just let you go on your way. It shouldn't take more than a few hours."

"A few hours! You can't be serious?"

"I'm afraid I am."

Duskov was worried. His papers contained signals from the German high command that he was supposed to take to the German Embassy in New York. They contained information and instructions about his trip to Hawaii. The use of microdots was new to the world of espionage. An entire page of written materials could be contained in a period at the end of a sentence. For Duskov, his instructions were written on the last period in a set of "tips for seeing America."

It was almost five hours later when the man Morton had sent with Duskov's briefcase returned. Duskov stifled a gasp when the man in the brown suit followed the agent into the room. The man walked straight up to him and introduced himself. "Mr. Popov, allow me to introduce myself. I am Lloyd Rose of His Majesty's Secret Service."

"British Intelligence?"

"MI6 actually."

"Then you know who I am."

Rose smiled, pushing his hands down into his pockets. "Yes, I know who you are. I know you've been working for the Germans and now for us. We tried to stop you from coming here when you were still in Lisbon because we knew what German intelligence was asking you to do."

Duskov watched as Morton picked up a phone after talking to the agent with the briefcase. He put his hands on his knees and leaned forward so that only Rose could hear his voice. "Then you know what I'm to do, and so do the Americans? I'm the only one who doesn't know?"

Rose folded his arms and stroked his chin. "That's about right. We would like you to follow through with your mission, however. There's no sense in letting the Germans believe that you've been compromised."

Duskov glanced at his gold Piaget watch. He patted his foot nervously. "Then you'd better get those men to release me. I'm already late. The people at the Embassy will be worried about what has happened to me. They'll think the worst, and there will be questions."

Rose looked around to where Morton was still talking on the phone. "You do have a point there."

Morton put down the phone and walked over to where Duskov and Rose were talking. He was forcing a smile. "I just spoke to the director, and you can go, Mr. Popov."

"I can go?"

"Yes, he said you were nothing more than a Balkan playboy. However, he has denied you permission to go to Hawaii."

"Why?"

"You'd have to take that up with Mr. Hoover. We'll put your bags back together and call you a taxi." With that, Morton turned and walked away.

Duskov and Rose exchanged glances. "And do you mind telling me what it is I'm supposed to know? What it is that you and everyone else in this room knows but me?"

Rose cleared his throat. "It seems the Germans are carrying out a request from their friends the Japanese. Your instructions were to go to Hawaii and get information on the navy's stronghold at Pearl Harbor."

"I see. I was told I would be going to the islands there, but I wasn't told why. And if I fail to do that, what will become of me?"

Rose glanced back at the American agents. "That would seem to be the question, Mr. Popov. If you'll allow me, I'll work on it. We wouldn't want Adolf and his henchmen to feel that they can't trust you, now would we?"

Duskov got to his feet. "No, we wouldn't." He started to step toward his bags but then turned around for a final word with Rose. "One thing more. What about that man in Lisbon, the man selling fish?"

Rose's face was cold and expressionless. "What you did there might actually help you with the Germans. He was one of our agents. Like I said, we were trying to stop you from coming here." He cleared his throat once again. "But now that you're here, we'll have to make the best of it, won't we?"

SAN FRANCISCO
AUGUST 26, 1941

CHAPTER 4

Gwen's office couldn't really be called an office. It was more like a warehouse with a small metal table serving as a desk, a goose-neck lamp, and a gray, government-issue filing cabinet. Her gray desk chair had stripes of black tape to keep the meager padding from spilling out. There were no windows, and the only door was uncomfortably close to her desk. There was hardly any room for personal effects, just a picture of her parents in their Japanese costumes and her little brother in a Giants baseball uniform. Overhead, a series of caged lights hung in rows, their bare bulbs glaring down on a wooden floor that Gwen was certain had last been polished before the Spanish-American War.

Gwen had left the door open to the dark hal!. There was very little traffic in the basement, and just the thought that her desk wasn't in the file room eased her mind. When she closed the door she heard sounds in the stacks that she imagined to be rats. She fully expected one to come bounding around the corner of the files like some Great Dane with bared teeth. The open door at least gave her the illusion of escape, and when she worked late at night, any illusion was a godsend.

Gwen Williams had been working in the Office of Naval Intelligence for two years while she was completing her Ph.D. in Far Eastern Languages at Stanford. The extra money allowed her to help with the support of her parents in their missionary work and to keep a cat in her small apartment on Telegraph Hill.

She did her best to keep up her masquerade as a member of the typing pool. It wasn't an official disguise, more of a matter of self-protection. Male naval officers had little understanding of a woman working with top secret information. Since men often acted like they had a monopoly on brains, they would have viewed a female doctoral candidate as a threat. She would come and go from the building, flashing her badge and making her way down the stairs to her lair among the musty files. It was there she could work in peace.

She also made it a point not to attract a man's attention, sticking to pleated skirts, plain sweaters, and loafers. She was far from plain, though, and she knew it. Her short, chestnut-brown hair tumbled around her face. Her high cheekbones, straight nose, and full lips had always caused her to present herself well at formal affairs. She was thought of as leggy.

She took no pleasure in her looks. Her upbringing in a missionary home in Japan had hit her with feminine modesty from both directions, parents who were moral to a fault and a culture that viewed woman as objects without souls and certainly without passion. She might be American on the outside, but she was most definitely Japanese on the inside. It often caused her to walk with her head down and her eyes on the floor.

Her gray eyes were penetrating, and she took effort to conceal them with glasses that she didn't need. They allowed her to be seen as a woman with brains and not just legs. Most men didn't even allow a woman to speak and dispel what notions they might have about her. Gwen had learned that where men were concerned, what they saw drowned out anything else they might have to think about.

Gwen had found little comfort in her attempts to be less than she was. At times she felt like a teenager who had spent the last ten years of her life frozen in a time capsule. She would stifle her rage in a mature and condescending Japanese manner, only to have it erupt when she least expected it. The American inside of her was coming of age much too late in life. It should have happened in high school, not while she was busy becoming Dr. Gwen Williams.

"Hey there, pretty lady."

Gwen didn't have to turn around to know who was at her door. Lieutenant Jack Hershey was a man full of self-importance. He was used to getting what he wanted, and for some time he had wanted her. She didn't kid herself, however. He didn't really want her. She was simply handy. She even suspected that he was married.

Gwen swung her chair around and pushed her glasses down the bridge of her nose, staring at the man. His hat was cocked back, showing a lock of blond hair across his forehead. It was a look he thought to be especially appealing to women, and his twinkling blue eyes showed it.

"To what do I owe the honor of your company today, Lieutenant?"

He reached into his inside pocket and produced two tickets. Holding them in front of his face, he grinned. "I have two tickets to the opera tonight."

Gwen reached out and took the tickets, smiling. "How thought-ful of you. My landlady would love to go with me."

"Well, no . . . er," he stammered. "I was thinking I'd go."

Gwen blinked her eyes innocently. "With my landlady? Sure." It did her heart good to toy with the man. There was some power to be found in her sexuality, a power she had never used. Jack Hershey and men like him provided her with the best target possible to try out her new wings. "She'd enjoy that very much, and you'd just love her. Since she's gotten her new set of teeth you can even understand her."

A dull glow of red formed in Hershey's cheeks. "No, Gwen, you and me. From what I hear, women can't refuse an opera." He smiled. "I'd wear my dress uniform for you."

She swung her chair back around and opened the folder on her desk. "I'm afraid I'm going to be busy tonight, working. You should be too."

Hershey stepped into the room and over to her desk. He put his hand on the back of her chair and turned her around to face him. "You know the old saying, all work and no play makes Jack a dull boy. Somehow, I always had the feeling that was written just for me. And I've taken the advice very seriously."

"I'm sure you have, all too seriously." Gwen shrugged. "Then feel free to take my landlady. She's a widow and very available." Gwen flipped through the file on her desk. "As you can see, though, I have a full plate of office work to do and schoolwork to do when I'm fin-ished with this."

He reached out and took her glasses, lifting them off her face. "There now, that's better. No use trying to hide behind that schoolgirl look. I know better. I saw you at the Navy Ball last year, remember?"

"How could I forget?" Gwen couldn't forget the impression she had made at the ball with a new red dress. It showed off her shape and caused men who had ignored her to stop and ask her name. There was something about it that sent a shiver of power up and down her spine.

"I remember. You looked at me as if I were cheap, but that's nothing new for you I'm sure. I sort of have the impression that cheap women are your forte, Lieutenant."

He held up the tickets. "These things aren't cheap."

"And neither am I. Besides, wouldn't your wife be upset?"

"My wife? Who said anything about me being married?"

Gwen grabbed her glasses and pulled them out of his hand.

"You think you know me? Maybe that's the way it is with all you college girls. You get a little education and it goes to your head. You start to think you know all about life and men too."

Gwen wiped her glasses with a silk handkerchief and slid them back on to her face with both hands. "And if you knew anything about women, you'd know I'm not a college girl. I'm a woman, and education is supposed to go to my head. That's where it belongs."

"You don't know what you're missing, Miss High-and-Mighty."

Gwen turned back to the papers on her desk. "A pleasure I plan to continue to enjoy." She wagged her hand in his direction as if she were sending an alley cat on his way without so much as feeding him a morsel. "Now find your hole, Lieutenant, and crawl back into it."

She glanced up moments later and breathed a sign of relief at the sight of the empty doorway. Questioning the integrity of men was something that had been strange to her at first. It went against everything she had ever known, but it was one of the things she had learned quickly since coming back to the States six years ago with her parents. She was a quick study, and if there was one thing she had learned since starting her work for the navy, it was that many men viewed a uniform as some special mark of masculine virility. For some, the bars of an officer were a means of obtaining the respect they couldn't earn in any other way.

Giggles from the stacks of files behind her drew her to full attention. Someone had been listening. "All right, come out of there."

A small man in a rumpled suit stepped out from behind the stacks of files. She knew him right away. It was Sammy Lee. The man was Chinese but very loyal to the work of the navy.

"I sorry, Miss Williams. I back there working, and when I come to go, he was there. I could not step out and break up your talk."

"I wish you had. I needed some interruption."

He was carrying a file folder and took several steps closer to her. "I did want to talk to you, though." He held out the folder. "About this."

"What is that?"

"It Japanese transmission we picked up from Honolulu a week ago, or I should say was picked up for us by an English steamer in the Pacific, the *Nautique*. The radio operator is Chinese, and the characters are all in Chinese. He speak Japanese too. He and me is good friends."

"You know this man?"

Sammy nodded. "Yes, I know him. He give this to me yesterday when he come in cause he's my friend. We going out tonight. He ain't been in town for four months."

"Hmm." Gwen stroked her chin. "Have you translated it?"

"I try, but me not get very far. I thought maybe you could help. It seem to be a Japanese weather report, but there other things here too. And you have the code books."

"You say it came from Honolulu?"

"That what he said, from an official communication company on the island. But it come from the Japanese."

"You know this is illegal, don't you?"

Sammy grinned. "It's only against the law if we listen to the signals. It not against the law if we hold a piece of paper with the signals on them."

Gwen narrowed her eyes and shot him a sly smile. "You are a cunning sort, aren't you?"

"I am Chinese. I am supposed to be cunning."

Gwen knew full well that most Japanese was written in Chinese characters called *kanji* but that it could also be written in a phonetic syllabary called *kana*. The *romanji* form of *kana* employs Roman letters but has its own telegraphic code to represent the fifty-one symbols in the system. Most of the Japanese radio traffic was in *kana* code, but the numerals were in the international telegraphic code. It was necessary for an operator to be adept at both *kana* telegraphic code and the international telegraphic code in order to copy it. The rendering of a foreign place name in Japanese *kana* generally resulted in weird spelling and pronunciation, incomprehensible to anyone who did not speak Japanese fluently. If the steamer had a Chinese telegraphic operator who could speak Japanese, then that represented a very unusual combination to be found on the high seas, something the Japanese would never have suspected.

"Here, let me see it. Pull up a chair and we can work on it together."

Sammy pulled up a chair, and the two of them spent the better part of the next two hours working on the Japanese transmissions. Gwen then pulled out her copy of the latest Japanese codes, breaking the message down. She pushed back her chair and took off her glasses. "Do you know what we're looking at here?"

"Maybe a Japanese navy base?"

"No, these names used—states in America—are not code words. They are the names of American battleships anchored in Pearl Harbor."

Sammy blinked at her, almost refusing to understand the meaning of what she was trying to convey.

"The Japanese high command is receiving messages on the location of the American fleet at anchor, messages being sent from the island of Oahu, messages sent by a spy."

"You don't think . . ."

"It's not my job to think." She leaned closer to him. "You forget, I'm a woman. We're not supposed to think. We're here to take notes and make coffee."

"Well, you should take these transmissions to the Captain. Let him think, then."

CHAPTER 5

Captain Pete Allen was a man of fifty-five, called back into the navy because no one else would take the job. He had left his retirement and the work of engineering he loved so much to take this spot with the navy.

Gwen thought he looked like a kindly grandfather in spite of the fact that he could explode when facing incompetence. He didn't suffer fools well. The man's face looked like a worn catcher's mitt with oversize ears. Sandy gray hair, which he carefully pulled over the top, trimmed his balding head. When he smiled, it was as if the Grand Canyon had opened up all over his face.

Gwen slipped into the briefing room and took a seat in the rear. Allen noticed her at once and nodded but said nothing. The room was gray, like the rest of the building. It had large windows with blinds open to the typing pool outside. Rows of red leather chairs were set in straight lines and filled to capacity with uniformed officers and civilian workers.

Allen paced back and forth and cleared his throat. "Men." Allen corrected himself. "And ladies." His eyes twinkled as he glanced at Gwen. "You obviously know what we're facing here. Feelings are running high all over the Intelligence community. Many of you believe your hands have been tied behind your backs. Congress has made it illegal to eavesdrop on communication, largely due to the annoyance of the telephone party line." A sneer formed on his lips as he said the words.

"It might easily be said that everything we're doing is now against the law. The public doesn't care one whit about foreign powers or some attack that might be about to take place. They just want to be sure small-town gossip stays among their own circle of friends."

He lifted the lid of a cedar box on the table in front of him and pulled out a large dark cigar. Biting off the end, he leaned over and spit it into the wastebasket. He slid open a large red-white-and-blue box of Diamond safety matches, his stubby fingers tumbling over them until he found one to his liking. Striking it on the side of the box, he touched the flame to the end of his cigar, puffing the cigar to life. A smile formed on his face. He took the cigar out of his mouth and grinned at it. "The Cubans are good for something."

He waved his hand at the room. "Smoke 'em if you got 'em."

Gwen watched as almost the entire room of men fished in their pockets for cigarettes. She knew within minutes the place would be an indoor cloud of stifling smoke. It made her long for the cold, lonely room in the basement she called home.

Allen continued his pacing as he puffed on his cigar. "Perhaps for some of you this is a history lesson you don't need, but there are others who need to know just what we're up against here. In 1929 Secretary of State Stimson condemned cryptanalysis as unethical. Right now the State Department has no service for the reading of potential enemy communication of its own. With Japan brandishing its army and navy in the Pacific and sending its envoys to Washington to negotiate a peace, the State Department's only link to the truth comes through what they can milk out of us. Because of the vacuum, diplomatic codes and information have become our highest priority. To make matters worse, Henry Stimson is now the Secretary of War. His finger is now on the only means of obtaining information, and its something he's already gone on record as opposing."

One of the officers in the front of the room spoke up. "Sir, are you telling us we could be out of business?"

Allen puffed out a large cloud of smoke. "That's exactly what I'm telling you. The jugheads in Washington seem determined to be blind. I want to make sure you say nothing about what we're doing here with regard to the interception of foreign radio traffic. You don't tell your wife or kids. You don't tell the cab driver who takes you to the movies. You don't tell the bartender who pours you a drink."

He leaned forward on the table, his hands wrapped around the edge. "In short, say nothing to no one. You do, and you could find yourselves rocking across the water in a tin can cleaning your popguns for an enemy we can't listen to. Have I made myself understood?"

Gwen watched as everyone in the room nodded.

Allen waved at the assembly. "All right then, get back to work. Just keep your mouths shut."

The entire room got to their feet and made their way past Gwen and out the door.

Gwen walked to the front of the room and stepped up to the captain as he was busy stuffing papers into his black leather briefcase. She noticed that Lieutenant Hershey had also chosen to remain behind. She only hoped it wasn't because of her.

Allen looked up at her. "Something bothering you, Miss Williams?"

Gwen pushed her glasses up her nose and rocked back and forth on the balls of her feet. She clamped down harder on the manila folder under her arm. "I have something here you should see, Captain. For your eyes only."

"I'm all ears." He grinned slightly. "But you can see that."

"Captain—" Gwen shot a glance at Hershey and then out the large windows—"I think this would be better discussed in private. Given what you've just talked about, it's not only a matter of secrecy, but it could be illegal too."

Hershey snickered. "The missionary lady doing something illegal. What's next?"

"All right. We'll go into my office. Hershey, you can come too. This might involve you."

Gwen didn't much like the idea of Jack Hershey listening to her information, but she sheepishly followed the two men into Allen's office next to the briefing room. The captain circled his worn pine desk and took a seat in a swivel chair. He kicked open a file drawer and sticking his feet into it, leaned back, still puffing on his cigar.

The room was the same shade of constant gray but with personal pictures and a purple banner marked WASHINGTON HUSKIES hanging on the wall. Several photos of football players, and one of Allen in his leather helmet, made up the collage of mementos hanging on the wall behind his desk.

He waved the cigar at her. "All right, Miss Williams, the floor is all yours."

Gwen opened the folder under her arm and laid it down in front of him. "Sir, we intercepted a Japanese message in code that contains some disturbing language. It could be very important, and I thought you should see it right away. It's not diplomatic, though. I believe it's of military importance."

Allen dropped his feet to the floor and leaned over his desk to read the message. His eyes widened as he read it. "Where did you come by this, Miss Williams?"

"From an English freighter in the Pacific. Technically we didn't intercept this over the air, so I suppose that means they can't put us in jail."

Allen stared at her, blinking his eyes. "The Brits passed this on to you?"

Hershey stepped around behind the Captain and read the message over his shoulder.

"No, sir. One of our men, Sammy Lee, got it from a friend who was the radio operator on the ship. I helped him translate it this morning. Then I decoded it."

"You sure this is accurate?" Hershey asked.

Gwen's eyes bored into the Lieutenant. "The Japanese language is inscrutable. Few Americans can read it, and only a dozen or so naval officers have any knowledge of the special idioms and ideographs particular to naval operations. Even after a Japanese naval message has been decoded, it often remains a mystery wrapped in a riddle. But this is my native tongue. I'm sure of what it says and what it means."

Allen looked up at Hershey. "Satisfied, Lieutenant? We've got us one bright lady working here."

He inched closer to the edge of the desk, turning his gaze to Gwen. "You know anyone at the British Embassy? I know how you government women can keep close touch with your counterparts."

Gwen nodded. "Yes, sir, I do."

"Would she know anything about this?"

"No doubt she would, if there's anything to know. She works for the military attaché."

"Fine, then why don't you plan on dinner with her." He motioned with his cigar. "Make nice talk and find out if she's heard anything about what the Japanese are up to. I can't help but feel that our cousins over the pond know much more than they're telling us. It's their war right now, and they'd give anything to make it our war as well." A frown creased his face. "Also, we seem to have a president who would like us to come to John Bull's rescue. Being caught asleep at the switch is one thing, but having someone put knockout drops in your drink and rock you to sleep is another. I don't want that on my watch."

"This woman's a language specialist," Hershey said. "She's no cloak-and-dagger type."

Allen once again looked up at him. "Are you questioning my judgment, Lieutenant?"

"No, sir."

"Good. For a moment it sounded like that was exactly what you were doing. Miss Williams knows all the particulars of how we came upon this communication and, so far as I can tell, she's the only one who could possibly decipher it." He glanced at her. "Besides, she's bright. She can recognize water that's over her head when she sees it. You can do that, can't you, Miss Williams?"

"Yes, sir. I won't do anything that's unnecessary."

Allen passed the folder back over to her. "See that you don't. What you have here could be the trigger to a shooting war. Plenty of people would pay dearly to make sure we can't confirm it."

It was evening before Gwen left the building and headed for Chinatown. She had called Jill Ashley, whom she had met two years before at an Embassy ball. Jill was somewhat of a hardened woman of the world with long black hair and a chiseled look. She had taken to Gwen right away, offering advice on how to work with men and meeting with her on numerous occasions just to go shopping. Gwen's tastes were simple, but she had always enjoyed watching Jill plow through the dresses in the shops along Market Street. They had decided to meet at Kow Wo's, a place where both had dined on several occasions.

Gwen picked up her pace. She always wanted to be early for a meeting. It was much better to be waiting for someone and relaxing than to feel frantic and arrive out of breath and embarrassed. She passed by the shop windows, noticing the items for sale, items she didn't need and couldn't afford. It always made it easy for her to accept that she couldn't afford something when she knew it was something she didn't need. Her experience with many working women, however, was that they wanted the most what they could afford the least.

She stopped at a window to look at cut-glass crystal. Behind her, a man in a gray suit paused to look in an adjoining window. She studied him, trying to think if she'd seen him before.

The window he was staring stonily into contained ladies' shoes, items he couldn't possibly be interested in. *Odd*, Gwen thought. *A man would never look at women's shoes, not even for his wife. Most men have no idea of their wife's shoe size, and most women would never tell them.*

Gwen turned and hurried down the street, under the golden dragon's gate that led to Chinatown. The street was ablaze with light; paper lanterns hung on the street signs, which were labeled in both English and the Cantonese dialect. Gwen could read and speak Cantonese, although for the most part she kept her natural gift with the language to herself. What people didn't know or suspect about her gave her an edge. She had once surprised her dinner companion, an older American woman, by dressing down a rude waiter in his native tongue and demanding to see his manager.

She stopped and glanced back, pretending to read the signs and look into the windows. The man in the gray suit was still there, becoming more conspicuous against the bustling backdrop that was Chinatown.

She walked briskly, more curious than fearful. The streets teemed with people. Work had stopped for many of them, and if Chinatown wasn't their destination, it most surely was a way to get to the tenderloin district where many of them lived. She smiled and nodded at passersby, occasionally speaking to the children in their own tongue. They laughed and ran away at the sight of a white woman speaking their language. Gwen was comfortable here. It all seemed normal and almost fun had it not been for the pounding of her heart. But she could easily lose the tall stranger.

She spotted a large restaurant filled with people. Some sort of party was going on. Children were in the aisles, and people crowded the tables. Gwen ducked inside and broke into a fast walk between the tables. She pushed her way past people, excusing herself and making for the kitchen and, hopefully, a door to the back alley.

She stepped back as the swinging doors crashed open. A waiter with trays balanced over his head rushed past her. Allowing him to pass, she hit the doors as they swung back. She stepped boldly into the steaming kitchen.

Smoke was rising from the stove, and three men in dirty white aprons were screaming at one another. Cleavers seemed to be flying. Pots banged on the stove, and dishes rattled on the sideboards.

All at once they spotted her. The world of the kitchen came to a jarring halt.

Gwen nodded politely at them, then spoke in Cantonese. "Can you show me the way to the back door?" she asked.

They blinked in unison, wide-eyed with wonder. Not only was a woman in their kitchen, but she was a white woman speaking to them in their own language.

"A man is chasing me," she said. "I need your help. Where is your back door?"

One of the cooks, a young man with a thick swatch of black hair hanging over his eyes, lifted his arm and pointed to a hidden door behind a hanging curtain of ducks. The other two nodded in mute agreement, mouths slightly agape.

Gwen thanked them all, nodding politely again as she hurried past the ducks, opened the steel door, and scampered down the stairs into the alley. She began to run, lifting up her skirt and maneuvering past several merchants who were pushing carts of fresh produce to the back doors of the restaurants.

She ran to the side street, making her way to Kow Wo's. Gleeful, she knew she'd lost him. If this man really had been following her, the last thing she wanted was to lead him to the place she was meeting Jill. *Maybe all the intrigue and secrecy at work is making me paranoid*, she thought. Now, as she moved confidently toward Kow Wo's, she wondered if she hadn't eluded an innocent tourist or a businessman shopping for trinkets for the wife and kids.

By the time she reached Kow Wo's, she'd decided she had let her imagination run away with her. She felt slightly silly as she darted through the front door to the restaurant. Rounding a corner, she ran smack into a man in a blue suit. He held her tight, his hands gripping her arms.

CHAPTER 6

Gwen hung on to the man, her fingers twisting into his suit coat. It was all she could do to keep from screaming, or at the very least falling backward onto her behind right there in Kow Wo's.

"I'm sorry, Miss. I must have startled you."

Gwen gulped a big swallow. She wasn't certain if it was because she'd been followed and had to make an escape, or because a total stranger had seemed to manhandle her in the restaurant. "No," she said. "It's my fault. I was in a hurry."

He smiled. "Well, lucky thing for me that you weren't in a big hurry. You might have knocked me on my keister."

The man released her, and she stood there for a moment, straightening her blouse. He was a nice looking man with a long face and lantern jaw. His soft brown hair tumbled across his forehead, and he pushed it back, giving her a better view of his eyes. They were brown with soft wrinkles at the corners. He looked to be in his early forties. She noticed a small scar on his chin.

"I'm terribly sorry," she said. "I just wasn't looking."

"That's quite all right." He straightened his tie. "Are you sure you're all right?"

"Yes, I'm fine."

"Can I buy you a drink?" His eyes twinkled.

"No, I'm afraid not. I'm here to meet a friend."

He chuckled. "Not a boyfriend, I hope. That would be just my luck."

"No, a girlfriend. Perhaps some other time, but I think it's I who owe you the drink."

"Just so I get some time with you. I don't really care who pays. Do you have a card or some way I can find you?"

Gwen snapped open her purse and produced a card. She handed it over to him.

"Hmm." He read the card. "Language specialist for the Office of Naval Intelligence, I see."

She smiled. "It's a job."

"And I'll bet you're good at it." He waved the card and slipped it into his pocket, grinning. "All right, Miss Gwen Williams, I'll know where to find you now. I can collect on my drink, or you can collect on yours."

"Fine." She smiled and stepped around him. "I should be getting to my dinner companion now. Nice meeting you. But I didn't get your name?"

"Charles Bauer."

Gwen wound her way through the tables to the screen that separated the main dining room from a small alcove where she usually sat with Jill. She stepped around the screen and saw Jill, dressed in a petite black dress and pillbox hat, seated at their usual table. "I am sorry I'm late. I got tangled up at the door."

Jill smiled and motioned to the chair in front of her. "Tangled up? Did you run into a vegetable cart?"

Gwen smiled, slipping her purse under her chair. "No, a man."

"Ah." A broad smile formed across Jill's lips. "Men are always nice to get tangled up with."

"We almost knocked each other over."

Jill glanced at her expensive-looking diamond watch. "Well, you aren't late. In fact, you're still early. If I hadn't cut my shopping short, you would have been the one waiting for me."

The waiter's head peered around the screen. He was a young man with thick black hair and small wire-rimmed glasses. "You ladies want dim sum or you want order something else?"

Using her native Cantonese, Gwen ordered appetizers. The man's eyes widened. He seemed almost speechless. Moments later, he was gone.

Jill laughed. "You do have quite the effect on men, my dear girl."

"Only when I walk and talk."

Jill patted her hand. "Well, whatever you're doing, you just keep it up. Before long you'll have every man in the United States Navy eating out of your hand."

"There are more than a few that I'd like to lose, mostly those who think they're God's gifts to womankind."

It was only a matter of a few minutes before the waiter returned with over a dozen others from the staff. There were even a few children who bussed tables. The man stepped over to Gwen. "Please, Miss, say something."

"Say what?" Gwen asked in English, knowing what they wanted.

"No, no. Say something in Cantonese. It very hard language. How you learn it?"

"What do you mean it's a hard language?" Gwen asked the question using Cantonese. She pointed to the children, continuing to entertain them by using their language. "It's an easy language. Even your children know how to speak it."

The staff began to laugh, nudging one another and pointing at Gwen. It was plain to see that they were enjoying not only the sight of a white woman speaking their tongue but also one who had a sense of humor.

A short time later they were enjoying their order of orange beef and shrimp with noodles. Jill looked up at her. "I was surprised when you called me today. We haven't talked in a couple of months."

"Yes, I feel bad about that. I thought perhaps we could catch up."

Jill held her fork. "It didn't sound like that. I thought I detected a sense of panic in your voice over the phone. For a moment I was afraid you were having trouble in school." She smiled. "But then I realized that was impossible. You're too smart to have trouble in school. I figured you must be having trouble with the men at work. Being smart can be a liability where men are concerned."

"Yes, I suppose so. I am having trouble with one man in particular. He keeps hovering around me like a pesky fly. He's away from home, if you know what I mean."

"Going off the reservation?"

"I think so. He hasn't said he was married, but all the signs indicate it. It's not exactly normal for a single man in San Francisco to take leave and go back to Wakefield, Nebraska, to spend two weeks, now is it?"

Jill shook her head and continued to eat.

"I'm not sure I could spend two hours there much less two weeks, and my parents come from the Midwest," Gwen said. "This guy's a playboy in his own mind. I really don't think tractor parades would have much fascination for him. He's got to be going back there to spend time with a wife and a string of kids."

"Why wouldn't he bring his family here?"

"You'd have to know the man. A man like Jack Hershey in a uniform in a place like San Francisco. He no doubt would convince her that he wouldn't be here long enough to uproot the family." Gwen chuckled. "Also, consider the miserable weather here compared to Wakefield."

Jill laughed. "You are quite the detective, girl. Your mind's always whirling." They both continued to eat. "Are you sure there isn't some other problem at work?"

"Well, there is one thing, but you probably don't know anything about it."

"What's that?"

"What can you tell me about a British steamer, the *Nautique?*"

The question brought Jill's fork to a halt. Gwen could see a forced coolness in Jill's usual calm expression. Her mind was turning the matter over. It was almost like a large row of dominoes had fallen in her brain. She put a forkful of beef into her mouth and chewed slowly. "It's more of a personal matter, I'm afraid."

Jill smiled. "A personal matter? You've got me there. I've never heard of the *Nautique*. It's not exactly in my department, you know. I work for the military attaché. We have little to do with commercial traffic. They come and go as they please." Jill used her singsong voice in an attempt to make light of the matter. "But they don't report to me."

Gwen knew she was lying.

"What do you care about a British ship, anyway?" Jill went on. "You're a language specialist, as we've already seen."

"I have a coworker, a Chinese man by the name of Sammy Lee. I guess he has a friend on that ship. I just thought you might know where it was heading next and how long it would be in port. I'd like to pass it on to Sammy."

Gwen had given her the opportunity of volunteering any information she might have. The British Embassy must have had a copy of Sammy's friend's wireless notes, perhaps the originals. Something as important as Japanese transmissions about Pearl Harbor would have to come across Jill's desk, but for some strange reason she wasn't saying anything about it. It was a curious puzzle.

"Well, you'll just have to tell your friend Lee to take it up with his radio operator friend."

Gwen paused. She hadn't mentioned the fact that Sammy's friend was a radio operator. "I can see that would be best." She shook her head. "I go to butting into matters that aren't my concern. I guess Sammy hasn't seen the man in such a long time that I thought it would cheer him up if I brought him back news that he would be in port for a while."

Jill shrugged. "I wish I could help."

When they finished their dinner, Gwen patted her lips with her napkin. She started to reach under her seat for her purse.

"That won't be necessary," Jill said. "Dinner is on me tonight. You can buy next time."

"Won't this set you back a pair of shoes?" Gwen chuckled.

"Hardly. Not the kind I buy." She lifted a rolled up newspaper from the seat next to her. "You just get on back to your studies and leave the bill with me. I'll stay here and read for a bit."

Gwen got to her feet. "Thank you, Jill, and thank you for your time."

"I'm sorry I couldn't have helped you more."

"But you did." Gwen smiled. "You brightened my day considerably. Let's do this again soon."

Jill nodded at her. "Yes, let's do that."

Gwen walked out of the small alcove and made her way to the entrance of the place. She looked down at her hands. She had forgotten her purse.

Whirling around she retraced her steps through the restaurant and to the alcove where they had eaten dinner. The sound of voices stopped her, Jill's voice and that of a man. She leaned closer to get a better listen to what was being said.

"Do you think she knows?" the man's voice asked.

"Of course she knows. She's the language expert for those people. Anything like that would come to her right away."

Gwen backed away from the screen. The man's voice was familiar. It was the man she had bumped into when running into the restaurant, the man who had called himself Charles Bauer.

CHAPTER 7

T he two of them were like peas in a pod, Sammy Lee and Quon Eng. They had played together as boys in the streets of San Francisco. Quon had gone to school to learn the radio and Sammy had gone on to college. Sammy's job with the Office of Naval Intelligence gave him the thrill of working in an office with a suit and tie, but often he envied Quon and the world of travel the man seemed to enjoy.

Barely any mention at all was made of Quon's interception of the Japanese radio transmission during dinner. The two of them talked only about family and what great friends their mothers were. The waiters brought over tray after tray of food, and both of them took portions, filling their plates and laughing as they stabbed and sampled what was being offered.

Like Sammy, Quon wore thick glasses. His hair was thick and parted, but it still fell down over his eyes. He had to push it away as they laughed about their sisters and what homely women they were. They were both dressed identically except for a few modifications. Both men were wearing khaki trousers that dropped around their black heavy-soled shoes. Quon wore a T-shirt that showed under his white shirt, which was buttoned from the third button down. He thought it made him look sexy to let his undershirt show. Sammy was wearing a light blue shirt, buttoned to the top as befitted his desk job.

"You know, I show that communication of yours to the woman I work for," Sammy said.

Quon's eyes grew bigger. "You did? Why you do that? That was for you."

"I can't keep something like that a secret from my people. It might be too important." Sammy reached over the table and gently pushed at Quon's chest. "You a big man now where I work. People think you really important."

Quon shook his head. "I don't want to lose my job. It's a good job."

Sammy waved at him like he was swatting away a mosquito. "Don't worry about that. They don't know who you are. I never used your name. How they gonna know?"

Quon shrugged his shoulders. "They know. They always know. You don't know how those people are. When they hear about something, they are like a dog digging under a fence. You shoo them away and still they come back and dig. They dig and dig until they make a hole, and then they crawl under. Those people are like that. They never give up."

Sammy speared a pot sticker and pushed it into his mouth. "Don't worry. Nobody know." He waved his chopsticks in an inviting circular motion. "Just eat and be happy. You in San Francisco now. You home. You can be sad later tonight when you have to go home to your mother and sisters."

Quon grinned. "I'm gonna get very drunk first. Then I won't hear their yelling at me. I can just fall in bed and wake up when they're gone."

Sammy pointed at Quon's stomach with his chopsticks. "That's good. First you get real full. You don't get this on that ship of yours."

The two men spent the better part of the next hour stuffing themselves with food, finally staggering out onto the street and looking for a bar. Quon pointed to a place that had a picture of ruby red lips in the window. A neon sign was flashing, BAR—BAR—BAR. He tugged at Sammy's shirt sleeve. "Let's go there. Maybe there's women there."

Sammy twisted the brass knob on the shiny black door and they stepped into a dark, smoke-filled room. A juke box was blaring out "String of Pearls" in the corner, and a sailor was dancing with a short, squatty blonde while three of his shipmates clapped and cheered him on, waiting their turns.

Sammy followed Quon to the bar.

"Rum and Coke," Quon said.

The bartender was a large man with rolled-up sleeves that showed bulging arms and an anchor tattooed on the bicep of his right arm. He had black curly hair piled high on his head in waves. His drooping jaw showed a day's growth of black beard. "What about your friend?" he mumbled.

"I'll have one too," Sammy said.

The man smiled and poured their drinks. Quon paid him out of a roll of bills he'd collected that morning from his sea pay, and the two of them walked to a table in the back of the room. They settled down into two worn red Naugahyde chairs.

Quon watched as the blonde swung her hips to the music and twirled on the floor in the sailor's arms. Sammy could see that the sailor hadn't seen much of women in the last few months. Almost any woman would have looked good to him.

"You wanna go somewhere and dance?" Sammy asked.

Quon looked at him. "Not with your sister."

"Oh no. My sister don't go there. She better not."

Quon smiled as he watched the woman. "One of the sailors on my ship has a woman like her."

"He does? Here in San Francisco?"

Quon laughed. "No, everywhere he goes. He keeps her beside his bed on a chair." He continued to giggle. "She wear a hula grass skirt and her head is joined to her big body by a wire. When he shakes her, she dances for him."

"A hula doll?"

Quon smacked his lips. "Yeah, but she is fine all right." He held his hand up to a spot about a foot off the table. "She about this big, but he thinks she's all right for him. A real handy woman."

Sammy laughed. "There aren't many handy women."

Quon shook his head. "No, there aren't. You always got to feed them, take them to the zoo, and talk to them too. Women can be a real bother. My friend says a sailor can't afford a real woman, only his kind."

Sammy noticed a tall Caucasian man wearing a gray suit step into the bar. His presence was unusual for a place like this since he was neither Chinese nor a sailor. The man surveyed the room before he locked eyes with Sammy. He was tall, dark haired, and clean shaven. His eyes were sunken hollows of dark shadows in the darkness of the bar with no light to them whatsoever. He turned away and walked to the bar.

Sammy nudged Quon. It was hard for him to distract Quon's eyes from the dancing woman. "Do you know that man?"

"What man?"

Sammy pointed to the man at the bar in the gray suit. "That man. The one at the bar."

Quon leaned forward, adjusting his glasses. He settled back into his chair and shook his head. "No. I don't know him. Why would I know him?"

"I just thought you might have seen him before."

Quon sipped his drink. "Nah. He's a stranger to me. He must be policeman."

Sammy gave Quon a double take. "Police. Why would you say that?"

"It's nighttime. He no sailor, and he wearing a suit. Why else would a man like that come in here?"

Sammy nodded. "You could be right. I hadn't thought of that."

Quon snickered. "You people where you work always see too much. You look but you see more than there is to see. I have a cat on the ship who is like you. He always looking for rats and he never find any. He looks under boxes and then look some more." Quon smiled. "If he found one, he'd probably be scared, run and hide."

Sammy finished his drink and continued to watch the man at the bar. Quon had already turned his attention back to the blonde dancing with the sailors. The first sailor had switched with one of his shipmates and now was taking his turn watching the woman dance.

"So you want to go dance with a woman?" Sammy asked.

"That woman?" Quon asked.

Sammy shook his head. "No, not that woman. She's too busy already. Chinese woman, and not my sister, either."

"OK." Quon got to his feet. "You show me, and I'll go. I can't dance much, though."

Sammy pushed back his chair. "You don't want to dance anyway. You just want to hold a woman."

Quon chuckled. "Yeah. You're right about that. OK, let's go."

Sammy followed Quon toward the door. They wound themselves around the tables, which had been filling up with people. Couples who had been dining in Chinatown were having a drink and listening to music before going home.

Suddenly, the man in the gray suit pulled away from the bar and ran into Sammy as Quon left the bar. "Hey, you should watch where you're going."

Sammy stopped and looked up at the man. "I was watching. It was you who wasn't watching."

The man grabbed his shirt. "You're just looking for it, aren't you?" He glanced back at the bartender. "Did you see this goon run into me?"

With that, Sammy quickly pulled himself away and ran through the door, catching up with Quon. He was out of breath, and his heart was beating rapidly. "That man is no policeman. He ran into me and tried to pick a fight."

Quon stopped and looked at him. "You mean that guy back in the bar?"

"Yes."

Quon laughed and tried to ease Sammy's mind about what had happened. "The man's a clumsy drunk. If he was trying to fight with you, you'd still be in there. Don't worry none about him. I'm here to protect you now."

"Yeah, and who's going to protect you?"

Quon stopped and gently pushed at Sammy. "That's your job at the next bar. You have to protect me from some jealous husband." He drew himself to his full height of five feet four. "I make lots of men jealous, you know."

"Oh yeah," Sammy laughed. "I'm sure you do."

The traffic on the street was thinning out, and a few people were stopping to look into the darkened store windows. Most of them were busy going into the bars, and up ahead several drunken sailors were singing a tune. With their voices raised they sang, "I'm looking over a four-leaf clover," as they swayed arm in arm, exploring the darkened streets of San Francisco. There was something about an Irish song that seemed strangely out of place in Chinatown, but then so did the sailors.

"You sure this place will be open?" Quon asked.

Sammy smiled. "It's Friday night in San Francisco. Of course they're open. You know this place. San Francisco never closes, and on the weekends it adds two or three hours to every night."

Quon laughed. "We gonna need three more hours tonight, buddy."

Sammy heard a black sedan start its engine and begin a slow roll down the steep hill toward them with its lights still dark.

"We better cross the street," Sammy said.

He grabbed Quon's arm and pulled him across the street.

Suddenly the car burst into life, its wheels spinning, its engine racing, its bright beam flashing full on. The car made a direct line toward the two of them, its lights bathing them with an intense glare.

Sammy and Quon raced toward the curb, but the vehicle steered toward them, the dark figure inside guiding the car in a determined and steady manner. The car hit them with a sickening thud, sending Quon toppling over the hood and into the air and crushing Sammy with the wicked sound of crunching metal and gyrating wheels.

The last thing Sammy heard before everything went black was the sound of the car spinning away, followed by squealing tires and the sound of his friend's moaning cry.

HONOLULU, HAWAII

AUGUST 28, 1941

CHAPTER 8

Aki Kawa looked for all the world like she should still be in school someplace wearing a pleated checked skirt and nuns with rulers standing guard over her. Her straight brown hair fell just over her shoulders. It set off her warm, brown, almond-shaped eyes. Her high forehead and well-formed eyebrows gave her the look of a girl, but her full lips were definitely those of a woman. The young woman had soft, custard-colored skin that made her look fragile and appealing at the same time. She had been valedictorian at her high school and had graduated magna cum laude from the University of Hawaii with a degree in Far Eastern Studies. She had met Brian at a dance there. They knew at once there was something special between them, and both of them had been paying a price for it ever since.

The heights above Pearl Harbor were windy, but it was a gentle breeze and warm that August day. Brian Picard was an ensign on the USS *Arizona*. Aki knew he loved to take her picnicking on the heights just so he could feel a sense of pride at gazing down on the big battleship. It made him feel manly, almost as if he were a part of the floating steel. He was that, all right, and Aki was proud of him. Brian had graduated from the Naval Academy. His father was an admiral, and Brian had always known he would follow in the old man's footsteps. Only his love for Aki was holding him back. His father had made that very plain. No officer would get very far married to a Japanese girl.

Aki took the basket out of the car and walked over to where the heights overlooked the harbor. Brian was right behind her with a blanket. He tossed the end of the thing into the breeze and settled it flat on the sandy grass. "What's for lunch, sweetie? I don't have much time, I'm afraid."

She smiled at him and set down the basket. Opening it up, she removed plates and glasses. "I made your favorite, egg salad sandwiches."

Brian put his hands together and rubbed them. "Faaantastic. You're the best, babe."

Aki loved to watch Brian eat. He was so enthusiastic. He ripped into the sandwiches, a wide smile forming on his face. She hated egg salad sandwiches, but Brian loved them. It did her heart good to see Brian enjoying himself. It was far more important to please Brian than to eat food that she liked but he didn't. Food was meaningless. Brian was not.

His brown hair was short and neatly combed, and his heavy eyebrows looked manly to her. But it was his eyes that melted her soul. They were blue, sort of an icy blue, the color of a tidal pool on a volcanic beach. She could swear that those eyes of his could almost shine in the darkness. They were so clear that at times she felt she could see all the way through them and into his soul.

"You're not eating, doll."

Aki smiled, lost in thought. "I will. Just watching you is more than enough for me." She started to finger the small gold cross around her neck. It was unusual in that it had a black pearl in the center.

He reached over and stroked her cheek. "Sweetie, you're the best. You like that cross?"

"Oh yes, especially since you gave it to me. It reminds me of you."

Brian smiled. "I saw myself as the black pearl and you as the gold cross when I bought it. I want to be right in the middle of you, feel what you feel, see what you see."

"I want that too."

He turned away and looked at the ships in the harbor. "That's quite a sight, isn't it?"

"Yes," she nodded.

Brian shook his head. "It's hard to believe how stupid the navy can be. The kind of nonsense they play with their own people is just hard to imagine."

Aki giggled. "You forget. I work for Naval Intelligence. It's my job to think for them."

Brian laughed. "Yes, and if they let you do more than translate Japanese weather reports, they'd be a whole lot better off. Can you believe that when I first got here and asked them where to find my ship I had some petty officer tell me it was a secret? He told me only the captain of the yard had information on the ship's berthing assignments."

He bowed his head and shook it once more. "Shoot fire, all a feller has to do is come up here and look. You can pick out every ship in the fleet and know exactly where it's berthed. And the *Arizona*, how could anyone think they could hide that? Stupid navy. They believe

everything except what's right before their eyes, and they'll do anything to comply with regulations set by people who have never seen
Pearl Harbor."

Aki took a small bite out of her sandwich. "They are like every
other government. The people who make decisions are seldom the
people who see what needs to be done. They decide what they decide
from an office with no windows."

Brian watched as she took a second bite. "That guy been bothering you lately?"

"What guy?"

"You know, that sugar planter's son. What's his name, Mitch
Krinkle?"

Aki dropped her gaze to the blanket. "No, I'm fine." She looked
up at him, a spark in her eye. "I can take care of myself."

"I'm sure you can. I just don't like it. Guys like that are used to
getting their way. They take what they want, use it up, and throw it
away. When they stumble across something they can't have, it eats
away at them. They become like vicious dogs, jumping for a piece of
meat. You snatch it away and they forget about the meat and tear you
to pieces. I don't want that happening to you. I don't want him bothering you."

"I'll be fine. You'll just get into trouble."

"Maybe a little trouble is what that guy needs."

Aki put her hand on his arm. "Don't do anything. Let me handle
it. Promise me."

He rubbed his chin with the back of his hand, almost in an
attempt to remove a nagging itch. "I'll just have a word with the man,
make him see that you're already spoken for and that he'd be better
off to find some other local girl to harass."

"No, now promise me you won't do or say anything. You know my
brother works for his family."

"I don't care if Yasuo does work for the family." He leaned closer to her. "I wish he'd never met you."

"Me too. I wish the navy hadn't ordered me to go to that ball. But I had to go. It was orders. They were afraid there would not be enough women. I just sat there drinking punch, not dancing with anyone. He came up to me."

"Lousy bum. He's had every woman on the island. He just wants what he can't have."

She dug her fingers into his arm. "I can take care of it. I'm a big girl now. If I let other people decide for me and do for me, then I'd be listening to my parents and not seeing you. Promise me that you won't say or do anything."

Brian looked her in the eye. "I'll promise if you promise me something."

"What is that?"

Brian scooted closer to her. "You've got to promise me that you will tell me everything. I want to know every time that guy comes on to you, what he does and what he says. I know you. You're going to clam up and shut me out of this. You're going to try to protect me when I should be protecting you. If we're going to have a life together, then we have to tell each other everything. No secrets. You've got to tell me what your parents say, and I have to tell you what my old man wants. And you've got to tell me everything that happens with this sugar deadhead. Total honesty all the time. You promise?"

Aki nodded. "I promise."

Brian smiled. "OK, then I promise too. I'll leave this guy to you. But if things get out of hand, then the sugar baby is going to have the United States Navy to deal with in the person of Brian Picard."

Aki put the plates back into the basket and got to her knees. Brian shook out the blanket and folded it up. They slowly walked back to the car.

As Brian stuffed the blanket into the trunk of the car, he noticed that Aki seemed distracted. She had a faraway look. "What's wrong, sweetie?"

"That man."

Brian looked down the bluffs and saw a man in a charcoal gray suit. He had a pair of binoculars along with a notebook. He was looking through the binoculars and taking notes. "Do you know that man?"

Aki nodded her head. "Yes, that is Takeo Yoshikawa, a special vice-consul at the Japanese Embassy."

"You're kidding."

"I most certainly am not. You're forgetting, Japan may not be a free country any longer, but the United States is. We even allow him to send radio transmissions to Tokyo free from interference or encryptic deciphering."

"I can't believe that. Our own sailors can't be told where to find their ships in the yard, and this bird has them scoped out and is telling Tokyo everything." He looked at her and frowned. "And if you know who the man is, then your office must know. Intelligence has to have a clue."

"They know. They just can't do anything."

"They can't stop him from sending information to Tojo and the boys with the guns?"

She shook her head. "Every day in Honolulu the Consul General of the Imperial Japanese Embassy, Nagao Kita, files coded messages to be sent to Tokyo. These messages are protected from interception by the Federal Communications Act of 1934. The Japanese don't trust our laws, believing they would be violated by our own intelligence community on behalf of our national interest."

She looked him in the eye. "Of course they have every reason to think that because they are a military state without respect for civilian law. They are simply measuring us by their own standards. So they depend on their codes to protect them, not our laws."

She smiled. "We have already broken their codes, so they're trusting in the wrong thing. The one thing we haven't broken is our own silly laws. Do you know that if I or anyone else tried to intercept Consul Kita's messages to Tokyo that we could be fined ten thousand dollars and sent to prison for a year?"

Brian threw his hands up. "Man, I ain't believing this."

"You'd better believe it, because it's true."

Brian put his hands on his hips and stared out toward Pearl Harbor. "Our guys are sitting ducks, and the hunter is pacing the distance to shoot."

"That's about it."

"What if some other ship at sea picked up their signals? Suppose they wrote the messages down? Suppose they weren't even an American ship and weren't scared of our lousy laws?"

Aki loaded the basket into the backseat of the car. "It wouldn't do them any good if they didn't know the Japanese codes. You see, the way this works is that the only people who can read the codes are the ones who have laws against getting the messages in the first place."

Brian looked back at the man in the charcoal suit and watched him continue to make notes. "Then God help us," he said. "God help us."

CHAPTER 9

It was later in the evening when Gwen climbed the stairs to her boarding house. She had caught a cab from Chinatown and had spent most of the night at the Stanford library. It was a long cab ride, and she was suddenly feeling cash poor. She was glad Jill had volunteered to pay for dinner. But the fact that Jill had been conspiring about her when she went back to claim her purse was more than a little disturbing. Waiting across the street from the restaurant to go back for her purse had been worth it. It gave her an opportunity to see the man who had been talking with Jill, the man calling himself Charles Bauer. The sight of the two of them together filled Gwen's mind with questions. *Was it really that important for the British to conceal the communication intercepted from the Japanese?* she wondered. *Why?* Her mind raced.

She lifted the lid on her mailbox and took out a small stack of bills and circulars from Stanford along with a letter from her parents. They were continuing their missionary work among the Japanese even though they could no longer be in Japan. They had been in Honolulu, Hawaii, for three years now, missing Japan but still loving the Japanese. It was just like them. They saw only the best in people. Her parents were idealists whose calling was from God. Gwen understood that. Responding to what God wanted you to do always brought about the best that someone had to offer. Higher education and her work for the navy had turned her into what she saw as more of a realist. It was something she didn't like. Innocence was to be treasured, never thrown away.

She pushed open the heavy beveled-glass door and stepped inside onto Mrs. Malone's fine oriental carpet. Before the woman's husband had died he had been a sea captain, and the evidence of his wanderings were to be found all over the house. Chairs from India, fine oriental china, and shelves of carved ivory figures stood at various places throughout the house.

She put her hand on the banister of the dark mahogany staircase but turned away when she saw the light in the kitchen. She really needed to tell Mrs. Malone that she was home. The woman would be worried about her. One of the nice things about renting a room at the Malone house was the sense of being in a home and having a mother away from home. Sarah Malone was that.

Gwen rounded the hall and walked through the dining room into the kitchen. Sarah was in a pink bathrobe, and pink slippers dangled from her feet. She was sipping a cup of chamomile tea. The woman's gray hair was in a tight bun. "I'm home. Just wanted to let you know."

Sarah turned and smiled. "I was worried about you." She started to get up. "Have you had something to eat?"

"No, please don't trouble yourself." Gwen laid the mail on the table and, rolling her shoulders back and forth, leaned on one of the polished wooden chairs. "I'm stuffed. I had dinner with Jill in Chinatown tonight. You would have liked it."

"I'm sure I would have. Oh, dear, don't let me forget." Sarah got up from her chair and walked over to the corner of the room. "I picked up your umbrella today, the one you sent in for repair."

She reached into a large brass milk can and pulled out a black umbrella with silver-colored tips and a wooden handle. Turning around to face Gwen she shook it and slid the thing open. "See? Good as new." She closed it. "You were wise to have it repaired in the summer. You're going to need it in a couple of months. You know how bad the rain gets here from time to time."

"Thank you. I'm sure I'll use it." Gwen hung it on the back of her chair. "Can I pay you later? I won't have my check for another week."

"Of course, dear."

The refrigerator was a gleaming white General Electric that tended to buzz when it was working extra hard. The summer months kept it buzzing, but it was a comfort on August nights like this one. It made Gwen think of milk, something she enjoyed before going to bed. She didn't like warm milk. There was something about the coating of cold milk on her throat that soothed her. She stepped over to the refrigerator and pulled on the handle, springing the door open. Reaching in, she took out a bottle of milk. "My parents are so faithful about writing. They must send me four or five letters to every one I write."

"That's to be expected, child. You're busy with both school and work. I honestly don't know how you do it."

Gwen pulled open one of the metal cabinet doors, taking down a tall glass. Mrs. Malone had replaced her wooden cabinets with metal, to be modern and up-to-date, Gwen imagined. She poured herself a glass of the milk. "It gets easier with time. You get used to it. It pays the bills." She chuckled, "Occasionally it even makes me think."

"And are you meeting any nice men there?"

Gwen silently returned the milk bottle. She knew what was coming. It was so much like a mother. She meandered over to her chair and took a seat.

"You know, you're well into the age when you should be thinking about such things," Sarah went on. "A woman can't stay single forever. I don't know what I would have done if Amos hadn't come along when he did."

"Well, I meet men but very few nice men." She sipped her milk. "When I meet one like Amos, you'll be the first to know."

Sarah sipped on her tea. "You should find a stable man, someone with substance who can care for a lady. My Amos was gone a lot, but he always took care of me." She smiled. "Whenever he came back into port it was almost like a holiday." Sarah seemed to look back in time, her smile widening as she thought about life with Amos. "A life of holidays is what I would call it."

"I think I want a man I can really live with," Gwen said. "A best friend. The idea of being with a man who excites me and makes me laugh but who also holds my interest is very appealing to me. Of course I want one who shares my values, a Christian."

Sarah reached over and patted her hand. "Single women have so many ideals about men. Men are not that way. You have to choose. Most women I know either found a dependable man who bored them to tears or a man who caused their blood to race but one they had to look for every other night. They were wild. So there you are." Sarah smiled. "Bored or wild."

Gwen took a deep gulp of her milk, then wiped her mouth. "Sounds like what I have right now. Most of my days are boring, and a few get wild."

"And how was your day today, dearie?"

"Wild, I'd say." Gwen smiled. "Things were popping at work, and I was sure a man followed me tonight."

Sarah leaned closer. "A man followed you?"

"Yes, in Chinatown. He looked out of place. Where I walked, he walked. When I stopped, he stopped."

"Oh, dear. That sounds serious."

"Yeah," Gwen laughed. "No doubt he was a man planning on stepping out on his wife and just trying to build up his nerve. There's some wild woman in San Francisco tonight looking for him and wondering when he's going to get home to her and the kids."

"I hate that."

"Me too, but it happens all the time. They have no values, nothing that tells them right from wrong, no roots. But some women pick them every time and for all the wrong reasons."

Shortly after that Gwen climbed the stairs to her bedroom. Gwen's bedroom was roomy and had a sitting area next to the window. Sarah had brought up a chocolate-brown overstuffed club chair and footstool when she moved in, along with a table and lamp. It made for a comfortable reading area, and Gwen usually took the time to read mysteries before going to bed. It helped her relax, although for many people it would only have kept them up during the night. Normally, however, her job was so mundane and dull that any amount of excitement seemed to relax her. She also kept her Bible and a devotional book on the table. Every morning was dedicated to reading them.

She set her milk on a lace doily, leaned the umbrella on the edge of the table, and tossed her mail onto the double bed. Her bed was spread with a bright purple and gold quilt designed with lilies and orchids. At times the size of the four-poster bed reminded Gwen how lonely she was; but at other times she appreciated being able to toss and turn whenever she felt like it.

Quickly she hung up her dress in the wardrobe and then put on her nightgown, a blue robe, and slippers. She cracked open her window to allow a breeze and settled into the chair. Turning on the lamp, she picked up a volume of Agatha Christie.

It was hard to tell just how long it took, but before she had finished more than two or three chapters she could feel her eyes getting heavy. She placed a lace bookmark where she was reading and turned off the lamp. The fresh air coming through the window felt good.

She walked to the door, switched off the overhead light, and hung up her robe. Kicking off her slippers, she climbed into bed.

It didn't take long for her to fall asleep, but some time later her eyes bolted wide open. A cat had screamed in the alley, which wasn't that unusual. She glanced over at the glowing hands of her alarm clock, listening to the incessant ticking. 1:35 A.M. If it hadn't been for the sounds that followed, she would have drifted back to sleep.

She heard the slow squeak of metal outside her window, a sound that could only have come from her fire escape. It caused her heart to race. She listened closer and then heard what sounded like the placement of the metal ladder on the cobblestones of the alley. *Someone is trying to climb up the fire escape*, she thought.

She tossed back the covers and swung her legs over the side, feeling for her slippers. Pushing her toes into them, she got to her feet.

She had to see this. It would be too easy to turn the light on and perhaps scare off whoever it was that seemed determined to climb up to her window. She reasoned if she did that the man might very well return some other night when there was no cat to bother with, some night when Gwen might remain asleep. She was determined to teach whoever this was a lesson he wouldn't soon forget. He might even find some other line of work.

She crept over to the table and picked up the umbrella she had leaned there. It was snapped shut. She didn't really want to have to repair the thing again, but if it came to that she would. She stepped back to the edge of the curtains where she had a good view of the window. It would allow her a couple of feet between the chair and the window, more than enough space to flail away at anyone who had the audacity to stick his head in her room.

The sky was clear outside, and a half-moon bathed the rooftops with a gold hue. Moonlight streamed through her window. She gripped the wooden handle of the umbrella tightly. Sweat formed in the palms of her hands, and her heart began to thump.

The man's feet scraped the metal as he climbed the ladder, first one foot then the other. It wouldn't be long now. He would be at her window. Then the next move would be hers.

Moments later she saw his outline in the moonlight. He was standing on the landing just outside her window, bending down to see in. Gwen glanced over to her bed. The quilt was balled up where she had left it and her pillows were scattered, giving the bed the appearance of someone sleeping in it. She was thankful for that.

She raised the umbrella to her shoulder. She smiled. Miss Marple would have done the same thing she was doing. The old lady in Christie's stories wouldn't have played it safe and called the police. She would have gone after the man like a pit bull.

Gwen watched as the man put his hands under her window. He gently tugged on it, sliding it up to a point to where it was now half open. *Any burglar would pick a warm summer night in San Francisco,* Gwen reasoned. *Most of the windows in the city are open.*

She watched as he bent low and pushed his head through the window. *Should I do it now?* she wondered. *No, I'll wait until he can't pull himself out so quick,* she thought. *I don't want him getting away that easy.*

He pushed his shoulders and arms through the window, raising up slightly to open it farther. Gwen struck. Without saying a word, she stepped forward and brought the umbrella down on his head with all her might. It landed with a sharp crack.

The man let out a yelp, jerking his head up and banging it on the window. That might have done more damage to him than her original blow, but she was determined not to let up. She continued to bang his head with the umbrella as he cried out with screams and moans.

Jerking back on the umbrella, she suddenly decided to make certain that he got the message. She rammed the metal tip directly into the side of his head. He jerked, slamming back against the opposite side of the window. His cry was painful, and she then brought the umbrella down on him again, raining on his skull with a series of hard deliberate blows.

The man squirmed ferociously, finally freeing his body from the window. He fell backward onto the landing. Stumbling to the ladder, he tried to put his foot on the rung, but fell instead. Gwen could hear the fall, a series of sharp metal crashes followed by the sound of the man hitting the cobblestones below.

Gwen pushed her head out the window. She could see the dark outline of the man hobbling down the alley in the direction of the street. "Let that be a lesson to you," she yelled. "Don't come back, not ever."

An hour later Gwen and Sarah were sitting in the kitchen with two uniformed policemen. One was taking notes, and the other one was examining her umbrella, which was now beyond repair. Gwen would need a new one.

The officer with the umbrella held it up to her. "You must have really done a number on him with this, miss."

Gwen nodded, sipping her milk. "Yes, he felt it."

"I'm sure he did," the man grinned.

Sarah put her arm around Gwen. "Poor child. You must have been frightened to death."

The officer taking notes looked up at her. "You say it was one-thirty when this happened?"

"Yes, I looked at my clock."

"That's unusual." The man continued to take notes.

"Why is that?" Gwen asked.

The officer looked up. "It's Friday night. We don't get many cat burglars out before three or four A.M. on a Friday night. People normally stay up later those nights. Cat burglars strike on a Sunday through Thursday, but never before three. I'd say your man was a rookie."

"Or maybe not a burglar," Gwen added.

AUGUST 30, 1941

CHAPTER 10

Sam Diamond was an ambitious man, but one who never placed much stock in simply pleasing the people who counted. His squash game had become legendary in Washington, something he proved over and over to his bosses on the *Washington Post*. When they were on the court with him, they could count on the man never to show mercy. No matter how far ahead he was, putting an opponent away was something he took pride in. A muscular man of thirty, he had been a reporter with the *Post* for seven years. It was long enough for him to make friends, and of course, it never took Sam that long to make enemies.

That late August day when he finished his game with Jeff Walsh, his city editor, Walsh walked out of the court behind him and put his arm over Sam's shoulder. "Sam, I'm going to do you a favor."

"Oh boy, a favor from you. If you want me to cover the sailing of the *Titanic*, the ship's already sailed, Jeff, and sunk too."

Walsh laughed. "No, it's something a little more current than that. But it might be kind of similar."

Sam took his small white towel and patted his head. He pointed to the polished running track around the outer wall of the athletic club. "Come run with me and tell me what you've got on your mind."

Walsh bent over, his hands on his knees. "Oh man, you kill me on the court and it's not enough for you. Now you want to bury me on the running track."

Sam began to jog. "Come on, Jeff. It'll be good for you."

Walsh raised his head and slowly began his chase of Sam Diamond. He raised his voice. "I really am doing you a favor. I'm sending you to Hawaii."

That slowed Sam down. He looked back at Walsh. "Hawaii? Why don't you do that in December when it might do me some good?"

"Hey, you can work on that pretty-boy tan of yours. Don't knock it. It might just turn out to be a vacation for you that the paper's paying for."

"Favors from the boss." Sam shook his head. "There's something wrong with that. There must be something really big about to pop here, something the old man wants me out of town for so I don't embarrass him."

"No, I just know what a stubborn mule you are, and right now I need a mule, someone who won't take no for an answer. You like to go up against the brass. I'm sending you to a place with wall-to-wall brass."

"Hawaii? Nobody's there except retired people and a few generals who want to play golf in the winter. It's not winter, though, so even they're here."

"The Japanese are there, and the people here are too stupid to know what they're doing. The Pacific fleet is there too. You read the papers, don't you?" Walsh grinned and tried to keep up his jogging. "Oh, I forget, you only read your own stories."

Sam picked up his pace. It was his way of making Walsh suffer.

Walsh reached out and grabbed Sam's shirt, tugging him to a halt. "Hold on there, cowboy." He bent over and started to pant. Looking up at Sam, Walsh forced a smile. "Look, something may be breaking there, and I want you there until it does. I have a friend with the FBI who occasionally does me a favor."

"One of Hoover's men?"

"Yeah, but he hates the guy." Walsh grabbed his stomach and forced a grin. "Just like you hate your boss." He took a deep breath. "He told me we have a German spy in New York who's also working for the Brits. I guess the man has orders to go to Hawaii and look over the naval base at Pearl Harbor. He has orders from the German high command. They want it done as a favor to their buddies the Japanese."

"Are they planning an attack there?"

"What do you think?"

"What are we doing about it?"

"Nothing." Walsh spit out the word. "That's where we come in. My friend who reports to Hoover says Edgar's just sitting on this, figuring this spy doesn't count. My friend thinks if we were to break the story with some hard facts that it just might wake the whole country up."

Walsh stood up straight, gently swaying and looking Sam in the eye. "Now wouldn't you like for the *Post* to be responsible for waking the country up? Wouldn't you like your name on the story?"

It was late in the afternoon before Sam could meet with the Man. Sam always called him "the Man" because he could confirm or deny almost any story that happened to float across Sam's desk. He and Sam's father had been best friends, and Sam figured even if he couldn't seem to make friends of his own, he should trade on his father's good name for as long as that dog could hunt. He'd never been above using people to get what he needed, and he wasn't about to start now.

Sam walked along the grassy mall with his tie loose around his neck and his shirt unbuttoned at the collar. His suit coat was slung over his shoulder. The sun was low and the air was heavy with humidity. He knew he should look his best, but with the steamy heat in the air around Washington, he could easily set protocol aside.

He took his seat on the bench he had always used when he met with the Man and glanced at his watch. The guy was late today, but that wasn't unusual. It served to remind Sam of who the important person really was here. The Man had come far since his father had known him at Yale. They had both been members of the Fellowship of the Bones, a secret Yale society that followed a graduate into life. It was why the Man even recognized Sam. The secret society evidently gave Sam some right to call on his father's old classmate for help. Before his father had died a few years back, he told Sam about a few of his connections with the society, people he could call on and a few he couldn't. Sam had never been refused by the Man.

Sam watched a black government limousine circle the block in long sweeping turns. This was always true to form. He had to make sure Sam was there and that he was alone. The car pulled up to a curb almost a half-mile away, and the chauffeur got out and opened the door for Sam's appointment.

Sam watched him walk in his direction as the vehicle drove away. A lanky figure in a light blue suit, he looked almost cool in the distance with his neatly combed gray hair. There was an air of power to him that was not undeserved. He was, after all, one of the most powerful members of Roosevelt's cabinet. He was listened to and relied upon almost without reservation. To be close to him was to be close to the power that seemed to sweep through this city. It was intoxicating. Normally, Sam would never trust someone this high up in the government. Sam reasoned they were where they were because they couldn't be trusted. But this was different. The Fellowship of the Bones had made it very different.

Sam got to his feet. "Good afternoon, sir."

"Please take your seat, Sam." He smiled. "I'm glad I got your message. It's good to see you, one of our gentlemen from the fourth estate." He unbuttoned his suit jacket, put his hands on his hips, and looked Sam over. "You do look so much like your father, that powerful build and that dark curly hair of yours. You must be fighting the young ladies off with a stick."

Sam sat down as ordered. "No, sir. I'm too busy, much too busy."

"What a pity." Sam watched him sit down. "Our ladies are losing out then, when it comes to staking a claim on you."

"What they don't know won't hurt them, I'm sure."

"My sentiments exactly. These days people know too much. It makes them worry needlessly."

Sam cocked one eye, knowing the conversation was no longer about his love life. "Sometimes what they don't know can kill them."

"I should hope not." He swung his wrist limply in Sam's direction, egging him on and showing a glint of his gold cuff links. "But you called this meeting, Sam. What do you want to know? If I can help you, I will."

"Are we expecting an attack by the Japanese?"

The sudden abruptness of Sam's question took the Man by surprise. His jaw tightened slightly and his lips clamped closed. "Where did you hear that?"

"I have my sources, the same as you do."

"The Japanese are sending a diplomatic delegation to Washington to work out our tensions. They ought to be here in November."

"But you don't really expect that to succeed, do you?"

"No, I don't."

"Then that will mean war."

"We hope not."

There were times when Sam could tell what the Man was thinking by what he didn't say. At times he dodged questions, thereby giving away what the answers would have been had he given Sam a straight answer. It was political speak, and this guy was very good at it.

"I understand we have a German double agent cooling his heels in New York who wants to go to Hawaii to do a favor for the Japanese."

That statement brought a slight smile to the Man's face. "You do have good information, Sam. You should be proud of it."

"I am, but is it true?"

"What makes you think it's a favor for the Japanese?"

"He's working for Germany."

"Is that so? Only Germany?"

Sam's mind raced. He knew the man was a double agent for both the German and the British governments. Normally that would have placed both of those powers at odds, but would it this time? Suppose both Germany and England wanted their agent to succeed? He shook his head, getting the man's drift. "I can't believe England wants an attack on us."

"Why can't you? They're on the ropes over there. Some would say their only chance of survival is America coming into the war."

"And what would be the Roosevelt administration's view on that?"

"Sam, you know we have a nation full of pacifists. The Germans have a following in this country that goes way back. It might take a shock to win those people over."

"What kind of shock?"

He shook his head and bowed it slightly. "Say the Philippines, or the islands of New Guinea."

"Why not the Hawaiian Islands?"

He looked almost pained by the suggestion, as if Sam had slowly drilled a hole into the pit of his stomach. "They wouldn't do that. They couldn't do that. It's much too far for them to come, and our wrath would be much too great."

"Don't count on their knowing that," Sam said.

"When will you go, Sam?"

"My orders are to follow this spy. When he goes, I go. It might be tomorrow or it might be a month from now. It all depends on when Hoover's men let him loose."

"I'll see what I can do for you then."

CHAPTER 11

E arly Monday morning Gwen tapped lightly on Pete Allen's door. The man seemed preoccupied, standing with his back to her and staring at the wall. He glanced over his shoulder, "Come on in." He then turned back and continued to look at his pictures on the wall. "That seems like another time and place." He was speaking almost as if he were thinking to himself, but out loud. "We were boys then, full of life, hopes, and dreams. We didn't know the world was turning upside down. We didn't know we had a short life ahead of us in the trenches of France, and we didn't know that most of us would never come back."

Gwen waited patiently. She had learned that some men did their best thinking when they were talking. The sound of the words floating through the air caused them to make sense out of whatever they were grappling with. The thoughts and ideas were slower. They could pick out the best thoughts and return to them later. They could be examined and studied; a few could even be reeled back into the brain and judged as wrong. Of course some of the words could never be taken back. They hung there like ugly pictures bolted on the wall, like the photographs Captain Allen was looking at.

Allen stepped closer to the photos and pointed out one of the players in a uniform. "That was me back then, the dumb one. I had the world by the tail, and we were going to the Rose Bowl. Nothing else mattered. Fact is, I didn't think anything else would ever matter again. That's the way it is with a young man. What's standing right in front of him is the only thing that counts."

"Yes, sir."

He continued to stare at the photographs. "We have boys just like that in the navy right now. They don't know what's coming. They're trusting us to tell them, and we're stuck here trying to please Washington while they think we're trying to do the right thing." He crossed his arms and shook his head. "They're fools, just like we were back then."

He glanced back at Gwen. "Do you understand anything I'm saying, Miss Williams?"

"Yes, sir. I just have faith. That's all."

"Faith in what?"

"Captain, I have faith in a sovereign God who controls this planet when everything around us would suggest otherwise. I'm not privy to His plans, but I know they include my welfare. It isn't the circumstances that I believe in; it's Him."

"I wish I had your faith, Miss Williams."

"I do too, Captain."

He turned around. "You know where we came up with the name *Purple*, don't you? Why we labeled the Jap code the *Purple code* and our machines the *Purple machines?*"

"No, sir," Gwen replied.

They had broken the "unbreakable" Japanese ciphers the year before, quickly building four of the so-called Purple machines. Already the intelligence community had two hundred people who were working deep-secret communications from Japan, and Gwen knew she was just one of them. With the Purple machines they were often able to deliver decrypted Japanese diplomatic dispatches to Secretary of State Cordell Hull and the President before the clerks at the Japanese Embassy could take the message to their own ambassador. Of course the priority was always diplomatic communication, never military.

He smiled broadly, jerking his thumb back in the direction of his wall. "Husky colors, my dear. Man's got to take some pride in his work even if it's borrowed from the past."

"You sent for me, sir?" Gwen wanted to bring him back to task. She had piles of papers to go through and with very little help.

"Yes." Allen scrambled under some papers on his desk before pulling up a pink note. "That man of yours, Sammy Lee."

"Yes, sir. I haven't seen him today."

He handed over the piece of paper. "That's his room number at Saint Francis Hospital. He was struck by a hit-and-run driver on Friday night somewhere in Chinatown."

Gwen took the paper and opened it to read. "Do you know how he's doing?"

"He's pretty serious, I guess. But he did fare better than his friend. The other guy was killed."

Gwen looked up at him. "Do you know the man who was killed?"

"Nope. Should I?"

Gwen nodded. "Yes, Captain, you should. When I talked to Sammy on Friday he told me who he was going out to dinner with. I'm pretty certain the man Sammy was with was the one who intercepted the Japanese message at sea, the one I showed you on Friday."

"The one with the details on berthing assignments at Pearl Harbor?"

Gwen nodded. "Yes. He's the man who took down the message we decoded. We used one of the codes from the Purple machine."

"And you think this hit-and-run was no accident?"

"I don't know what to think. I should think anybody would realize the damage has already been done, unless . . ."

"Unless what?"

"Unless they thought all of the message hadn't been delivered to us, or perhaps there was a second message, one that we haven't seen."

"Well, you'd better go see this Lee fellow. I don't know if he's awake enough to talk, but he might have been told something. You'd get it before anyone else."

Gwen turned and started to leave, then stopped and turned around. "One thing more, Captain. This probably isn't important, probably unrelated."

"What is it?"

"On Friday night someone tried to come in through my window at the boarding house. He climbed a fire escape. At first I thought it was a simple burglary, but now I'm not so sure."

"You think they might be looking for whatever it is that we're supposed to know?"

"That wouldn't be likely. I'm not exactly in the habit of taking secret homework with me to my room. They might think I know too much, though."

Allen stepped around his desk and over to where she was standing. "All of us think that, Miss Williams." He smiled. "I wouldn't worry about it. More than likely it was a burglary attempt by a rank amateur."

"Well, whoever it was got the business end of my umbrella and fell down the fire escape too."

Allen laughed. "He ought to remember that."

Gwen lifted her chin, feeling a slight momentary surge of bravado. "He won't forget it. I'm sure of that."

Gwen spent the rest of the morning doing a combination of things she knew she should do and getting ready to do something she knew she should never do. She saw Sammy Lee, and he told her Quon's name and the name of his ship. She then caught the cable car for the docks. She was going to find some way to inspect Quon's berth on board the ship and see for herself if the man had held back a portion of the communication from them.

She got off the cable car and walked to the office of the harbor master. It was in a red board building that looked like it had made it through all the storms of the last century but could never make it through another one. The shutters were painted a dull olive green, and the sides were a washed out red. She walked through the door, taking care not to step through the broken stairs.

The man behind the counter was wearing a long-sleeve T-shirt smeared with grease; a lengthy black leather belt undergirded his ample belly. He had on a black fisherman's cap that was pulled down to eye level.

She stepped up to the counter. "Excuse me, sir."

The sound of a woman's voice got his attention. He walked over to where she was standing and pushed his cap back, showing off a pair of blue eyes. He flashed a smile. "Can I help you, miss?"

"If you would be so kind as to direct me to the *Nautique*. I believe it docked last Friday."

Leaning back to a window behind him, the man stuck out a stubby finger. "It's down there, miss, about three ships away. You can't miss it." He leaned back on the counter and grinned. "Would you like me to show you?"

Normally the very idea would have made Gwen gag, but she swallowed hard. Having a harbor master let her on board the ship might be just what she needed. "Yes, that would be nice." She forced a smile. "Would you?"

He grinned and wiped his hands on his shirt. Stepping out from behind the counter, he walked over to the door and held it open for her. "After you, miss."

"Thank you." Gwen stepped outside, once again taking care that she didn't put her foot in a hole. She then followed the man down the docks and listened as he babbled on about the ships they were passing. He took a great deal of pride in knowing what he was talking about, describing each ship and its flag, along with when and where it was made.

When they got to the *Nautique*, the man paused at the gangplank. "And here is the *Nautique*, a British steamer with the keel laid in Liverpool. You ever been to Liverpool, miss?"

"No, I'm afraid I haven't."

"Too bad." He shook his head. "Rip-roaring place, that Liverpool is." He signaled for her to follow him. "Come along and let me take you aboard. You can see the old gal firsthand."

Gwen followed along behind him as he led her up and onto the deck. As was typical of the British, the deck was neatly arranged with coiled ropes and a bright new coat of gray paint. The grates were painted black, and the glass looked like it had just been cleaned.

"Who goes there?" A man stepped out on the flying bridge and peered down at them.

"It's the harbor master," the man bellowed back. "I brought me a lady who wants to see your ship."

"Hold on then. I'll be right down."

Moments later a sailor in striped shirt and white pants joined them. The young man looked to be only in his teens. Gwen figured most of the men were seeing the sights of San Francisco; it figured they would have left a boy to watch the ship.

He ripped off his cap and smiled. "What can I do for you, ma'am?"

The use of the term *ma'am* startled her. Maybe Sarah Malone was right. She suddenly felt very old. Reaching into her purse she pulled out her Naval Intelligence badge. It didn't really have any power. It was used mostly as a means of identification to let her into her office building, but Gwen didn't think a man the age of this particular sailor would know the difference. And even though it was a United States naval badge and this was a British ship, she doubted it would cause him great concern. They were, after all, in an American port. She flashed the badge. "You have a radio operator on board, a Quon Eng?"

The man hung his head. "Yeah, but I heard he got killed."

"I'd like to see his berth, and maybe the radio room."

"That's funny." The sailor put his hat back on his head. "Two blokes just came aboard looking for the same thing. These gents were British, though." He looked up at the bridge. "I believe they're still about the ship."

Gwen gulped. "Could you show me the man's quarters?"

"Certainly, ma'am. Follow me."

Gwen followed him around the deck to where he opened a door that led to a narrow hallway. She walked behind him. There was scarcely room for more than one person at a time. Passing several doors, the man stopped and opened one. "Here it is, ma'am. I'll show you Quon's bunk."

She followed him inside. The room was small and contained three bunk beds, each with a cot suspended on chains. On one small chair stood a grass-skirted Hawaiian Kewpie doll, the kind that danced when you shook it. Three trunks were tucked under the three cots. The sailor pulled one of them out.

"This here is Quon's. We don't have much space for personal stuff, but we make do."

Gwen stooped over and began to rummage through the personal effects of Sammy Lee's friend. A number of shirts, along with three pairs of trousers and socks of assorted colors, were folded neatly. There was also one pair of worn shoes. She picked up a collection of post-cards, no doubt purchased because they contained pictures of women in various stages of undress. The man's toothbrush and hairbrush were laid side by side.

Then she spotted a notebook and pen. She opened the book and instantly saw that it was some sort of journal, written neatly in Cantonese. She could make out the dates clearly and could see instantly that it was current.

"What's that over there?" She drew the young sailor's attention to a stack of magazines on a table in the corner. When he stepped over to examine them, she slipped the notebook into her purse. Her conscience nipped at her slightly. The very idea of taking something that didn't belong to her was appalling. But she had to see the man's writing more closely. She had to look for the day he had made the interception of the Japanese message.

"Oh, ma'am, you don't want to look at those magazines." He turned back to her, an embarrassed grin on his face. "They are men's magazines."

"I see." Gwen got to her feet. "Well, why don't you take me to the radio room?"

"Just follow me. I'll show you the way."

Moving out into the hallway again, they scurried up a set of metal stairs that emptied out into a small dining area. The man led her past the metal tables and, opening a door, stepped in.

She could hear him. "You fellas still here? I got me somebody else that wants to look too."

Gwen stepped into the radio room. One man in a blue suit was standing near the radio table, looking through a stack of wireless communications. A second man in a gray suit was going through a filing cabinet. He turned around. It was Charles Bauer, the man she had bumped into at Kow Wo's, the man who had met with Jill.

His look of surprise quickly turned into a smile. "Gwen Williams. How good of you to come. How nice to see you again."

He stepped forward to shake her hand, and she thought she detected a limp.

CHAPTER 12

ki had been through a tiring, frustrating day. Being Japanese caused her to be distrusted by every white face that looked at her, especially the men she worked for. Naval Intelligence was always looking in the wrong direction when so much that was wrong was going on under their noses. Aki had sent off a communication to the office of Naval Intelligence in San Francisco, asking if they knew what was being sent by the Japanese Embassy in Hawaii to Tokyo. It was a long shot, but if she could uncover a Japanese spy ring in Hawaii, then perhaps people would trust her.

She got off the bus and started on the walk to her house. Her cool summer dress, bright green with orange and yellow flowers, blew in the breeze. Color was everywhere in Hawaii, and the bright colors seemed to pick up her spirits. The trade winds brought some relief to an otherwise sweltering day. The street was quiet with palm trees and flowering shrubs. Hawaii was in bloom year-round, but the shade and flowering vines of the warm summer made the foliage especially appreciated.

She rounded the block and slowed her pace when she saw what was waiting for her. Mitch had his red MG sports car parked in front of her house. The top was down, and he was sitting on the hood, reading a newspaper. She took small steps, rehearsing what to say to the man. There was one good thing about having him here. Her house was close. He couldn't do much here, and when she finished telling him what she had to say, she could at least go inside and put him and her job behind her.

He lowered the paper and spotted her, breaking into a wide, toothy grin. Mitch Krinkle appealed to most of the women she knew. Not only did he have wealth, but his boyish good looks swept one woman after another into a world of daydreams and fantasy. Women swooned when they saw him and closed their eyes just imagining themselves in his arms.

His blond hair was tousled, and he was wearing a white shirt open at the first few buttons. White pants and white bucks completed his ensemble of put-on purity. He would have presented an angelic appearance had Aki not known better.

He slipped off the hood of the car and walked toward her. "Hey, beautiful. I've been waiting for you. I thought maybe you'd like to go for a drive and have some pu pus and steak. We could swim and enjoy the moonlight."

Aki walked past him. "No, thank you. I've had a hard day." She knew right then she should have said more, let him know exactly what she thought of him. It was too easy to blame her total disgust for the man on the hassles of work.

He stepped quickly to catch up with her. "Angel, you shouldn't be working there. I can find you a job with my father's business that pays you twice as much."

"I'm not interested." Again she knew she hadn't made herself clear. He might have thought her disinterest was in the job when actually it was in him. *Why am I such a coward?* she wondered.

He then reached out and grabbed her arm. "What is it with you, beautiful? Here I am practically throwing myself at you, and you treat me like I'm one of the lepers of Molokai."

She turned to face him. "Look, I told you I have a boyfriend. I'm not interested in you. Why don't you understand that?" That did her heart good. She had made herself clear.

"Because I'm not used to it. I see what I want and I go get it. I don't take no very well."

The very idea of this spoiled rich boy sickened her. He was from a different world. He had no idea what it was like to earn his way in life, to have something because he'd worked for it. "Get used to it. It's part of life."

"It's not a part of mine."

She knew that was true. Most likely from the time of Mitch Krinkle's birth, no one had ever told him no. There had never been any boundaries for the man.

"Honey, I just want a good time. I could show you one too." He reached out and stroked her lips with the tips of his fingers. "And I could put a smile on that pretty face of yours if you'd let me."

His touch made her feel queasy. She pulled herself free and started to walk away, but he caught up and stepped in front of her. "Hey, this doesn't even require you to think." His voice rose, almost in a note of frustration. "It's a no-lose proposition for you. I get what I want, and you get what you need."

That was part of Mitch Krinkle's problem, and Aki knew it. Women didn't have to think. It was better if they didn't. Women were not for talking to or for companionship. They were to use, to have fun with, and then to be cast aside. "What you want, I don't want. Like I told you, I'm taken."

"By that miserable swabby ensign?"

Aki looked surprised. She hadn't said anything about the identity of her boyfriend. He had been asking questions. The thought frightened her and made her angry at the same time. He was obviously serious enough to dig under the surface when it came to her.

"You don't think his papa is going to go for him dating a Japanese girl, do you? I don't think so. Don't kid yourself, beautiful. This thing you have with him is going nowhere. All you're going to wind up with is a broken heart." His smile widened. "With me you're going to get a good time and some pretty things too. I'll treat you right. I know what you want."

"You don't know the first thing about me other than that I wear a skirt."

"Beautiful, all you need is one kiss from me and every other man will melt away from your pretty little head." With that he grabbed Aki's head with both hands, leaned into her, and planted a kiss on her lips.

She swung her hand up and landed a hard slap on the left side of his face.

He drew back in a combination of shock and pain, rubbing his cheek. "You shouldn't have done that."

"And you shouldn't have done what you did. Now leave me alone. Stay away from me. Far away."

She hurried past him, running through the chain-link fence that led up to her house. The sight of her parents stopped her. Her mother was on her knees digging at the roots of a red torch ginger plant, and her father was pruning some of the broad green leaves that formed cradles for the stalks of red blossoms. The flowers looked like a bright explosion of flame surrounded by cool green broad leaves.

Her father was wearing a torn T-shirt, shorts, and sandals, while her mother was in the yellow sundress she liked to wear while working in the garden. They both enjoyed caring for plants. Aki always thought it was because they did more than nurture them and watch them grow; they could also control them. In a way, she saw their love for gardening as an extension of their desire to keep things in their place.

Her father lowered his shears and frowned at her. His close-cut gray hair seemed wrinkled up into a series of waves on his forehead as he arched his eyebrows. "Why are you with that white sugar boy? Isn't it enough that you see that white sailor without shaming us by taunting the son of the man your brother and I work for?"

"I am not with him, Father. He came here to meet me. I didn't ask him to come."

Her mother got up from her knees, brushing the dirt from her dress. Her eyes were sad as she stared up at Aki. "Why don't you like Japanese boys? Didn't we raise you right in the ways of your people?"

Aki bowed slightly to them. "Yes, I am sorry to disappoint you. I like Brian because of what he is like on the inside. I don't care what his race is." She bowed again. "Please excuse me. I must go inside and change clothes."

Aki had been part of many discussions with her parents on the subject of Brian Picard. She knew exactly where such talk would lead, and it was never favorable for her. It always came down to her being disrespectful of her parents' wishes. She was their daughter, but she wasn't a flower in their bed of carefully tended blossoms.

Turning the polished brass knob, she opened the door and stepped inside. She slammed the door and pressed her back to it, breathing hard. Mitch Krinkle was behind her now, and so were her parents. She was certain Mitch would never bother her again. Even though she knew she would have to face her parents over and over about what she was doing with her life, she knew she had spoken her mind. Brian would be proud of her.

The sound of laughter brought her to full attention. Her brother, Yasuo, and three of his friends were in the living room. She didn't know how much they had seen, but it was all too plain to see that they were having a good time at her feeling of panic.

"Hey, Sister, what's the problem? You don't like being treated like a woman?" Yasuo grinned at his friends and snickered, making her the object of their collective humor.

She stood up straight, adjusting her dress. "If by that you mean not being treated like a human being, then no, I don't like it at all."

She glared at the four of them spread out over their living room. Yasuo and Hiroki, his ringleader best friend, were seated on the blond rattan couch. The cushions were yellow with large, bold red flowers on them and the two men looked like lizards perched on the branches between the flowers. The other two were seated on chairs turned backward. They were leaning forward on the backs of the chairs, trying their best to appear tough.

"You ain't no woman yet," Hiroki offered. "You just look like it on the outside. But you jes a cheap local girl for the sailor boy. If you were a woman, you'd be more Japanese."

Hiroki had always maintained a pride in what the Japanese empire was doing. He saw it as a matter of "Asian masculinity" to trample on the territory of China and to beat one's chest shouting about domination. Aki knew that life in the sugar fields was hard for Yasuo and his friends. As the years had gone by, their hatred for the white race had grown. The rise of the Empire of Japan had given them and a few like them some cause for hope. But young men like her brother and his friends were causing the navy to mistrust her.

"I am an American. I was born an American."

"You just a white slant eye," Hiroki said. "You even becoming a Christian." He shook his head. "That is shame for your ancestors. You not respect them."

"I've started going to a Japanese church. The pastor there lived in Japan. You haven't. Jesus is for everyone, not just white people. And I do respect my ancestors. I just don't burn incense in front of their pictures. I don't worship them. They were people the same as I am."

Hiroki shook his head.

"You think that by becoming a Christian that sailor's father is going to approve of you?" Yasuo asked. "Because he won't. He just looks at you on the outside the same as they all do. To him you're Japanese, and that's all you'll ever be."

"I'm not in love with him. I love his son."

"And what about our parents? You know you're breaking their hearts?"

"Not as much as you are." Aki shot a quick glance at Yasuo's friends. "You think they like you being a tough guy and hanging out with hoodlums, these sons of the rising sun?"

Hiroki shot to his feet and shook his finger at her. "You a traitor. You spy for the Americans. When our army does take these islands, they will throw you in jail. You'll be with those white-skinned devils then. You'll be one of them, an enemy."

Hiroki had always been a hothead, and Aki knew it. She had hoped that his friendship with her brother would mellow him out, but instead she was seeing more and more of his influence on Yasuo. Together they seemed bent on destruction.

Aki started to walk away. "This is getting us nowhere. As long as you continue taking pride in some man on a white horse in Japan and taking no pride in what you are and what you can do, then you'll always just be angry men who come to no good."

She started to move out of the living room and into the kitchen, but Hiroki stepped closer to her. He pushed his face closer to hers.

"You may be the sister of my friend, but you're an enemy of Japan. You're just a spy, and you should be shot."

CHAPTER 13

Gwen raced up to Pete Allen's office and walked in the door without knocking. It was something she had never done before, and she was more than a little embarrassed when she saw that Jack Hershey was there. Hershey was standing over Allen's shoulder pointing out new communications. He had a bruise on his forehead and several cuts and scrapes on his nose and cheek. She shuddered.

Pete Allen lifted his head. "You have a problem, Miss Williams?" Allen's uniform jacket hung on a worn wooden coat and hat tree. Even there it looked wrinkled. His tie was loose; his top button was not only undone, but it was also hanging by a thread. He had on his reading glasses, two small half-moons of polished tortoiseshell rims that made him look intelligent and busy at the same time. Stacks of paper were placed in rows on his desk.

"I'm sorry, sir. I didn't mean to interrupt. I can come back later." She knew better than to walk into the department head's office without an invitation. She felt like a rookie who didn't know how to do her job. She had let the events of the day run away with her without thinking.

"No. It's all right." He waved her in. "Lieutenant Hershey was just finishing up." He picked up a communiqué and lifted it for her to see. "We have something here that might fit in your department."

Gwen stepped over and took the mint green sheet from Allen's hand. She glanced at Hershey and then made eye contact with Allen. "I really can come back when you're finished here."

"Nonsense. We're done, aren't we, Lieutenant?"

"I suppose we are." Hershey looked at Gwen. She saw irritation in his glance as he lifted his eyebrows. That didn't trouble her. If the man saw himself on the other side of the fence when it came to competing for the old man's attention, then perhaps he would stop trying to pursue her.

She quickly glanced over the communiqué. Allen's phone rang, and he picked it up and began to talk.

The communiqué piqued her interest when she saw it was from a woman working for Naval Intelligence at Pearl Harbor, and a woman of Japanese descent at that. The woman wanted to know about Japanese communication from the island. Maybe there was something there that might prove useful.

"You think you can help this Aki fella?" Hershey asked.

Gwen looked at him. She knew that Jack Hershey knew very little about names associated with the Japanese culture. There was no reason he should. "Aki is a female Japanese name."

"You've got to be kidding. What are they doing with a Japanese working for Naval Intelligence?"

Gwen took a deep breath and blew it out slowly. "Maybe she's the most qualified."

"That doesn't make any difference. She's Japanese."

Allen hung up the phone. "You two having a spat?"

"No spat," Hershey said. "Our little lady here just wants to help the Japanese. That's all. This Aki person is Japanese and, to make matters worse, a woman."

Allen silently looked at her, but the challenge from Hershey was not something she was going to allow. She placed her hands on Allen's desk and leaned forward. "Let me tell you something. I was born in Japan. When I went to school I was the only white person in the entire building. I was a female. I had something to prove, and that made me work harder. There were no off days for me. To relax even for an instant was to allow someone to gloat and think he was right about me. If this woman is working for the navy in Hawaii, then she has a lot to prove. She has to live down both her gender and her race at the same time. Frankly, I'd rather have her working for me than ten men."

Allen looked over at Hershey and smiled. "You see, Lieutenant, we have a hard worker here in Miss Williams, and for a good reason." He leaned back in his chair, creating a squeaking noise. "Now why don't you tell me what's on your mind, Miss Williams, and then we can discuss this communiqué."

"Yes, sir. I went to see Sammy Lee today."

"How is he?"

"Not good. It's touch and go, I'm afraid. I did talk to him enough to find out that he thinks the accident Friday night was deliberate. Whoever was driving that car wanted both of them dead." Gwen felt guilty. She knew she hadn't gotten him into this thing. Sammy had approached her. But without her help, Sammy would never have known what he was looking at.

Allen's phone rang again, and he picked it up. He then swung around in his chair, turning his back to them both.

"Maybe you're trying too hard with this one," Hershey said. "You're letting your imagination run away with you. It's one thing to feel important because somebody gives you a Japanese transmission that turns out to be consequential, but that doesn't mean you have to let your suspicions run wild here."

Pete Allen swung his chair around. Even though he was talking on the phone, this subject held his interest.

"I don't think the police are going to find the car that killed Sammy's friend," she said.

"Why not?" Hershey asked.

"Because I think this so-called accident is connected to the Japanese transmission that we worked on last week. The man with Sammy was the radio operator from the *Nautique*. That's just too much of a coincidence. Whoever did this wanted to seal the man's lips."

"And you think the people responsible may have diplomatic immunity?"

"Yes, I do. I believe they're connected in some way with the intelligence community."

Pete Allen hung up the phone and shook his head. "Look, I've been listening to you. This idea about Sammy's accident not being an accident sounds screwy."

Hershey's smile widened.

"I don't get why anybody would do such a thing," Allen went on. "I'd say the cat's out of the bag now. They don't have much to gain at this point. We know what the transmission is all about, and this guy who was run down was no more than a radio operator. Why go to all the trouble?"

"Yes, sir. That's what I thought too. Then I got to thinking. What if we don't know everything? What if the radio operator had other things he wrote down and didn't pass on to Sammy? That might be cause for certain people to want him dead, and Sammy just happened to be there."

"Interesting theory." Allen glanced up at Hershey. "Don't you think so, Lieutenant?"

Hershey grunted at the notion.

"Well, sir, it made me do something that I probably shouldn't have done, at least not without your approval."

Allen stroked his chin. "And what would that be?"

"I went to the man's ship, the *Nautique*. I wanted to see if there was another part of that message that he didn't bring with him and turn over to Sammy." Gwen shook her head. "I know I was out of place to do that. I should have told you and let you take care of it."

"It might have been a dangerous thing for you to do on your own," Allen said.

"And foolish," Hershey offered.

"Those same people who ran that man down could have been there," Allen said. "At the very least they might know you were there." He smiled. "How am I going to explain to your parents if something happens to you? You have a safe job, you know, as a language expert."

"Yes, sir. I know and I'm sorry."

"How did you get aboard the ship?" Hershey asked.

Gwen smiled and looked at Allen. "Let's just say I flashed my badge. The young man pulling watch duty had no way of knowing just how unofficial I was."

She opened her purse and pulled out the notebook she had taken from Quon Eng's footlocker. "I did get this out of his locker. It seems to be a diary. It has dates and writing, but in Cantonese."

Allen reached out and took it from her hand. He opened it and began to leaf through the pages. "When do you expect to have this translated?"

"It shouldn't take me more than an hour or two. I did see something else, though, and it presents a problem. I think it's something you're going to have to handle."

"What's that?"

"I wasn't the only one there looking into the radio operator's personal effects. I found two members of British Intelligence. One of them was a man I have seen before. He was in the restaurant where I met with my contact from the British Embassy for dinner on Friday night, a man by the name of Charles Bauer."

"Charlie? Really?"

"You know him?"

"Of course." He leaned back and looked at Hershey. "We know old Charlie pretty well, don't we, Lieutenant?"

Hershey nodded.

Gwen eyed Hershey. His facial cuts were deep. They could have been made by her umbrella. "It did make me wonder," Gwen went on. "Wonder why they would be there. This radio operator was American. He was working on a British steamer, but they had no rights to his personal things. They aren't the man's next of kin."

Allen smiled. "You mean things like diaries?"

"Yes." Gwen hung her head. "I know it was wrong of me to take it. I'll return it to his family. I just had to get it, and I didn't want them to have it."

Allen's phone rang again. He picked it up. Gwen could tell there was a different tone to his voice, almost surly. She did feel bad about the theft of someone else's private property. It went against everything she believed. She could also see how addictive this business could become. If she was willing to violate even one of her basic principles in order to stay on top of the problem, what else might she be willing to do?

She turned to Hershey. "So, how was your opera?"

"What opera?"

"You remember, the one you were trying to interest me in."

"Oh, fine. It went just fine."

"And did you find someone else for the other ticket?" She smiled. "I know you didn't take my landlady."

"Yes, I did."

"Someone from work here?"

Hershey stepped back, thinking. Then he quickly shook his head. "No, just a friend."

"I'm just glad your accident didn't prevent you from having a good time."

"What accident?"

She pointed to his face. "The one that caused that. Looks like you took some bad bruises and cuts there."

Hershey put his fingers up to the bruises on his face. He blushed. His face almost turned red. "I got these in a bike accident. The hills in town are deadly."

Allen hung up the phone then leaned forward on his desk. "OK, so Charlie Bauer and the MI6 were at the man's ship. That does seem odd."

"Too odd," Gwen agreed. "It just seems to be too much of a coincidence to me. It's almost like we're on the same trail and keep bumping into each other. I'd just like to know what possible interest British Intelligence has with our naval base at Pearl Harbor, or the interception of a coded message. I thought maybe that is something you could look into, since you appear to be somewhat cozy with these people."

"All right. I will look into it." He jotted down a note. "I must admit, it's more than a little intriguing. You have to remember, though, we're not an espionage unit here. Our responsibility is simply the interception and deciphering of foreign communication."

He looked up at Hershey. "You see, Hershey, Miss Williams may be a cloak-and-dagger woman yet."

"Let's hope it doesn't come to that," Hershey shot back.

"Now as to this other matter, Miss Williams, this communiqué from an Aki Kawa. She's at the place we're all curious about and asking questions that we know at least some of the answers to."

"Yes, sir. It would appear so."

"Aren't your parents living in Hawaii?"

"Yes, sir, they are."

Allen folded his arms. "I was just wondering. If you took a short-term assignment there, you might be able to help us out along with lending a hand to this Kawa person." He held up both hands as if to back her off. "Of course I would only want you doing safe things. I don't want you being the shore patrol over there."

Gwen nodded. Pete Allen was a fatherly figure. Since he had taken notice of her, the man seemed bent on protecting her.

"You might even consider taking a short cruise on a foreign national vessel and spending some time in the radio room. See if there are other transmissions going to Tokyo. Of course, we couldn't give you the code books. We'll have them in the office at Pearl Harbor, though. You never know. There could be all sorts of interesting things being transmitted to Japan."

"Yes, sir. I could do that." The fact was, Gwen would love to do that. She had no doubt that she would be able to uncover other communication being sent to Japan and, with the right help, she wouldn't even break the law.

"It would help a great deal if you could find me a neutral ship, sir, one where they would cooperate."

"I think I can do that. Of course it would allow you to spend some time with your parents too." He smiled. "You probably wouldn't mind that."

"No, sir. I wouldn't mind that at all." Gwen started to leave and then turned around. "Sir, we may have a bigger problem here at the office."

"What's that?" Allen asked.

"If the people who did this thing to Sammy and his friend were trying to find information he might have known about but didn't pass on to us, that would mean they would have to know what he did give us."

"Yes, I suppose it would."

"I was followed on Friday. So someone must know I was the one who had the information. And if the attempted break-in of my room is connected with this, that would mean someone knows what we are dealing with and who is responsible."

"Go on," Allen said. "Get to the point."

"Then there's the matter of the message itself and the identity of the person we got it from. British Intelligence was at the man's ship today. How did they know anything was wrong? How did they know the identity of the person who gave the information to Sammy?"

Allen and Hershey exchanged glances. Allen was worried, and Gwen could see it. She had to make her point. "So as I figure it, the only way that would be possible is if there is a leak somewhere in this building, someone who knows the names and particulars of the people involved."

"Are you suggesting a traitor, Miss Williams?"

Gwen nodded. "Yes, sir. That's exactly what I'm suggesting."

SEPTEMBER 12, 1941

CHAPTER 14

Autumn in New York came early that year, and it was the one good thing Sam Diamond could see about having to find and tail the man Jeff had sent him to follow, that and the expense account he had from the *Post*. He had a photograph of the man and stationed himself outside the German Embassy to watch the comings and goings of everyone doing business with the Nazi government. The most pathetic were the Jews, who were trying desperately to get their relatives away from Hitler's clutches.

Sam spent the most of his days on a park bench with a copy of the *Times* in his face, doing his best to keep from falling asleep. So great was his desperation, he had even taken to doing the crossword puzzles. The people making decisions in the FBI ought to be shot as far as he was concerned. Whatever they were doing, it was certain they hadn't approved this spy's further travel, at least not yet. They also seemed to be shortsighted. If they allowed the man to travel, they could find out his contacts. Such knowledge might prove invaluable.

He got up, folded the paper under his arm, and walked over to a hot-dog vendor. The dark-complexioned man looked to be Italian. He had a black handlebar mustache and dark, dancing eyes. He spotted Sam right away. He smiled. "Hot dog, sir?"

"Might as well," Sam said.

The man opened the lid on his cooking tray and extracted a long wiener. Tearing a bun from a sheet of the things, the man set the dog down on it and folded it together. He pointed to the end of the cart. "I got mustard, relish, and onions. Help yourself. Would you like a beer?"

"I'd love one." Sam reached over and took several napkins. He hated the light blue seersucker suit he was wearing, even though it was cool. He just didn't hate it enough to spill catsup on the thing.

The man set down the frothy beer. "That'll be fifty cents, mister."

Sam pulled two quarters out of his pocket and slapped them on the counter. Picking up his cup of beer, he walked back to the bench.

It was close to four in the afternoon when he spotted the man. He reached into his pocket and took out the photo he was carrying of Duskov Popov. He studied the picture and then glanced across the street. *It could be him*, Sam thought.

Popov appeared to be about five-foot-eight or nine, with dark hair graying at the temples. He had a thin mustache and looked to be two hundred forty or fifty pounds. Sam smiled. Obviously this fella wouldn't make much of a match on the squash court. He'd have to find some other way to meet him. From the looks of the man, Sam guessed a restaurant would be best. He was obviously fond of eating.

The idea that he had finally found Popov excited him. Something must be happening. Popov had kept his distance from the embassy for over two weeks now, and all that time Sam had been waiting. It irritated him not to be writing. Just sitting on his bench and thinking about the stories he could have been writing was enough to make him explode. While some people might actually enjoy this early retirement to a park bench, the very idea made Sam Diamond sick. The only thing that kept him going was the idea that he might actually be on to a story that would shake up the entire country. It could be the kind of a story that would make him as a reporter.

Popov stopped in front of the embassy steps and looked across the street in Sam's direction. Sam instantly raised the paper up in front of his face. He would look no different from the average man on a sunny September day. Popov had never seen him before, and Sam just wanted to blend in to the women passing by with their baby buggies and the old men wandering the streets. The only one who could possibly know different would be the man selling hot dogs.

He lowered the paper in time to see Popov going in the door. It would be time to move now. He didn't want to be on the bench when the man came back out.

He got to his feet and walked past the hot-dog vendor to the bus stop where a crowd of people had gathered. He would work at trying to blend in. Surely Popov wouldn't be long at the embassy, and then he could follow him. He had to find out just where Popov was staying and even if the man was meeting anyone.

Two hours later the door opened and Popov came down the stairs. Sam watched him walk away, then trailed him from a distance, sticking to his side of the street. He watched Popov call and then step into a taxi. Sam stepped out into the street to call his own. Putting his fingers into his mouth, he let out a bloodcurdling whistle.

Jumping into a yellow cab, Sam nudged the driver on the shoulder and pointed to the cab Popov had just gotten into. "Follow that cab."

The cabby turned to face him. He was a large man with flaming red hair and ears that stuck out like the open doors of a car. "Are you serious?" The man smiled.

"You bet I am."

The cabby grinned and threw the taxi into gear. "Good. I've always wanted to do this. Are you trailing some man making time with your wife?"

Sam sat back in the seat. It was good to have something soft on his back after the park bench, even if it was the seat of a taxicab. "Yes. How'd you know?"

"Just figured it might be. Most folks don't go around following people. Man's got to have a good reason for that, and in my book, that's the best there is. Whatcha gonna do when you catch him?"

"I'm going to try to catch him with my wife."

The cabby let out a low whistle. "Man oh man, ain't that gonna be something? You reckon he's going to meet up with her in a hotel somewhere?"

"I sure hope so." He clapped his hands. "I want to catch them together."

"Boy," the cabby shook his head, "Ain't that gonna be a scene. You just gonna yell at them, or you gonna give him a whipping?"

Sam grinned. Making up stories was something he did best as long as it wasn't going to press. "Nah, I ain't going to touch him. It's her who's getting the whipping."

The cabby turned around and grinned. "That's the boy. That's just what I'd do too, if I found my old lady with another man. I'd put some welts on her, sure enough."

They drove for another ten to fifteen blocks before the cab up ahead pulled over. Sam's cabby edged over to the curb to a spot some one hundred yards behind the lead cab. "You think this'll do, mister? I don't want to get too close. He might spot you."

Sam pulled out two dollars and handed it over to the man. "Keep the change."

Taking the money, the man stuffed it into his shirt pocket. "Thanks, mister. Why don't I just wait out here for a spell. It looks like he's going into Clancy's. Maybe he's making a phone call to her. You just might need me to take you to the hotel."

Sam got out and leaned into the window. "Great. You just wait then."

Sam walked through the doors at Clancy's and spotted Popov right away. He was seated at a table across the room, wearing a powder-blue suit with white shoes and a dark blue hamburg hat. The man appeared to be a dandy. He looked to be dressed more appropriately for Palm Beach than for New York City. Sam stepped right up to the bar. "I'll take a draft beer."

The bartender picked up a shiny beer glass, held it under the spigot, and pulled back on the wooden handle. He slid the foam-filled glass over the bar.

Sam slapped down two quarters and held the glass up to his lips. He could see Popov in the mirror behind the bar. The man had his large fist wrapped around a small whiskey glass. He was lifting the glass and sipping it like a Kentucky colonel enjoying an after-dinner drink of sour mash, sniffing it and rolling his eyes as he held the glass up to his lips. It made Sam smile. *The man can sure enjoy life*, he thought. *He must be used to the finer things.*

Popov got to his feet and walked over to the phone booth in the corner of the room. He closed the door, lighting up the small glass booth. Taking out some change, the man fed the phone and dialed.

Sam sipped his beer. He reached up and loosened his solid blue tie, then unbuttoned his top button. Being a policeman was something he didn't enjoy. He'd always thought that if the facts weren't readily available, then it was a story that wasn't ready to be written. This one was different, though. Something was afoot that could make the difference between war and peace, and for some reason the people who should be looking out for it were asleep at the switch. It might take his story to wake them up, and if the *Post* thought it was worth months of his time and thousands of their dollars to get it, then who was he to argue? It was flattering, as long as he didn't have to live through all the dead time to get it.

Looking into the mirror behind the bar, Sam saw Popov finish his call, come out of the booth, and walk to his table. Popov pulled a bill from his pocket and dropped it on the table. Lifting his chin and sticking out his chest, he walked out the door.

Sam finished his beer and slipped off the stool. He walked out of the bar and looked down the street. Popov was signaling for a cab. Glancing over to the curb, Sam spotted his own cab driver. His cabby was leaning out the window, smiling.

Sam raced over, opened the door, tumbled into the backseat.

"He tried to hire me," the cabby said, grinning, "but I sent him on his way. I told him I was off duty."

They watched as Popov finally hailed a cab and got in. Then they pulled out into traffic behind him.

"You ain't got much to worry about from that guy," the cabby said. "He ain't so much to look at, and besides that, he's got himself a steering-wheel blister." The man laughed and turned, then slapped his belly several times. "That's what we call this big belly in the cab business. It seems the longer a man sits behind one of these steering wheels, the bigger his belly gets."

Sam chuckled.

"So I wouldn't worry about him stealing her heart, if I was you. He must be rich, though. Maybe you should be on the lookout for jewels around the house that she's got stashed away. That has to be it. It can't be the man, 'cause you're a good-looking guy."

It was about a twenty-minute drive through busy Manhattan before Popov's cab pulled over in front of a hotel.

"That's the Mayflower Hotel. That man's got to be rich." The cabby swung the cab over to the curb.

Sam pulled out another bill and handed it over the seat to the man.

"I'll wait for you, same as last time." The cabby took the bill and stuffed it into his pocket. "You do what you've a mind to do, and you just might want to catch my cab to get outta here."

"That won't be necessary. You can go."

"Oh, no charge." The man split open a wide smile. "I ain't had me fun like this in a month or so. You just come out and tell me what happened, and I'll take you anywhere you like."

Sam ran up to the large revolving glass doors and pushed his way around them into the lobby. The place had a large crystal chandelier hanging in the middle of the room. Sam heard music and looked up to see a string quartet dressed in red waistcoats playing in the balcony.

Popov was taking his key from the clerk at the large mahogany desk. The dark, wooded front-desk reception area swept around the lobby with a freshly waxed shine and crystal vases filled with white lilies.

A group of people stood at the brass-caged elevators, and Sam made his way to the back of the group. Popov stood aside and let them get on, then took the next one with only a few people to compete for space.

Sam opened the cage and jumped into a third elevator, followed by a tall man in a simple blue suit. Sam looked over at Popov's elevator and could see the man looking at him for the first time. Popov smiled and, lifting his hat slightly, seemed to acknowledge Sam. It was as if he had been waiting for him. He watched Popov rise in the air and disappear into the floor above him.

The tall man pressed the button for the twelfth floor, and their own lift began to rise. Sam continued to look out the cage. He at least might be able to spot where Popov stopped. Failing that, he would try to bribe the desk clerk.

Sam's elevator suddenly stopped on the third floor. A short stumpy man got on. The man was powerfully built, and his suit bulged at the buttons. A five o'clock shadow darkened his face.

As the elevator began its rise once again, the tall man reached over to the control box and pressed the stop button just as their lift was closing in on the next floor. Sam saw him reach into his pocket and slip on a pair of brass knuckles.

"Now hold on, boys." Sam backed up to the far side of the elevator. "I'm not carrying that much money, but you're welcome to what I've got."

The shorter man spoke up. "We don't want your money." He looked over at the taller man and smiled, showing his greasy looking teeth. "Do we?"

Sam knew he was in trouble then. His only chance might be an unexpected punch. He figured he had to make it count, one punch, one man. There wasn't much choice for a man outnumbered and outweighed. He shrugged his shoulders and smiled, holding out his hands. "Well, you must have me mistaken for somebody else. I'm a real simple guy."

With that he launched a powerful roundhouse into the jaw of the tall man with the brass knuckles. The man's bones crunched under his fist. The man slammed against the cage and sank slowly to the floor. Sam wouldn't be so lucky with the shorter man.

The short stocky man sent a flurry of blows into Sam's midsection, stinging his ribs and doubling him over.

Sam turned and spun into the far side of the cage, breathing hard.

The man came on, this time sending a punch into Sam's jaw. It was a hard jab that showed some experience.

Sam weaved with his head and flung a punch into the man's face. It didn't seem to faze him in the least. The short man just kept plodding forward, his fists up.

Sam ducked several punches, sending blows into the man's midsection. Then he knew. The man was large but definitely not soft. Sam's fists seemed to bounce off his belly.

The man landed a punch to the side of Sam's head, and Sam crashed into the cage. The short man took Sam by the collar and turned him around.

Sam didn't exactly know where the blow came from. He figured it must have been from the tall man, who had evidently regained his senses. But it came down on the back of his head like a hammer, dropping Sam to his knees. The entire world was spinning, not just the elevator. Flashes of light exploded inside his brain. Then he could see nothing. He went limp.

SEPTEMBER 13, 1941

CHAPTER 15

Aki walked up the rocky walkway to her grandmother's house. The rocks were volcanic, a deep rich black that seemed to shine even in the dark. Colorful shells had been set into them, blinking out with deep blues and pink. Palm trees lined the walk, and large numbers of hibiscus flowers were in bloom, their rose and plum colors waving in the soft trade winds. It was peaceful here, and guests could feel it long before they knocked on the door. The old woman had worked the pineapple and sugarcane fields her whole life. She knew what it meant to stoop the entire day in the hot, blistering sun. Grandma Dai had saved her pennies and bought the house long ago. Now it had become an oasis for Aki, the one place she could go to find love and understanding.

Aki kicked off her shoes and knocked on the bright green door with the plumed peacocks carved into it. She waited for the woman to come to the door, and when it opened, she beamed. Grandmother Dai was in a red kimono. The woman's gray hair was in a bun with a bright black tortoiseshell comb in the back. Her arms and legs were frail, but she held herself steady as she bowed. She smiled at Aki and then hugged her. "Come in, child. Let's have some tea." Grandmother Dai's love was constant. She gave it without expecting anything in return.

Aki padded through the door and followed her grandmother into the kitchen. The house was beautiful, cool, and shady. The pink and white tiles on the floor depicted a delicate orchid. Paintings of birds hung on the walls, and the old lady stopped to playfully tease a pair of turtledoves in a bamboo cage. "You sing nice and love each other. I be back to you soon." The old lady had an enduring relationship with the birds. They were more than house pets.

After she had carefully made a pot of tea, the two of them sat on the shady veranda and sipped from small cups. Dai reached over and patted Aki's hand. "You feeling loved today, child?"

"Yes, but sometimes it's confusing."

Dai smiled and sipped her tea. "Love is not confusing. It is the people who are not in love who are confused."

"Yes, I know. I love a man my parents do not approve of."

"Because he is not Japanese?"

"Yes, how did you know?"

"You are a child. Sometimes parents see more than the heart of a child. It makes them dizzy with all the things they see."

"But you don't, Grandma. You just see me."

Dai shook her head. "Nothing is more important than a child's heart. It is pure like the streams of the mountains. It is surrounded by the flowers, and the birds bathe in it to make themselves clean all over."

"Why are they like that? Why can't they let me be me and make my own decisions?"

Dai nodded her head in a rocking motion. "You feel angry with them when you should feel sorrow."

Aki was puzzled by this remark.

"You should feel sorrow," Dai went on, "because their lives have become wrapped up in yours for their own reasons, not because of you. When a mother or father are unhappy with their own lives, they start to live the life of the child. If they can make their child turn out the way they wanted their own lives to be, then it makes it easier for them to deaden the pain of feeling empty. The more hollow they are, the harder they try to steer their children."

"And you think my parents' lives are empty?"

"They work the cane fields with your brother, only they fight against it. They hate the sun, but they are in it every day. When I work there, I always love the sun. I work hard because I love the work. It is not a curse to me. It a blessing. You go to school and then to the university. You are a smart girl, and they want so much for you because they are living their lives through you."

Dai held up her hands and positioned her fingers to form a frame around Aki's face. "Your parents have a beautiful picture in their head of their lives through you. They know they will never have it, but they take pleasure in dreaming you can." She put her hands down and smiled. "Part of their picture is you being a good Japanese girl and marrying a Japanese boy whose family they know. They think it's best for you even when it's only best for them."

It took Aki several hours with her grandmother to feel refreshed and at peace before it was time to leave. Brian had loaned her his old Ford car, and when she jumped in and slammed the door, she took a deep breath. *Will I ever have my grandmother's wisdom?* she wondered.

She started the car and drove up to the bluffs overlooking Pearl Harbor. Brian was working that day on the *Arizona*, and if she could see the ship, it would make her feel a little bit closer to him.

She pulled the car up to the turnaround, turned off the ignition, and put on the brake. Getting out, she stepped over to the guardrail. There it was, the *Arizona*. Something about the power of the ship reminded her of Brian. It was a serious ship with a mission, and so was Brian. The man knew what he wanted, and he wanted her. It warmed Aki's heart.

She turned to go but stopped when she looked down the bluff and saw the familiar sight of Yoshikawa, the Japanese vice-consul. Already she had taken the time to do a little background work on the man. He had at one time been an ensign with the Japanese navy. It was highly unusual for a man to leave the military to join the diplomatic corps. That was certainly true during these times. The future of Japan was in its military, not in its diplomacy. It would seem that Yoshikawa had taken a backseat when it came to his future, but Aki knew that wasn't true. Everything she had heard about the man showed him to be bright and ambitious. He was here as a member of the Japanese consulate for a reason, a military reason.

She watched him look through his binoculars at the fleet below and then make notes in the small notebook he was carrying. He then turned around and made his way back to his car.

Aki's heart raced. She knew she shouldn't do it, but she was determined to follow him. The man obviously had a routine, and she was going to discover what it was. If military intelligence was asleep at the switch, she was going to make sure she was wide awake.

She walked back to her car and got in, waiting until Yoshikawa's car passed by on the highway. Then she began her slow pursuit of the man. It took them some time to wind down the bluffs, but Aki wasn't concerned about getting lost. She knew, however, if she was going to follow him through Honolulu, she would have to stay close. She just hoped he wouldn't get suspicious.

They took the turn on to King Street and drove past the Aliiolani Hale, or the House of the Heavenly King. Kamehameha's statue stood imposingly at the front of the unused palace, frozen in his dignity. Then turning on Richards Street, they drove past the YMCA building. Aki saw him pull into a parking place in the next block. She drove past him, looking for a place to park.

It took a minute or so before a spot opened up and she could pull in. It was a loading zone parking place, but that didn't stop her. She jumped out of the Ford and shut the door, not bothering to lock it.

She scampered down the block before she caught sight of the man. He was going into Saint Andrew's Cathedral, and she was certain it wasn't because he was an Episcopalian. She rushed past the tall, thin statue of Saint Andrew. He seemed to be pointing to her.

She pushed open the heavy door to the church and slipped inside. It was somewhat dark, but some light poured though a series of stained-glass windows. The church had been built in 1867. Kamehameha IV had been an Anglophile, and he had brought the Anglican religion to Hawaii after a trip to England. Everything English and white had to be good, and everything brown and Hawaiian must be old and out-of-date. It was one of the attitudes that were snuffing out the Hawaiian culture.

Aki strained to see to the front of the church, finally spotting Yoshikawa. The man was seated in a pew near the front, talking with a second man. Aki knew she couldn't get close enough to overhear what the two of them were saying. That would stop this adventure of hers in a minute. But she wanted desperately to see who Yoshikawa was talking to. She could see even from that distance that the man wasn't Japanese. He was an Anglo. It made her heart race. *Is it a military man?* she wondered. *Perhaps even someone I know?* She slipped around to the side aisle. The two men's voices were muffled, but it was obvious they weren't worshiping. They were talking.

The altar was imposing and distant. She didn't much like it. It was so very different from her own small missionary church led by Pastor Williams. It made God feel cold to her, and she knew He wasn't that. The God she was learning about had made every effort to span time and space to be a man Himself, not to remain aloof in the heavens and simply pity the plight of mankind.

She said a small prayer, hoping she could remain invisible to the two men, if only for a moment. Normally she wouldn't have to worry. Women were usually invisible on their own. They had nothing important to accomplish in the eyes of most men, and if they were not in a place to be admired and desired, men simply looked through them. Aki hoped that would be the case for her today.

She slowly padded forward, straining her ears to hear. But it was what she was looking for that mattered most to her. She had to see what the second man looked like. He had on a white shirt with wet-looking, jet-black hair combed straight back.

Suddenly the man turned, his massive shoulders stretching the fabric of his shirt. He looked in her direction with a scowling face. She didn't recognize him. He nudged Yoshikawa, who also turned to look at her.

Aki bowed her knee and crossed herself. Then slipping into a pew she knelt, bowed her head, and began to pray.

PART 2
RED SUN RISING

SEPTEMBER 16, 1941

CHAPTER 16

G wen scrambled down the ramp of the plane and held her straw bonnet down on her head. The prop wash was mixing with the trade winds in a swirl of warm air, and the bright Hawaiian sun hit her eyes like a bolt of white lightning. The green hills were lush with dotted flowers in bright colors. Near the door of the terminal, two young women in grass skirts were swaying to hula music while another beautiful young woman was hanging leis around the necks of the passengers and greeting each man with a kiss. It was a traditional Hawaiian greeting for anyone who had caught the early flight from San Francisco.

Gwen bent her head and allowed the woman to circle her neck with a lei made of fragrant pink carnations. Joining the throng of passengers, she scurried through the doors like one more member of the flock of sheep called tourists. It was her father's smile that awakened her to the fact that she wasn't a tourist. She was home now, not because she had ever known the place, but because this was where she was loved.

Her father was tall and had a shock of white hair and a white mustache. He smiled at her and held out another lei made from jasmine and white ginger blossoms. The smell was like a sweet perfume. He pushed the lei over her head and kissed her. "It's so good to see you, honey. Your mother and I have been waiting a long time for you to visit us here."

Gwen looked over his shoulder at her mother. She was still beautiful, thought Gwen, with a broad angular smile and dark hair mixed with gray. Her dark brown eyes were much like Gwen's. She held out her arms without saying a word.

Gwen rushed to her mother and hugged her. It felt good to hold her mother in her arms.

Her mother removed Gwen's hat and stroked her hair. "It's so good to see you, baby. I don't know why you think you're here, but your father and I believe the Lord sent you." She pushed her back slightly and looked her over. "And you look wonderful. A little pale," she laughed, "but good."

Gwen smiled. "I'm sure this sun of yours will cure that. The sky can be so gray in San Francisco. Why don't we go to the Pink Palace and you can let me buy you lunch. I'll try to explain what I'm doing here. Frankly, I don't know how long I'll be staying. I will need some transportation, though."

"We can loan you our car," her father said.

Her mother wrapped her arm around her father's waist. "We don't use it much anymore. You're welcome to it."

The trip to the Royal Hawaiian Hotel wound through the streets of Honolulu and into the district known as Waikiki. The place was known for its beach, and it was one of the things Gwen wanted to see right away. King Kamehameha I had built a bungalow facing the water after he had conquered the chiefs on the island of Oahu. It had been built close to where the Royal Hawaiian Hotel now stood. He had evidently enjoyed the ocean view, and the majestic sight of Diamond Head behind it made it even more awe-inspiring. Just the sight of the place caused Gwen to appreciate the taste the man had in location. The beach was sandy white, and men stood on surfboards in the water, riding the waves toward the white stretch of sand.

Gwen's father took a turn with the Ford onto a side street and parked the car near a spot frequented by picnickers. "I thought we could walk along the beach to the hotel," he said. "The view is much better this way."

It was a beautiful view of the breaking waves and silver sand. Gwen slipped off her shoes and followed them onto the beach. She could see the men on their surfboards riding the waves in front of her, and in the distance an outrigger canoe was being paddled into the breaking surf, filled to the brim with tourists who were anxious to feel the thrill of the surf, even if they couldn't stand on one of the monstrous boards.

Stepping over to the wet sand, she lifted her skirt and waded into the foaming water. It felt good on her lower calves, warm and inviting. It would be easy to forget why she had come to Hawaii. She would have to remember to schedule a day off for herself.

The sight of the Royal Hawaiian Hotel was almost overwhelming. The Pink Palace was aptly named. It was coral pink from top to bottom with a Moorish design. Banyan and palm tress crisscrossed the front of the place with a small forest of pink and white umbrellas scattered over the emerald lawns. Within minutes Gwen and her parents had seated themselves at a glass-topped white wrought-iron table, but Gwen found it hard to take her eyes off the water.

Her father leaned across the table. "I know just how you feel. I never tire of this place."

"How long will you be here?" her mother asked.

The question brought Gwen's mind back to the purpose of lunch. She did want to communicate with her parents, even though there wasn't much she could tell them. "I really don't know. It might be days. It might be months."

"So I take it you're here on Navy business?" her father asked.

Gwen nodded. "Yes, I'm afraid I am. I will have other things on my mind while I'm here that I wish I didn't have to deal with."

"I won't ask you what that is," her father added.

Jack Williams had always been a lighthearted man who seemed to look on the positive side of whatever disaster they were in the middle of. He had a quick mind as well as a sharp wit. He always seemed to know just when it was best to leave things alone and ask no questions.

Gwen shook her head slightly. "I'm afraid I couldn't tell you." She swallowed hard. "I'm also afraid I need to ask you a favor"—she shot a glance at her mother—"a big favor."

"What is that, baby?" her mother asked.

Gwen inched closer to the table. "I need for you to tell people I'm here just to visit you and take a break from my studies. I know you minister to the Japanese, and I don't want my visit linked to anything official. That may be difficult for both of you because I know you're scrupulously honest."

Jack reached over and patted her hand. "Just so you actually do spend some time with us. Doris and I would never want to put you in any danger." He leaned closer to her. "Is this a dangerous situation?"

"It could be."

"But I thought you were just a language specialist for those navy people," her mother said.

"I am. I'm sorry I can't tell you any more than that. I have no intention of dragging you into my problems or compromising any of your work here."

Jack patted her hand once again. "Sweetheart, you dragged us into your problems the day you were born. There's nothing you go through that we don't go through ourselves."

"Just trust me on this, Daddy. It's best that you stay out of it, the both of you. It's nothing serious. Don't worry. Just the usual government paranoia."

They finished their leisurely lunch while watching people playing in the surf. Gwen had a papaya filled with plump pink shrimp. The fresh pineapple juice tasted especially good. Gwen was finishing her third glass when something caught her eye. A pudgy man in a rumpled and dingy white suit nervously settled into a seat across from a stone-faced Japanese businessman who was sporting a thin, black mustache. What attracted her attention even more was a third man who seemed to be following the pudgy man. He took a seat at a distance. Even though he had on dark sunglasses, Gwen could see at once that his eyes were fastened on the man in the white suit. He shook open a newspaper but lowered it slightly to make certain the man in the white suit was in view. It was one of those silent movie moments, Gwen thought, where you could see what was happening but had no words or thoughts to accompany your observations, only what appeared in plain sight.

"Are you all right?" Jack asked, dabbing his narrow mouth with his starched white napkin.

"Yes. I'm sorry. I seem to get lost so easily these days. Any little thing at all can set my mind adrift."

"Is work bothering you, dear?" Doris asked.

Gwen let out a sigh. "Right now it's the worst, and yet it's the best I could have hoped for. Don't ask me to explain that. I'm doing things

I never bargained for. They are important things, and somehow I seem to be the only one who can do them."

"You feel necessary," Jack said.

"Yes, that's exactly it. Very necessary."

Gwen watched the man in the white suit get to his feet, followed by the Japanese man. She nudged her father's arm. "Do you know that man, the Japanese man in the blue suit?"

Jack turned his head to spot the man, then quickly looked back at Gwen. "Yes, that's the vice-consul at the Japanese Embassy. His name is Takeo Yoshikawa. I don't know the other man. Never seen him before."

As the two men left, Gwen watched to see what the other man would do. True to what she thought, he got to his feet, dropped a bill on the table, and followed the two men at a respectable distance.

"Will you be reporting to Pearl Harbor today?" Jack asked.

Gwen shook her head. "No, it's Saturday. I don't think the person I need to see will be there until Monday."

Jack laughed. "Yes, you won't find anybody there who knows anything until Monday morning. It's Hawaii, you know. This seems to be the playground for everyone over the rank of corporal."

"Then you'll be going to church with us tomorrow?" Doris asked.

"Yes, I'd love to do that."

"I think we have a young woman there who works for the navy," Doris said. "You can ask her about where to report. Her name is Aki Kawa."

Gwen put down her juice. "Really? Aki Kawa? That's the woman I need to see first."

CHAPTER 17

Aki got off the bus and walked slowly toward the beach. She was wearing a red-flowered sarong to cover her swimsuit, but even then her movement attracted attention from the sailors she passed. They turned their heads to watch her walk by. A few even raised their eyebrows and whistled. Such things used to bother her. Now she just saw them as feeble-minded compliments from guys too backward to make conversation. It wasn't exactly their fault. Poor family structure only produced rudeness. It actually made her feel sorry for them. In spite of their faults, her family had bred a sense of pride in her.

Kuhio Beach Park stretched along Kalakaua Avenue. Palm trees were bent over in the breeze, appearing to touch their toes. The grass was green and well kept, and small children ran around the trees, playing tag and laughing. Barbecue pits smoldered in the late afternoon sun. She and Brian loved to come to this place. The ring of children's voices made each of them think about the family they were going to make together.

She had spent most of her day doing what she could to make her parents happy. She had toiled in the vegetable garden, doing her best to clear the weeds out of the rows of yams. It had taken some time to clean up, and her nails had taken quite a beating. The *Arizona* was on a short shakedown cruise, and Brian wouldn't be back on the island until late in the afternoon. The beach at Kuhio would be the perfect spot for her to watch the big ship steam into Pearl Harbor. And it would be a nice place to dream about Brian.

She walked over the small hill and stepped onto the sand. Unwrapping the large beach towel, she spread it out. She then stepped out of her sandals and took off her sarong. The afternoon sun would be cooler. She had been through the heat of the day in the garden, and she knew this would be far more pleasant. Taking a copy of Mark Twain's *Roughing It* from her handbag, she lay down and began to read. Twain always made her laugh, and his observations about the American West struck her as almost Japanese. They were wrapped in self-effacing humor with a very dry wit.

She read for a short time and then looked up to see an old man in a straw hat making his way down the beach in her direction. The man's dirty T-shirt hung from where he'd tied it around his waist, and his shoulders and arms were practically glowing with the effects of the sun. He had a small yellow pail in one hand and a rake in the other, which he was using to sift through the sand. His scraggly beard was snow white and his face beet red with large flakes of peeling skin coming off his exposed nose. Even from where she was lying, she could tell the man was a drinker. Spiderweb veins stood out on his burned nose and through the patches of beard that were missing from his cheeks. His legs were thin and spindly and stood out from his dirty brown shorts like clay pipe stems from the bottom of a paper bag.

As he moved closer, he spotted her and broke out into a wide grin. He lifted his hat to politely acknowledge her presence. "Afternoon, little lady."

"Good afternoon." Aki put down her book.

He glanced at the sand. "I'm just out here looking for some spare change. Folks run around and drop all kinds of whatnots in the sand, you know. They don't miss them, and I'd sure appreciate finding them."

"I haven't seen any, but you could be right."

The man shook his pail. Coins clanked in the bottom of the yellow bucket, and the man's grin widened with each shake. "You bet I is right. This here beach is my own rice bowl. I knows it backwards and forwards. Where else can a man scrape up a few bucks and watch pretty girls too." His blue eyes twinkled in Aki's direction. "Old Homer knows what to do with his self. That's more than I can say for most folks hereabouts."

He turned around and stretched. White hair on his back stood up like a frosty forest on a field of snow, pink from the setting sun. "Whew," he said, pointing a long arm and extending a crooked finger. "Look out there. It's the *Arizona* coming in."

Aki sat up. The man was right. Brian's ship was coming in. She lightly fingered the cross around her neck. Just the sight of the big ship filled her with warmth. She could imagine that just then he was standing on the deck of the great ship and was looking off in the direction of Kuhio Beach. Even now their eyes could be meeting, even if they couldn't see one another.

Homer squatted down and stared at her. "You all right, ma'am? You seen a battleship before, ain't you?"

Aki swallowed and smiled. "Yes. I'm sorry. My mind was drifting. My boyfriend is on that ship. I came here so I could see it come in and know just how soon he'd be here."

Homer grinned, showing several spaces where teeth once had been. "That sure is sweet, mighty sweet. I jes craves seeing young folks who is in love." He stood upright and threw his shoulders back. "Homer here was in love too once. Had me a wife and kids, I did."

"What happened to them?"

He turned and stared off across the open Pacific. "I reckon they is still over there in Iowa. I had me a hankering to travel, I did. I hitched to Frisco and then shipped out on a steamer for Hong Kong. Had me a high old time too." He hung his head. "But I guess life ain't jes about high old times. There's got to be more than that. The times end, and a body winds up raking through sand for nickels, dimes, and quarters."

"Why don't you get a job and earn enough for passage back home?"

Homer kicked at the sand with his bare feet, then stirred it with his toe. "I reckon old Homer here ain't much fer doing any more. I'm more cut out for dreaming and thinking about doing. Guess I'm past caring about, 'cause I don't care so much myself anymore."

"I might know a place where you could find help."

He cocked his head and stared at her over the bridge of his crooked nose. "Where might that be? I ain't much for charity. People who set themselves to giving to other folks usually wind up taking."

Aki forced a smile. "You can come tomorrow to the Rainbow Community Church on Duke's Lane. I have friends there who can find you a job and maybe a place to live. It wouldn't take long to earn your way to Iowa. Who knows, maybe the people there who love you are thinking and praying for you right now."

"I never was much of a church person."

Aki smiled. This time it was genuine. "That's all right. Rainbow Church isn't that much of a church. Most of the people there are

Japanese. You'd like the pastor though, Reverend Jack Williams. He'd like you too, I think."

"I've seen the place. I jes might take you up on that."

"I'll be there tomorrow at ten. You'd at least have one friend."

Homer nodded his head slowly. "That's mighty nice of you. It's been a long time since I had me a friend."

"Well, you have one now. My name is Aki."

Homer reached down and shook her hand. "Pleased to meet you, Aki. Will yer feller be there with you?"

"Yes, I think so."

"That's nice. Good to see young folks going where they ought to go." He shook his bucket and gripped his rake. "I'll be moving on down the beach now." A small smile cracked his lips. "You never know, I jes might find me something for that offering basket."

Aki watched him as he moved slowly down the beach, raking and pawing at the sand, occasionally bending over to pick up a part of the treasure of Kuhio Beach. Then she settled back in the sand to read and wait for Brian. He would know where to come. This was always where she liked to go when he was coming back into Pearl Harbor.

Time passed as she read. If it wasn't for the writings of Mark Twain, the time would have crept by. As it was, the book made the waiting bearable. It made her laugh, and she needed to laugh.

The sound of loud voices and laughter caused her head to turn. What she saw made her skin crawl. Coming over the grassy hill onto the beach was Hiroki Fujiyama, leading a few of his Japanese mafia in blue jeans and tennis shoes. Her brother wasn't one of them, and that meant trouble. They had spotted her, and Hiroki was pointing in her direction. Evidently, she was going to be the object of their evening fun.

Aki put her book on the ground and jumped to her feet. The thugs with Hiroki fanned out around her, smiling and cackling like a group of hens who had spotted a juicy worm in the barnyard.

"What are you doing here?" she asked.

Hiroki lifted his chin and stared at her down the length of his straight nose. "We were looking for you. You here to meet your sailor?"

"Yes, I am." Aki glanced at her watch. "He ought to be here any minute."

Hiroki laughed. "You lie. We saw his ship pull in. He not be here for an hour or more." He glanced at the men around him and smiled. "That leaves us plenty of time with you here in the sand."

"You are shaming yourself. You call yourself a friend of my brother, but you're no more than gangsters."

"We are Japanese. We find what we want and we take it." Hiroki held out his hand and slowly squeezed his fist into a tight ball. "We don't need the permission of the Americans. Those people you work for can't save you now. You belong to us."

Aki backed up. The men with Hiroki had managed to place themselves between her and the rest of the beach. They were on either side of her and, while they were anxious to join in on the fun that Hiroki had in mind, they were going to wait for him to make the first move. That much was apparent.

"I will tell my father, and he will come after you."

Hiroki smiled and shook his head. "Be serious. Your father and mother are ashamed of you already. They see you as dirt under the white man's boot. I don't really think you're going to shame yourself even more in their eyes by telling them or anyone else what happens to you here tonight. And I don't think you're going to tell your sailor, either. Do you really think he would have anything further to do with you if he knew you had been the concubine to Japanese men? He would spit on you and walk away. He would go back to his father. You are a fool, Aki."

Aki continued to back up until her feet hit the water. She could see the look of determination written on Hiroki's face.

"Look at it this way. We are doing you a favor. Now you will have nowhere to go but back to your own kind."

"Just leave me alone." Aki waded into the water. It lapped through her legs and around her knees.

CHAPTER 18

Brian Picard worked feverishly on the deck of the *Arizona* as the big battle wagon slowly slipped into her berth. She had performed well during the sea trials, and Brian's men had made their drills with very few flaws. He was in charge of a set of anti-aircraft batteries on the port side of the ship, and he took pride in his men executing their assignments with speed. He shouted orders, commanding the men to stow the ammunition in an accessible location and then fasten the containers securely. Everything had to be inspection-ready before he could leave the ship, and he wanted to see

Aki as soon as possible. She would be waiting for him in their usual spot at Kuhio Beach.

One of the men working beside him nudged him and pointed over the side. "Admiral's launch," he said.

Brian stopped work and stared out at the boat below. It was white with polished oak rails and a flag with two stars flying. He didn't think there was an inspection in the wind, but one could never be sure. He strained to see who was on board the launch, but he couldn't see anyone who looked like an admiral. Several sailors manned the engine and rudder of the vessel, and one lone junior officer stood in the bow. "You better alert the deck officer," he told the man.

Brian and the men continued to store the supplies and ammunition. It was several minutes later before he saw the officer from the launch come up the boarding ladder. The man asked a crew member a question, and the sailor pointed Brian out. It began to dawn on Brian why he was being singled out, but he tried to push the thought out of his mind.

The young officer walked in Brian's direction. The man was in his dress white uniform. He looked uncomfortable, high starched collar and all. He stepped up to Brian and saluted. "Admiral Picard's compliments, sir. He's asked you to accompany me back to the fleet headquarters."

"My father's here in Pearl? When did he get in?"

"About noon today."

Brian turned over what remained of his duties to the chief working next to him and picked up a washcloth to clean his hands. He was wearing his khaki uniform, and he glanced at it to make certain it was presentable. He knew he had to be careful of his appearance around his father. The man cut slack for no one, especially his own son. His shoes were a bit scuffy, but other than that he seemed to be OK.

He dropped the cloth into the bucket and turned to the ensign. "Let's go. I guess we can't put this off."

The man snappily turned on his heels and led the way to the ladder. He went over the side, and Brian followed. It wasn't long before the launch was cutting through the water and heading for the docks. Chugging up to the wooden dock a short time later, the sailors edged the craft next to it and cast lines to the men waiting above. Brian headed up the ramp behind the ensign and began the walk to the place where he would meet with his father.

Being the son of an admiral had always been a difficult proposition. Even as a child there had never been any question about what was expected of Brian Picard. He was going to be a naval officer, and that was that. His first toys had been boats. Sailing was a matter of virtue for him, a test of masculinity mixed with intelligence. It had always seemed to Brian that his father carefully watched his life for flaws, for any weakness that might prevent his rise in the ranks. Brian had grown weary of it before he'd ever gotten into kindergarten.

Brian's time at the Naval Academy had perhaps been the worst experience of his life. His father's scrutiny had been replaced by that of hundreds of others. Everywhere he went he was Admiral James Picard's son, never just Brian Picard. He had no life of his own. He was merely an extension of his father's career.

A man like his father had been measured in every way possible, including how well he could manage and control his family. Brian's mother had disappeared into a haze of party dresses and cocktails, and now Brian was fading into the oblivion of white dress uniforms in his father's shadow. Brian had become the ultimate test of how high an admiral like James Picard could rise in the eyes of his peers.

Brian ran up the gray concrete stairs behind the young ensign. A pair of white uniformed shore patrol sailors stood by the door of the building. They were wearing black spats and leggings with shines that equaled the black, mirrorlike shoes on their feet. Both men snapped to attention and saluted as Brian followed the ensign inside.

The walls of the long hallway, bleached white, were dotted with pictures of dead heroes. It was as if the men in the photographs were taking stock of his character and trying to see if he measured up to what they expected in a navy officer. There was no way he could ever fill one of those polished frames. What was more, he didn't want to.

The ensign pushed open a double door and stepped inside, saluting the two admirals who were standing beside a massive, polished mahogany desk in the center of the large room. A plush blue carpet adorned the hardwood floor. Books on shelves and trophies behind leaded glass flanked the room. Red, overstuffed leather furniture, two wing chairs, and a couch surrounded a polished driftwood coffee table with a heavy glass top.

Brian's father returned the young officer's salute. Beside him stood a man that Brian had only seen in photographs and at a distance from a reviewing stand—Admiral Husband E. Kimmel, commander-in-chief of the Asiatic fleet.

"Sir," the young officer squeaked, "I brought Ensign Picard as ordered."

"I see you have." The older Picard laughed. "That'll be all. You're dismissed."

The young ensign dropped his salute and awkwardly turned an about-face maneuver. Brian could see the embarrassment registered all over the young man's face as he almost tripped. He marched out of the room, picking up speed as he hit the hallway outside. There was a rat-a-tat to his polished heels that sounded like distant machine gun fire. No doubt the man was trying to cover his retreat. Brian only wished he could.

"Stand at ease, young man," Kimmel said.

Brian went to parade rest. It was about as at-ease as he could be under the circumstances.

"Your father has brought you some good news."

Brian watched his father's expression. The man was tall, over six-feet-two. Height seemed to be a prerequisite for command in the navy, and Brian could thank or curse whatever circumstance had made him turn out to be six-feet-four.

His father's carefully parted gray hair didn't have one single lock out of place except for one over his forehead that the man habitually pushed back into position. His barrel-sized chest allowed his decorations to shine with an array of colors that matched the aurora of a rainbow. He was otherwise trim for his age. His lantern jaw had a stern sense of command about it, and his short stubby nose was flanked by brown eyes that looked like puddles of fresh oil being poured into the crankcase of a purring engine.

He reached back to the desk he was standing in front of and produced a small, velvet-covered purple box. "Yes, very good news. I brought you something else too."

He opened the box and held it out for Brian.

Brian stepped forward and took the box from his father's hand. In it were a matched pair of silver bars, the silver bars of a lieutenant.

"Your promotion has come though," his father said. He reached into the box in Brian's hand and took out the insignias. "I brought you my old lieutenant's bars. I've been saving them for you. I just wanted to get a chance to tell you myself and pin them on you."

Brian swallowed hard as his father unpinned the single bars of the ensign rank from his khaki collars and then stapled the lieutenant's bars into position, pushing the pin stays into place. There was a brief moment of pride for Brian at wearing the new rank, but only a brief one. He knew it marked a moment of pride for his father, but it also singled him out as an admiral's son. Few other officers had made grade as fast as Brian Picard, and now there would be evidence as to why that was. "Thank you, Admiral," Brian said.

Brian's father slapped both of his shoulders with his hands. "No need for that admiral crap right now, son. Dad will do just fine."

"Thank you, Dad." Brian said the word hesitatingly. It seemed much too informal for the man. Admiral, yes. Sir, definitely. But Dad? Seldom. The man had always commanded respect and awe. It was affection he seldom got. Brian knew that was because it was something he seldom if ever gave.

"Admiral Kimmel and I were planning on taking you out to the Officer's Club tonight to celebrate. We can get some beefsteaks, some beer," he chuckled, "and watch you chase a few skirts."

Brian hung his head, the air escaping his lungs slowly.

"Of course, you can go back to your ship and change into your dress whites."

"Dad, I'm afraid I have plans for tonight."

"Change them! Whoever you're playing poker with won't mind this once. I'd say this is an important occasion." He cast a glance at Kimmel and grinned.

"Yes, sir." Brian looked him in the eye. "But I'm afraid they can't be changed. They're plans I've made with a woman."

"Hey, you're going to have plenty of women all over you tonight. One less won't mean much."

"This is a very special woman to me, Dad."

"Special? How special?"

Kimmel cleared his throat and smiled. "Look, it would seem you two have a lot to talk about. Jimmy, I'll be at the O Club at eighteen hundred hours. If you're there with young Brian, that will be great. Otherwise, we'll just tell lies to each other." He stepped over to where Brian was standing and put his hand on Brian's shoulder. "Son, your father and I go back a long ways. If you ever need anything, you just sing out. You've got a listening ear with me."

Brian nodded at him and smiled. "Thank you, sir. I appreciate that."

Kimmel doffed a semisalute in the direction of Brian's father and strode out of the room. Brian could feel a chill from his father as soon as Kimmel stepped out.

The man looked at him, his eyes hardening. "This woman you're with tonight, is this the Japanese girl I've been hearing about?"

"How did you hear anything?"

"I have my sources. Admirals do have some pull, you know."

Brian reached up and fingered the bars on his collar. "Yes, I can see that."

"So, is it? I don't mind you going out with a few of the locals now and then. It's good for a man. Makes him figure out the keepers from the throwaways. But going out with the enemy, that is out of the question."

"She isn't the enemy. She works for the Office of Naval Intelligence as a language specialist." Brian could see that his words made his father angry. The old man's face turned hard. His chin tightened, and his lower lip pushed out.

"A Japanese working for Naval Intelligence? That's a blame fool thing to do. I'd call it dangerous. We could be fighting those people any minute, and I wouldn't want one under the sheets with me. We'll have to see what we can do about that."

Brian reached out and took his arm. He squeezed it hard. "Don't say or do anything. This is the woman I'm planning to marry."

The old man's face turned white as the T-shirt peeking out over his collar. "Marry? Now you're the one doing the fool thing. Do you have any idea what that would do to your career? People won't speak to you, and you'll be cut out of receiving any classified information. You'll be ruined."

"I don't care. I love the girl and I'm going to marry her."

"Who is she, and where does she live? If my hunch is right, I'd say all she wants is money. I can take care of that. If there's a baby on the way, I can take care of that too."

Brian shook his head. "There's no baby. We haven't slept together. She's not that kind of girl, and I haven't been that kind of man since I met Aki. She's different. She's good and pure."

CHAPTER 19

The twilight moon over Kuhio Beach hung low in the sky. The Royal Hawaiian Hotel stood out in the pale silver silhouette of the moon, cutting into the bottom half. Its Moorish arches and pink tower were like fingers pointing into the sky. It reminded Aki to pray, and she did. She had often needed God's help but rarely with the note of desperation she was feeling. Usually when she prayed, it was with thanks in mind, and on occasion when she asked for something, it was for something on the distant horizon of her life. Now her need was immediate.

Aki backed into the surf, letting the waves slam into her back. With each lapping wave, a force seemed to push her toward the waiting arms of the men who were leering at her from the beach. They were laughing and taunting her like jackals surrounding a wounded gazelle on the African plain, hungry, eager to pounce, but circling and draining all hope before finally finishing her off.

"Come on out," one man said. "We won't hurt you"—"much." His cackling laugh rumbled with enthusiasm and filled her with despair.

Aki was trembling. Her feet dug into the sandy bottom of the beach, and each crashing sound of the surf behind her caused her to gasp, sucking the heavy salty air deep into her lungs. She could only hope that the next large wave wouldn't pick her up and send her headfirst into the gang of thugs waiting for her. "Go away," she shouted. "Stop bothering me."

Hiroki bent over, placing his hands on his knees. He started laughing. "Why do you think we came here to find you?" He shouted to make himself heard over the sound of the waves. "We aren't just going to watch you swim. Even if you do, we'll be waiting for you out here. It might even be better if you tire yourself out. You won't fight us then. You'll be a nice little Japanese girl."

Aki put her hands to her mouth and began to jump and shout, "Help! Help me! Help me, please!"

That only made them laugh all the more. One of the young men with Hiroki was particularly seedy looking. His black hair fell down across his face, and his T-shirt was torn and dirty. A scar across his cheek showed him to be a man accustomed to trouble. "You don't think someone's going to hear you, do you?" he shouted. "They'll only think it's somebody playing in the water."

Aki continued to jump and shout. "Help! Somebody, please help me!"

"I hope you're not waiting for that sailor of yours," Hiroki yelled. "He's not coming yet, and when he gets here it'll be too late for you."

Hiroki yelled at the men on either side of him. "Go get her." He waved his hands at them. "I'm tired of waiting. Get her if you have to drag her out of there."

The men looked at each other, blinking, wondering who would brave the surf first. Finally, the man that Aki thought to be the toughest one in the group, the man with the scar on his face, made the first move. He shrugged his shoulders and marched off into the water. The others followed more cautiously, hanging back but finally getting their feet wet.

Aki backed up farther into the oncoming surf. She could swim for it, but she had never been that good of a swimmer. Besides, they were right. Kuhio Beach was a long beach. They would simply walk along the sand and watch her, waiting for her to tire or even drown. She might have the strength to struggle if she let them take her now, but after swimming, she would be powerless. Placing her hands beside her mouth once again, she screamed and then followed her scream with another weaker cry for help. "Help me, please. Somebody, anybody, help me!"

There was a sense about the scene that seemed almost like a dream, a childhood nightmare that she would wake up from in the arms of her grandmother. She could see the old lady's smiling face and feel her hand stroking her forehead. There was a melody to her grandmother's voice, a comforting song of love and warmth. Nothing could hurt Aki when she was in her grandmother's arms, so strong was the love the old woman had for her. The same thing was true about God. Even now, His arms were reaching out to her and His words seemed to fill her ears. *The Lord is my shepherd,* she thought. He loves me more than anyone, even my grandmother.

The men in the water moved closer to her. She could tell they were none too happy about having to get their clothes wet, but that wasn't going to stop them, not any more.

Just then she looked up at the grassy hill and saw the old man she had met earlier. He wasn't looking for coins any more. He looked down the hill and then began running, waving the rake over his head like a sword in the hand of an officer leading a desperate cavalry charge. He had the bucket in his hand. The coins were rattling, and he started to yell at the top of his lungs. "A-e-e y-a-a-a." It was like the scream of a banshee, bloodcurdling and angry.

The charge of the old man stopped the men in their tracks. They froze and then lunged back toward the shore, pulling their legs against the water and straining to get back before the sudden reinforcement arrived.

Hiroki drew a switchblade from his pants and sprang the blade open. He lowered his body and went into a crouch, trying his best to present a formidable obstacle to the onrushing wild man.

That didn't stop Homer, however. He opened his mouth wide and gave out a roar that sounded like a lion just released from a cage. The loud echo carried itself down the beach. Homer dropped his bucket and whirled his rake in the air, cracking Hiroki across the arms and sending his open blade spinning off into the evening air. Once again raising his rusty weapon, he cracked Hiroki across the shoulders and head, lifting the rake and bringing it down hard again and again on the man. The young gangster dropped to the ground and became a whimpering dog, holding up his hands and arms for protection against the beach bum's fury. He crawled off swiftly, a wounded crab seeking the shelter of some wet rock.

Homer stepped past him, wasting no more time on the man. He headed straight for the four thugs who were now stumbling out of the surf. The man swung the old rake like a windmill in a stiff breeze. He clipped the first man out of the water across the face, dropping him screaming in pain to his knees. Two others ran down the beach in the direction Hiroki had retreated, their clothes dripping water. That left only the man with the scar. He had been so close to Aki that he was the last to leave the water.

He raised his hands. "Just stop," he said. "I know when I had enough."

"Enough!" Homer yelled, raising the rake. "You ain't had any yet."

"Don't hit me with that thing. I know who you are, and I know where to find you."

Homer grinned. "You bet you do, and I'll be right here waitin' fer you."

The man with the scar stepped toward where the others had run, keeping an eye on Homer. But the temptation was evidently too much for the old man. He cocked the rake and came down on the man's arm.

The scar-faced man reached out quickly and grabbed the rake, pulling Homer toward him, but Homer didn't hesitate. He charged the man with his head down, crashing into the man's belly and sending them both sprawling onto the wet sand.

As the two men rolled around in the wet sand and surf, Aki waded out of the water. It was hard for Aki to tell who was who with the waves lapping up against their struggling bodies.

Homer rolled away and struggled to his feet. He grabbed the man by the shirt and pulled him up, shaking him. "You better leave my little lady alone or you'll have old Homer and his mates to deal with. It won't go so easy on you, either." With that, Homer delivered a hard blow to the man's midsection, still holding him upright. "I don't care none how young you is, mister. Old Homer is twice the man you is on his worst day."

He then pushed the man over on his backside and picked up his rake.

The man scrambled to his feet and ran down the beach. He was wide-eyed and panicky, looking back to where Homer was standing.

Aki could tell that those men of Hiroki's were creatures of the crowd. They had no stomach to stand alone.

Homer held the rake up in the air, yelling defiant shouts in the man's direction. "You come on back here and pay old Homer a call, ya hear? I'll be waiting for you, and it ain't gonna be so pretty."

Aki stepped out of the water. She was shivering.

Homer turned and stepped over to where she was standing. He put his arm around her. "Is you all right, missy? Them men didn't hurt you none, did they?"

Aki shook her head. "No, they just scared me. I know one or two of them."

"Then I'd be a talking to the police, iffen I was you. Ain't no call for a woman to be scared of coming to the beach. It ain't right. It jes ain't right. I'll be happy to be a witness for you, should it come to that. The cops 'round about here all know old Homer. I may not seem like much, but they'll believe me, I'd bet."

Aki forced a smile. "I'm sure they would. No matter whatever else you are, you certainly are trustworthy. How did you see what was happening here?"

Homer grinned. "I may not see so well any more, but I got me a good set of ears. You was screaming bloody murder down in that water. At first I thought it was a woman drowning and I come arunning. Then when I came over the hill, I saw them fellers had you in the water. They looked like they was coming after you. Well, that made old Homer here mad."

Homer bent down to pick up his spilled pail, and Aki joined him on her hands and knees. They spent some time running their fingers through the sand, trying as best they could to pull up every coin that had been spilled.

Aki didn't know how long they had been on their hands and knees, but the next thing she heard was the sound of Brian's voice coming over the hill. He spotted her and ran in her direction.

Aki and Homer got to their feet. Aki fell into Brian's arms, sobbing.

"The little lady here's been through quite a fright," Homer said. "Are you her feller?"

Brian nodded and continued to hold Aki in his arms.

"Well, you best take her home then. She's plum stove in, I'm a betting."

Aki turned back to Homer and put her hand on his arm. "Thank you. Thank you so much. God sent you to me tonight. I believe that. You may not know it or believe it, but you were his angel."

Homer smiled. "I ain't never been sent by God before, nowhere to nobody. I figure He can pick whole lots more reliable folks than old Homer here."

Aki dug her fingers into his arm. "Not tonight He couldn't. You were an answer to prayer." She turned to walk away, but then looked back at him. "Will you be in church tomorrow?"

Homer grinned. "Now, how is they gonna keep an answer to prayer out of church? Doesn't angels belong in the church?"

"Tonight they belonged on the beach," she said. "I tell you what. If you come to church tomorrow, I'll buy you lunch. It's the least I can do."

"Ma'am, that would be mighty nice. An angel being taken to lunch by a real angel." He laughed. "It would be my pleasure."

CHAPTER 20

The bright November Sunday morning was like any other morning in Honolulu. Local people often grinned and called each day "another day in paradise," and truly it was. Gwen brushed her teeth and looked out the window at a rare ania-niau. The small yellow bird with its black wings and tiny black eyes was hopping from branch to branch in the large banyan tree in the backyard of her parent's home as if it didn't have a care in the world. Gwen was envious.

She could never explain to her parents just what was expected of her on this trip to their home. The task seemed to be enormous. How

could she convince the brass at Pearl Harbor that they were in immediate danger? Would they listen to her? To make matters worse, everything she had heard about Hawaii was true. The weekends were quiet
and peaceful. No doubt the brass played golf or cavorted on the beach
from 4 P.M. on Friday afternoon until 9 A.M. on Monday morning.
There would be no one over the grade of E-5 minding the store during that time. No one would be able to make decisions. And from
what she had already seen, people thought of Hawaii as untouchable,
an oasis in the middle of the Pacific.

There was also the fact that she was a woman. Men didn't expect
women to have serious thoughts. One man she had dated several years
before had told her that "when women think, it robs them of their
charm." It had been her first and last date with that man, but she
knew that he merely had the chutzpa to say to her what other men
only contemplated and talked about among themselves.

She dropped her toothbrush into the glass beside the sink and
turned on a burst of water. Dipping her hands into the sink, she
splashed her face. She had never been much for makeup, didn't like
the fuss of powder or the feeling of not being clean. She squinted into
the mirror and pinched her cheeks. There was a knock at the door.

"Are you ready, dear?"

"Yes, mother. I'm all done here." She grabbed a towel, patting her
cheeks down. She then replaced the towel and straightened it.
Tidiness had always been a fault of hers, and while others might com-
plain about her fastidiousness, it never drew a protest from her parents. She knew that her years of living in Japan had no doubt made
her this way. Japan was, after all, a neat and clean country. There was
a place for everything with everything in its place. It was one of the
things she was glad she had taken with her out of the country.

She straightened her dress and turned to the large mirror that
showed it at full length. Her dress was typically Hawaiian, orange with
bright yellow and green flowers. It hung on her nicely and did manage

to show her figure. She had taken the time to run earlier that morning. Staying in shape was something she took pride in. No matter what other people thought, what she felt about who she was and how she looked was very important to her. She stepped into her white sandals and, bending over, fastened the buckles. There. She looked in the mirror. She was ready.

Her parents' home was comfortable enough by Hawaiian standards. It was a low-ceiling stucco house surrounded by large trees that gave it shade. The bright flowers in the beds that circled the home would have been the envy of the *Ladies' Home Journal*. Brilliant colors and tall bamboo gave it a tropical feel. The furniture was oriented to the beach, white wood with yellow, green, and red pillows. Grass mats and Persian rugs were laid out over a parquet floor.

Her mother was waiting for her with the car keys in her hand. She glanced down at Gwen's feet and smiled. "You forget so soon, dear. We're Japanese here."

Gwen glanced down at the sandals on her feet. Her mother was right. It was the Japanese custom to remove one's shoes before entering a home. It made the entryway and the front porch look like a pile of used footwear on sale at a local shoe store, but it did keep the floors clean and polished. She had gotten out of the habit since coming to California. Most people there would have been quite shocked had she removed her shoes upon entering their home. "I'm sorry, Mother. You're right. I've gotten out of the habit. When I unpacked, I just left my shoes in the room."

"Well, dear, you'll get used to it soon. Things come back to you. Your father preaches both in Japanese and English, you know." She laughed. "You'll get to hear him twice."

Gwen nodded. "I'm looking forward to it. I've missed his preaching."

Her mother bounced the car keys in her hand. "He left us the Ford and walked this morning. You know how much he loves to pray before he preaches."

They both went out and got into the car. In a matter of minutes they were driving the few miles to the little Rainbow Community Church, pulling up outside and taking a few moments to collect their purses and Bibles.

At first glance Gwen loved the small wooden structure with picket fence and flowers. Palm trees bent low in the front yard. Gwen got out and felt the slight breeze. It rippled through the fronds on the palm trees with almost a musical lilt.

In a short time they had taken their seats at the back of the church and people had begun to file in. Most of them were Japanese, but the oddest sight was the man on the front row. He was wearing a dirty T-shirt. His gray hair was long, extending past his shoulders, and beside him sat a young Japanese woman. Gwen thought she looked quite attractive. She also thought they looked unusually out of place together. She would never be able to size the two of them up as a match.

Gwen's mother nudged her and motioned in the direction of the young woman Gwen was looking at. "That's the woman we told you about, the one who works for Naval Intelligence."

Gwen settled back and enjoyed the service. It was a small crowd, fewer than forty people, but her father's preaching was just as she remembered. The man had fire mixed with a soft sensitivity. Even the songs were sung in both English and Japanese. It felt good to be in an assembly of Japanese once again. She knew the racial hatred for them was strong on the island, but everything she had ever seen or heard showed them to be the finest Americans imaginable.

When the service was over, Gwen and her mother were the first ones out the door. Gwen's mother took her place, shaking hands and talking to each person who came out the door. She held Gwen by her side, carefully introducing her to every family leaving the church. It was a duty Gwen had been participating in all her life, the charming and pretty preacher's daughter. She bowed to each one and spoke her greeting in Japanese.

Before too long her mother became engaged in a conversation and Gwen slipped away to a spot under the palm tree. She watched as the old man and the young Japanese woman came out of the church. Her father and mother greeted them and began to engage the man in conversation. Gwen's mother spoke to the Japanese woman and, looking around for Gwen, pointed to where she was standing.

The young Japanese woman looked at Gwen and walked over to speak to her. She held out her hand. "I'm Aki Kawa. Your mother tells me you work for Naval Intelligence too, in San Francisco."

"Yes, I do." Gwen smiled. "In fact, you're part of the reason I'm here."

"I am?"

"Yes, your transmission to our office. You asked about possible Japanese communication from Hawaii to Tokyo."

Aki nodded.

"It just so happens that I know about that. I even have the substance of one of their transmissions translated and decoded."

"You do?" Aki smiled. "Would you like to see who it comes from?"

"Yes, indeed. I really would. Do you know the man?"

"I've seen him a number of times. He goes to the same place every day and writes down everything he sees about our fleet. He's probably there right now." Aki smiled. "I don't think he goes to church."

"Is it far?"

"Not far. Just on the bluffs overlooking Pearl Harbor."

Gwen glanced back at her parents. They were continuing to talk to the old man in the dirty shorts. "I might be able to get us a car, if you'd like to take me there. My parents like to take a walk after church, and it's not far for them. I'd like to see this man for myself."

"I can do that. There's just one thing."

"What's that?"

"That man I'm with, Homer. We'd have to take him with us. He saved my life last night on the beach, most certainly my honor. I promised him lunch if he came to church today."

"All right, but that will be a little tricky. We'll have to see what you want to show me but with no discussion on it until we're alone. We are dealing with secrets, you know." Gwen shot a glance in Homer's direction. "He looks harmless enough, but we'll just be sightseeing while I'm with you."

"That's fine with me," Aki said.

Gwen made the explanations to her parents, and the three of them drove up to the bluffs overlooking Pearl Harbor. Gwen parked the car and put on the brake. They could see the ships below, men working on them and others transporting ordnance and supplies by truck, then ferrying supplies to the ships. It was a beehive of activity, even on a Sunday.

They stepped out of the car and walked over to the bluffs. Aki pointed. "That's the *Arizona*. My boyfriend is an officer on that ship."

Gwen nodded. "Boyfriend? Is it serious?"

"Oh yes." Aki smiled. "Very serious." She reached down and held up the cross around her neck. "He gave this to me. He said it reminded him of us and how he wanted to be in the middle of everything I felt and saw." She smiled. "He's sort of a romantic that way. He likes to see the meaning of things."

Gwen looked at her. She was taking a liking to the woman. She was obviously bright. "It's lovely. He shows good taste. Must be nice to have a romantic boyfriend. Not many men are like that, you know."

"Yes, I know. Brian is."

"This may be none of my business, but he doesn't mind that you're Japanese, does he?"

"Whew-ee." Homer interrupted their thoughts as he looked at the ships below. "Them boys stay mighty busy, I'd say. They must be stocking up for some kind of sea duty." The man looked animated, waving his arms and pointing at the activity below. There was an innocence about him that didn't seem to fit with his demeanor.

Aki pulled Gwen a few steps away. "You see. Not only can you see the American fleet from here, but you can actually tell what supplies are being loaded. A person could keep track of all the comings and goings of the fleet, and the man I have in mind does just that."

"No doubt Tokyo knows exactly what is going on here on a day-by-day basis," Gwen said.

The three of them walked back and forth over the edge of the bank. Finding a spot where a path cut to the clearing below, they began to walk carefully down the sides of the bluff. Aki would occasionally glance back at the parking area above. It didn't take long. Aki nudged Gwen. "There he is."

A dark sedan had parked above them, and a man in a dark business suit stepped out of the car. He moved to the front of the car and took out a pair of binoculars. Peering through them, he began to survey the fleet below.

"I'm only sorry we didn't bring a picnic lunch," Gwen said. "We do look a little out of place down here."

"Let's go up so we can get a better look at him." Aki watched as Homer skipped down the hill. The man was enjoying himself, lost in a new world. She called out to him. "Homer. Let's go now."

He turned and looked back at them, then waved. They waited for him to make the hike back to where they were standing.

Gwen glanced back up the bluffs and nudged Aki. "That man up there isn't watching the fleet any more. He's watching us."

Aki turned to look.

The man had his binoculars trained directly on them.

CHAPTER 21

Gwen finished breakfast with her parents and did the dishes. It felt good to have a hand in the kitchen for a change. In the boarding house in San Francisco, she seldom got the opportunity to cook.

"Are you going to Pearl Harbor today?" Jack asked.

Gwen smiled and stepped over to the table where they were having a cup of tea. "Yes, if I can borrow the car."

"Of course you can. Today's my day off. I can make do as long as you need it."

"Thank you, Daddy." Gwen bent over and kissed his cheek. She stepped to the glass-covered bamboo table next to the door where she had left her purse and the brown leather briefcase that contained her papers. The papers were important. The truth was, she never should have had them overnight outside of a vault. The problem was, there was no other place to put them. Pearl Harbor was a ghost town in terms of responsibility on the weekends. There was also the matter of trust. With what she had to do, it might be simpler for the Office of Naval Intelligence here to misplace the evidence she had than to deal with it and with her. No one liked to be upstaged, especially by a woman who was claiming they weren't doing their job. She wasn't about to allow that. She had felt herself in danger in San Francisco, but in her parents' home in Honolulu she felt safe, at least for now.

Gwen had taken care in dressing that day. She had on a dark blue pleated skirt and white ruffled blouse. Her stockings were straight, and her hair was pinned into a bun. With the black pumps she was planning on wearing, she would look all business, at least as much as a woman could look on a navy base. Her orders from San Francisco would take care of the rest. At least she hoped so.

A short time later she was in the Ford driving to Pearl Harbor. She had spent some time with Aki yesterday, listening to the woman's impressions of the men she worked with in her office. There were certain men who would present an obstacle to what she had to do; one or two of them could not be avoided. She would just have to do her best. The least she could hope for was that she wouldn't be ignored.

She drove to the gate and presented her badge to the uniformed guard, who directed her where she needed to go. Winding her way through the manicured lawns, she pulled up outside a long, low concrete building. It was gray with very few windows. She pulled a pair of brass handcuffs out of her handbag and snapped one of them to her left wrist, then clamped the other end to the briefcase. At least the precautions she was taking wouldn't make her appear to be an amateur. Reaching inside her blouse, she felt for the key on a chain around her neck. It was there. She got out of the car and headed up the long set of steps that led to the building, pausing once again to show her identification and to get directions.

Once inside, she headed down the main hall and turned into a corridor lined with tables stacked with paper. Above the tables were glass-windowed bookcases filled with gold-lettered blue military binders. The descriptions of their contents were coded. Gwen smirked. It had been her experience that the more paper a place generated, the less attention they paid to it.

She headed down to the basement. From talking with Aki, she knew this was the place she would have to penetrate in order to gain a hearing. A sailor with a medium build, brown hair, and a pressed white uniform sat at a table near a set of double doors. He was drinking a cup of coffee and watching her walk toward him. From the way he surveyed her, she got the distinct impression that it was her blouse and hips that attracted his attention. She tucked the thought away for future use should that prove necessary. The ashtray at his elbow was already filled with cigarette butts.

"Good morning," she said. Noticing the man's name tag, she added, "Edwards." She then reached into her handbag and pulled out her identification badge, sliding it across the table at him. He took it and looked up at her, comparing the photograph with what was standing before him.

He nodded. "Morning."

Gwen produced her orders, opening them and laying them on the table.

Edwards looked them over, a frown forming on his face. Slowly he slid his chair back and got to his feet, picking up her orders. "I'll have to show these to Chief Morrow. Nobody spits 'round here without his say-so."

He pointed to a padded metal chair with the padding ripped and huge wads of gray stuffing oozing out the slits of Naugahyde. "You just sit yourself down and I'll fetch him."

Gwen paced the floor, refusing to sit in the spot he designated. She glanced at her watch and repeatedly read and reread the bulletin board, LOOSE LIPS SINK SHIPS. It contained warnings of security breaches and no doubt was repeatedly ignored.

It was some time before the double doors opened and Edwards stepped out smiling. It was more like a grin on his face, something that showed that he knew something that she didn't. "The chief will see you now. He's got your orders. His office is the third door to your left." Tipping his head slightly, his grin turned into a smirk. "Nice knowing you."

She ignored the remark and walked through the open green metal door. The walls of the hallway were littered with bulletin boards, many of them marked with the same familiar slogan about loose lips. It seemed to be a recurring theme.

She rounded the corner to the third office on her left and stepped into an oversize, windowless room. The man behind the wooden desk would have been hard to ignore in a crowd. His hair was close cut with what looked like beeswax holding the short stubs in place. His massive head seemed to sit directly on a pair of broad shoulders, and the decorations on his starched khaki uniform spread across his chest. "Chief Morrow, I'm Gwen Williams."

He looked up from the papers on his desk and coldly stared at her. Reaching to the stack of papers on the side of his desk, he picked up her orders. "What am I supposed to do with this nonsense?"

Gwen forced a slight smile. "You're supposed to do exactly what it says: cooperate and get me in to see the fleet commander."

He tossed the set of orders in her direction, and Gwen watched them float to the floor. "I can't get you in to see the admiral on this say-so. The man's busy. He doesn't have nearly enough time to worry about what some civilian skirt from San Francisco has to say. If you think you can march in here and get us to fall all over ourselves because you think you heard something thousands of miles away that we don't already know here, then you're more than a little silly. You're a fool."

Gwen stepped over to his desk and leaned over to look him directly in the eye. "Chief, you're in greater danger here than you realize. Don't kid yourself. The Japanese watch Pearl Harbor every day. They make notes about which of our ships are in port and what supplies are being loaded, then take those notes and send them directly to Tokyo."

"Who says so?"

Gwen placed her briefcase on the desk and, taking out her key, unlocked it. Reaching into it, she pulled out her copy of the Japanese transmission that had been intercepted, then pushed the papers across the desk. "I have here a listing of all of your ships in Pearl Harbor. If you look at the date and then look back at what you know to be the disposition of the fleet on that day, you'll be able to see how accurate it is. It even has the berths where each ship was located, a detailed description that could only be used in preparing a battle plan."

Morrow picked up the papers and looked them over, then looked back up at her. "How do you know where this came from?"

"It was intercepted by an English freighter at sea."

"And you expect me to believe the limeys?"

"The radio operator who copied the message was killed in San Francisco. His friend who gave the message to me was struck by a hit-and-run driver. My room was broken into."

"And how do you know the message is accurate?"

"I translated and decoded it myself."

"You decoded this?" He looked at her and arched his eyebrows. The Purple code was top secret, and Morrow knew it.

"Yes, it's part of my job."

"Look, Miss Williams, I know you think you've got a time bomb here, but the Japanese know what we have in our fleet. They're ready for us, and we're ready for them. We keep an eye on their movements, and they watch ours. This stuff doesn't mean a thing to me, and it certainly isn't new."

Gwen took the transmission from his hands and put it back into her briefcase. "There is one big difference, Chief. It isn't the fact that they know our ships are here that ought to concern you. It's the fact that they know exactly where they are located in the harbor. We might know the strength of the Japanese fleet, but we don't know where they lie at anchor. There can be only one reason why they would want to know such a thing."

Morrow folded his hands. "And what would that be?"

"If they planned an attack on Pearl Harbor, they would want to know just where every ship was situated. It would make their bombing run more accurate. They could fly in and know exactly where to hit."

"And you know this from your vast military experience, I take it." A faint smile crossed his face.

"No, Chief. I know this from common sense."

"Then perhaps this common sense of yours, along with a little clairvoyance, can tell us when this attack will occur."

"I can narrow it down somewhat. From what I've seen already after having been here over the weekend, I would place the attack on a Saturday or Sunday. People are on the golf course. You don't have anyone here who can make a decision."

Morrow got to his feet. "All right, Miss Williams. Since you don't have any confidence in our ability to figure out when to chew and when to spit, suppose you follow me and let me show you something."

"Gladly, Chief Morrow."

He rounded his desk, and Gwen reached out and grabbed his arm. "Aren't you forgetting something, Chief?"

"What?"

"My orders there on the floor where you dropped them." She smiled. "I'm certain your mother raised you better than that."

He grunted, then reached down and picked them up. Shuffling them into a stack, he handed them back to her. "There, satisfied?"

"Quite. After all, I am a lady, Chief."

She followed him out the door and down the hall to another set of double doors. A guard was standing at attention, and he snapped his heels together and opened the door when Morrow approached. They both headed down another flight of stairs. The room below was a beehive of activity with some men on the phone and others standing over maps and adjusting pins.

"This is the joint Army-Navy Defense Center for the Hawaiian frontier, Miss Williams." He waved his arm at the maps that covered the walls. "We have the location of every Japanese ship in the Pacific on this wall. We may not know where they're anchored, but we know where they are."

He rocked back and forth on the balls of his feet, giving off an air of smugness. "So you see, if we ever get word that Japanese carriers are anchored offshore, then we'll look into what you have to say and be as scared as you want us to be. In spite of what you may think, we're on top of things down here. We know the comings and goings of every Japanese tin can in this ocean, so you can sleep easy tonight. You're unnecessary."

Gwen saw an officer spot the two of them and walk in their direction. He was a man with a long face and thin mustache that sloped down the edges of his narrow lips. He smiled at her when he got closer.

"To what do we owe the honor of your presence today, Chief Morrow?"

Morrow shook his head slightly in Gwen's direction. "This is Gwen Williams. She's a language specialist from the office in San

Francisco. She thinks she's uncovered a secret Japanese communication targeting Pearl Harbor. I tried to tell her that we've got the situation well in hand without her worrying, but I figured seeing the center here would put her pretty little head to rest."

The officer extended his hand to Gwen. "Lieutenant Jack Rorke. Nice to have you aboard, Miss Williams." He turned and pointed to the maps. "We have the location of the Japanese fleet on our board here at all times. I can tell you exactly where their carriers are located."

"Have you ever misplaced one?"

Rorke dropped his gaze to the floor, but only for a moment. "We do occasionally lose one, but they turn up."

Gwen looked at Rorke, then at Morrow. "Well, let's hope you don't misplace some of their carriers and have them turn up attacking you. By then it will be too late."

She continued to stare at Morrow. "If you don't mind, Chief, I'm just going to continue to do the job I was sent here to do. I'm going to find further confirmation of the Japanese intentions, and when I do, I'll expect you to get me in to see the admiral. I just hope I'm not too late."

"Where are you staying, Miss Williams?" Morrow asked.

"Here." Gwen took out a pen and a note card and scrawled the address and phone number of her parents on it. She handed it to Morrow. "I am staying at my parents' home, but I'd appreciate it if you'd keep my location to yourselves." She smiled slightly. "Loose lips sink ships, you know."

CHAPTER 22

S am paced back and forth in his room, then stepped out onto the balcony. His copy of the *Washington Post* was five days old, and he was glad to have even that. He had already read the thing twice and had started in on Hemingway's *The Sun Also Rises*. He felt a lot like the old man in the little boat, alone and surrounded by nothing but ocean so far as the eye could see. He didn't like being cooped up, even in the fancy digs of the Royal Hawaiian.

His room had a large picture window that opened out onto the balcony. White steel rails curled around the small mezzanine, and the stones and sand embedded in its floor gave the illusion of a beach, even though the mezzanine was ten stories up. Below him, carefully maintained lawns showed beneath the tops of palm trees. Two men were once again mowing the grass, shaving it slightly to perfection. So far as he was concerned, they had more purpose to what they were doing than he had experienced in almost two months.

He gawked at the ocean. Waves were breaking up on the sand, an endless drumming of water that lapped at his ears without letup. Several of the locals had huge surfboards out in the water, hamming it up for the gawking tourists with their cameras. So much was for show in Hawaii, and Sam had seen more than enough of the performance. The Pacific had ceased to have its charm as far as he was concerned. Every day was like the last, and each wave like the one that had gone before. He had tired of trailing Duskov Popov. By now the man was getting predictable. Sam could forecast just where the man would turn up at any given moment.

He turned and stepped back into the room. The furniture was blond and rattan, and blue-and-green overstuffed pillows covered his chairs and love seat. He stared at the large painting that stood out over his bed—white orchids and red and blue parrots.

His phone rang. He dashed to his bedside table and picked up the receiver. "Sam Diamond."

For a moment he listened to the scratchy and distant voice of the overseas operator. "Yes, operator, I have a call in to the *Washington Post*. To a Jeff Walsh."

He strained to hear. "Jeff, this is Sam. Get me out of here."

He nodded as Jeff talked, but his face was growing redder by the minute. "Look Jeff, I got beat up in New York, but I'm bored to death here. Frankly, I'll take the beating any day. Yeah," he nodded as if it made a difference, "so you say. Of course, you can't prove that any of this will amount to a hill of beans, if you ask me. The Japanese will come to Washington, they'll cut a deal, things will go on as usual, and I'll be out two months of my life. It's no trade so far as I'm concerned."

He listened carefully, trying to make out what was being said. "Look, you've gotten my reports. I've followed the man until I'm blue in the face. He meets with the Japanese, talks to them, and then goes to a bar and smokes a cigar. He buys the same paper every day, eats at one of three restaurants, and occasionally dresses in gaudy shorts and a shirt to walk on the beach. Do you think we could talk the man into playing a little golf?"

Sam nervously ran his hand through his hair, pressing the receiver into his ear. "Ball? What Ball? Do I have a tux? No, I didn't think to bring a tuxedo with me to Hawaii. Now do you think we could get serious for a change?"

He sat on the bed, trying his best to focus on what Jeff Walsh was trying to say. "All right, that's a good idea. We'll try a different angle here. Maybe I can actually find out something. Of course, I doubt it. You know how it is. Nobody knows anything about their own incompetence, especially the navy."

After a few more minutes of chatter, made more difficult by the poor connection, he slammed the phone down with a bang. He would have to get a tuxedo. Jeff Walsh had managed to finagle an invitation to the Navy Ball at Pearl Harbor for him. His job would be to question the brass there about what was being done, if anything, about the Japanese threat. He knew the most he could hope for would be some background on the real story, if there ever was a real story. Something about newspaper reporters always seemed to cause high-ranking officers to develop lockjaw. Only one thing gave him any sort of hope. He might be able to meet an attractive woman. Someone, anyone, to take his mind off of the boredom of his job would be a welcome relief.

Four days later Sam stood at the mirror adjusting his black bow tie. The tux looked great, and he had shaved especially close. He thought he looked devastating, much too good to resist for any woman who wasn't caught up in the mystique of a uniform. He had to admit, at least this relieved the boredom of the last few days. Picking up the invitation Jeff had sent by airmail, he folded it and slipped it into his jacket pocket. In a matter of minutes he was getting into a taxi and heading for Pearl Harbor.

He had made the drive before, but without getting far. Pearl Harbor hadn't proved very friendly to the Washington press, and the time spent with the information officer had only added to his impression that the whole experience was a waste of time.

The cab sputtered up to the gate, and Sam produced the invitation for the swabby who looked to be a kid in dress-up clothes. The young sailor bent down and stuck his head in the cab driver's window, then motioned to the Officers Club. The cabby pulled up beside a long row of redbrick buildings. The lights were on, and as far as Sam was concerned, that was a good sign.

He bounced out of the cab. Peeling a couple of bills from his gold money clip, he paid the driver. Couples climbed the stairs and filed into the building. The men wore gleaming white dress uniforms, and the women wore floating chiffon clouds that passed for ball gowns.

Sam took the stairs two at a time. Formal dances had never been his thing; they had been a means to an end. In that way he suspected he was like all the other men inside. Men went to formal dances to find a woman in a moment of weakness, when her head was swimming from dim lights, soft music, and too much champagne. Others went to line up business or maybe a bridge partner. Sam had already worked out his priorities. He would look for a woman he could have a few laughs with and, failing that, find a man who played squash. If he could get one who liked to put a buck or two on the line, that would be all the better. Then and only then would he worry about questioning these people about the Japanese. He was sure they wouldn't tell him anything, and at the moment his boredom had squeezed out almost every ounce of his interest in the matter. For tonight he would concentrate on showing off.

He went through the reception line, dragging himself behind a file of couples who were bent on shaking the hand of Admiral Kimmel. The man, with his mousy-haired wife standing next to him, was dutifully performing his function as host. He stepped out of line and allowed the couple behind him to get ahead. Being last in line for the moment might allow a word with Kimmel.

He waited his turn and stepped in front of Kimmel's wife as the admiral was continuing to talk to the couple Sam had allowed to get ahead. Taking her hand, he did the unexpected. He smiled at her and then bowed his head, planting a kiss on the woman's bare knuckles. "Enchanté," he grinned. "I'm Sam Diamond of the *Washington Post*."

The woman's eyes fluttered, and Sam could see a blush in her cheeks. "A reporter?"

"Yes, but so far tonight, you're the best thing I've seen." He grinned. He shot a glance at the admiral as the man continued to talk to the couple next to him. "I was hoping to get an interview with your husband, but the man's hard to see."

She tightened her lips. "Yes, I know—all too well."

"Maybe you can put in a good word for me." His smile widened. "And when I see him, I'll put in a good word for you."

"I'll see what I can do." The admiral's wife was rather plain looking, but Sam imagined that came from years of neglect. When a woman gives up on getting a man's attention, it becomes all too easy to simply quit. Her eyes were glassy, and it looked like she'd been drinking. It wasn't even 8 o'clock. Sam could tell that she had just as much difficulty with being in this place as he did.

She put her hand on Kimmel's arm, squeezing it. "Dear, I'd like to introduce you to a Mr. Sam Diamond. He's a reporter for the *Washington Post*, and he'd like to do an interview with you."

Kimmel swiveled his head around and drilled a hole in Sam with his dark eyes. "The *Post*, huh?"

"Yes, sir. We've got quite a bit of clout on Capitol Hill."

"That's just what I'm afraid of. Right now, publicity is something we could do without."

"But what about you, Admiral?" Sam glanced at Mrs. Kimmel, who was following the conversation closely. "Wouldn't you like some notice of the fine work you've done here? I'm sure it would give our readers some measure of confidence to know that a man like you has his hands on the wheel in these troubled waters. You'd like the people of America to feel secure wouldn't you, Admiral?"

"Go ahead," his wife finally blurted out. Sam saw the look in her eyes. Most women wanted their husbands to be successful, even if they weren't all that successful in their marriage. It was the mark of a loyal woman—a sense of self-sacrifice sadly nourished for a soul starving for self-esteem. "Give the man his interview. What harm could it do? You could always refuse any questions you thought were too sensitive."

Kimmel swallowed hard. Sam could tell that saying no to his wife in public was hard to do. "All right, be at my office at oh-nine hundred hours on Monday morning. You can have your interview then."

Sam walked away feeling somewhat smug. At least he was earning his pay, even though he thought he was tilting at windmills. Now he could be free to pursue his personal agenda—finding a woman who could laugh.

He stepped over to the punch bowl, which was a mark of creative genius or, at the very least, an eighth-grade science project gone awry. A mold had been cast in the shape of a volcano, and pink punch poured down the carefully painted green sides of the cinder cone into an oversize lagoon. Dry ice floated in the frothy lagoon, and formed a gentle fog. There was no way he was going to touch that stuff. He picked up a glass of champagne instead.

He surveyed the room. Most of the people were coupled, but there were some single women. A few could truly be classified as wallflowers, while others were no doubt the underage daughters of some brass button going out with Daddy and Mommy for a night at the club. These were to be avoided at all cost.

Sizing up a woman had its own special delights as far as Sam was concerned. Innocence was to be avoided. In Sam's book, innocence almost equaled stupidity, and stupidity meant outright boredom. Spotting a fairly attractive blonde, Sam cruised in her direction.

He spent some time trying to make conversation with her. She was attractive enough and predictably flirtatious, but she had no real wit. He found his mind wandering and then his eyes.

Then he sighted the kind of woman he'd been looking for. She was coming down the receiving line, a tall and attractive brunette. The woman was shapely but athletic looking. Her long neck arched elegantly from a red Japanese kimono with a gold dragon emblazoned across it. The design gave her a note of danger. She was a sleek and confident figure slicing through the crowd of puffy pastel chiffon that dominated the room. Even though the stunning goddess who captured his fancy wasn't Japanese, she had enough moxie to wear a Japanese dress when events in the Pacific would have advised against it. He liked arrogance in a woman. Shoot, he liked it in anyone, but especially in a woman.

He grinned and excused himself from the blonde he had been talking to, or rather at. He watched her carefully as she left the line and stepped away from Kimmel, walking in his direction. She looked somewhat disappointed. Her face was drawn.

He smiled. "What's the matter? Your boyfriend didn't get his promotion?"

Her eyes bored into him. "And just who are you?"

The woman certainly could manufacture an icy stare. "Sam Diamond." He clicked his Brooks Brothers heels together. "Sorry I can't give him the promotion. I'll bet your smile looks a whole lot prettier than the long face you're wearing now."

"I don't have a boyfriend." She turned to look at the overflowing volcano, trying her best to ignore him.

"Here, let me get you a glass of that stuff." He set his champagne glass down on the table and picked up one of the glasses with the navy logo on it. "I avoided it myself and went for the champagne." He nodded at the volcano. "Never much cared for disasters."

Filling her glass, he turned around and handed it to her. "I didn't get your name. If you ask me, you and I are the only ones around here who don't look like we belong. I guess that means we should get to know one another."

She took the glass and sipped it. "It was foolish of me to come."

"I thought that same thing"—his smile widened ever so slightly—"until I saw you."

She looked up from her glass at him. It was the look of a school-teacher when a spitball has been thrown. "In Japan we have a phrase for what you're doing." She set her glass down on the punch table and circled her closed fist above the palm of her left hand. "*Gomasuri,* grinding the sesame seeds. It's said about a person who tries very hard to ingratiate himself to someone else. You see, ground sesame seeds stick to everything."

"I didn't know you were Japanese."

"A little too much on the inside at times, I suppose. I was born in Japan. Missionary parents."

"And you think I'm a little too sticky then?"

"Let's just put it this way. I work for the navy in San Francisco. I meet sticky men every day."

"I bet you do." Sam laughed. "Well, you'd better get used to it. You are a knockout, like it or not. I don't think I could treat you like one of the guys."

"Just so you treat me like someone with a brain." She held out her hand. "I'm Gwen Williams."

He shook her hand. "Pleased to meet you, Gwen Williams. Now make my day complete and tell me you play squash."

Gwen smiled. "As a matter of fact, I do. Now you make mine complete and tell me you can get me in to see Admiral Kimmel."

Sam laughed. "As a matter of fact, I just might be able to do that." He glanced back to where Kimmel and his wife were still shaking hands. "I did some sesame grinding with the admiral's wife a little earlier tonight." He glanced back at her. The admiral's wife had been almost too easy, a piece of cake. Ignored women were always hungry for attention from any direction.

"I'm a reporter for the *Washington Post,* and I've got an appointment to see the man at nine A.M., Monday morning. I might be able to drag you along. Tell you what. Why don't you and I play some squash at the Y at six. I'll buy you breakfast and we can talk. Then I'll just take you with me. We can get you in the old man's front door, and the rest is up to you."

Gwen stared at him. There was a long pause. "I don't really like being dragged anywhere. I work for Naval Intelligence. I'm afraid what I have to discuss with the admiral is something you can't hear."

Sam clapped his hands and rubbed them together. "Hot dog! Now that does sound delicious." He laughed. "You sure I can't have you tonight, get you drunk on lava over there, and take advantage of you?"

Gwen smiled. "What do you think?"

"I'd guess not if I had to lay a bet, but it's good to see a smile on your face all the same."

He glanced back at the receiving line, and his mouth dropped open. Coming though the line in a white dinner jacket was Duskov Popov. The man had a red carnation in his lapel. His hair looked darker and was smoothed back into place with a crisp part.

"You know that man?" Gwen asked.

"You might say that."

"How do you know him?"

"Part of my job. Hopefully you'll be able to read about it in the *Post*, but at times I've had my doubts."

Gwen smiled once again. "I've seen him myself the last three days."

"How do you know him?"

Her eyes twinkled. "It's part of my job."

Sam grinned. "Well here we are, two people with secrets who know how to play squash."

CHAPTER 23

Gwen padded along South King Street early Saturday morning, drinking in the sights and listening to the birds. Her feet hit a rhythm, drumming a soft rubber beat on the hard pavement. She had decided to meet with Aki at the end of her morning run. In her white shorts, T-shirt, and tennis shoes, she didn't look all that different from the other tourists in Honolulu, except for the fact that she was up and running and they were no doubt still in bed.

She ran past the old Kawaiaha'o Church, tucked away from the traffic of King Street by the trees and lawns. The old stones were gray and imposing, making the church look like it had been there forever, but actually it was not quite a hundred years old. Westerners were the newcomers to this place. They had brought their ways and their dress with them, and they hadn't always been welcomed. It was one of the attitudes that were helping to form the Japanese Empire. The Japanese saw themselves as a people who belonged to the Pacific while seeing the West as an interloper.

A red-crested cardinal hopped along the grass, probing the ground with its pale beak. The bird had black wings and a creamy white breast. A bright red splash of color covered its face and neck and painted the tips of the feathers that stood up from its head, giving it the appearance of an Indian in a war bonnet. Suddenly, the cardinal took wing and flew off.

Escape was not nearly so easy for human beings, Gwen thought. *Humans were never free to simply fly away.*

Gwen kept up her pace as she ran past the black and bronze statue of Kamehameha. The imposing figure was holding a spear in one hand while extending his other hand in a gesture of welcome. Occasionally people would drape leis over the arm of the king, but today his arms were bare and black. Gwen smiled. *If the man had known what was good for him, he would have used the spear.*

She passed the post office and rounded the corner onto Richards Street. The YMCA was on her left. Aki had called her to set up the meeting and had given her good directions. The bandstand near the Iolani Palace was across the street from the YMCA and shouldn't be too hard to find. She was playing squash there on Monday morning with the reporter, Sam Diamond. The man was cocky and self-assured, a typical squash player. She smiled at the thought of teaching him a little humility. She had actually enjoyed the man in spite of how obvious he was. Over the years she had given some thought to the kind of man who would be best for her, and it always seemed that the ones she would let get close enough to count were the type she could run over like a steamroller. They weren't confident; they were

shy and anything but dangerous. Most of all, they were safe. Gwen
had begun to see that those men, while they might give her the feeling of being a woman, were much too content to run wide circles
around her for fear of causing a conflict. She quickly became bored
with them. Sam didn't strike her like that at all. However, it was a first
impression. Usually men like Sam Diamond didn't last long enough
to form a second impression. She never let them.

Directly in front of the YMCA, she turned right and into the park
that surrounded the Iolani Palace. Palm trees, with stout banyan trees
behind them, lined the drive, spreading out their branches like
ancient cradles suspended in midair. She jogged through the palms
toward the bandstand. Luxuriant Victorian rails surrounded the white
base of the bandstand. The cupola was a burnished green metal with
ornate gables of white wood jutting out from the sides. Gwen could
see Aki and a man inside the stand.

She ran up to the concrete stairs and stopped, leaning on a pillar.
Breathing deeply, she began to pant. There was something about the
pain of hard exercise that did something for Gwen's soul. To be in
pain was to be alive, to feel something more than the deadness of
comfort. To her the life of ease was a life that was mediocre at best. To
push and live hard meant the difference between making a difference
or merely forming the backdrop for somebody to make a difference.

Aki got up and walked toward her, followed by the man. "You ran
all the way here?"

"Yes," Gwen gasped. "I try to run in the mornings, and I figured
my dad could use the car today."

Aki motioned with her hand to the man with her. "This is Brian.
I told you about him."

"Yes, the boyfriend." Gwen smiled. "The serious boyfriend."

Brian was wearing a pair of khaki slacks that looked suspiciously
like the trousers from his uniform. He had on a blue checked shirt,
which was a departure from his normal dress of the day. Brian's brown

hair was curly and combed back, and his brown eyes looked soft, almost warm. She held out her hand. "I'm Gwen Williams. Nice to meet you."

Brian reached out and shook her hand. "Likewise." He glanced at Aki. "Aki has told me so much about you and your parents. I've heard your dad preach several times. Enjoyed it very much."

"He'd be pleased to hear that."

"I know you and Aki have matters to discuss that I'm not cleared to hear, so I can just walk off a ways and leave you two to talk. I just wanted to come with her. I don't like her being out alone so early in the morning without people around."

"That's very protective of you. I like that."

Brian walked off the bandstand and started on a slow stroll of the grounds. Aki turned to Gwen. "He's like that, always worried about me."

Gwen put her hand on her arm. "That's good. So many people have no one to worry or care about them. You're blessed."

Aki nodded and looked off at Brian. "I know I am. He's so tender and kind to me; he treats me like a precious jewel."

"And you love him."

"Yes, I do. With all my heart."

Gwen began to swing her arms to work out the kinks from all the exercise of the morning. "Maybe we could go for a walk and I can cool down."

"Of course. We might even be able to get into the Iolani Palace. You'd like that."

"Yes, I would."

The two of them began a brisk walk around the grounds, and Gwen noticed that Brian was keeping pace with them at a distance. He seemed determined not to let them out of his sight. "I see Brian is *Yoraba Taiju no kage.*" Gwen used the Japanese expression for the shelter of a big tree.

Aki smiled. "I forgot you speak Japanese."

"Yes. Actually it's more my native tongue than English. I've gotten a little out of practice though."

"An easy thing to do."

They walked past the flower gardens. The plumeria blossoms had opened, showing a bright reddish pink color. They were like the wet strokes of a brush, vivid and uncurled.

"I went to the Navy Ball the other night. Thought I might see you there."

Aki hung her head. "Yes, we could have gone, but Brian was afraid he'd run into his father. He's an admiral, you know."

"No, I didn't know. Must be nice for Brian."

"Not really. Brian wants to put as much distance between the two of them as possible." Aki glanced back at Brian. "He wants to be his own man and make it without his father."

"I see. Might be hard to do, what with Brian being in the navy." Gwen knew it was always a problem to be in the shadow of one's father. Preacher's kids experienced it all the time, people pointing and demanding more than what ordinarily might be expected. Life for her had been on her best behavior, and she was certain the same was true for Brian. "Does Brian's father approve of you?"

Aki shook her head. "Not in the least. Brian told me his father wants to get rid of me. He thought I might be expecting a child and offered to buy me off. He thinks I am going to be bad for Brian's career, his future."

"You don't believe that, do you?"

"Sometimes I don't know what to believe. I just know I don't want to hurt Brian." She forced a smile and tried to change the subject. "So, how was the ball?"

Gwen laughed. "It was typically navy. People trying to impress the right people and single men trying to impress single women. I did meet a reporter, though, who seems to know a man I saw with the Japanese vice-consul."

"Is that right? That reminds me. I wanted to pass on to you something I've turned up from our boys in the basement. It seems we have a German spy in Hawaii. The man's name is Otto Kuen, a German national who has lived here for several years. He has a house in Kailua. We know he's a Nazi sympathizer." Aki let a thin smile cross her lips. "His pride won't let him keep his mouth shut. He brags about Germany and its victories in Europe. I don't really think he's a spy, though. He's more like a collaborator. But we have our eyes on him."

"*Iwanu ga hana.*"

"Yes, silence is golden," Aki repeated. The meaning, however, was the same. "We know that the man is outspoken and that he's the kind of man who would go to great lengths to assist the Nazi war machine."

"You've been digging into this, haven't you?"

"Yes. I'm Japanese. I am determined to do whatever I can to expose this group. I have to. I have no choice. We are loyal Americans too, you know. Germans look American with their white skin and blond hair, which is why they will not be persecuted should this war happen. We Japanese will be, however. I want to make sure that I can do whatever possible to keep that from happening."

"I understand. I've experienced the prejudice too, and I'm not even Japanese, at least on the outside."

Aki stroked her chin. "We might have something else coming up, but we'll have to be patient. Sometimes dealing with powerful men can be an exercise in futility. No amount of persuasion can get them to move."

"Perhaps an appeal to their vanity." Gwen chuckled. "That always seems to move the unmovable."

"We have a Captain Mayfield who is trying to get around the Federal Communications Act," Aki said, "but it's been tough."

"I know. We could go to jail for doing our job. If a friend of a coworker of mine hadn't picked up the Japanese transmission from the island here on an English ship, I wouldn't be here talking to you."

They walked up the stairs to the Palace and went in through the front door. The hallway was a cream color with polished koa doors. The wood of the koa tree looked like honey poured out of a jar, almost liquid. A staircase of koa stood in the middle of the room and wound itself to the floors above. Aki continued to speak. "I guess David Sarnoff is coming to Hawaii this month. He's the president of Radio Corporation of America. They own the radio office the Japanese have been using to send their messages to Tokyo. Admiral Bloch is going to try to convince him to deliver file copies of the Japanese messages to Captain Mayfield. That ought to give them something they can believe." Aki paused, looking Gwen in the eye. "After all, it would come from a man."

"Unless Japan strikes before then."

Aki hung her head. "Yes, let's hope they hold off until December."

CHAPTER 24

Aki got off the bus and watched it pull away. A stifling plume of diesel exhaust left a trail of gray smoke behind the green giant. Her spirits lifted almost immediately as she started the walk toward her grandmother's house. She had never known anyone as wise as her grandmother. It was like the old woman could read her thoughts, and the best part was that Grandma Dai liked what she read.

She turned the corner and spotted the rusty chain-link fence that surrounded her grandmother's home. Opening the gate she stepped onto the rocky walkway. The black volcanic rocks glistened with pools of water; evidently her grandmother had just washed the walk-way. The tiny shells embedded in the black rock sparkled beneath her feet, and the shade from the palm trees cast shadows along the way to the door.

Aki slipped off her shoes and knocked. Her grandmother's hearing was still good, but Aki knew it might take a few minutes for Grandma Dai to get to the door. The old woman didn't move as fast as she used to. She knocked again.

A short time later, Grandma Dai opened the door. She smiled.

Aki bowed. "I hope you are feeling well, Grandmother."

Dai bowed in return. "*Ogenkisio' na no de anshin itashimashita,*" which meant, "I feel much better now that I see you looking so well."

Aki shuffled in the door and closed it behind them.

"I have tea, and we can take it in the garden," Dai said. "Follow me and you can get the cups." The woman waddled toward the kitchen, talking as she went. "I hoped you would come to see me today."

A few minutes later they were seated at the table under the tree. It was peaceful there. The shade was cool, and the flowers seemed to smile as they waved in the soft breeze. As Dai poured the tea, Aki reached into her pocket and took out a piece of folded yellow paper.

"Something troubling you?"

Aki drummed the folded-up paper on the palm of her hand. "It's a note from Brian. He wants to meet me at our beach tonight."

Dai lifted her cup and held it to her lips. "And why should that bother you, my child?"

"Because of what I have to tell him."

Dai sipped her tea. Aki knew she was just waiting to hear. Her grandmother seldom spoke unless she knew what the question was. What Aki had to say to Brian was something that cut into her heart, and she knew that she could never share her heart without first running the matter past her grandmother.

"His father is here in Hawaii."

"Yes." Dai continued to sip her tea.

"He does not approve of Brian seeing me. He thinks it will hurt Brian's career to marry a Japanese girl."

Dai put down her cup. "And what do you think?"

Aki shook her head and picked up her cup of tea. She knew that what she had to say must be said, but it was almost as if the delay would make it less painful. "I've worked for the navy for three years now, ever since I graduated from college, and I think Brian's father is right. I've seen how they look at me, and I've heard the whispers."

"And you want to do the honorable thing and take yourself out of Brian's life? To let him, *hane o nobasu?*" Dai used the Japanese expression for stretching one's wings, cutting one's self free from restraints.

"Yes, Grandma." Aki sipped her tea. "Brian would never do such a thing, but I fear for him, and I fear for us should he not. He is too honorable, but he is a boy. I know him. He will go ahead with what is on his mind and ask me to marry him. Of course only later will he realize his mistake, but by then it will be too late."

Dai picked up her cup. "Perhaps then you should do that." She smiled. "You have made the right decision."

Aki put down her cup and nervously shuffled her feet. "Why do you say that, Grandma?"

Dai's smile widened. "Not for the same reason you have given."

"Then why?"

"Because if you have so little respect for him now that you are willing to act in a manner that is contrary to his wishes, then you will respect him even less if you do marry him. You see him as a boy. Perhaps he can never grow up to be a man in your eyes."

"I just don't think he understands the hatred his people have for people unlike themselves. He loves me, and it has blinded him."

"But you think that you see more clearly than he does. When will that change? When will he see clearly enough to do what is best for you? Isn't that what he wants, to care for you and to make you happy?"

"Yes it is. I just don't think he understands. The navy is his dream. He's always wanted to be successful and to rise in the ranks of his peers."

"Do you know this for certain? Perhaps this is his father's dream and not Brian's. Your parents have their dreams for you. Do you want to subject this young man to your mother and father's dreams for their daughter? When will he come to know your own dreams?"

Aki felt flustered. She blinked her eyes and felt for a tissue in her purse. Pulling one out, she dabbed the corners of her eyes. "I don't understand what you're saying. I love him, and I want what is best for him."

"And Brian feels that what is best for him is to marry the woman he loves. You seem to want the man to be successful but lonely, to clutch a hollow feeling to his heart every time he thinks of you and wonders what his life would have been like with the woman he loves." Dai shook her head. "This would be a painful life for both you and Brian, but you want it rather than disappoint Brian's father. It should be his decision, but you are making it for him. I am sad." Dai dropped her gaze to the table, then lifted her head and looked Aki in the eye. "To be with a man is to respect and honor him. You are not showing honor."

Aki dabbed her eyes. "Then this is his decision?"

"Yes, and you must respect it."

"You remember how God sent his son into the world to suffer and endure pain?"

Aki nodded. "Yes, Grandma."

"And you will have pain too. Rain firms up the ground, but you must submit and obey. You must have a gentle spirit and accept what God has for you."

"Yes, Grandma, you are right." Aki unfolded the note and looked at it. "All right, Grandma, I will see him and tell him my heart." She reached up and touched the cross around her neck.

"And?"

Aki swallowed hard. "And I will tell him that it is his decision. That I will respect his decision no matter what it is." She reached over and took the old woman's hand, squeezing it gently. "I do love him, Grandma, with all my heart."

Dai patted her hand. "I know you do, child. I wish you every happiness."

Aki spent the rest of the afternoon helping her grandmother clean her house. It gave her great satisfaction to be of use to the old woman, to scrub when her grandmother would be too weak to get into the places that needed to be cleaned and to reach for high things so that her grandmother wouldn't take the risk of falling. Saturdays had always been a day for Aki to help her grandmother.

When she finished the last of the sweeping, she set the broom back in the narrow closet and closed the door. Her grandmother was reading her Bible. She mouthed the words as she read, her small frail fingertips gliding across the worn pages. Dai eagerly turned the tissue-thin pages, lovingly smoothing the paper and nodding as she continued. This was a very unusual thing for an older Japanese woman. Aki's own parents hadn't become Christians, but her grandmother had listened to Aki explain her faith and had taken the time to read the message that Aki had spoken to her about. It comforted the old woman that there was more to life than the grave.

Dai looked up at Aki and smiled, pointing to a passage. "You see what this prophet Habakkuk says, my child. Right here. He says, 'Behold, his soul which is lifted up is not upright within him: but the just shall live by his faith.'" Dai smiled. "You cannot make all your decisions because of what you see or think. Sometimes you have to trust and wait. You must trust God, and you must trust Brian." She lifted her finger and shook it. "Most of all you have to wait."

"Yes, Grandma." Aki bowed her head. "I know you are right. Sometimes I just need to hear my own words to realize how wrong they are. I do want to be a person who believes, and I want to respect and believe in Brian. I will tell him that tonight when I meet him on the beach."

Later that evening Aki walked along Kuhio Beach. She glanced up the hill, hoping to see Brian. She had changed into a yellow sarong that hung gently around her shoulders and was wearing her brown-strapped sandals. She had also taken the time to go to the market and buy two leis, which hung around her neck. They were uncommon, with white orchids fanning out like butterflies with splashes of yellow in the middle. This was to be a special night.

The sun had set, leaving a ribbon of purple like crushed plums, and palm trees formed dark lines that sliced through the fading splash of color. The tide was outgoing; the sand was wet and spongy. Aki watched the swirling water back away from her like a whimpering dog. The foam melted with each retreating lap of the waves on the sand, and the sea looked dark, a deep indigo blue.

Brian was late, but she wasn't worried. Today had been a working day for Brian. Most high-ranking officers were at play on the weekends, and that left the duty for the junior officers like Brian to perform. It was like him to be diligent, even when he wanted to be somewhere else.

She looked back up the dark hill. She saw a lone figure walking with a determined step. Her heart leaped. *Brian,* she thought. She would let him come to her.

A few moments later she heard her name, "Aki."

It wasn't Brian. She turned to look. "You. What are you doing here?"

"I have come here for you."

Aki backed away, but the man kept coming closer.

"I am waiting here for Brian."

"You needn't bother. He's not coming. I sent you that note at work."

Aki turned and began to run. She picked up her dress, doing her best to scamper along the wet sand. She could hear his steps getting closer. Her heart was pounding.

CHAPTER 25

am laughed as they stumbled out of the squash court, and he put his arm gently around Gwen's shoulder. Sweat was trickling down his back. "I gotta tell you, girl, you're a terror with a racket in your hand. I wouldn't be a mosquito with you and a fly swatter for all the tea in China. Your kill shots were right on the money."

The fans were spinning overhead, large wooden blades that chopped at the air and drove the musty smells down in puffs of gymnasium odors. Gwen reached up and slipped his hand off her shoulder, smiling all the while. "I'm glad I could keep up with you. You've obviously had a lot of practice."

Sam knew he'd gone a bit far with the hand on her shoulder, but for a moment she had been one of the boys. Only for a moment, though. It had been hard to play squash with Gwen when all he had wanted to do was watch her run. He chuckled. "They call me the killer in D.C."

"I can see why." Gwen laid the towel over her shoulders and stepped out onto the track, pulling back to allow two joggers to pass. The two men slogged past them, breathing hard.

"But you were the best tussle I've had in a long time." Sam ran his hand over his face, wiping off the sweat, then pushed his fingers through his curly black hair. "I've wanted to have the chance to play ever since I got on this island." He motioned at the set of locker room doors at the far end of the circular track. "We'd better get ourselves presentable for the admiral. I'll take you out to breakfast, and then we'll get over to Pearl."

"Are you sure you should do this? I mean, I talked to the admiral at the ball, and he made some noises about seeing me later, even though he didn't sound very enthusiastic."

"I don't see how it could hurt. We'll say I just ran into you." Sam laughed, thinking about their furious struggle on the squash court. "And I did, if you recall, several times on the court."

Gwen bowed her head and smiled. "Yes, I recall. Quite hard too."

Sam shook his head. "I'm sorry about that. I'm not used to playing with a woman. It seemed kind of strange at first, but you weren't exactly holding back." Sam knew she wouldn't let a man win to shore up his ego. Of course Sam had never needed that. He was too good for that, and his ego was far beyond the need for a woman to make him look good. He looked at her. "In fact, it almost seemed like your life depended on it."

"When a woman competes with a man, her life does depend on it."

A short time later their taxicab pulled up outside the Moana Hotel, one of the venerable grand hotels in Waikiki. The series of rooftops were flat, and a row of white pillars held up the entranceway with arches running along the entire facade of the building. Tall stately palms lined the entrance. The place had a colonial look to it, and that was no accident. Hawaii was nothing more than a colony when it was built up in 1901 to cater to the steamship crowd.

Sam paid the driver, and Gwen and he took to the stairs and walked through the oversize doors.

"Which way to the coffee shop?" Sam asked the porter.

The man motioned to the side of the lobby. A minute later, Sam and Gwen slid into the leather booth. A white tablecloth covered the copper-colored table, and yellow and white gardenias swam in the middle of a large crystal bowl.

"This looks expensive," Gwen said.

"I hope so." He smiled. "I'm on an expense account, and I have to make those people pay in some way."

A waitress in a tight-fitting sarong presented them with gilded menus, and they took some time in looking over the delicacies offered by the hotel.

"Have whatever you like. I'm having flapjacks. A guy has got to feel at home." He stroked his chin. "And I'm going to drink a gallon of the Kona coffee they serve here, black of course. No sense diluting the stuff."

Gwen ordered the fresh fruit and tea, and Sam hunched over a cup of black coffee. "So, Gwen, why don't you tell me why it's so important for you to see the admiral? You tell me your secrets, and I'll tell you mine."

Gwen poured cream into her tea and stirred it. "Wouldn't that be the way to end my career with the navy, giving secret information to the press? I might as well just quit and go to school full time."

"Well, it has to be about Japan or you wouldn't be here. Am I right?"

Gwen nodded. "Yes, you're right about that." She smiled, sipping her tea. "Of course that puts you on a par with everyone else on this island. Everybody here is edgy about the Japanese Empire."

"But not edgy enough to suit you, I take it."

Gwen smiled. "No, I'm afraid not. The navy seems to have an untouchable attitude here. They see Hawaii as too far away from what is taking place in the Pacific to make any difference."

"But we both know that's not true. The American fleet is here. What better target could the Japanese have?"

Sam tried hard to hide his frustration during breakfast. He watched Gwen taking careful slices of her pineapple, strawberries, and papaya. It seemed to him that each time he asked a sensitive question, Gwen would pop another piece of fruit into her mouth and smile while she chewed.

"Why don't I just tell you why I'm here?" he asked.

Gwen rolled her wrist, flashing her fork in his direction. "Go ahead. You're paying."

He laughed. "That's right. I am. Well, I'm here following a German spy. To be more specific, he's a German and English spy, a double agent. Sort of makes it hard to figure just who he's working for. I've followed him all over Waikiki. I know the man's habits. I know where he eats and where he spits."

"The man you saw at the ball?"

"Yep, that's the feller. A slimy sort, I'd say. He meets pretty regular with people from the Japanese Embassy here. I'd say they've become close buddies by now. The way I figure it, the man's a conduit from the Nazis. If he doesn't give them information, he gives them pats on the back."

"I've seen your spy." Gwen put down her fork and leaned over in his direction. "I even saw you following him the first day I arrived. I had lunch with my parents at the Royal Hawaiian."

"You are a sharp lady. I like that."

"It's part of my job to notice things."

Sam related the man's travels on the island, watching for her reactions. But she was somber, merely nodding and keeping her thoughts to herself. Sam couldn't detect a single note of surprise in her expression. He dabbed his mouth with his napkin and then dropped the napkin beside his plate. "I got to say this about you, Gwen, you'd make a heck of a poker player. I wouldn't want to face you with two pair in my hand."

It was close to 8:45 when they arrived at the fleet headquarters building. A young sailor in denims was pushing a lawn mower, yanking it back and jamming it over the top of the green grass in an attempt to give the lawn that groomed, manicured look so highly sought after in the semitropical climate of Hawaii. It required a great deal of effort, but manpower was never a problem in the navy. The man was down to his T-shirt, and sweat was pouring off his forehead. A package of Lucky Strike cigarettes was rolled up in one sleeve. His day had just started, but already he looked exhausted.

"How's it coming?" Sam asked as they walked by. He always made a point to speak to the people on the periphery of a story.

The man stopped his mowing, pulled his hands off the mower, and shook his arms. "It's coming, but I'm beat." He looked down at the grass and shook his head. "Man, this stuff comes up overnight. I think Hawaii makes everything grow, especially the stuff you don't want to grow."

Sam smiled. "You're doing a great job. Keep it up."

Tulips were laid out in rows that formed a pink, yellow, and white pathway along the sidewalk and up to the stairs. The native blooms of Hawaii were missing in favor of flowers that made the Naval station look like it was located somewhere in the heart of Ohio. Red brick gave the sidewalk a distinctive, almost red-carpet look.

They made their way down the walkway. Sam glanced back at the man who had once again started his mowing. "Showing somebody he really counts doesn't take a whole lot of time and effort, and sometimes it really pays off. You can't imagine how many good leads I've gotten from laundry women and maids."

They walked up the stairs, and Sam pushed open the glass door, holding it for Gwen. The hallway was a dull, military gray with a dark Oriental credenza halfway down the hall and against the wall. It had an arrangement of roses on it and a photograph of Admiral Kimmel above the flowers. Sam thought the flowers and the picture made it seem like Kimmel was dead.

The two doors at the end of the corridor were open, and an attractive secretary with flaming red hair was at her desk, slowly typing a letter. Sam thought she filled out her white blouse rather nicely. "I'll be with you in a minute," she said in a high-pitched twang.

"No problem," Sam replied. "We're in no hurry."

The woman pushed a key and then frowned, uttering a curse under her breath. She opened the drawer in front of her and rummaged with her hand until at last she pulled out an eraser. Lifting the bar over the paper in the typewriter, she rubbed furiously at the mistake. Dropping the bar back into place, she looked up at them. "You have an appointment?"

Sam grinned and stepped forward. Putting his hands on the desk, he leaned forward. "I'm Sam Diamond and, yes, I have an appointment." Turning on his charm with secretaries was something he could make a living at. He flashed a smile, showing his teeth. "Of course, right now I wish I didn't. I'd love to just sit here and talk to you."

She batted her eyes and returned his smile. Wiggling in her seat, she reached over to pick up a clipboard. She held it closer, scanning the page. Finally locating his name, she pointed to it. "Yeah, here you are, Sam Diamond." She looked up at him, letting the name and Sam's face sink in.

"Well, good," Sam said. "Nice to know you haven't lost me before you found me."

"Yes." The woman got to her feet, straightening her tight black skirt. "I'll tell the admiral you're here."

Moving around her desk, she swayed over to a side door, swinging her ample hips. She opened the door without knocking and stepped inside, closing the door behind her.

Sam stepped back to join Gwen. He flashed her a smile. "Gwen, my lady, I'd be willing to bet that this is an office where that charm of yours will work better than the hard-working, no-nonsense approach you usually use. You saw how that woman typed that letter. She obviously wasn't hired for her secretarial skills."

Gwen frowned, sticking out her lower lip.

"Just a suggestion, but I think I'd try a smile if I were you."

Moments later, the woman stepped back out. "He'll see you now, Mr. Diamond."

Sam tugged on Gwen's arm. "Come on, deary, it's our turn to strut our stuff."

Both Sam and Gwen walked into Kimmel's office. The place had been paneled in pecan, the grains standing out in dark lines. A white wicker planter along the wall overflowed with voluptuous ferns, their fronds hanging to the floor. Photographs of ships studded the wall, and models of ships filled a bookcase.

Kimmel's gray hair was pulled over the top of his head to hide a bald spot. He got to his feet. He forced a smile and pointed to a red leather couch and chair that were arranged in front of his desk. "Please, have a seat."

"Sure," Sam said. "I bumped into Miss Williams and asked her to come along. You don't mind, do you? I think you two met at the Navy Ball last week."

Gwen forced a smile, but it was a good one. "Nice to see you again, Admiral."

"No, I don't mind. I'm not going to say anything that Miss Williams can't hear."

Sam could bet that was right. He had no doubt that the man was going to stonewall him and say nothing of any importance. He was just that type. Living in D.C. had taught Sam about dealing with men like this. All Sam had to do was tell part of what he knew was the truth. Kimmel's silence would do the rest.

Sam and Gwen sank into the overstuffed couch, and Kimmel returned to his seat behind the massive desk. "It was nice of you to see me." Sam reached into his pocket and produced a small spiral notebook and pen. "I know you're a busy man. I think our readers would be interested to know just how you plan to prepare for Japan. We've got a lot of nervous people back home, Admiral."

Kimmel started to speak when his door opened and the secretary stepped in. She seemed a little flustered, wringing her hands. "I am sorry to disturb you, sir, but the police are here."

"Police?" Kimmel's eyes opened wide.

"Yes, sir. A Sergeant Lowry."

"Show him in."

Kimmel got to his feet, along with Sam, and waited for the unexpected visitor.

The policeman, who wore a wrinkled brown suit and brown fedora hat, looked the part of someone who was not given to making a good impression. His rather thin face was unshaven, and he had dark circles around his eyes. He was carrying a spiral notebook.

"Sorry to bother you, Admiral, but I don't have anybody else to turn to to get what I want." He leafed through the notebook. "It seems we have a murder victim that is connected to you folks here, a Miss Aki Kawa."

Gwen gasped, and Sam reached down to grab her hand.

"She worked for your Office of Naval Intelligence, and I can't even get in the door there to find someone who might know her and identify the body. We'd rather not call on the girl's parents just yet if we can help it. No sense in dragging folks down to see a body that might not belong to them. The body had some identification on it, but we can't know for sure until someone identifies it."

Kimmel put his hands on his desk. "What do you want from me?"

"Just the name of someone that you can call out to see me, someone who worked with the girl."

Gwen looked up at Kimmel. "I knew Aki. I saw her just the other day."

"There you are, Sergeant. Maybe Miss Williams here will work for you."

CHAPTER 26

Gwen slumped over on Sam's shoulder in the backseat of the police sedan. It gave her some comfort, even if she didn't know the man that well. There was something about him that she trusted. He was plain-speaking and honest. Many men who had been interested in her had tried tactics that were cunning and self-serving, but Sam Diamond was a man who said what was on his mind. She liked that.

The news about Aki's death had shaken her. In the short time she had known the woman, she had come to respect and care for her.

There had been an innocence to Aki Kawa. She was smart, and she seemed to know what could be done and what couldn't.

They drove down King Street through the downtown section of Honolulu and turned right onto Punchbowl Street. Queen's Hospital was on their right, and Lowry pulled into a spot behind the big gray building and parked. "The morgue is in here," he said. "You'll have to follow me."

Both Gwen and Sam got out of the car. Gwen took Sam's hand. "Thank you for coming here with me."

Sam reached around her and put his arm around her shoulder. "That's all right. I'm happy to do it. I wouldn't let you go here alone."

The back door of the hospital was the ambulance entrance as well as the entrance to the Emergency Room. A red-and-white ambulance, its back doors open, was parked next to the door. They walked past the ambulance and into the Emergency Room. Nurses dressed in crisp white uniforms hurried through the hall while children cried and other patients waited on Naugahyde chairs and settees. A large clock on the wall read 9:42. Time was standing still for Gwen. There were no smiles in this place, only pain.

Lowry opened the caged doors to the elevator and stepped aside for Gwen and Sam. He closed the door behind them and pushed the B button for basement. The elevator lurched to life and sucked them beneath the concrete slab of the first floor. Seconds later it jerked to a halt and Lowry opened the door.

Gwen and Sam stepped out into the hall. It was long and dim with caged lights overhead. Their steps echoed as they walked down the cool hallway.

Lowry paused in front of the door that said MORGUE and looked at them. "OK, now we don't know for sure if this is your friend. It might not be. There were some papers on her that gave us a name, but they could have belonged to her and been on someone else. I've taken people in here before and had them shocked to see someone they didn't recognize."

"I'll be all right," Gwen said.

Sam held her closer, and Lowry opened the door.

They walked into the large room. The overhead lights bathed the place with a stark white light. The creamy walls were trimmed in steel, and the floor was tile. It was like walking into a large shower stall. Across the room, a man was working on a corpse. The man turned and spotted them, pulling up a sheet to cover the body.

"We're here to identify the Kawa woman," Lowry said.

The man nodded and stripped off his rubber gloves. He walked over to a row of shiny steel lockers. Grabbing one of the handles, he cranked it open and reached in. The rattle of the rollers on the bottom of the gurney was unsettling.

Sam held Gwen. The attendant reached up and pulled the green sheet off the victim's face and shoulders. It was Aki, her eyes seemingly closed in sleep.

Gwen's fingers dug into Sam's arm, but she lifted her head high. She wasn't going to break down, even though everything inside of her wanted to cry. "That's her. That's Aki. Where did you find her?"

Suddenly Gwen turned back to look at Aki once again. "Do you have her personal effects?"

"Yes," the attendant said. "They're over in a locker."

"Did you find a cross? It's a gold cross with a black pearl in it. She wouldn't have been without it. Brian gave it to her."

The man shook his head. "No, we didn't find any jewelry on her."

Lowry motioned for the attendant to put the body back in place. "Why don't we step outside?"

The three of them moved out into the hall. Lowry looked Gwen in the eye. "She had been in the water for twenty-four hours or more. We found her washed up on the beach near Barber's Point. Figured the tide must have carried her that far."

"Are you sure she didn't drown?" Gwen asked.

Lowry nodded. "Pretty sure. The woman was strangled. There are bruises on her neck." He swallowed hard. "Her skull was also fractured with a blunt object. It's hard to tell what killed her, the strangulation or the blow on the head. Look, why don't we go over to my office. I'd like to get your statement and anything else that you think might help us."

A short time later they were making their way through the squad room. Cigarette smoke curled around the air, a gray semitransparent snake that refused to settle in the room. Bright sunlight filtered through venetian blinds that were buckled and bent, casting shadows on the tile floor that looked like twisted prison bars. The place wasn't exactly a beehive of activity. Several detectives sat around an empty desk playing cards. They didn't even glance up as Gwen and Sam walked by. One detective was leaning back in his chair with his feet on his desk, taking a report from a caller. He rolled his eyes as Gwen walked by, bored but murmuring a series of uh-huhs. Putting his hand over the receiver, he called back to Lowry. "You got a swabby in your office."

The sergeant stepped over to the man. "When you finish with that, why don't you call the Kawa woman's parents. Go down to the hospital and take them to the morgue. Tell them we've found their daughter. You'll have to stay with them until they make an identification and then take their story. Tell them also that I'll be paying them a visit later in the day." He shook his head.

The man shrugged and let out a sigh.

Lowry took off his hat and squashed it on a wooden coatrack outside his door. He then opened the door that had HOMICIDE emblazoned on the smoky glass and led Gwen and Sam into the room.

A navy officer in a pressed khaki uniform paced back and forth near the open window. A black armband on his short sleeve had SP boldly printed in white letters. The chief petty officer drilled his brown eyes into Lowry. "I'm Chief Gardner. I was ordered to come down here and see what you have on this dead woman."

"Not much." Lowry stepped around his desk and took a seat. He motioned to a dull green sofa that had shiny curved steel bars for the arms. "You two can have a seat. I just brought in Miss Williams here in hopes she could answer a few questions so we know where to start. But if you ask me, this looks like a few drunken sailors got carried away with having a good time on Saturday night. You know how it goes, too much to drink and not a woman in sight who's willing to say yes."

Both Gwen and Sam sat down.

"Sounds like it's our problem then," Gardner said.

"I wouldn't be so sure of that. The woman was a civilian and was found on a beach. She was obviously murdered in Honolulu because the tide took her to Barber's Point."

"But she's our employee and in a very sensitive position."

Lowry leaned back in his chair. "Why don't you tell me about that. I'm interested."

Gwen spoke up. "I suppose I would know more about that than anyone else here." She glanced at Gardner. "Aki was a language specialist, Japanese. She worked in the basement of the Naval Intelligence Office. Recently she had been involved with a series of Japanese communications to Tokyo. It's very sensitive material, and she's the reason I came to Hawaii."

Gwen glanced at Gardner. "The rest is navy business. I really can't say more."

Lowry looked at her, leaned forward, and opened his notebook. He shuffled through the pages until he found his place and took out a fountain pen. "I'm all ears."

"Unfortunately, there isn't much I can tell you about what we were working on. The people involved have diplomatic immunity."

Lowry rolled his wrist in Gwen's direction. "So you're telling me if her killer was the guy you two ladies have been working on that we couldn't arrest him?"

Gwen nodded. "That's exactly what I'm telling you."

"All right. Why don't we find out what you can tell me. Did she have any enemies, anyone who might want to see her dead?"

"None that I can think of. She had a boyfriend in the navy, a Lieutenant Brian Picard on the *Arizona*. He might be able to tell you more."

Lowry reached into his coat pocket and pulled out a waxed-paper-wrapped yellow piece of paper. He unfolded it and pulled out the paper, laying it on his desk. "We found this note in her pocket. It has her full name on it, which is why we knew where to look. It appears to be sent by this Brian and has his first name on the bottom." He looked up at her. "You know the beach this Brian referred to as their beach in this note?"

"I believe it's Kuhio Beach. Aki talked to me about the place."

"Yeah, popular spot."

Gwen went on. "Aki didn't talk much about her personal life. I know her parents weren't all that happy about her dating a non-Japanese."

"Not much reason to kill their own daughter," Lowry offered.

"Brian's father was equally unhappy with him dating her."

"Unhappy enough to kill the woman?"

"Now hold on." Gardner stepped forward. "Brian Picard's father is Admiral Picard. You're not suggesting . . ."

"I'm not suggesting anything." Lowry shot him a quick look. "Is the man here on the island?"

"Yes, but he couldn't have done such a thing."

"Why don't you let me be the judge of that? I'll talk to him and see what he has to say for himself. Also find out just where he was on Saturday night."

"He's a busy man," Gardner said, "and I'm sure he had nothing to do with this."

Lowry drummed his pen on the desk. "Chief, you here to find a killer or to protect an admiral?"

"Look," Gardner drawled, "if that woman was killed by the President of the United States, I'd put the cuffs on him myself."

Sam patted Gwen's hand. "Can we go now?"

Lowry looked at her. "You can if that's all you can tell me."

Gwen wrinkled her brow. "There was a man that Aki met on Kuhio Beach. She brought him to church with her last week." Gwen cast a gaze to the floor. "I think his name is Homer."

Lowry scratched down the name. "All right, we'll find this Homer fella and bring him in for questioning."

"He's harmless."

Lowry replaced the cap on his fountain pen and screwed it tight. "Obviously someone wasn't harmless here. We'll just have to find out who."

Gwen and Sam were out on the street a short time later. "Thank you for coming with me."

"Hey, this is a story and I'm a reporter. I didn't just do it for you." He smiled at her. "Mostly you, but not all."

"Well, thank you anyway."

"What say we don't leave this thing to those two yokels up there."

"What do you mean?"

"I mean, why don't we do some digging of our own? This thing crosses your job and my story. I'd say it falls in both our ballparks. If we can find a murderer, that makes your story more credible, then they'll have to listen to you. It wouldn't hurt to spice up my story, either. What do you say?" Sam stuck out his hand to shake hers.

She shook it. "All right. I'm game. I liked Aki."

"Great." Sam grinned. "Besides, it'll give me an excuse to see you again."

Gwen turned to walk away but then stopped and looked back at Sam. "There is one more place I'd like you to go with me."

"Where's that?"

"To see Brian. I'd rather he hear this from me."

CHAPTER 27

Gwen had a sick feeling in her stomach when the cab rolled up to the gates of Pearl Harbor. Even though she knew that Aki would have wanted Brian to hear the news from her and not from some seaman dropping off a note from headquarters, it didn't make it any easier. She could hardly bear the thought of Brian's face when she told him. Gwen knew she would just have to prepare herself for it.

The taxi dropped them off just inside the gate at Pearl Harbor, and Gwen and Sam walked over to the small compound that served as headquarters for the duty officer of the day. Sam politely opened the door and stood aside for Gwen, then walked in behind her.

The seaman seated behind the desk had his feet propped up on an open drawer. He was reading a magazine, which he quickly dropped to his side when the two of them walked in. Slumping forward, the man banged his feet to the floor. "Can I help you?"

"We would like to locate a Lieutenant Brian Picard," Sam said. "Does he have duty today?"

"Hang on and I'll get the officer of the day." He got to his feet and stepped into the back office. A few minutes later, a young ensign in a starched khaki uniform joined them. The man caught sight of them and smiled. Gwen wasn't sure if it was because he wanted to make a good impression on her or because they were both in civilian clothes and he didn't need to impress them at all.

He put his hands on the desk and leaned forward, smiling at Gwen. "Can I be of assistance?"

"You can tell us where to find Lieutenant Brian Picard," Sam said.

The officer barely looked in Sam's direction. He continued to stare straight into Gwen's eyes, making her uncomfortable. The man grinned. "Are you relatives of his?"

"No," Gwen said. "Friends of a friend."

The young ensign was evidently feeling his oats and wanted Gwen to know it. He straightened himself up and stretched, then picked up a clipboard, leafing through the sheets of paper. "Let's see where we can find daddy's little boy today. No doubt he's probably got some cushy duty on the back of a golf cart. Oh, yeah, here it is." He smiled. "Figures. Picard is off today. Guess he had weekend duty. He's probably at his quarters, number two-zero-two in the bachelor officers' quarters." He grinned. "You'd better hurry, though, before his daddy takes him to the next ship he's greased to command."

Once again, he leaned over his desk and flashed a smile at Gwen. "I can tell you, though, the man's got a woman. He's been had, but he ain't worth having."

They both turned without a reply and walked out the door and down the walkway. "I take it Picard isn't too popular with his fellow officers," Sam said.

"At least with the junior officers, it would appear," Gwen replied.

They walked over to the bachelor officers' quarters and headed up the concrete stairs. Moving down the row of numbered apartments, they found 202. Gwen knocked on the door. The place looked simple from the outside; a set of flimsy white curtains blew from an open window on the second-story corridor.

Moments later Brian opened the door. He was standing there in a pair of cutoff jeans. He had no shirt on, and his eyes were red.

"Can we come in?" Gwen asked.

Brian stepped back. "Sure, come on in. I can't very well stop you." Walking back into what appeared to be a living room area, he collapsed into a plaid chair, dropping his feet straight out in front of him. Brian motioned in the direction of the couch. "Have a seat."

Gwen sat down, but Sam chose to stand.

"We have some bad news," Gwen said.

"You mean about Aki?"

"Yes." Gwen could see the pained expression on Brian's face. She should have guessed that somehow he had found out about Aki by the way he opened the door. "How did you find out?"

"My father called me this morning and told me over the phone." Brian had a distant look in his eye. He stared out the living room window, watching the thin white curtains flutter in the breeze.

Gwen reached out and put her hand on his. "I am so very sorry, Brian. We wanted to tell you ourselves. We just came from the morgue where we identified her."

"How did your dad find out?" Sam asked.

Brian waited a moment, letting Sam's words soak in. It was a simple question, but his mind was elsewhere. He slowly shook his head. "I don't know. The man has moles everywhere. He probably knows I'm wearing shorts with no shirt on right now." He looked up at Sam. "He wouldn't approve of that, you know. An officer is a gentleman at all times, even though that means being dead to your feelings on the inside and a snake in the grass to your family."

His words seemed to animate him and stir his emotions. He looked over at Gwen and then up at Sam, a wild-eyed expression on his face. "Do you know what it's like to be a grown man and feel as if you're still in a high chair? I'll never be an adult as long as my father has a breath in him."

Looking off to the curtains once again, his face softened and his eyes grew heavy. "Aki respected me. She actually admired me and wanted to follow me wherever I wanted to go and support me in whatever I wanted to do. I felt ten feet tall when I was around her."

Sam thought he saw Brian's lower lip quiver. "Can you tell me if she had any enemies?" he asked. "Anyone at all who would want to hurt her?"

Brian looked up, his distant gaze suddenly transformed into a blaze of hatred. "She did have one guy who kept after her. He wouldn't leave her alone, and he wouldn't take no for an answer." He shook his head. "I tried to get her to let me handle the guy, but she wanted to do it herself. She was always like that, brave and self-sufficient."

Gwen watched his face quiver and then harden. He clenched his fists into tight balls, wanting to focus his mind on the anger he was feeling inside. "The guy's name is Mitchell Krinkle, the sugar man's beloved son." His words dripped with sarcasm. "He met Aki at a dance while I was at sea. She never paid any attention to him, but still the guy was determined. He kept on"—Brian slammed his right fist into the palm of his hand and ground it—"and kept on. And kept on. I would have put a stop to it once and for all, but she wouldn't let me."

He looked back up at Sam. His face abruptly turning pitiful as his lip quivered. There was a whimper in his voice. "Why wouldn't she let me?" Eyeing Gwen, he repeated the question. "Why wouldn't she let me?"

S am took Gwen to lunch at the Royal Hawaiian. As he cut into his Kalua pork, he tried to make something out of what they had found out thus far. "We might have to get Brian to go with us to see his old man. Admiral Picard will be hard to reach, and we have no official status in this investigation."

"Do you really think there's a connection?" Gwen found it hard to put together any possible connection between Brian's father and Aki. She had little doubt that the man disapproved of his son's choice in a wife, but murder seemed to be going much too far.

"How could he know about Aki's murder? We had barely gotten out of the morgue." He stabbed a bite of pork on his plate and pushed it into his mouth.

He nodded his head as he continued to eat. Gwen could tell that he was trying hard to make a case, and, like other men, there was something about hearing the words that helped him to think. "Now maybe, just maybe, he did kill her." He pointed his fork at her. "Follow me on this. He goes to try to talk her out of seeing his son. He makes a fatherly plea for her to consider Brian's career."

Dropping his knife and fork, Sam jerked up his napkin and patted the corners of his mouth. He smiled a sly smile. It was as if he had a secret he was letting Gwen in on. "She says no, but things get out of hand. He shakes her to try to jar her around to his thinking, but she still says no. Finally"—Sam held his hands out in midair as if gripping someone by the neck—"He takes her by the throat and begins to squeeze. Harder and harder he squeezes until she goes limp. He's horrified at the idea that he's killed her. He puts her in the water and waits. As soon as he finds out that someone's been in to identify her, he calls Brian. He's going to help his son grieve, but he's the killer."

Gwen reached out and took his hands, lowering them to the table. She smiled, looking from side to side. "Not so fast. You've got a good plot for a novel, but you're scaring our waiter over there." She smiled. It felt good to smile, even if it was a bit forced. "Personally, I'm in favor of us going to the sugar heir Brian talked about."

Sam pulled his napkin back to his lap. "Yeah, I doubt that. I'm sure Picard was a bit jealous; maybe he wants to make the guy hurt a little for trying to make time with his girl. But why would a kid like Krinkle risk so much for something he gets with the flick of a wrist? The kid's loaded, and his daddy is superrich."

"Yes, I know." Gwen put down her salad fork. "Both these ideas seem a little farfetched, even if they are all we have to go on." She stirred the remains of the salad on her plate.

"Maybe we shouldn't forget the obvious." Gwen looked up to catch Sam's eye. "Aki was getting too close to the Japanese conduit of information coming off this island. Possibly we could consider her death to be work-related."

"The Japanese?"

"It's a possibility. A week ago Sunday Aki and I went to the bluffs overlooking Pearl. Aki said one of the consulate's men was always there taking notes on what we have in port. She had seen him before. When we started up the hill from where we were standing, the man was watching us though his binoculars. He must have recognized Aki. They could have had her murdered. I had a coworker almost killed by someone believed to be their agent in San Francisco. There's no reason for them to stop with almost killing someone."

"If that's true, then the guy will have diplomatic immunity." He scooted forward and put his hand on Gwen's. "Something else too. If the man saw Aki, he saw you. That puts you in danger."

Gwen swallowed hard. She knew he was right. It also meant some danger for her parents.

"Our best bet in that regard might be to share the wealth." He smiled. "I'll go with you to see the guy. They can't kill us all, you know."

It was then that they saw Sergeant Lowry winding his way through the tables. The man's hat was pushed back. His suit was still wrinkled, but at least he'd gotten a shave. He stopped at their table. "They told me I'd find you here. I just came from the home of the Kawas. I thought you'd want to know. We've found Aki's murderer. Hauled him into jail this morning after you left. The boys are working him over now, so it shouldn't be any time at all before we have a confession."

"Who?" Gwen asked.

"That beach bum you told us about, Homer."

CHAPTER 28

Gwen parked her car and got out. It was after sunset, and the plum-colored rays of sun that had streaked across the sky only minutes before were dying with the darkness. The shadows grew longer, spreading across the street, and lights were glowing inside the house. This was one visit she had mixed feelings about. Gwen knew it was worth a try even though it would be painful.

She stepped up on the curb, studying the brass numbers on the door. The squatty house covered with blooming wisteria was the place. Even from where she stood, she could smell the aroma of the sweet purple blossoms. They hung like colorful little bells on the branches of the thick vine. A rocky walkway led up to the door. Palm trees bowed slightly, their branches making dark shapes against the sky. Small lights set inside stone-shaped lanterns were already glowing along the path.

Gwen opened the gate, walked along the path, and stepped up to the wooden porch. She knocked lightly on the door. She could hear the sound of violins playing soft music inside, "The Old Rugged Cross." She knocked louder.

The door cracked open. The old woman peered though the crack in the open door, a brass chain holding it in place.

"*Kono tabi wa goshushosama de gozaimasu.*" Gwen gave the Japanese expression for "Please accept my condolences on this sad occasion." She hoped opening her conversation with the woman in her Japanese language would help to ease her mind and to convince her that she was a friend. "I am Gwen Williams. Aki and I were friends. Do you think I could have a few minutes of your time?"

The door closed and she could hear the woman fumbling with the chain. Slowly the door opened again. The old woman's eyes filled with moisture. She was wearing a red kimono and white socks. "Yes, please come in." She bowed her head. "You are welcome to my humble home."

Gwen kicked off her shoes and stepped inside. "I am so sorry to be intruding in your time of grief." She bowed her head to the woman, and Aki's grandmother returned the gesture. "I thought your grand-daughter was a wonderful woman, and I am going to miss her very much."

"Would you like some tea?"

Gwen bowed her head. "Yes, of course, if it would not be too much trouble."

Gwen followed the woman though the small living room. It was simple with bamboo table lamps that gave off a soft light. A birdcage had been covered with a dark green pillowcase. The kitchen had yellow wallpaper with red and blue birds printed on it. A small Formica table with blue plastic chairs was next to the wall. The woman walked over to the stove and turned on a burner under a white kettle. She glanced back at Gwen. "Please be seated. It won't take a minute."

"Thank you very much." Gwen pulled out one of the blue chairs and took a seat.

"You speak very good Japanese."

"Thank you. I was born there. My parents are missionaries. In fact, my father was Aki's pastor."

"Yes." A ray of recognition spread over the old woman's face and then a slight smile. "Pastor Williams. He came to see me today. He is a very nice man."

"Thank you. Yes, he is." Gwen could see the softness in the old woman's face.

"Aki thought well of him, respected him highly."

"Thank you. My father spoke to me about her when I came to visit. He liked her very much. She is part of the reason I came to Hawaii."

The woman's eye's widened. "Is that so?"

"Yes. I work for Naval Intelligence in San Francisco. She sent us a wire asking for our help, and they sent me."

"I see. So this is business?"

"No. The navy doesn't know I'm here. This is more of a personal thing with me. As I said, I liked Aki very much."

The kettle began to whistle, and the old woman picked it off the stove and turned off the burner. Reaching up to a shelf, she pulled down a small red can of tea. She opened a small ceramic teapot and shook some of the tea into it, then filled the pot with the boiling water. Setting the pot and two small cups onto a bamboo platter, she brought them over to the table. "I didn't know Aki worked with such nice people."

"Yes, the navy can be quite hard on a woman."

The woman poured tea into the two cups, smiling. "Yes, especially a Japanese woman. There is no trust left for the Japanese, especially on these islands." She held out her hand. "I am Dai."

Gwen shook her hand. "You are being very kind to me at a most trying time."

"Trying to gain the trust of the navy is *takane no hana*."

Dai used the Japanese expression meaning "flower on a high peak," conveying the idea of something desired but unreachable and also a great danger. "Yes, I know. That will change, but it will take time, I am afraid."

Dai bowed her head. "Yes, anything that is valuable takes great patience and time. Let me read you something." She reached over and picked up a small black Bible that had obviously seen much use. The pages were worn. "I have loved reading the words of the prophet Habakkuk lately." She turned the pages gently, wetting the tip of her finger and pulling the thin onionskin pages to the side, one at a time. When she reached the spot she had in mind, she ran her finger over the place where the binding held the pages in place and pulled the book closer to her eyes. "It is in chapter two. 'For the vision is yet for an appointed time, but at the end it shall speak, and not lie: though it tarry, wait for it; because it will surely come, it will not tarry.' This is a fine thought, don't you think?"

"Yes, I do."

"It promises us that there is an appointed time for what God has in mind." She smiled and pointed her frail finger at the words. "And that His plan is a certainty. We want everything now, but God wants everything in His plan. We are very impatient with our small plans, and they will only bring us unhappiness in the end. His plan is always perfect, even if it is not our own."

Dai's gaze drifted out the window. "Aki and I discussed this many times."

Gwen sipped her cup of tea. "Did Aki ever speak to you about her work at Pearl Harbor?"

Dai shook her head. "No, we seldom talked about such matters. I knew she was worried. I could see it in her eyes." She picked up her cup and warmed her hands with it, then held it up to her nose to smell the aroma. "There were times when she was distressed about matters of the heart, and these were things she spoke to me about. I could tell she was troubled with other things that she couldn't speak about. I never asked. One should not have to open the door to another person's heart. When they open the door and invite you inside, it is better."

"Did she talk to you about that night she was going to the beach?"

Dai sipped her tea and nodded. "Yes. She did. She was going to meet her navy man." Dai smiled. "She was going to tell him that she trusted him and respected him. Of course, she was concerned."

"About his father?"

Dai nodded. "And his career. She was trying to protect him."

"That sounds like her."

"There is something you may want to see." Dai stared off to the back bedroom and lowered her eyebrows. It was an expression of doubt. "It was a personal thing, but perhaps you should see it."

"What is it?"

"Her diary. She kept it here so that her parents wouldn't find it and read her thoughts. Much of it was about her feelings toward them. I wouldn't want it seen. The pain it would cause now could do no good."

"Would it have work-related matters in it?"

Once again Dai shook her head. "I don't know."

"Maybe I could see it. I would only be interested in her thoughts about work. It might contain something that would help in trying to find out who is responsible for her death."

"Haven't they already caught the man?"

Gwen took a deep breath. "Yes, but I believe he's the wrong man. The man they have was Aki's friend. I don't see how he could possibly do anything like this. Aki cared for him."

"Wait a moment, and I will get it for you." With that Dai got up from the table and disappeared into the back bedroom area. Minutes later, she returned with a small red book. She laid it on the table in front of Gwen. "This is it. I don't know what is in it, but Aki called it her diary. I'll go back into the living room, and you can read it if you like."

"Thank you."

Gwen spent the next two hours sipping her tea and reading Aki's diary at the kitchen table. Two things caught her eye. *Prison at Wailea Point—for us.* Aki had written those words in June and underlined them. Several pages later, she came upon other words that stood out. *List of names in grandfather's mausoleum. Hold them for no one to see.*

Gwen got up from the table and stepped into the living room. Dai was in her chair, reading the old Bible. "Thank you very much." She set the diary down on a small table.

"Is there anything there that can be of help to you?"

"There might be." Gwen paused. "One thing. In the diary Aki talked about a list of names she had placed in her grandfather's crypt."

Dai smiled. "Yes, my husband. He and Aki were close while he was alive. We often went together to place flowers there and pray." She bowed her head slightly. "And now she will be buried in the crypt tomorrow morning. One can never imagine attending a grandchild's funeral."

"What did your husband do?"

Dai smiled. "He was a bookkeeper for the Krinkle Sugar Company. He also handled their investments. Numbers were of great interest to him. Perhaps this is the type of list she was writing about."

"Where is this crypt?"

"The old Oahu Cemetery on Nu'uanu Avenue. Do you know the place?"

Gwen nodded. "Yes, I have passed it a number of times."

"Our crypt is near the center of the cemetery, next to the tall obelisk."

"Perhaps I should go there tonight to see if I can find this list. I wouldn't want it discovered by someone tomorrow morning."

Dai closed her Bible and got to her feet. "Yes, this is fine with me. I still own it, and you have my permission."

Gwen bowed. "You have been most kind. I wish there was some way I could repay you."

"I am an old woman. I will see my granddaughter soon in the arms of Jesus. All kindness will be repaid there."

Gwen stepped out the door and pushed her feet into her black pumps. She headed down the walk and toward the car. She knew her father kept a flashlight in the glove compartment of the Ford, and that would prove helpful. There had been one more note of significance in Aki's dairy: *Message under my ink blotter. Admiral must see.* Getting into the Naval Intelligence Office and past the double doors guarded by Chief Morrow had been difficult enough. Getting in to see Aki's office and perhaps taking something out would be almost impossible.

She started the car and, as was her habit, looked behind her to see if anyone had crept up on her blind side. The last thing she needed was an accident in her parents' car. She spotted a dark sedan parked on the other side of the street about thirty yards behind her. She could see the glow of a cigarette.

She jerked the wheel, moving the Ford out into the street. Stepping on the gas, she zoomed down the small street and turned the corner. She spent the next ten minutes checking her rearview mirror. Cars were moving along the street with her, but she didn't think she could see the same dark sedan. Perhaps she had been overanxious.

People who did what she did for a living tended to see things even when they were not there.

She turned onto Nu'uanu Avenue by the canal and was soon pulling up alongside the old Oahu Cemetery. Gwen took out the flashlight and, opening the door, stepped out into the street.

She headed into the first section of graves. The sound of a car and the appearance of its lights caused her to freeze in place. She looked back but couldn't quite make out the shape of the vehicle. It seemed to be moving on. Gwen breathed a sign of relief.

The first section of graves was surrounded by a mean-looking rusty fence made to look like spears pointing up from the ground. It was almost as if whoever was laid out there was angry at his or her final resting place. *Are they keeping people in or out?* Gwen wondered.

Gwen looked up. She couldn't quite make out the monument Dai had spoken about. No doubt she'd have to move into the middle of the burial ground and see if she could find it from there.

She stepped around the fence and moved into the scattered monuments that covered the ground. Angels made of white marble and red stone were in attendance. Some were kneeling in prayer, and others were taking wing. Cherubs contemplated the cold ground, leaning on their elbows as if to study the whys of death itself. White stone crosses stood erect alongside tombstones and small monuments with marble containers designed to hold flowers. Most of them were empty and forgotten.

Gwen kept her flashlight turned off. If she could see with the light, no doubt anyone close by could see her. There weren't any lights in the old Oahu Cemetery, and she wasn't about to add hers.

She moved through the hedges. It was the first place she had felt any fear. The tall bushes cut her off from any view except the overhead stars. They seemed to press in on her from all sides. She turned on her light for the first time. She had to find the opening to the other side. She moved swiftly along the hedge, swinging the beam of light from side to side, before spotting the opening. Turning off the flashlight, she stepped out to the area that rose to the hilltop. A large monument was near the top of the small hill. It might be the obelisk Dai had mentioned. The mausoleum would be close by.

She made her way up the hill, past ground that was covered with small plaques and crosses. Odd-shaped monuments studded the ground, flat fences with spikes and headstones with verses. Many of the stones were flat on the ground and required that she step carefully. The heels on her pumps weren't very high, but they weren't exactly cut out for a walk through a dark graveyard.

She found the obelisk and, looking around, saw a crypt close by. It looked like a small house made of gray stone. Moss was creeping up the side of the large granite blocks, giving it the appearance of a castle set in a small forest. She walked over to it and turned on her flashlight to read the inscription over the door, KAWA. This was the place.

The door was green metal with a small window. Shining the flashlight inside, she could see the marble covers of six stone caskets with doors along the side that contained the names of other family members. No doubt the walls of this place were filled with Kawa family members.

Turning off the light, she stuck it in her purse and took hold of the bar on the latch. The thing was tight, and she had to push up hard. The bar slid slowly in her hand, then finally sprang out from the latch that was holding it in place.

Gwen pulled on the door. It swung open with a mournful creak. Stepping inside, she reached for the flashlight and switched it on. Now to find Aki's grandfather and the list. She shivered slightly, a sudden coolness gripping her. The place smelled like old clothes left far too long in a closet. The large marble coffins stood mute and silent.

Gwen studied the dates on each of the structures. No doubt Aki's grandfather had died not more than ten or fifteen years earlier. He might represent a branch on the family tree not too far removed. She ran her fingers over the walls, looking for dates, then moved to the marble coffins on the floor. Then she spotted a bouquet of silk flowers, white and yellow orchids. Silk flowers would need no water. It would be a perfect place for Aki's list.

She stepped over to the coffin and looked at the name and dates. AKIO KAWA—born June 4, 1868—died November 20, 1936. Gwen thought this just might be Aki's grandfather. She had been a teenager when he had died five years earlier. She slowly lowered herself to her knees and lifted the silk flowers from the vase. Reaching her hand down into the dark confines of the cold marble, she felt something. It was paper. Moving closer, she groped for a better grip, then pulled up the papers.

She heard a noise outside—a snap, the sound of someone stepping on a dried palm branch. She clicked off the flashlight and jumped to her feet.

Hurrying to the open door, she poked her head outside. She could see two dark figures not ten yards away. At the same moment they saw her.

One shadow raised a hand and pointed. "There she is, over there."

Gwen stuffed the papers and the flashlight into her purse and bolted out the door and down the hill. She could hear them behind her, panting and mumbling as they clomped along the ground. She could only take comfort in the fact that this particular obstacle course showed no favoritism. The stones were just as hard and unmovable for them as they were for her. But she had one advantage. Running was something she did every day.

She stopped and removed her pumps, holding them in her hand. She would have to be very careful. With just her bare feet, she would have no protection should she smash a toe on one of the low markers.

Such a blow might devastate her and spoil any advantage she might have.

She circled the stones and markers. Jumping over one set of stones, her feet churned beneath her. What she wanted most of all was a flat surface, where she could stretch out and run.

She burst through the opening in the hedge and her foot hit a root, spilling her onto the ground, her arms and elbows out in front of her. Pain shot through her body, but she stumbled to her feet. The men behind her were yelling, looking for the opening she had already found. She could only hope they also found the root she had found.

She scrambled down the hedge, feeling for the opening that led to the lower cemetery and to the street below. Spotting a towering banyan tree, she made for it. The hedge wouldn't go through the tree and, no matter where her opening was, she could always get out that way.

When she came to the tree, she squeezed herself between it and the hedge and out into the open graveyard. The street was in the distance, below her. She started to run once again, dodging stones and leaping over contemplating cherubs.

Hitting the street, she jerked open her car door and jumped inside. She fumbled in her purse for the car keys. Men were right. You could never find anything in a woman's purse, especially when you needed a set of keys.

CHAPTER 29

T

he bar was dark except for the tiki lights that crisscrossed the ceiling and gave the appearance of a gigantic thatched hut. The small dolls with lights in their bellies that showed through their faces glared down, dancing on their electrical cords and laughing.

Sam was wearing appropriate attire for Hawaii, a black Hawaiian shirt with white orchids and bold green stems that slanted across his chest. His khakis were cuffed and slopped over the sides of his loafers. He wore no socks.

He walked over to the bar and sat down on a leather-backed red stool. It was kind of convenient, he thought. If a man had too much and did fall over, at least he wouldn't fall over backward. Raising his hand, he caught the bartender's attention. The man looked Samoan, large and imposing with a broad flat nose and jet-black hair. His blue-and-white Hawaiian shirt fit over him like a tent.

He stepped over to Sam, his large lips spreading into a broad, toothy smile. "What'll it be?"

"Gin and tonic," Sam shot back.

"Sure thing." Stepping over to the racks of polished colored bottles and glasses, the man picked up the appropriate bottle of Beefeaters and poured him a stiff one, then shot a guzzle of tonic into the tall smooth glass. He ambled back over to Sam and set the drink on a pink-and-gold napkin labeled *The Royal Hawaiian Hotel*. He smiled. "That'll be a half-dollar."

Sam reached into his pants pocket and pulled out the roll of small bills he carried there in his money clip and slapped a single bill on the counter. He stared for a while at his reflection in the mirror, through the bottles and glasses. Just being there gave him an empty, hollow feeling.

He had just taken his first sip when a large woman with red hair came over and sat next to him. She was all there and then some, with green eyes and a mile of teeth. Her white ruffled blouse was pulled down around her shoulders, showing freckles and other attractions that she evidently wanted to feature. "Would you like to buy me a drink?"

Sam looked up from his glass. He usually gave this kind of woman a quick dismissal, but he couldn't make up his mind this time. "Sure, whatcha havin'?" He wasn't sure if this was an act of desperation or if the loneliness of the place was finally getting to him. He didn't really want conversation. He just wanted to be alone with his thoughts.

"Rum and Coke."

Looking up, he saw that the bartender had overheard the woman's request. Evidently the sight of the voluptuous woman coming on to Sam had focused the man's attention. Sam nodded at the man, who turned to mix the drink.

The woman leaned into him, wrapping her arm through Sam's bent elbow. "Thanks, sugar. You in Hawaii on vacation?"

"What makes you think that?"

She smiled and batted her eyes. They were a remarkable shade of green, like peeled grapes floating in a glass of milk. "This is the Royal Hawaiian, sugar. It ain't exactly a hangout for the locals."

The bartender brought the rum and Coke, and Sam pushed the bill across the bar. "I'm here on business."

"Oh." Once again she batted her eyes. The corners on her mouth turned up in a sly smile. "I like that." She took her right hand and rubbed his arm slightly. "You must be getting lonely."

Sam picked up his drink and sloshed it around in the glass, staring at the ice cubes. "Not really. A little bored, but not lonely."

"What do you do?"

"I'm a reporter."

"Really? I just talked to a reporter." She leaned back and pointed to a man in a blue seersucker suit in the far corner. "John Welsh, comes in here all the time."

Sam slid off his stool and picked up his drink. He shot her a slight grin. "I better go pay my respects." He made his way over to the man she had pointed out, weaving his way through the tables. A singer had just begun to croon Crosby's "Going My Way." Hawaii was like that, native until the pineapple juice came out your ears, and then just enough of home to make you realize you could never stay with your toes wiggling in the sand. He stepped up to the man's table and grinned. "I'm Sam Diamond of the *Washington Post*. I understand you're a reporter."

The man looked up at him and pushed back his cream-colored Panama hat, showing a long narrow nose and a set of beady dark eyes that had seen far too little in the way of sleep. They had dark circles under them. A smile spread out under his pencil-thin mustache. "Sam Diamond, I've read your stuff. Sit down." He pointed to the chair directly across from him. "Sit down."

He reached out to shake Sam's hand. "John Welsh from the *Honolulu Advertiser*." He chuckled. "What brings you to our glamorous but seedy neck of the globe?"

"Just getting a little rest and relaxation." Sam shook his hand and took a seat.

"Oh, sure, right." The man's smile broadened, and he arched his bushy eyebrows in a repeated rhythmic manner. "You don't expect me to believe that, do you?" He waved his hand. "But never mind, we'll get your story and print it. Of course it'll be a week after it's real news."

"Nice to meet you, John. You been working on this local murder?"

Welsh sat back, eyeing Sam with some suspicion. "Sure I have, but there's nothing here for you. Strictly local stuff. Girl goes for walk on beach. Old white man with too much cheap wine in him decides to have a good time. That's all, just the regular murder."

"Have you talked to this old white man?"

"Sure." Welsh chucked. "Homer is his name. He claims to have saved that same girl a few days ago on that same beach." He leaned forward. "He said the girl's brother had some Japanese friends who were trying some funny business with her and that he came to her rescue."

"Might be easy to check that out."

"Why bother? The man's lying." Welsh shook his head. "He's pretty far gone. Makes you wonder why he would even bother with such a cock-and-bull story."

Sam glanced across the bar and was startled to see Gwen. She had just stepped into the darkness of the room and was surveying the place. He knew she must be looking for him. She would never have any other reason to be in a place like this. "I see my date just showed up." He got to his feet. "Nice talking to you."

"Hey." Welsh grabbed his wrist. "You know anything about this story?"

"You just told me more than I knew when I came in. Keep grinding on it." He glanced at Gwen and then smiled. "I'm getting rest and relaxation, remember?"

He made his way across the room, and Gwen spotted him about halfway across the floor. "Hello, sweet thing. Fancy seeing you here." He could see almost instantly that she was more than a little troubled. Sweat formed a glossy shine across her neck, and her eyes were wide. "Is there a problem?"

"The man at the desk told me I could find you here. Yes, there is a problem, a big problem."

Sam took her elbow and led her into the dark foyer. "What has you so upset?"

"I found something tonight that may have something to do with Aki's death, found it in the Oahu Cemetery where she put it down to sleep with her grandfather."

"This sounds interesting."

"If it's as bad as I think it is, it would have given any number of people a reason to kill her, including her employer."

"The U.S. Navy?"

Gwen nodded. "I'm afraid so. And I was followed into the cemetery and chased out of it by two men. They could have been navy people, tailing me. We have to go see for ourselves."

"Go where?"

"Wailea Point. It's on the other side of the island."

"We'd better take my car, then. I rented a car, got tired of taxicabs. If you had people following you, they will stay by your car. They might have known that you would come here too." He chuckled. "We can drive right past them, and they'd never know you with what I'm driving."

Sam led her out a side door and into the parking lot. Several lights on ornate cast-iron poles were casting warm beams of yellow light with swarms of bugs swishing around them like dive bombers headed in for the kill. He led the way to a small green roadster with the white top pulled back and snapped into place. Cranking down the polished silver handle of the door, he held it open for her. "It's an MG roadster. It's supposed to handle well around the turns."

Gwen got in. "If we don't die first."

Sam slammed the car door. "Don't worry about a thing, angel. The wind will feel good in your hair." He grinned. "Besides, the *Post* is paying for it." Circling the car, he vaulted over the door without opening it and landed in the driver seat. "I'm going to have to get me one of these when I get back to D.C. I think I'm falling in love."

With that he pushed in the key and started the ignition. Pressing the clutch and then gas, he raced the engine. "There is one stop we have to make first."

"Where is that?"

Sam threw the little car into gear and lurched toward the entrance of the parking lot. "We have to go to Aki's house. Do you have the address?"

"I think so, someplace, but why?"

They rolled out of the parking lot, and Sam turned right. He wanted to go past the front of the hotel, just to see if anyone had Gwen's car staked out. "We need to see her brother. I just talked to a reporter in there who interviewed this Homer guy in jail. The man said that her brother had some friends who came on to her big time at that same beach where she was killed." He glanced ahead. "You point out your car when we get close to it."

They rolled past the front of the hotel, and Gwen motioned toward the curb where the Ford was parked. Across the street was a dark sedan with two men inside. One was smoking a cigarette. Sam stepped on the gas, and the MG roared to life. Coming to the next street, he took a vicious left-hand turn and stomped on the accelerator.

It took Gwen some time to find Aki's address and it took Sam even more time, winding through the streets of Honolulu, to get to the house. Lights were on inside the house, and Sam jumped out of the car. "Wait here, angel."

He walked through the gate and up to the house, then rang the bell. A short time later an older Japanese man answered the door. "Sir, I am very sorry about your daughter. I'm from the newspaper, and I'd like to talk to your son if he is in."

"My son?"

"Yes, sir, your son. It's about a job."

The comment seemed to brighten the man's spirits somewhat. He gave a slight smile and bowed his head. "Please come in. I will get him."

"No. I would rather not intrude on you just now. I'll just wait for him outside, if you don't mind."

"Just a minute." He bowed once again. "I will get him."

A short time later, a slender young man stepped outside. "What's this business about a job?"

Aki's brother was wearing dungarees with a T-shirt and had on sandals made of wood and rubber straps. A scruffy goatee was beginning to appear below his bottom lip, something Sam was sure he was very proud of.

Sam pulled his press pass out of his pocket and flashed it too quickly for the man to read. "I'm John Welsh from the *Advertiser*. Why don't we step over here a second, away from the house and talk."

The man shrugged his shoulders and followed Sam to the large tree. "Now, what's this all about?"

"It's about your sister's murder."

"My sister's murder? What's that got to do with a job?"

Sam smiled. "You give me the right answers and it might mean some money for you."

"I don't know nothing about that."

"I understand a few of your buddies roughed your sister up on that beach last week. What do you know about that?"

"Nothing! I don't know nothing. You're here just bothering me, and I don't like it. You go away and leave us alone."

He started to turn and walk away, but Sam reached out and grabbed him by the shirt. Spinning him around, he shoved him up next to the Banyan tree next to the walkway. Sam placed his forearm directly into the man's throat and pressed on it. "You know just what I'm talking about, and you know who."

"I don't know nothing."

Reaching into his pocket, Sam pulled out a long, pearl-handled switchblade knife. He held it up to the man's face and pressed the button, springing a large shiny blade into the man's face. "Listen here, I ain't the cops. Nothing you tell me will go to them, but if you don't tell me, then you won't be able to tell anybody anything. Now you tell me what I want to know or I'm going to gut you like a fish, right here in your own front yard."

The man's eyes focused on the blade. Sweat beads were forming on his forehead. Sam always made it a point to be believed, even if he wasn't telling the truth.

"Hiroki Fujiyama," the man croaked out the words. "He said they were just scaring her."

Sam let up his grip on the man. "Yeah, scaring her. But he might have just come back to finish the job. You ever think of that?"

The man shook his head, and Sam walked off, leaving him to massage his throat. Sam jumped into the roadster and started the engine with a roar.

"Did you find out anything?" Gwen asked.

"Yes, the name of a suspect, and he's not in the U.S. Navy either."

CHAPTER 30

The Pali Highway wound up the spine of the island and down to the sleepy little town of Kane'ohe. It was called the leeward side of the island because they didn't have a great deal of surf there, just good fishing and roads of nothingness. Gwen had been up the highway once before on a previous visit, but in the daylight and at a much slower speed.

Sam downshifted the MG as they roared around the curves, then opened it up on the turn. The high beams whipped around every curve, bathing what appeared to be a lush jungle with instant glare. They could see birds taking flight, an instant flurry of colorful wings spooked by the sound of the car and the sudden light. The wind whipped through Gwen's hair, lashing it across her face.

"What do you think of this machine?" Sam raised his voice and was positively bubbling as he shifted gears.

"You seem to like it," Gwen shouted back at him.

"I love it. I love anything that gives me a thrill. It makes me feel alive."

Gwen knew that all men had an affection for cars. Their hands on the wheel of anything with power made them feel invincible. It seemed juvenile to her, but then Sam was playful. It was one of the things she liked about him. He didn't take himself all that seriously.

They rounded a sharp curve that sent Gwen's body pressing against the hard door handle. "You keep taking those turns like that, and neither of us will feel alive, at least not for long."

He grinned at her and laughed. "Hey, angel, don't tell me you don't like thrills. I've seen you on the squash court, remember? You dive to make shots as if your life depended on it."

"But my life doesn't depend on it," Gwen yelled. "That's the difference." She leaned into him as they hugged a curve, almost brushing up against a white guardrail. "And if I fall, I skin my knee. If you make a mistake here, we're both dead."

"Then we'll just have to make sure I don't, won't we?"

"Yes, we will. I can tell you, I've had enough thrills for one night. I'd just as soon get to where we're going." Something in men made conquest very validating, and Gwen wanted to be sure that he knew she was crying uncle.

"Just where are we going?" Sam practically had to shout. The roar of the engine mixed with the wind made subtle conversation impossible.

"We're going to a secret prison."

"A secret prison? For whom?"

"For the Japanese."

"You're kidding?" He stared at her. "We're not at war with them yet. We don't have any prisoners."

"This isn't a prison for Japanese soldiers. It's a prison for Japanese Americans who live on this island." Sam shot her another quick glance, a look of doubt.

"Where did you get this information?"

"Aki's diary. She has a list of a hundred and eighty Japanese Americans who would be thrown into this prison. They would just disappear."

"That's bad."

"Yes, and I'd like to see it for myself."

"And you think they might have killed her because she knew about this concentration camp that we were building?"

"I don't know. I'd just like to see for myself."

Sam backed off the gas only slightly as they headed downhill. Suddenly he caught a sign in the glare of his headlights, and he pulled off sharply to the right, slamming on his brakes and skidding to a halt. The car sat idling in a cloud of dust.

"Why did we stop?"

"Didn't you see that sign? Pali Lookout."

Gwen looked over the hood of the car and could see the shimmering lights of the small towns below them. The ocean was beyond, dark with the moon bathing it in a soft light. "It is beautiful."

Sam looked at her. "Not nearly as beautiful as you, sugar." He put his arm around her. "We may be in a hurry here, but I'm still a romantic."

Gwen pulled his hand off her shoulder. "Not now. This may be the place, but it's certainly not the time. And I'd rather you call me Gwen, not 'sugar'"

"You're not about to tell me that you're sweet sixteen and never been kissed, are you?"

Gwen turned to face him. "And you're what, 40 and never been told no?"

"Ouch," Sam's handsome face fell. "And you won't love anyone unless you're ready to fall in love for good. Have I got that right?"

"Something like that. I believe God has a plan for me that includes a special man. Unless you're ready to be that special man, I don't want to waste my time or yours."

"It wouldn't be a waste of my time, believe me. I don't think it would be a waste of yours, either. Do you really think God has a certain someone picked out and that no one else will do?"

Gwen nodded. "Yes."

Sam jammed the gears into place and lurched out into the road. "Well, sugar, uh . . . Gwen, I sure hope yours comes along fast, 'cause you're certainly going to waste."

They continued down the winding road until they rolled into Maunawili, a sleepy little town that had a post office where someone had forgotten to take down the flag, a garage with padlocked gas pumps, and an empty diner with only the waitress, seen through the window, rubbing down the tables. "Man, this place is almost like a scene from a Rockwell painting, except it's more boring."

"You seem to like busyness."

"I wouldn't call it that. I like to contemplate more than most men. I like poetry, and I love a good book. I like art, especially contemporary stuff where you have to think to appreciate it. But I suppose you could say I like action. I need to be tested to grow. Otherwise, why live at all?"

"You like poetry? I wouldn't suspect a hard-bitten newsman to care anything about verse."

"That's where you're wrong, sugar, uh Gwen. Like I said, I'm a romantic."

Gwen laughed. "You're funny. But I guess being called 'uh Gwen' is an improvement."

"I'm a slow learner, I guess, but I'll get it down."

Gwen let a slight smile cross her face. She was almost beginning to like the term *sugar*. Coming from Sam, it sounded sort of cute. And it was so like him.

Gwen watched the little town disappear as they rolled past the one flashing light on the street. "Once in a while I would just like to be someplace where I could find my own mind and think thoughts because I want to, not because I have to."

Sam laughed. "Then you'd love that place. You'd have to force yourself to think or you'd go crazy." He cleared his throat and began to recite a familiar poem, using a Scottish brogue for effect. "The wind was a torrent of darkness among the gusty trees. The moon was a ghostly galleon tossed upon cloudy seas. The road was a ribbon of moonlight over the purple moor, when a highwayman came riding, riding, riding, a highwayman came riding up to the old inn door."

They drove for another twenty minutes or so before turning right at Kailua Beach Park. The waves were lapping up on the sand, and hundreds of palm trees were standing sentinel over the empty beach. The moon shone over the top of the white sand, bathing the place in a warm glow. It did seem to be a ghostly galleon in the distance, rocking on the surface of the dark water.

It took them just a short time before they came to Laniki. This would be the closest town to Wailea Point, the place Aki had indicated as the site of the prison. The town was typical for this side of the island, clapboard whitewashed houses with shingles. Nets hung from porches for decoration with glass balls in them. They passed a house with a ceramic seagull standing guard on a perch of driftwood. Another had an overturned boat in the front yard. The people had their names printed on the side in bold red letters, SNYDERS.

Sam spotted a small gas station with a light on inside. A large drum of petroleum was set in steel on the roof. Red paint had been applied to the front window, and the paint bled down the stems of the letters from the constant rain on this side of the island. The barely legible letters read JOE'S SPEEDY SERVICE.

Sam rumbled up to the only pump and turned off the ignition. "We'll get some gas here, and you can turn on that charm of yours and see if this fella knows anything about where to find this supposed camp." He leaned over closer to her. "You do know how to be charming and flirtatious, don't you?"

"Is this really necessary?" Sam seemed determined to extract femininity out of her at all cost. It wasn't that she didn't know how to be a flirtatious woman; it was summoning up the act on demand that bothered her. It made her feel cheap and insincere. "You think that all any man ever wants is a woman to bat her eyes at him and look pretty. If that were the case, there would be no need for a woman ever to go past the fourth grade."

"I know some men who would agree with that."

"I'm sure you do. Close friends, no doubt."

"Well, it's what we need right now, unless you want to drive around here all night in search of a place that may not exist." Sam spotted the attendant coming out of the garage area. "People around here don't take kindly to strangers," Sam went on. "They wouldn't tell an outsider where to drop over dead, much less give up the location of some Army post." He smiled. "But they might talk to a pretty woman like you. Listen, sugar, this garage man may not be the man of God's special plan for you, but please be nice. I'd like to get to bed sometime tonight."

Gwen narrowed her eyes at Sam. Then she turned to watch the man in the greasy overalls.

Sam grinned and cranked open his car door. "We'd like a full tank of high-test. You got rest rooms?"

The man spit out a stream of brown tobacco juice and jerked his thumb rearward. "Sure. We got a privy 'round back."

Sam smiled at Gwen. "Be right back, honey bun."

These little expressions of endearment that came pouring out of Sam were starting to make her feel remarkably like a housewife.

The attendant picked up the pump nozzle and, unscrewing the gas cap, inserted the nozzle into the tank with a series of sharp thuds. He reached over to the pump and began the task of getting the gas to flow. Gwen could see the gas bubble up in the dirty glass cage.

"Do you get many trucks on this road?" She asked.

The man spit out another torrent of tobacco juice onto the ground and then wiped his mouth with the back of his hand. "Used to. Not so much any more."

"We had an Army truck, at least I think it was an Army truck, almost run us off the road."

The man grinned, showing a set of teeth that were brown with tobacco juice. "It was Army, all right. Them fellers was real busy a ways back, but not so much any more."

Gwen batted her eyes. It was hard to play dumb. "Mercy me." She slapped her chest in a plaintive expression of bewilderment. "I didn't know there was an Army camp anywhere near here. It says nothing about it on the map."

The man rocked back and forth, chewing feverously on his wad of tobacco. "Ain't much of a camp, if you ask me." He took out a dirty cloth and picked up a bottle of spray wash, splashing it on the windshield. He then leaned toward her, staring at her through the glass. "I figure they is storing something dangerous there, though. They brung in lots of wire and stuff." Laying the cloth on the windshield, he began a circular motion. "Near as I can figure, this whole durn place could go kerflooie anytime at all."

"That sounds dangerous. Is this camp close?"

"You bet. Second road on the right down the highway yonder. That place is in the hills, but them bombs go off, and we're all going to feel it 'round here."

A minute later Sam came around the building. He was whistling and had a grin on his face. Walking up to the roadster, he pushed down on the handle, then jumped in and slammed the door.

"That'll be two dollars and fifty cents, mister."

Reaching into his pocket, Sam took out two one dollar bills and a pair of quarters. "There you are, pal. Thanks."

He started the car and drove out onto the road. "OK, sugar, where to?"

"Turn right at the second road."

Sam laughed. "That's great. I knew you had it in you in spite of all that education. You're a wonder."

They turned at a small dirt road and headed up a hill through the cane fields. The sugarcane was high, its blades towering in either direction as far as the eye could see. It would be easy to hide anything in these hills. They rounded a curve and roared up a hill, then stopped. There below them was a small camp. It was laid out with Quonset huts and two small blockhouses. They could see a fence with barbed wire and a gate that was wide open.

Sam spotted a small road that led off to their right through the cane fields. "We'll park in there and walk the rest of the way."

A few minutes later they were walking down the hill toward the camp. Sam had taken a flashlight out of the glove compartment of the roadster, but he left it turned off. The place was totally dark except for a light in the window of one of the blockhouses.

"Why is the gate open?" Gwen asked.

"No need to close it until they have prisoners."

They walked though the gate and heard music coming from the concrete building where the light was on. The radio was playing local Hawaiian music, directly from the lounge of the Royal Hawaiian Hotel.

"Let's check out one of these huts," Sam said.

They moved to the first one, and Sam twisted the metal doorknob and stepped inside. He turned on his flashlight and trailed the beam of light over the room. It was a room full of bunk beds. Trunks positioned at the foot of each bed gave the place the look of a barracks. Sam moved around the inside of the room and stopped at a window. "Look here."

Gwen stepped up to see the window. It had bars on it.

"This place is a prison," Sam remarked. He opened the door at the end of the hut and pushed the light inside. They saw toilets and showers on slatted wooden floors. There were no curtains or dividers; there was no privacy whatsoever. Bars of soap still in their wrappers were stacked on a shelf attached to the wall. The place had the aroma of ammonia. "Let's take a look at the other huts."

He turned and walked back through the empty barracks with Gwen right behind him. They checked two more huts, each looking like the first one they had seen. Finally, they came to the fourth one. Sam pushed open the door and stepped inside. It was a dining room. Tables were laid out with metal chairs. Shelves filled with tin plates, cups, and eating utensils were lined up along the walls. Large lights hanging by poles in cages were scattered throughout the room.

They walked through the room, and Sam opened a door at the end of the hut and stepped though it. It was the kitchen. The place had a stove and a large walk-in freezer. It stood silent and dark, its door wide open. Moving along the wall they could see that supplies had been laid out on a series of metal shelves. Gwen took Sam's hand with the light in it and pushed it to show what was in the bags on the shelves. "Rice," she said. "Rice for the Japanese."

"It would appear so."

"I've seen enough," Gwen said. "These people may not be prepared for a Japanese attack, but they're sure ready to incarcerate Japanese citizens."

"More than ready."

Sam switched off the flashlight, and they stepped out of the kitchen. Moving back out into the darkened dining room, both of them were silent. The thought of what they had just seen held them in its grip. Suddenly, the lights came on. Standing at the door was Chief Gardner, along with two shore patrol police. "Well, what have we here?" He smiled, his hand on his holster. The two sailors with rifles stepped to either side of the chief. "Search them," Gardner growled.

CHAPTER 31

T he gray jeep pulled up to the house and came to a screeching stop, jerking the two men forward. The Chief and the Lieutenant piled out of the vehicle and headed up the walkway. Gwen had been watching from her parents' living room window. Gardner had said they were coming to get her the next day, and she had been expecting the worst. She could get fired or at the very least disciplined. It made her sick to think that she might in any way disappoint Captain Allen back in San Francisco. He had trusted her.

She watched them come up the walkway and then turned to go to the kitchen. Her father had been standing in the doorway, his eyes trained on Gwen. She had told her parents what had happened the night before. She didn't tell them about her suspicions, however, nor did she tell them how angry she was at being followed. Her father, being the kind of man he was, had guessed at that.

The knock at the door sent her father past her to answer it. He opened the door. "Good morning, gentlemen. Please come in."

The men stepped in the door, and her father pointed to their shoes. "We run a Japanese house here. You'll both have to remove your shoes."

Gwen could see that neither man was terribly happy with having to take off his shoes. She could also see the smile on her father's face. It was almost as if he took some pride in humbling them.

"I am Gwen's father. I didn't get your names."

"Gardner," the Chief spoke up. "This is Lieutenant Rorke."

"Pleased to meet you, sir." Rorke stuck out his hand.

Her father simply turned away. "I'll see if my daughter can see you two men now."

Gwen had backed up into the kitchen. It made it hard for them to see her, but she could see them very well. There was a cockiness to both of them, and she could tell that they were angry.

Her father stepped into the kitchen and motioned with his head in the direction of the living room. "The navy. For you. Frankly, I wouldn't give them the time of day after the way they've treated you. One would think you were here to take their jobs away rather than to save their hides."

"Dad, it's the navy. Nobody likes anyone, especially a woman, looking over his shoulder."

He glanced back at the living room. "Somebody needs to. It might as well be you."

Gwen stepped through the door and into the living room. She was wearing army fatigue pants with large pockets sewn into the legs and a shirt that was sparkling white. It gave her an almost military look and hid her shape somewhat. If they had to see her, she wanted to make sure they weren't distracted. "Good morning, gentlemen. I'm glad to see you found the place."

"It was no trouble," Gardner said. "You remember Lieutenant Rorke."

"From the basement, sure. Nice to see you, Lieutenant."

"We need to have a little discussion," Rorke said, "And there's someplace we'd like to take you."

"Where's that, the guardhouse? Will I need a lawyer?"

"No," Gardner said. "Not now, at least."

"All right then, gentlemen, my time is yours." She stepped outside and watched them fumble with their shoes. Placing her feet into a pair of black boots, she tugged on the laces, wrapped them around the boots twice, and tied them off. She followed them to the jeep and waited for them to open the door.

"The Lieutenant will ride in the jump seat, and you can ride up here with me," Gardner said. He opened the door for her and she climbed in.

Gardner started the jeep and shoved it into gear. They then sped off.

"Where are we going?"

"First of all, we just wanted to show you how well prepared we are. You seem to be worried about a Japanese surprise attack, and you need to see that's not possible."

"Not possible. Why is that?"

"You'll see." Gardner said. "It's on the other side of the island."

The drive to the other side of the island was a long one, cutting up the middle of the island and past the Schofield barracks. Cane fields and hundreds of acres of pineapple fields covered the ground. Women stooped over the fruit, whacking away with machetes, harvesting the fruit. Men stomped up and down the rows, watching them and shouting for them to work harder. The jeep hit the coast and turned north, along the most deadly of Hawaii's beaches. The surf was high, and gigantic waves were crashing onto the shore. Just above an area labeled Sunset Beach, Gardner pulled the jeep over to a ledge overlooking the deep blue Pacific.

"Why are we stopping?"

Gardner put on the hand brake. "Thought we could stretch our legs a bit." He smiled. "Besides, it'll give you a chance to see some of our nicest beaches."

Gwen looked over the hood of the jeep. "Sort of rocky and high up, isn't it?"

"But it's got a great view," Rorke responded. He piled out of the back of the vehicle and stretched his arms.

Gwen noticed for the first time that both men were wearing their sidearms. "Is there a reason for the guns?"

Gardner grinned. "You never can tell."

"I think I'll just sit in the jeep, if you don't mind."

Rorke stepped over to the cliff. "And miss this view? You don't want to do that."

Gwen forced a smile. "I think I do."

Gardner climbed out from behind the steering wheel. He turned around and stared at her. It was a distant stare, as if the man had some other time or some other place in mind. "Now why don't you tell us what you were doing in that camp last night with that reporter?"

"We were taking a drive and stumbled upon the place." She shrugged. "I guess we got curious."

"Didn't you see the GOVERNMENT PROPERTY NO TRESPASSING signs?"

"Must have missed them."

"You don't lie very well, Miss Williams."

"I've never had to before." Gwen felt more than a little fear of the two men, especially if she was right about the navy being responsible for Aki's murder. For all she knew, these two might have been the ones who killed her.

"Well, you don't have to now. We're on your side, you know."

"Are you? Are you going to give me back what you took from me last night?"

Rorke had been listening. He stepped back from the cliff and crossed his arms. "I'm curious, Miss Williams. Where did you get that list?"

"I found it."

Rorke's face turned red. She could see the anger. "Where did you find it?" He asked the question with a growl in his voice.

"It wasn't on government property, if that's what you want to know."

Rorke stepped closer to her. "But that list is government property. It's secret government property."

"Now just how was I supposed to know that? It didn't have any designation on it, just the names of almost two hundred Japanese citizens who live in Hawaii."

"Two hundred subversives, you mean," Gardner added.

"Is that so? Has that been proven in a court of law?"

Rorke sat down on the door of the jeep next to her. "Listen, Miss Williams, our country is facing a war. If we don't take every precaution, we might just find this whole island burning down around our ears. Those people are dangerous."

"Just because they're Japanese?" Gwen looked the man in the eye. She didn't much like being taken for a drive to a cliff for interrogation. No doubt these men were just following orders from the men she really should fear, but it made her furious all the same. "Those people are American citizens. If you ask me, the dangerous men are people like you who will go around the law to accomplish your purpose. This country needs protecting, but so do our laws."

"Look," Gardner spoke up, raising his voice, "We know whose side you're on. You were born and raised in Japan. You're from a long line of do-gooders who go around trying to save souls even if the souls are beyond saving. You're not fooling anybody here, not after last night."

Gwen looked over the hood and out at the crashing waves on the cliffs below. "Is this where you're taking me today, to a set of cliffs to threaten me? Because if it is, you're wasting your time. I'm not going to be intimidated. I'm here under orders, and I'm going to see that they're carried out. If you try to coerce me or strong-arm me in any way, then you're going to be up on charges to show cause why."

Rorke looked at Gardner. "Let's go, Chief. We're wasting our time here."

"Should we show her the installation?"

Rorke studied Gwen, then looked back at Gardner. "I suppose so. We've already come this far. But I still think we're wasting our time."

Rorke jumped back into the small backseat of the jeep, and Gardner climbed in behind the wheel. He started the ignition and they roared off the dirt track and back onto the highway.

Gwen silently watched Gardner. His jaw was clenched tight, and he stared at the road like a man in a shooting gallery. She figured he, like most men, must have assumed that she was a pushover.

They passed through a number of small towns and, when the highway left the beach at the northernmost point of the island, they turned off onto a dirt road that led through the cane fields. Gardner kept up his speed, and the jeep bounced over the road.

They cleared the top of a hill, and Gwen could see power lines cutting over the top of the hill to their left and down the hill below them. Gardner kept up the pressure on the accelerator, and the jeep bounced over the next set of dried sinkholes and down the next hill.

The Pacific came into full view, along with a shack, some army trucks, and a large platform truck with machinery set up inside. There was also a large array of antennas. The wires and antennas were joined together in a pattern that stretched some forty feet across.

Gardner downshifted, then stepped on the brakes, skidding to a stop. He just sat there, his hands digging into the steering wheel.

Rorke jumped out of the backseat and opened Gwen's door. "I have something to show you, Miss Williams. It's only one of the reasons we're not afraid of a Japanese sneak attack. On this island, the only thing we have to fear are the enemies already living here, the people you seem bound and determined to protect."

Gwen climbed out. "This is a radar installation, I take it. I've seen pictures of them."

"Do you know what they do?"

Gwen nodded. "I've got a pretty good idea."

"Well, let me show you firsthand. It's an army operation, but maybe it will put your mind at ease."

An army officer bounced out of the truck and walked their way. He saluted. "Glad you could come to see us, Lieutenant."

Rorke nodded. "I just wanted to show you off to one of our civilian employees."

The man, an army captain, smiled. "Well, nice of you to favor us with a visit. We got our station up and running, mainly because we know there's not near enough scout planes possible." He then turned around and stared up at a set of large green palisades and mountains. "Of course we wanted to be up there," he pointed. "From that peak up there we could have an unobstructed view."

"Then why don't you move it there?" Rorke asked.

The captain turned back to face him and gave a diluted smile. "All that land belongs to the National Park Service, Department of Interior. It's part of the Hawaiian National Forrest. They won't let us get up there. And there's a wildlife conservation group that's raising bloody murder."

"What do you do when and if you spot something on your screen?" Gwen asked.

"We just call it in to headquarters."

Gwen looked up at the power lines. "I see you have power, but I don't see a phone line. Do you use your radio?"

The man smiled once again. "No, ma'am. Radio communication is too bad over those hills. Of course, if we were up there . . ."

"Then how do you contact your headquarters?"

"Well, ma'am, there's a gas station about a mile down the road. I'm sure they've got a phone. Of course, sometimes during the weekends the operators are just dropped off without a jeep. They have to hike to the station then."

"Thank you, Captain," Rorke said.

Gwen started to walk off in the direction of the radar unit to get a better look, then stopped and stared at him. "One thing I am curious about."

"What's that?"

"You seem to be so worried about Japanese saboteurs on Hawaii. Aki told me about a German spy you have operating right here under your noses."

"Otto Kuen? I wouldn't exactly say he's giving us the slip. We know the man, and we know what he does. We just haven't arrested him yet. I'll take you to see his place though, if you'd like. It's down the coast on the leeward side. Maybe I'll take you there later this week."

CHAPTER 32

S am didn't exactly get an early start, and room service had helped him with his hunger by not forcing him to be present-able downstairs in the café. The navy cops had kept him up questioning him until almost 3 A.M. They did go easy on him, though. After all, he was a member of the press, and the *Washington Post* had a lot of clout. It made men with stars on their shoulders get weak in the knee. Sam had rather enjoyed sitting back and not answering the navy boys' questions, while watching them grow more frustrated by the minute. He still didn't know how they had found them. Perhaps the tail they had put on Gwen was better than he imagined. Maybe it was just the direction Gwen and he were headed when they gave them the slip. The navy, no doubt, thought of the worst possibility and drove right to the place.

He stirred what was left of his eggs Benedict and dropped his napkin beside the plate of messy yellow goo. Picking up what was left of his cup of black coffee, he downed it with a flip of his wrist. He wasn't going to wear the traditional aloha shirt today. He'd already had more color than a body could stand. Instead, he had put on a simple pair of jeans and a starched white shirt. His saddle oxfords with the rubber soles would have to do.

He got up from the table and walked over to the sink. Running a comb through his hair, he stood back and admired how nice he looked. He picked up a washcloth, dabbing off what remained of the shaving cream on the lobe of his right ear. He grinned at his reflection in the mirror. He knew he was vain. He really didn't much care. A man had to be what he was. He had no patience with men who were filled with self-doubt only to take some pride in their self-effacing humility. They were boring, and if there was one thing Sam Diamond was not, it was boring.

Stepping out into the hallway, he closed his door. Losing any tail the navy had on him wouldn't be a problem. He would just have to think ahead of them, and, with what he had seen of Naval Intelligence the night before, he didn't think that would present too great of a challenge.

He took the stairs. Thirteen floors was quite a walk, but they wouldn't be looking for him to come out of the stairwell. The people who now knew his car would be another thing, but if he could lose the ones on foot first by coming down the stairs, then he could take care of the agents who might be watching his car. He had parked the MG out front, and he knew they would be there keeping an eye on it.

Sam came out of the stairwell on the lobby floor and took a side exit. Circling around the hotel, he came out onto Kalakaua Avenue.

He walked right up to the green MG and patted it the way one would give a dog a good morning swat on the head. Spotting what he thought were two agents in a large black sedan across the street, he ran across the street right in front of them, dodging the traffic. He wanted to make sure they didn't miss him. It might take them a few minutes to discover that his foot tail had lost him and join in the hunt themselves. These boys were kinda slow, but they'd be on him as soon as they figured out what to do. The shopping bazaar would be the perfect place to lose them too.

He stopped to look at the usual aggregate of colored Hawaiian shirts and glanced back to make sure the men in the car had taken the bait. They had. Stopping so soon after going into the market had given them the required think time, and he didn't want to lose them, not just yet. They were following him, doing their best to pretend to shop. One was tall and thin, the other rather short and squatty. They reminded Sam of Mutt and Jeff in the comic strips.

Strolling through the pants and shirts, he stopped periodically to ask for prices. He had to give the illusion of a man with nothing to do and no place to go, to lull them to sleep. He reached over and fingered a set of gaudy shells that no one in his right mind would ever wear off the island.

The marketplace was a blur of activity, housewives picking out fresh fruit and tourists working hard at finding that perfect souvenir to show the folks back home in Peoria that they had actually been to Hawaii. Chinese shopkeepers were haggling; shouts and squeals were mixed with occasional grins.

He spotted a restaurant, a genuine Hawaiian eating establishment that was complete with blazing torches in the middle of the day. Life-size Tiki gods stood on the deck, their mouths open and showing teeth in a constant state of angry appetite. No doubt the place would have waitresses in grass skirts, wiggling their way to better tips.

Bounding his way up the wooden deck, he rushed inside. Large nets hung from the open-beamed ceiling. Dried fish of every variety were caught in the net, puffer fish, marlin, tuna, and sharks, all with glassy eyes staring at the people who would soon be consuming their cousins. He quickly ignored the lady waiting to seat him and walked through the crowded tables like he knew where he was going or was looking for someone there to meet him.

He was right. The waitresses were all in grass skirts, women of all sorts, blondes, brunettes, and a cute little redhead with an appealing bounce to her step, along with a few locals. Given the nature of the people who came into a place like this, he was sure it would make no difference as to what type of woman was wearing the skirts, just so she could move when she walked.

He looked back and spotted Mutt and Jeff talking to the woman who was supposed to be the hostess. He also saw a set of rest rooms and a fire exit set in a small alcove. No doubt going through there would mark him as part of the dine-and-dash crowd, but he didn't much care. Stepping quickly over to the alcove, he pressed down on the steel bar and sprang the door open.

The alley was a straight shot to Kalakaua Avenue. He started to run and didn't quit until he hit the street. Dashing through the busy traffic, he jumped into the open cockpit of the green MG and started the engine. Throwing it into gear, he roared out into traffic, ignoring the horns that blared at him.

He took a sharp left turn away from the beach and then another left, buzzing past shopkeepers and pedestrians who had looks of panic at the sight of him. He laughed. The whole thing was fun for him.

He took the turn that led to the highway and Pearl Harbor. It wasn't long before he was buzzing past the trucks and cars that were jammed into a line, ready to turn into the navy base. The ships were in the distance, huge monoliths in the water, sitting ducks. The ships might be dangerous to the enemy at sea, but here in Hawaii they were nothing more than an open invitation.

Rolling through Pearl City, he took the turn north along the highway that marked the dividing line of the island, which would take him into the heartland of Hawaiian agriculture and directly to the door of the Krinkle empire. The pineapple fields were ripe, and workers dotted the green fields as they chopped and harvested the fruit. It was hard to imagine a life of bending over in the hot sun, making profits for other people who were sitting in open cars with lemonade. There had to be a certain amount of resolve to stay in one's place to allow that. From what he had seen of the Japanese, they fit the mold. That was precisely why the early colonial landholders had brought them to the islands. The Hawaiians themselves could never be counted on to work the land that had been stolen from them.

The sun was hot overhead, but Sam didn't have to worry about that. With the top down on the MG, the wind ripped through his hair and kept him cool. He passed Schofield barracks, the main Army camp on the island. Trucks carrying troops were just pulling into the gates. They rumbled and bounced, spewing out black diesel smoke.

After another twenty minutes of high-speed driving, Sam saw the sign, KRINKLE SUGAR. He turned off the road in the direction of the white buildings. The road was flanked by fields of sugarcane. On one side, the fields were being burned. Men with torches were setting fire to the ground, sending up billows of smoke and forming a choking fog over the road.

It took him a few minutes to drive through the gray cloud and pull into the lot that surrounded the Krinkle Sugar works. Some men were loading sugar onto trucks, and others were operating forklifts that were stacked with steel drums. He pulled over, turned off the engine, got out, and walked up to a man who was shouting orders. "'Scuse me. Where would I find Mitch Krinkle?"

The man looked at him and cocked an eyebrow. He was a short stocky man, shirtless and wearing shorts. His skin was the color of bronze, and sweat was forming a trickle down his chest. "You won't find him here. There's work going on here." He pointed to the road that led up a hill. "Follow that road. No doubt he's in the pool."

Sam thanked the man, then got back in his car and headed up the road. It wasn't long before the fields of pineapple turned into a valley filled with palm trees. A stream flowed down the valley that was lush with ferns and blooming flowers.

Rounding a bend, he could see the Krinkle plantation. The large house looked like something out of the Old South with its white colonnades, archways, and indoor brick plaza complete with fountain and surrounding forest of ferns. The roof of the house was a series of red tile ledges, each planted with blooming flowers. Acres of lush green lawns fronted the place. A series of sprinklers spewed out a fine, cloudlike mist.

Sam rolled up to the front of the house. He could see the open garage. Several expensive-looking sports cars were inside, and a man with white coveralls was giving them a fine dazzling polish. He got out of the MG and walked over to the garage where the man was working. "Do you know where I can find Mitch Krinkle?"

The older, stoop-shouldered man looked up from his work. "He's out in back, probably in that batting cage of his with his friends."

Sam suddenly heard the sound of deep growls. He turned around and saw a large Samoan man with three muscular Rottweiler dogs on chains. The man was huge, but he held the dogs back by leaning against the chains as the dogs made their way around the building and into the garage. They snapped and snarled in Sam's direction, straining against the chains. The beasts had fire in their eyes. They were barking furiously and straining to get to what Sam imagined would be his throat if they'd been given half a chance.

The garage man looked at the big Samoan. "You wanna take this man 'round back to see Mr. Krinkle? Put those dogs in their pens too. They'll scare people."

The Samoan grinned. "Yeah, I take him." He looked over at Sam. "You better go on ahead of me."

Sam made his way through the plaza and toward the back of the house. The sound of the dogs behind him only made him move faster. He didn't have to go far before he heard the sound of laughter.

Stepping out from the plaza, he could see how the other side of the economic circle really lived. A parking lot next to the tennis court was filled with expensive sports cars of every variety and color, although red seemed to be predominant. Next to the tennis court was an Olympic-size pool. Umbrellas and tables were scattered throughout the area surrounding the pool. Several waiters in white dinner jackets and black ties were circulating among the tables, evidently taking orders for drinks. Most of the guests were in swimsuits or robes, with a few in tennis outfits. Behind the pool, a small brass band, its members dressed in red jackets, was playing jazz. To the rear of the tennis court was a baseball diamond. A batting cage had been erected, and a machine was spewing out balls as a group mingled around to get a better view of the hitter.

Sam looked back at the Samoan as the man continued to hold the dogs. "Where do I find Mitch Krinkle?"

The man grinned. "He's the tall blond with the bat in his hand."

"Thanks." Sam walked through the tables and over to the batting cage. He watched as Krinkle continued to hit, all the while making jokes to his gathered guests. Krinkle finished his joke and then caught sight of Sam. He stepped forward as the ball whizzed behind him, slapping the wood at the rear of the backstop. "Who are you?"

"Name's Sam Diamond. I'm a reporter with the *Washington Post*."

"You don't look like a reporter." He grinned and looked about for approval from the collection of beautiful people surrounding him.

Sam knew the man was no doubt referring to his jeans. He smiled. "Well, you don't exactly look like an important industrialist."

The group laughed, but Mitch's sudden hard stare quieted them down. "That's my father. I'm just learning the business."

Sam eyeballed the group. "And what is today's lesson?"

One of the young men in the group raised a tall glass and rattled the ice in it. "How to have a good time."

Sam smiled. "Then I'd say you were learning your lessons well."

Krinkle grinned. "Yeah, Jerry here learns those lessons real well. And what can we do for you, Mr. Diamond? Did our subscription lapse?"

The remark brought another flurry of laughter from the group.

"I wasn't aware that you could read," Sam responded. The group fell silent, except for a few snickers. "Actually, I was here to interview you about a murder case."

"Murder? What would I have to do with murder?"

"That's exactly what I'd like to know."

"Well, ask your questions, Diamond."

Sam looked around at the people, who suddenly seemed to be all ears. "I think it would be better if I ask what I came to ask in private."

"There's no need for that. These people are all my friends."

Sam nodded. "Yes, but they might not be for long if they hear what I came to find out."

Some of the group tugged on the sleeves of others and began to trickle out of the area. A few like Jerry stayed behind to listen, grinning and hanging on every word.

"Mind telling me where you were last Saturday night?"

Mitch lifted his head and stared off at the low-hanging cloud of smoke over the cane fields. The ball machine continued to work, slapping the baseballs one after the other into the empty backstop. "Last Saturday night, hmm, let's see. Where was I?" His eyes suddenly brightened. "Oh yes." He glanced at a young attractive brunette in shorts standing nearby, then put his arm around her and pulled her to his side. "Heidi and I went for a drive around the island." He smiled down at the girl. "We like to find secluded beaches, you know, away from prying eyes."

"What time was this drive of yours?" Sam could tell the girl was gushing from the attention.

Once again a ball sailed through the air, striking the backstop. Krinkle shouted at the man working the batting machine. "Turn that thing off." Looking back at Sam, he went on. "It was from about five in the afternoon until somewhere, let's see, oh yes, I suppose it was way after three A.M."

"But, Mitch," Sam could see Jerry start to ask a question, but Krinkle ignored him and looked down at the still beaming girl and smiled. "We like long drives you know, don't we gorgeous? Why do you ask?"

"Do you know Aki Kawa?"

"Hmm." He rolled his eyes once again. "The name sounds somewhat familiar. Oh yes, she's the granddaughter of a man who used to work for my father. A Japanese girl."

"Yes. She was murdered last Saturday night."

"And you think I had something to do with it?"

"I don't think anything. I'm just asking questions."

Mitch smiled. "Unless Heidi and I did the girl in together, I'm here to tell you that I know nothing about the matter. I can't think of any reason why I'd ever want to do such a thing."

"Perhaps because she didn't want you and she was one of the few things on this island that your father couldn't serve up to you on a silver platter."

"I can have any woman I want." He looked down at the girl again. "Can't I, sweet cakes?" Looking back at Sam, he smiled. "You really think a girl like that could say no to me?"

"In a heartbeat. I met the girl. She wouldn't touch you with rubber gloves."

The remark instantly hardened Krinkle's glance. His face turned a slow shade of pink. He dropped his hand from around the girl's arm and gripped the bat with both hands. "I think it's time for you to go, Diamond."

Jerry laughed. "Yeah, you'd better go. He's pretty good with that bat. Best hitter on our team."

Looking over to the large Samoan who had been standing near the backstop, Krinkle signaled for him. The large burly Samoan walked over. His hands looked like hams, and his biceps were as large as Sam's legs. "Take Mr. Diamond back to his car and remind him of our rule against trespassing." He shot Sam a glance. "I really don't ever want to see you again, Diamond."

Sam turned to leave. "I'm not sure that what you want will make much difference, Krinkle. If I don't ask you questions, the police will, and you won't have anybody there to tell them otherwise."

He walked off behind the large Samoan, a man whom Sam had no interest in trying to cross. They strolled past the pen that held the dogs, and it was obvious they were still interested in Sam. They growled and barked, trying to climb over the fence to get to him. When he got to his car, he found another man waiting for him. Spotting Sam, the man stuck out his hand. "I'm James Krinkle. I understand you were here to see my son. One of his guests came and informed me."

"Yes sir. I had some questions about a murder."

"Are you referring to the Kawa girl? I just came from her funeral. Her grandfather was my bookkeeper and investment advisor."

"Yes."

"And you think my son might be involved in some way?"

"I don't think anything. I just ask questions. From what I hear, though, she rebuffed a number of his advances. You know your son. He doesn't strike me as a man used to hearing no."

The old man nodded. "Yes, his mother and I have spoiled him." He looked Sam in the eye. "But I don't think he could ever do anything like that. He would have no reason to."

"From what you tell me, saying no to him just might be plenty of reason. I'd try it if I were you, Mr. Krinkle. Say no to him for a change and see how he reacts."

CHAPTER 33

The long corridor in the city jail seemed to go on forever. Gwen felt totally out of place, and the men, pressing their faces into the bars and watching her go by, made her feel all the more uncomfortable. She was following the uniformed policeman as closely as she could, but right then she would have felt better being invisible.

It had taken her the better part of the day to finish with Gardner and Rorke; most of the time was spent with her pretending not to be terrified. Now some of those same feelings came floating back to her.

The men in here were all behind bars, but the ones she had just left had given her the same feelings.

The policeman came to a cell and raked his club across the bars. "Homer! You got yourself a visitor."

She could see the old man on the cot. He looked up at her and blinked his eyes, a look of disbelief written all over his face. Swinging his feet onto the floor, he got up and walked over to where Gwen was standing.

The policeman looked at her. "Miss, I'll just be standing over here in case you need me."

"Thank you."

Homer pushed his fingers through the bars and held a tight grip on them.

"Are you all right?"

He shook his head. "Not by a long shot. That woman was a friend of mine." His eyes looked sad, a droopy look with dark circles. "I would have put myself on the line for her anytime. I sure wouldn't have hurt her none." He looked up at Gwen. He had the look of a puppy. "Why they say I killed her?" Slowly he shook his head. "She was a fine Christian woman. She gave me some hope. She called me an angel, she did."

"I know she cared about you, Homer, cared about you a great deal. It would be a tribute to her if after you get out of here, you did the things that you were planning to do the last time you saw her."

Homer tried to shake the bars. "How am I gonna do that? How in blazes do I get myself back home now? These people plan to fry me— and for something I never did."

"Why don't you tell me about that night? What happened out there on the beach?"

He swallowed, then bit his lower lip. "I heard her screaming and yelling in the surf. First I figured it was some woman drowning, then I remember her. She and me talked earlier. I thought she was plenty nice. So I come arunning, and I seen her in the water with these men all around her, coming after her."

He took a deep breath. "Well sir, I weren't scared, no way. There was five of them and only one of old Homer, but I come off that hill like Sittin' Bull after Custer. I was swinging that rake of mine and yelling my durn head off." He smiled. "Well, I whipped 'em, whipped 'em good, I did. They lit out like foxes with their tails caught on fire."

"Do you think you could identify those men?"

"Sure I could, couple of them at least." He raised his hand and ran it along his cheek. "One of 'em had his self a long scar. They was Japanese boys. I seen a couple of them before. I know where they hang out."

"Where is that?"

"Old bar on Lemon Road called the Red Lips." He shook his head. "Don't you go in there, though, not by yourself, ya hear?"

"I'll be careful."

"That Aki girl called one of them fellers Hiroki. They was bad folks, so I'd be careful iffen I was you." He reached out to her through the bars. "Will you get me out of here?"

"We're going to try, Homer. I can't make any promises, but I think our best chance is in finding the person who is responsible for the murder."

"I sure hope you do. I liked that gal. She was one sweet child. Ain't many folks what pay Homer no nevermind, but she did. She treated me like a real person, she did."

Gwen parked her car on busy Kalakaua Avenue and walked the few blocks to Lemon Road. The entire district had been given over to honky-tonks and sailor bars. Music and smoke blared out the doors, and hand-painted signs in the windows advertised the cost of beer along with the price of a dance. Local girls would pick up money and tips by dancing with lonely sailors. Business was good too. Neon lights buzzed and blinked off and on. Brightly lit arrows pointed the way to a good time.

She saw the neon red lips. The puckered lips flashed off and on, and the name of the place was emblazoned on the smoky glass window in bold red letters. Gwen realized she should have heeded Homer's advice and not have come alone.

She pushed open the door and stepped inside to almost total darkness. It took some time for her eyes to adjust. The place had become a Japanese bar, and in the corner a band was playing a very loud, very poor imitation of one of Benny Goodman's hits.

She stepped up to the bar, and a Japanese man with a faint thin mustache and white shirt came over to her. He grinned. "You looking for some action, missy? Japanese men like white ladies. You do well here."

Gwen forced a smile. "You look busy. *Imo [no ko] o arau yoo.*" She used the Japanese expression for "like washing a bucketful of potatoes." It signified a jam-packed atmosphere where people were stirred together.

The man smiled. "You speak Japanese. How you do that?"

"I was born in Japan."

"Wow-eeee. Then sure enough, you come to the right place. You get all the dances you wanna have." He leaned forward on the bar. "You pretty lady too, very pretty lady."

"Thank you, but I'm here to find someone, a man named Hiroki."

The man slammed his fist on the bar. "That too bad. You do fine here, mighty fine." He pointed to a group of men seated around a far table. "Hiroki Fujiyama, he a regular here. He the one in the black leather jacket." He grinned at her. "You come back though sometime, you hear? You a mighty fine lady, and you be very popular gal here."

Gwen made her way over to the other side of the crowded room, weaving in and out of the tables and pushing away the dancers who jostled against her. The smoke was making her gag and she coughed.

She watched the women dancing, their eyes blurry, almost as if they were in a dreamlike state. Women like these were always the lowest link of the food chain. They lived for others, not for themselves.

Gwen walked up to the table the bartender had pointed out, and instantly several men at the table stopped talking. Their eyes were riveted on her, smiles spreading across their faces. She could see that one of the men at the table had a long scar across his cheek, the kind that Homer had told her about.

"I'm looking for a Hiroki Fujiyama."

The man had his back to her, but he turned around and met her eyes with a slithering stare. "That would be me. Have a seat." He swatted at the man beside him, as if he were shooing away some cat who had perched himself in the wrong seat. The man quickly moved to the other side of the table, and Gwen took his seat.

Fujiyama moved closer to her and put his arm around her chair. "Now, how can I help you?" His eyes flashed as his smile broadened.

The other men in the group began to laugh and make lewd suggestions in Japanese, all of which Hiroki responded to with an equally off-color phrase.

Gwen glared at them and responded. "I can see you're not used to women who make their own decisions. *Osato ga shiremasu yo.*" She used the Japanese expression for "it shows a lack of breeding." The idea of a white woman understanding and responding in their own language caused them to clamp their mouths shut. They stared at her, blinking their eyes.

"You know Japanese?" Hiroki asked.

Gwen nodded. "I was born there and, more importantly, was raised there."

Hiroki looked her in the eye. "Then what are you doing here?"

"I have a friend that you knew. I wanted to ask you some questions about her."

"Who?"

"Aki Kawa."

Hiroki leaned back and smiled. "Ah, yes, the pretty little spy. Are you a spy too?"

"I work for Naval Intelligence, if that's what you mean, but I'm no spy. And neither was Aki."

"That's a matter open to dispute."

"And as I understand it, you did dispute it with her. In fact, you and your friends threatened her."

"And you think we killed her?"

"I don't think anything. I just came here to ask a few questions."

"Like what?"

"Like where you were last Saturday night, the night Aki was killed?"

Hiroki glanced around the table. "We were all playing baseball in Kapo'olani Park. We work for Krinkle Sugar, and the company had a game."

"That's pretty close to Kuhio Beach isn't it?"

Hiroki nodded. "Right next door."

"What time was the game?"

"It was under the lights, so it started at sundown and went on till ten o'clock or so. You can ask anybody. People from the company were there, from the boss's son to the guy on the loading dock."

"You have much contact with Mitch Krinkle?"

"Some. He had the hots for Aki, I know that."

"And what about your threats to Aki the week before?"

Hiroki laughed. "We were just funning with her, trying to scare her. The woman was a spy. She had no loyalty to the Japanese, even though she was one."

"What makes you think that?"

Hiroki moved closer to her. He lowered his voice almost to a growl. "Her brother Yasuo found a list she had at her home, a list of Japanese that were going to be thrown into jail. My parents' names were on that list." He let the words drift into Gwen's mind. "She had an American sailor as a boyfriend. They used to meet all the time at Kuhio Beach from what Yasuo said."

Gwen figured that what he said was true. Yasuo had undoubtedly found the list. Yasuo, like his friends, had been suspicious of Aki. Perhaps it was this invasion of her privacy that had prompted Aki to move the list to her grandfather's grave.

"Did you discuss this with anyone else?"

"I might have."

"Did you talk about it with Mitch Krinkle?"

"Yeah, sure. Like I said, he had the hots for her. He didn't care if the woman was a spy. He knew Yasuo and I were friends. He was always asking me questions about her and what she was doing with this Brian guy. What did I care? If she could give herself to this sailor, then she could give herself to Krinkle. Japanese girls who go outside the Japanese can stay there for all I care."

"Aki was Japanese, but she was an American too."

"Yeah, too American if you ask me. I know she had found lots of stuff. She kept it in her office. It was like she had something to prove." He pointed his finger. "But those navy people wouldn't pay any mind to what she did. She was Japanese, and that was all she was ever going to be. She could have stayed loyal to her own people. Instead she traded her soul to people who could care less."

CHAPTER 34

rian wore his dress white uniform as he marched into the headquarters of the Asiatic fleet. He was determined to see his father and follow through on the suspicions that Sam had raised the morning they had come back from viewing Aki's body. Being at the funeral and seeing her parents weeping as she was placed in the family mausoleum had deepened his resolve to find out what he could about her murder. He knew his father was still here. The man had voiced his desire to bring Brian's mother to Hawaii so the three of them could spend Thanksgiving together. Brian couldn't think of a sadder occasion. There was nothing he was thankful for, not anymore.

He marched down the long hall, the sound of his dress shoes echoing with each step. No matter what else he did, he had to look navy. His father was using the guest flag officer's office, and his two-star flag was stuck in a guidon holder outside the door.

Without knocking, Brian walked through the door and marched up to his father's large ornate desk. The man was leaning over the desk and inspecting what Brian assumed were daily fitness reports or the results of the latest gunnery practice at sea.

He came to a halt, assumed a firm crisp posture of attention, and snapped a salute into place. "Sir, Lieutenant Brian Picard."

The admiral looked up at him and returned his salute. "At ease, Lieutenant."

Brian stared down at him and gritted his teeth slightly.

"What do you have on your mind, son?"

"Some questions, sir, if I have permission to speak freely."

His father leaned back in his high-backed brown leather chair. "Of course you do." He waved the back of his hand at Brian. "Go ahead. Get on with it. What's on your mind?"

"It's about Aki, sir." Brian's eyes were directly ahead of him, drilling a hole into the wall behind his father.

"What about her?"

He dropped his gaze to his father's eyes and narrowed his own. "It's about the day they found her body. You called me and told me about it almost before the people who identified her came out of the morgue. I'd just like to know how you knew she was dead."

His father picked up a brass letter opener and began to finger its sharp edge. "Why? Do you think I had something to do with it myself?"

"I don't know. I'd just like to know how you found out. It doesn't seem possible."

"You must think the navy is totally incompetent. Her identification was found on her. They knew who she was before those people went down there to confirm it. The police called Pearl to confirm her identity as an employee that morning. I got the word from the shore patrol. I've got people in there who knew you'd been seeing her."

"You seem to have me wired, sir. Don't you?"

Picard slammed his fist into the ink blotter on his desk, driving the point of the letter opener into it. He got to his feet so he could look directly into Brian's eyes. "You're my only son. Why wouldn't I want to know what you're doing? You were in the process of flushing your entire career down the john by sleeping with the enemy."

Brian took a step forward. "She was not the enemy. She was working hard at keeping this navy of yours out of a sling. The woman was determined to prove she was just as American as anybody else, more so, because she cared."

Brian walked around the desk and looked out the window that overlooked the harbor. He pointed to the ships. "Your navy is sitting in this landlocked duck pond just waiting for a Japanese attack. Aki was doing everything in her power to keep that from happening. Somehow, some way, she just saw the day when Japanese Zeros would be buzzing over your head, dropping torpedoes down your throat and sinking that fleet where it sits."

The admiral had turned to watch him. He chuckled, his smile spreading across his face. "You'd better stick to what you know about gunnery, son. Torpedoes that are dropped sink to seventy feet before coming up and leveling off. Pearl is no more than forty feet anywhere. They'd be stuck in the mud."

"The English sank three Italian battleships in a harbor no bigger than Pearl. If they can do it, so can the Japs. Then where will your navy be?"

"It's not *my* navy," the man raised his voice. "It's yours, too, in case you've forgotten. And if Aki was working all that hard, then maybe she actually found something. Have you ever considered that? It could be she found a nest of saboteurs among her own people and they killed her for it. Before you swagger around accusing your old man of murder, you'd better go and do your homework."

"And just where were you last Saturday night, Father?" He drew the word *father* out sarcastically.

"That's none of your business." The admiral took his seat once again.

"All right, I'll just find out for myself. I'll look into what Aki was investigating. It could be she just found a massive amount of incompetence in Naval Intelligence."

"Be careful."

"Why? Are you afraid I'm going to bring dishonor to the Picard name by going behind your back and rooting out stupidity?"

"No, if anything I'm afraid of your being labeled *stupid*. You seem bound and determined never to rise above the rank I've spent so much time and effort getting you to."

Brian's face flushed with anger. He clenched his fists and then reached up to his shoulder boards, unpinning his father's bars. He held them in his hand, bouncing them slightly, then slammed them down on the desk. "Here. If you earned them and not me, you keep them. I'll go out and get my own."

Without waiting for a reply, he snapped to attention and offered a quick salute. Most of the time when he had found himself angry with his father, he bottled it up inside. Today was different. Today his father would know it. Turning on his heels, he stepped out of the room and marched down the hall. He was more determined than ever to find out the truth. If Aki had been on to something, then he was going to find out just what. But if his father had somehow been involved in her murder, he would find that out too.

When he got back to his billet at the bachelor officers' quarters, he stripped off his dress uniform and flung it across the room. Just at that moment it represented something he hated, a mold he had been poured into, a lifetime of saying "yes, sir" to people he would liked to have screamed at, especially his father. Grabbing a pair of khaki trousers, he stuffed his legs into them and picked up a blue-and-black aloha shirt with flowers on it. He headed out the door, pulling his shirt on as he went. He knew Aki's routine. He had seen the man she had followed.

A short time later he was driving up to the bluffs overlooking Pearl Harbor. If the man Aki followed hadn't already been there, he soon would be. Aki had told him about the daily routine the man followed. This particular Japanese diplomat was constantly spying on the fleet and then meeting a man to pass on what he had seen. He then went to the American radio transmission station in Honolulu to send his messages straight to Tokyo. American law protected him and everything he said to those warlords who held his leash.

He took the curve on two wheels, gripping the steering wheel. Brian was determined to follow the man and then go farther than Aki had gone. Fear never crossed his mind, only anger that he was having to do what neither the police nor naval investigators had done or would do.

A short time later he pulled up to the spot alongside the road where he and Aki used to go. A wave of emotion went through him. There on a blanket on the ground was a couple with a picnic basket. The man was a navy enlisted man, and the woman appeared to be a local girl. He fought back the tears, wiping his eyes.

Taking several deep breaths, he got out of the car. He walked over to the rail that separated the road from the grass and bluff and looked out on the fleet. He hoped his father was right. Perhaps Pearl Harbor was too shallow for a torpedo attack. Then again, maybe that idea was just one more shaky element in a house of cards that could soon come crashing down.

He could see the couple on the grass. She was feeding him a sandwich, just as Aki used to feed him egg salad. There was a tenderness to them, a slow motion of caring that Brian missed. All of a sudden he felt painfully lonely. Aki had spoken to him often about her faith in God. He knew that she had been living for more than the here and now of this world. He only wished he could.

It was some time later when he saw the black sedan drive up to the pull-off beside the road. A man in a blue suit got out, and he carried his familiar pair of binoculars along with his notepad and pen. This was the man Gwen and Aki had seen, but was this the man responsible for Aki's death? That was the only question in Brian's mind. Had she gotten too close for him. Did she know too much? The same question haunted him about the navy. Did Aki know too much about their incompetence? He thought he knew her and her thinking, but now there was so much more that he wished he knew.

CHAPTER 35

Gwen took the elevator up to Sam's floor. She didn't like the idea of visiting a man in his hotel room, but she pushed it out of her mind. She had taken every precaution, parking five blocks away and weaving her way through the market on foot. She was even wearing sunglasses and was wearing her hair wrapped in a scarf. She wasn't quite sure she did it to disguise herself or to keep her hair in place should Sam decide to take the little sports car.

She knocked on his door. A few seconds later he opened it wide, a grin on his face. He was wearing a blue-and-white checked sport shirt, no doubt in his desire to remain distinctive as a mainlander, she thought. "Come on in, sugar. Good to see you."

Gwen stepped into the room as he closed the door. The bed was a mess; sheets rumpled with newspapers spread across them like a disheveled blanket. The chair was pulled over to the coffee table with an open book on the floor.

"I called you from a phone booth in the coffee shop," he said. "For all I know, the navy has my phones tapped."

"I'm glad you did. We have a lot to catch up on."

"You bet we do." Sam slid open a drawer and took out a camera. "I'd like to start by retracing Aki's steps. You say you went with her to the bluffs to watch the Japanese diplomat?"

"Yes."

"I can just bet who the man meets with after that. No doubt the guy I've been tailing for weeks now. Where do they meet?"

"Usually at Saint Andrew's Cathedral."

"And probably not for worship."

"I rather doubt it."

"We know where the Japanese goes after the meeting, straight to the radio office to send his message. I'd like to find out where my man goes when he's finished there. That's one end I'd like to tie up."

Gwen nodded. There was so much about Aki's death that puzzled her. She almost believed what Hiroki had told her. It sounded like him to try to prove how tough he was by scaring Aki. The only thing that really troubled her was how much it seemed that the navy was involved in her death. She had to be able to deliver concrete proof of Japan's intentions for Pearl Harbor, but if the navy had something to hide already, not only would they not believe her, but they would also fight her all the way.

"Why don't we take my car?" Gwen said. "I parked it a ways from here. We could go out the back and across the beach."

Sam smiled. "And you'd be able to drive."

Gwen almost breathed a sigh of relief at the thought. "Yes."

Sam motioned toward the door. "After you, my lady." They hurried toward the back set of stairs. Within minutes they were walking across the warm sand parallel to the breaking surf. The trade winds were blowing, and an outrigger canoe was riding a high wave. Tourists on board were screaming at the top of their lungs. Sam and Gwen would make a wide circle around any agents the navy might have left to follow them. With any luck, they hadn't noticed.

It took them some time to make the circuitous route to where Gwen's car was parked. The street was busy. Sam leaned over to her as they walked. "Look, when we get to your car, let's just walk past it. I'd like to see if they've got the thing staked out. They may have followed you from home."

As they got closer to the car, Gwen pointed it out. "The Ford is just ahead."

"OK. I'll cross the street and meet you at the end of the block."

She watched him cross the street, dodging traffic. The man had nerves of steel. She'd give him that. She couldn't shake the feeling that if the navy was behind Aki's murder, the closer they got to what really happened, the more their own lives would be in danger.

She walked past her car, looking both ways for the dark sedan with its sinister occupants. She saw nothing, at least nothing out of place. The street was busy with automobile and pedestrian traffic.

When she got to the end of the block, she stopped to wait for Sam. He ran across the street against the light and took her arm. "OK. I think we're fine here. Let's go."

"Where?"

"Saint Andrew's, of course."

It took them just a short time before they parked the car outside of Saint Andrew's Cathedral. They watched a few people going into the church, some there to pray, some there to gawk at the stained-glass windows and explore the old church.

It was then that they spotted the familiar dark sedan of the Japanese diplomat. The man pulled into a parking space, then carefully got out and locked his doors. Sam snickered. "He doesn't look out of place, does he?"

"He probably doesn't even think about it any more. He's been doing this for such a long time now that he doesn't even see himself."

"That's good. Then he won't see us."

Then they spotted a second car parking across the street. Sam nudged Gwen. "Isn't that Brian, Aki's boyfriend?"

"Yes." It seemed out of place for Brian to be there.

"Why do you think he'd be here? You don't think—"

Gwen cut him off. "No. He's probably doing the same thing we are. This is where he knows to start."

Sam opened the car door and leaned out. "Brian," he called out to the man who was getting out of his car. He waved him over.

Brian ran across the street and jumped into the backseat of the Ford. "What are you doing here?" Sam asked.

Brian leaned over on the seat between the two of them. "Following that Japanese from the Embassy. I just thought maybe I could find out something that would help. For all I know, he might just run across somebody I've seen before, somebody who could put the pieces together."

"Good thinking," Sam replied. "We know who he is meeting in there, a German spy that I've been following for months now. And when he's done with him, he'll be going to send his radio message to Tokyo."

"What do we do then?" Brian asked.

Sam glanced at Gwen. "I'd like to follow Popov. We haven't been in that direction before. We know what the Japanese is going to do." He leaned over in Gwen's direction. "That sound all right to you?"

"Sounds fine to me."

Sam and Gwen spent the next several minutes going over their last few days. Sam filled her in on the questions he'd put to Mitch Krinkle, and Gwen carefully related her trip to the cliffs with the navy men and her meeting with Hiroki. She then went through her time with Aki's grandmother, the diary, and her being chased through the graveyard. Brian's head swung back and forth, listening to the two of them.

"What about it, Brian?" Sam asked. "Do you think the navy could be involved in Aki's death?"

"It's possible, if they knew about that list. Stuff like that hitting the newspapers here on the island would be dynamite." He scooted closer. "I can tell you one thing. We've got to get to Aki's office and see what's under that ink blotter."

He hung his head slightly and then looked up at Sam. "I did talk to my father this morning. I wanted to see just how he knew about Aki's death." He spent a few minutes relating the conversation with his father.

"There he is," Gwen said. She was looking out the window at the Japanese vice-consul leaving the church. Duskov Popov soon followed him.

"There's my man," Sam said. Popov was wearing an ice-cream suit, a white suit, white shirt, and white tie. He had a cream-colored Panama hat on his head and was carrying a brown leather briefcase. "Let's follow him, but hang back. I don't want to get too close."

For the next half-hour they drove behind the man. Popov had rented a candy-apple red Dodge coupe, and they kept him in distant sight as they weaved their way in and out of Honolulu traffic. It was when he hit the Pali Highway and headed up the mountain toward the other side of the island that Gwen dropped back. "I think it's best that we stay out of sight for a while," she said. "He's not getting off this road until we get to the leeward side anyway."

Brian sat back thinking. "You say Krinkle had an airtight alibi for the night of Aki's murder?"

"I wouldn't call it airtight. More like a young female idol worshiper who would pay any price to stand in the man's shadow."

They hit the small town of Kaneohe before Gwen caught sight of the red coupe once again. Turning north along the highway, she worked at maintaining a distance that wouldn't attract the man's attention, while at the same time keeping him in view. They covered the length of peaceful Kaneohe Bay before coming to the Chinaman's Hat, a small grass-covered island in the bay that was shaped like the kind of hat that the Chinese wore to keep the sun off them in the pineapple fields.

The sun was setting, filling the water with a reddish hue. A bright ribbon of crimson painted the distant horizon as it dipped below the surface. Rounding the bend, they saw the red coupe turn toward the beach. Gwen pulled the Ford over and put on the hand brake.

"Good going, sugar. We'll have to go by foot from here."

They walked along the sandy road until they passed several houses, each of which had a marvelous view of the ocean. The rosy pink of the disappeared sun blanketed the water, making it look warm to the touch. Several minutes later they came to a house at the end of the road. The red coupe was parked out front.

The house was typical beachfront property, a weathered blue wooden structure, flat on top, with a broken-down, sand-covered picket fence out front. An orange lifesaving ring hung next to the door. "Can you make out the black letters on that?" Sam asked.

Gwen shook her head. "Not yet."

A short time later Gwen stretched out her hand, bringing Sam and Brian to a halt. "It says *Kuen*." She looked at them. "That's the German spy that Aki told me about."

"How did she know about the man?" Sam asked.

"I really couldn't say, but she did. She mentioned something about the boys in the basement knowing, but I don't know if she'd ever met the man."

"And you don't know if he'd ever met her?" Brian asked.

"No, I don't." Gwen knew that this was someone who could also be a suspect in Aki's murder. The military police and the intelligence community all knew about him, but that didn't mean he knew he'd been discovered. In this case what the man didn't know didn't hurt him, but it might have killed Aki.

"OK," Sam said. "Let's just lay low and see what happens." He pointed to a sandy hill on the other side of the road. "That looks like a good spot."

"How long are we going to stay here?" Gwen asked.

Sam shrugged. "I don't have any idea. I don't even know what we want to find out." He smiled. Sam had a way of maintaining his moxie even in the face of being thought a fool. "I guess we'll know when we see it."

They ran across the road and moved around to a spot behind the sandy hill where they could keep the house in view. Lying in the sand didn't appeal to Gwen, but she had little choice.

It was quite some time later, maybe an hour or two, before they saw the door open. Popov walked out of the house and climbed into the red coupe. He started it up and drove around the turn at the end of the road, then slowly moved past the sandy hill where the three were hiding.

"Now what?" asked Brian.

Sam rolled over on his back, staring up at the stars. "Well, I know where he's going because I live there. He's headed for room thirteen-ten at the Royal Hawaiian. I don't know what he's doing here, unless it's just visiting an old friend from the fatherland."

"Come on." Gwen jumped to her feet. "No sense sitting here." She dusted the sand off her pants and blouse. "Let's get a closer look."

Gwen led the way up to the house. There was a window in front. They could clearly see the woman of the house. She was tidying up, picking up cups and saucers and a small percolator. Behind her on the wall was a large Nazi flag.

"These people don't hide their sympathies, do they?" Sam remarked.

The sound of a small dog barking inside startled them. They moved back away from the window. Sam grabbed Gwen's sleeve and nodded for them to go around the house, and she bobbed her head in agreement. They began to circle the house to the left, stepping away from the light coming through the windows. They could hear the waves hitting the beach behind the house, not the surf of Waikiki, but the gentle lapping of the leeward side of the island.

When they had circled the house, Gwen grabbed Sam's arm and pulled him down. She turned to Brian and motioned for him to get low. There on the beach behind the cabin was a lone figure standing in the sand. The man had a boxed light on a tripod and was flashing signals out to sea.

"You reckon that's Kuen?" Sam questioned.

Gwen nodded. "I think so."

"What's he doing?" Brian asked.

"Sending signals," Gwen responded, "probably to a submarine."

"Well, I'll be," Sam said. "These people are spies." He had been carrying his camera on a strap over his shoulder, and he swung it into position and began to take pictures. He looked at Gwen and smiled. "Lucky thing for me I got film to allow me to do this. Can't promise how it'll turn out, though."

Just then they heard the scurrying of small feet on the sand behind them, accompanied by barking. They turned to see a small poodle yapping and snarling. Behind the dog stood a woman, a Mauser rifle in her hands.

"Who are you?" she asked. "And what are you doing here?"

PART 3
JUST ANOTHER SUNDAY

CHAPTER 36

The woman stood up on her toes and shouted over them. "Otto, come here quick, Otto." Her shrill, panicky voice was unsettling, especially with her holding a rifle in her hands.

The man on the dark beach dropped the small gate on his lantern. He looked back in their direction, straining to see what was happening. He left the lamp in place on its tripod and marched in their direction. The man was deliberate, stepping off his paces in the sand and holding his head high.

"You wait for my husband." The woman's voice had turned into a growl. She waved the barrel of the rifle back and forth, making her point that she was prepared to shoot any of them at any moment. "You have no business here. This is our beach, our property. You do not belong here."

Sam tried his best to calm the woman. He forced a smile and motioned with his hands in a downward motion. "Lower that thing, lady. Look, how were we to know this was your beach? We didn't see any signs. Now why don't you just put that thing down?" He glanced in Gwen's direction. "You're starting to scare the lady here."

"You just stand still and wait," she shouted. They could see the spray of spittle flying out of her mouth as she spewed out the words. Her lower lip drooped, forming a cascade of spittle over her red-painted lips. The woman was a hefty sort, with ringlets of blonde hair peeking out of a red-and-yellow scarf she had tied around her head. She pushed the rifle in Sam's direction. "You wait."

"Lady, we ain't going nowhere. Just calm down."

The small dog stayed at the woman's heels, yapping and gurgling. The dog peeked around her dress, and barked, and then backed up and growled.

The man stepped up to them, planting his hands on his hips. "What do we have here, trespassers?"

He was dressed in baggy blue dungarees and T-shirt. His hair was cut short, exposing a bald top with a fringe of gray hair.

"Yes," the woman said. "Fritz heard them, and I came out to see. They were watching you."

The man glared at them, sizing them up and considering what to do next.

"We were just out here to see the beach," Sam said. He motioned over to where the man had left his tripod. "Guess we couldn't help but see you out there. But there's no law that's been broken. We didn't see any signs."

"Are you in the habit of prowling other people's property at night?" Otto asked. "My wife might have shot you."

Sam chuckled and glanced back at the woman. "She still might if she doesn't put that thing down." He glanced back at Brian and Gwen. "We didn't mean any harm. Just out for a stroll, that's all."

Otto motioned toward the house. "Let's go inside and get a better look at you. We'll see if your story makes sense."

They padded their way through the sand and around the house, the tiny poodle circling them and continuing to bark.

"Quite the watchdog you got there," Sam smirked.

"He lets us know when anything is out of place," Otto replied. He stepped around them and pushed open the front door. Gwen stepped in, followed by Brian and Sam.

The interior was a hodgepodge of blond furniture with sharp, pointed legs that staked down a dirty green carpet. A checkered dog bed with pillow and rubber mouse marked the spot where the ferocious keeper of the Kuen's privacy slept. The thing trotted over to its bed and climbing in, shook itself.

Gwen noticed piles of magazines stacked waist-high along two walls. Many were *Popular Mechanics*, and the rest seemed to be copies of *National Geographic*. Piles of newspapers covered the dining room floor, neatly stacked and some yellow with age. The piles rose to almost the level of the ceiling, obscuring the windows on that side of the house and allowing only a narrow path to the kitchen.

What caught her eye, however, were the two German flags on the living room wall. One was the flag of the German Republic and the other a Nazi banner complete with swastika. Surrounding them were photographs of the Bavarian Alps, the Brandenburg Gate in Berlin, and numerous shots of Adolf Hitler. His hands were on his hips in the photographs, just like the pose Otto had struck on the beach.

Otto took the rifle from his wife's hands and motioned toward the couch in front of the large window. "Please be seated." He took a seat in a chair directly across from them and leaned the rifle up against the wall by his side. The rifle looked less dangerous against the wall than it had in his wife's hands, but it was still close enough to be used.

The three of them took seats on the sagging couch. Gwen noticed a small black phone on a table near the hall. "Aren't you going to call the police?" she asked.

Otto shot his wife a quick glance. "I don't think that will be necessary."

"Then you're going to shoot us yourself." Sam laughed.

The man glared at them, a twinkle in his icy blue eyes. "I just might, at that."

Sam shook his head. "Somehow I always had the impression that these islands were hospitable. What do they call it, the aloha spirit? Yeah, that's it."

"Helga and I don't like intruders."

"Then I'd suggest you put signs up." Sam glanced at the small poodle that still refused to lie down in its bed. "At the very least you could warn people about your vicious attack dog."

"You are quite the comedian, aren't you?"

Sam smirked. "Some things just strike me as funny, like holding a gun on people who are just out to see the moon on the beach. God forbid if we should have tried to fire up a hot-dog grill."

Otto glared at them, then scooted forward in his chair. "Then why don't you tell me who you are?" He waved his hand. "I heard your story about walking out here to see the beach, but there are beaches all over this island. Why here?"

"Why not?" Sam replied. He shrugged. "We were driving past here. The moon was up. The beach was here. So why not here?"

"Then you're all tourists?"

Sam turned his eyes to Brian. "Well, our friend here is in the navy. I guess that doesn't make him a tourist. I'm from the East Coast, and Gwen here is from San Francisco."

Gwen knew immediately that Sam had taken pains not to say that he was from Washington, D.C. There was no use in arousing the man's suspicions even further. "I see you're from Germany," she said.

"Yes, we are."

Gwen smiled. "You seem to be quite proud of that." She glanced up at the Nazi flag. "Even the politics."

"Why shouldn't I be? Hitler has unified the German nation. He has taken a people who were mired in poverty and shame and given them a reason to hold their heads up once again." He stuck out his chin, as if to fulfill his own words. "Any German would be proud."

"Then why are you so afraid of strangers?" Brian asked.

Otto shifted in his chair and stared into Brian's eyes. "Because of people like you. This is a military state. Your American navy owns this island. They find innocent people like my wife and me and harass us constantly because of our politics. We see them snooping around here all the time, looking as to what we're doing and who we are seeing."

Helga edged over to his side, trying her best to show support for what he was saying.

"No doubt you're nothing more than a long line of what we've already seen."

"And you think the military here is dangerous?" Brian asked.

"Of course they're dangerous." He began to wave his arms. "Their spies are all over this island, prying into people's lives, going where they shouldn't go. They follow us everywhere."

"You ever met any of these spies?" Gwen asked.

The man straightened himself up in his chair. "Yes, I've seen them, and I know who they are."

Sam got to his feet. "If you know them, then you know we're not a part of that bunch. I don't see the point of continuing this any longer." He motioned in the direction of the telephone. "If you're going to call the cops and report us as trespassers, then do it and we'll all wait for them. Otherwise, my friends and I have better things to do."

He nodded at Gwen, who also rose off the couch, followed by Brian. "If you'll keep that attack dog of yours at bay, then we'll just be going on our way. We won't be using your beach."

The man exchanged looks with his wife. There seemed to be a moment of doubt, but as Sam moved to the door, the man got to his feet and followed them. Gwen stepped through the door, followed by Sam and Brian. The three of them made their way up the sandy road in the direction of where the car was parked. A large hedge of sharp bamboo stood alongside the road. The breeze rippled through it.

Brian stopped and looked back at the two of them. "They're the spies," he growled.

Sam nodded. "That about sums it up."

Gwen had been walking behind them, but she turned to look back at the dark beach. "You know what he was doing out there, don't you?" she said. "He was sending signals to a submarine off shore."

"No doubt things they couldn't trust to the radio office in Honolulu with everything they had," Sam added.

"If he knew about Naval Intelligence watching him, do you think he'd ever seen Aki?" Brian asked.

Gwen looked at him. Brian still had grief written all over his face. "If Aki knew about him, then no doubt he knew about her."

They spent the next several minutes discussing what they had seen in the house. Whatever kind of spies the Kuens were, they weren't careful about it. It was doubtful that anybody who knew their way around the world of espionage would be so bold as to let their politics stand out so glaringly.

"They're amateurs," Sam said.

Gwen nodded. "But dedicated amateurs."

"Just the kind of people who make mistakes," Sam added.

Brian bowed his head. "Yes, like killing someone when they don't have to."

Gwen's eyes drifted across the road to the large set of sandy hills that were opposite them. She thought she saw movement, like someone running behind the hills.

"I'm not sure even those people could be that stupid," Sam said. "For someone who is supposed to be part of the master race, neither one of them struck me as very bright."

Suddenly Gwen saw something else. The soft moonlight had picked up a glint of gunmetal on the top of the hill opposite them. She reached out and grabbed Sam and Brian, pulling them into the ditch below the bamboo.

Shots rang out; several shots that ripped into the dirt on the road and then into the bamboo over their heads.

Sam nudged Gwen and Brian and nodded his head in the direction of the bamboo overhead. "Let's go out that way. I'm not going out into that road."

Heaving themselves out of the ditch, they rolled for the spaces under the tall plants, squeezing themselves past the thick branches and crawling past the hedge on the other side. Scrambling to their feet, they began to run parallel to the road, keeping the bamboo between them and the hills beyond.

CHAPTER 37

D uskov strolled along the street, swinging a silver-tipped cane and wearing his white ice-cream suit and cream-colored Panama hat. As he passed the windows in the shops on Hotel Street, he smiled at his own likeness. He thought he looked very much like the dapper figure of Fred Astaire with the cane he was wielding. Of course he was a good four inches shorter and sixty pounds heavier than Astaire, and his pudgy face with thin mustache didn't look a thing like the man. Still, he could imagine. The cane helped.

Duskov had been studying the city and the islands. He knew that when the war was finally over, it might be difficult to determine just where the final boundaries would be drawn. Of course, he had positioned himself so that no matter who finally won, he'd come out on top. There was no sense in putting himself at risk for something he didn't believe in, and Duskov Popov believed in only one thing, Duskov Popov.

This area of Honolulu was known for several things. It was a part of Chinatown and, as such, had suffered. The Chinese had been brought to Hawaii to work the sugar plantations, and it hadn't taken them long to wear out their welcome. The area had burned to the ground and then been subjected to another fire in 1900. The difference was that the fire of 1900 had been deliberately set by the island authorities to rid the place of bubonic plague. At least that was what the people were told. It was also the red-light district in Honolulu and had been for years. The shore patrol from Pearl Harbor regularly prowled these streets, dragging sailors out of bars by the scruff of their necks.

He walked by an open market, ignoring the noise of women who were squatting on the sidewalk. They rocked back and forth and waved their hands toward him, trying to attract his attention. Their sounds went from an almost silent nod to a murmur and then escalated to fast gibberish and were finally punctuated by shrieks of desperation as he passed. Ducks were hanging with their bills down, almost as if they were ashamed to be displayed with no feathers. The heads of salmon were turning slowly on wires. Glassy, amber eyes appeared to follow him as he walked by. Snakes hung side by side with ginger, the aromas pungent in the afternoon air.

He passed by a sailor who had a Chinese woman hanging on his arm, slouching so she could look up into his eyes and continue her cooing. The sailor was her dinner, and everybody knew it but him.

He hurried across Maunakea street. The Wo Fat Restaurant was on the corner. It was a white pagoda-style building with a turret facing the street. The corners of the green tile roof were pointed up, and a gold-colored spire jutted into the sky from the top of the turret. Long green wooden shutters flanked the wide windows and doors. Inside the place was crowded with people leaning on their elbows and stuffing their faces with Cantonese-style food. No doubt the shamefaced ducks that had hung in the market only yesterday now graced the plates of the people inside. The crowd would make it harder for him to be seen and even harder for anyone to overhear his conversation.

He stepped through the doors and up to a woman dressed in a long, slinky, blue dress. Her hair was pulled neatly into a bun with a tortoiseshell comb. She widened a smile in his direction, parting her painted red lips.

"I'm here to meet someone." He waved a hand to ward her off.

She bowed slightly and continued her perpetual customer grin, wiggling her hips slightly.

The waiters were weaving their way in and out of the round polished tables, holding trays of food overhead. Aprons wrapped around their middles were smeared with grease and orange- and red-colored sauces.

Duskov stepped into the middle of the confusion, turning his head back and forth to look for the man he had seen only once before. The place was full of Chinese, and he knew the man would be hard to pick out. It wouldn't be hard for the man to recognize him, though. His white suit set him apart in a world of black mixed with bold colors. He had only taken a few steps when he saw the man waving at him from a booth beside a long window. He was seated with a Chinese girl on his arm. She leaned into him in one of those possessive meal-ticket embraces.

Duskov stepped around several tables, fighting for a chance to move without jarring a chair or running into a waiter. He walked over to the table, and the young man motioned for him to take a seat across from him. Taking off his hat, Duskov slid into the booth.

"I thought we were going to meet alone."

"Oh, her?" He grinned at the woman who had hardly taken her eyes off the man to acknowledge Duskov's presence. He patted her hand. "Don't worry. She doesn't speak a word of English." He laughed. "I sort of like them that way, no trouble, no back talk, just nods and grins. You should try it."

"I'm sort of busy right now."

"A man gets too busy, it messes up his head." He motioned to the woman and then at the table in front of him. "You've got to live a little, enjoy yourself."

Duskov could see the array of food in front of them was something not even the three of them could begin to finish. It was almost as if the man had ordered from the menu to impress the young woman with the idea that she'd never go hungry as long as she was with him. The web feet of a duck stuck up from the opening of a clay jar. So great had been the shame of the duck to be hanging on display, it appeared as if the thing had taken a shallow dive into a sauce of greasy brown elixir, never to come up again.

"Besides, you called this meeting. You can't expect me to set my life aside at a moment's notice, now can you?"

Duskov reluctantly shook his head. He knew this man was an amateur, an effective one to be sure, but he was playing a game that was totally out of his league. Duskov would have known that no matter what his contact had told him.

"Go ahead, eat. We set a place for you." He smiled at the young woman leaning into him. "Didn't we, sugar?"

The young woman continued to stare up into his eyes, then smiled broadly and nodded.

The man laughed. "Yes, and you're an empty-headed idiot, aren't you, darling?"

The young woman's expression never changed. She snuggled up to him all the more and giggled.

"You see," he flashed a smile at Duskov. "It's just you and me here."

Duskov scooted closer. He picked up a piece of sliced pork, dabbed it into the bright yellow hot mustard, then popped it into his mouth like candy. Most people wouldn't have dreamed of such a thing, but the sting of the mustard was almost comforting to him. It made him feel alive. "We have a problem."

"Problem? What problem?" He seemed to ignore Duskov, staring into the woman's eyes and then running his finger over the girl's cheek, lightly brushing it as an artist would lay a stroke of bright paint to a fresh canvas.

"That Japanese woman you said you'd take care of."

"Yeah, what about her?" He barely cast a glance in Duskov's direction. "I did take care of her. She's finished." Turning to face Duskov, his eyes twinkled with a glimmer of satisfaction. "Fact is, I kind of enjoyed it."

"I'm sure you did." Duskov looked at the woman, who was continuing to look at the man with wide-eyed admiration. He wondered just what her reaction might be if she knew how terrible and deadly this man could be to a woman. "But it's created another problem for us. This woman Aki has friends."

"Yeah, I know. I've seen them."

"You have?"

"Sure. They've been asking questions. It's only reasonable they would ask me." He let out a rumbling giggle, which sounded like a car engine having trouble turning over. "Of course I played dumb, and, besides, I have an airtight alibi. I'm no fool. They can chase their tails all they want."

"Well, these friends of hers are causing trouble. They're digging where they don't belong, and I'm afraid they're going to find something."

"Like what?"

"Our contact at the embassy told me this Aki woman had pinned him down as to what he was doing and when. She had become like a shadow to the man and was starting to worry him."

"And he thinks these friends of hers are doing the same thing?"

"Worse. Aki was Japanese. These people are not."

The man laughed. "Yeah, I know what the navy thinks of the Japanese."

"Then you know that Naval Intelligence might just listen to them, and that makes them even more dangerous, especially now. I can't impress on you enough how delicate the timing is. Our contact at the embassy is more nervous than ever. If this is exposed, then all the careful work he's done for over a year is going to go down the drain and take him along with it." He leaned forward on his elbows to get closer. "And they might be trying to find out what happened to this woman and stumble across something that's potentially far more dangerous."

"The cops already have their man. They've stopped looking. The heat's off."

"Our worry isn't the police; it's these friends of the woman. Our contact wants them taken care of."

"Then let him take care of them if he's so worried."

"He can't do that. The man's a diplomat. One little slip-up and he'd explode the whole thing. You've got to remember, he's a military man at heart, not a killer."

"You mean he doesn't like to kill people one at a time, just in bunches."

"Yes, and that's where we come in."

The man laughed. "Yeah, he bellyaches to you, and you tell me to kill them."

Duskov shrugged his shoulders. "It's not exactly like that. You believe in what we're doing here. You've got a share of this the same as he has." A sly grin spread across Duskov's face. It was like he recognized what might motivate the man if he couldn't appeal to his ideology. After all, he was a born killer, even if no one else knew it. He cleared his throat and picked up a sparerib. "Besides the woman involved is something you might just enjoy."

A grin crossed the man's face. "Yeah, I've seen her. She is quite the looker. I might just enjoy it at that."

CHAPTER 38

Gwen put down the phone and sheepishly stared at her father in the living room. He was reading a book on the history of Palestine, and Gwen knew it must have been interesting to him. His chair was tucked into the corner under an iron lamp that stood beside him and peeked over his shoulder. The glowing flute-shaped lampshade had streaks of brown burns flaring out from the bulb, testimony to its constant use.

Her father's sock feet were stretched out in front of him on a plaid overstuffed ottoman. He had a big toe protruding from a hole in one of his socks. Her father often found himself in his favorite chair with comfortable socks, air-conditioning, and an absorbing book. He looked up from his reading, his eyes probing her.

"What's wrong, honey?" He held his finger in the place in the book where he'd been reading. It was a hardback leather book, old and cracked at the binding. No doubt it was the kind of scholarly work that her father enjoyed, the kind that had to be explained. Her father loved explaining things. It was what he did best, and his eyes always lit up when he was doing it.

Gwen laughed. "It's nothing. You just look so comfortable there, as if you were born to occupy that position."

He looked down at his feet and wiggled his toes, including the bare one. "I guess I am a creature of habit."

"Yes, you are. I like that about you, Daddy." She stepped away from the phone. "You have something you're good at and you stick to it."

He laid the book down on his lap, staring first at her and then at the phone. "Trouble, I take it?"

She stepped toward him, wringing her hands slightly and wiping them across her fatigues. No matter how hard she tried, she had never been able to hide anything from her father. He seemed to see right through her. It was his job to see through people. Still, there were times it made her uncomfortable. "It's just something I have to do."

He put down the book. "It must be something unpleasant. You look nervous."

Gwen laughed. "Am I all that obvious?"

"To me you are. Anything I can do to help?"

"I'm afraid not, Daddy. I really don't want to drag you and Mom in on what I'm doing. It's best if I just see it through." She swallowed hard. "Do you mind if I use the car tonight?"

"No, not at all. You know where the keys are." He looked her over. "You look like you're going for a hike, but it's kind of late for that."

He opened the book and held it back up to read, then spoke to her from the other side of the cover. "Tomorrow is Thanksgiving, you know, and your mother's already been hard at work. We're expecting you and that reporter friend of yours."

"I can already smell it. We'll be here, and Sam will be pleased. I think he's actually looking for something that's homelike."

He lowered his book, his eyes peering above his half-moon reading glasses. "Is he looking to make a home with you?"

Gwen laughed and shook her head. "A night no doubt, but not a home."

"Maybe he just doesn't know how nice a home feels. Just be careful. Your mother will worry if she gets up and finds that you're not here."

Gwen picked up the keys from the table beside the door. "I will, Daddy." Stepping outside the door, she mashed her feet into her boots on the front porch and grabbed the laces, tugging them into place.

Minutes later she was rolling through the dark streets of Honolulu and onto the highway that led to Pearl Harbor. Brian said that he would wait for her at the gate and take her in on foot so her car wouldn't be noticed. The precaution might be unnecessary, but she needed to take care. Her job might depend on it.

Some time later her headlights hit the wide spot next to the chain-link fence that separated the naval base from the rest of the world. A number of cars were parked there, some of them facing the road with prices affixed to their windshields in a poor man's attempt to scuttle his past life on the islands before being shipped back to the States. She pulled up next to an old Chevrolet that had FIFTY BUCKS written in bold red letters across a poster board tucked under the wiper blade. A name and phone number were under the words, and the rain had streaked the letters to bloody rivulets.

She got out of her car and locked the door.

"Psst."

Her head whipped around. Brian was standing on the other side of the fence in his khaki uniform.

"If you pull up closer, you can stand on the hood and come over the fence," he said.

She nodded and unlocked the door, sliding back into her seat. She edged the Ford up to the fence. When she saw the metal chain links bulge from the soft push of her bumper, she switched off the ignition and got out. Scampering onto the hood of the car, she placed her hands on the top of the fence, swinging her hips back and forth to make sure she got good movement into her jump. Brian was standing below her on the other side, his arms outstretched. He looked sure of himself, and that gave Gwen some comfort. She wasn't quite ready to wear a cast.

She jumped, landing her left foot on the top of the fence and then vaulting over the sharp edges and down into Brian's waiting arms. He staggered when she landed, but held her firm while easing her to the ground.

"I think it's a little too early to do what we planned. Too many people around," Brian said.

Gwen nodded. "Yes, you're probably right. I think I was a little overanxious about this. I'd like to get done with it. The longer we wait, the more time I have to think about it."

"The basement of the intelligence office will be empty," he said. "They've all gone home. It's much too late for the navy to be intelligent."

The two of them walked through the grounds and over to where Brian's quarters were situated. The night shadows of tree branches writhed across the walkway, hiding them from time to time from the soft glowing streetlights that illuminated the signs on the base. In a typically creative military way, the streets were numbered and then lettered so that a corner might be marked G-17. Brian's quarters were on K-24. It made perfect sense to the navy.

They sat in Brian's tiny apartment, making small talk and listening to the sunflower-shaped clock on the wall loudly tick away the hours. Unlike the rest of his beige, military-issue decor, the beaming yellow clock was strangely whimsical. Big bobbing petals framed the face. The hands were made of twisted green stems with broad leaves on the ends pointing to the numbers. It reminded Gwen of Aki, cheerful and happy. No doubt it was her handiwork, a gift that Brian would always look at and think of her.

"What do you hope to find in there?" Brian asked.

Gwen scooted to the edge of the chair. "I want to know what Aki knew. It might just be what got her murdered."

Brian shook his head. "Maybe, maybe not. It might not have had anything to do with her job. It might just have been her."

"Do you seriously think your father had anything to do with her being killed?"

Brian got to his feet and stepped over to the window. The late-night breeze was rippling the curtains, and he stared out at the darkness, his hands clamped behind his back. "I don't know what to think."

He shook his head, continuing to stare out the window. "He might have tried to talk with her and just got carried away. I don't think he's capable of planning such a thing."

Turning around, he looked at her, curling his lip slightly. "He's used to controlling things and people. Everything he does is for a reason. He knows just where he wants to go." He jabbed his finger in her direction. "And what's more, he knows where he wants you to go. You can go the easy way or you can go the hard way, but either way you go."

The anger on his face made Gwen uncomfortable. She wasn't used to that kind of emotion when a man spoke about his father. She had never known anything but love and trust for her own.

She got to her feet. "We'd better get going. No doubt the place is a ghost town by now, especially since tomorrow is Thanksgiving."

They hurried across the grounds to the building that housed Naval Intelligence. A young Marine stood guard outside, and Gwen took out her Naval Intelligence badge and held it up for him to see. He leaned over and tried to focus his bleary eyes, then blinked at her. "Kinda late, ain't it?"

Gwen nodded and smiled. "Yes. It won't take long."

The man opened the door and snapped his heels together lazily.

Gwen and Brian moved down the empty hall, the echo of their footsteps sounding down the corridor. They made the turn that led to the basement stairs, and Brian spotted the door he had in mind. He opened it and pulled her inside. It was a broom closet with mops and push brooms standing in a confused mass in the corner along with a collection of painted buckets. Gwen reached into her back pocket and pulled out the flashlight she had brought. Brian closed the door behind them as she turned it on.

He pulled a smaller light from his pocket and switched it on, flashing it on the ceiling. "There it is." He was pointing to a small opening with a plasterboard covering.

"It goes into the ventilation system," he went on. "We can get to the basement that way and won't have to go through the guard at the door. Here, I'll lift you up."

He stuck the light in his pocket and put his fingers together, forming a step.

Gwen stepped into his hands and heaved herself up. She pushed on the door to the opening, and it gave way. Shoving it aside, she lifted herself into the darkness. Soon she found herself inside the metal tunnel that wound its way under the skin of the building. She gave Brian a hand. Gwen was sweating.

Brian led the way. They moved along the dark passageway, Brian's light flashing back and forth ahead of them. Gwen moved carefully, sliding her boots forward so she wouldn't make noise.

Brian stopped at a corner. "This is where it leads to the basement. We'll have to slide down carefully, 'cause we'll be landing just above where the guard normally sits."

"Oh, fine," Gwen whispered.

"Here, come around me and I'll lower you as far as I can."

Gwen squeezed herself around him and positioned herself on her stomach, her feet dangling down the long metal slope that led to the basement area. Brian took both of her hands and lowered her as far as he could. She nodded and slipped down into the darkness, sliding along the smooth metal and doing as best she could to keep her speed down; stopping herself occasionally by digging her boots into the sides of the chute.

Shortly after she heard Brian coming. His shoes didn't have the traction of her boots, and that made his speed dangerously close to creating a tumble when he hit the landing. She braced herself. He hit her, forcing a stifled grunt.

Both of them got to their knees and stared into each other's faces. "One question," she asked. "How are we going to get out of here?"

"We'll just take that as it comes."

"Well, you'd better think of it. I don't want to be around when they all get back to work."

"They'll be gone for days. It's the Thanksgiving weekend."

They inched down to the offices that made up the nerve center of Naval Intelligence. Several grates in the metal passage marked openings to the floor below. Brian picked one and yanked on the bars. It gave way. He then lifted up the plasterboard and lowered himself over the side.

Moments later Gwen followed him, dropping into his arms in the darkness. She straightened herself up. "Do you know where we are?"

Brian switched on his light and shined it around the large collection of desks. "I'm not sure. I've been here once with Aki and got the tour." He held the light out, sending a stiff beam down a long hall. "It might be down there. She shared an office with five other people."

Gwen followed him down the hall, passing a series of maps with pins on them. The familiar LOOSE LIPS SINK SHIPS seemed to be everywhere. Obviously the confidence this saying inspired would have kept everyone quiet about what they were doing.

Brian stepped into an office and shone his light. "This is it, I think." He pointed to a desk in the corner. "That's Aki's desk over there."

"Do you think they've cleared out her things?"

"This is the navy. I doubt it."

Gwen moved to the desk. She could see that it was Aki's. There were photographs of her family, a small frame with Dai's picture in it, and one that had Brian in uniform. Fortunately, Gwen knew just where to look. Aki had made that clear. She lifted up the ink blotter on the desk and picked up several pieces of paper.

"Is that what we're looking for?"

Gwen put the beam of her flashlight on them. "Yes, I think so."

"All right. Put those things down your shirt and let's get out of here."

"How are we going to do that?"

Brian took a deep breath. "We're just going to walk out the door."

"You've got to be kidding?"

"Not in the least. That's a Marine guard out there. They follow strict orders. They keep people from getting in here, not from getting out."

Gwen shook her head. "Unbelievable."

"I doubt he'll even check our ID. Keep walking and follow my lead. Just smile and look like you know what you're doing."

Gwen folded the papers and stuffed them down her shirt. She followed Brian down the hall to the outer office and then down another hall to the small crack of light she could see beyond the two metal doors.

Brian opened the door and stepped into the light, then held it for her. "So who do you think will really win the Rose Bowl this year?"

Gwen could see the Marine guard at his desk. The man bounced forward in his chair and seemed to stagger as he braced himself at the small table. She could see the look of shock on his face.

"Good night, Corporal." Brian gave the man a slight wave of his hand. "We're finally done."

"And going home," Gwen added. She stepped quickly behind Brian. "USC, of course. Who else ever plays in the Rose Bowl?"

Brian laughed.

CHAPTER 39

S am finished shaving, wiping the last of the foam away from
the lower portion of his right ear with a damp washcloth. The
rose-colored towels and washcloths were beginning to wear
on him. What had once seemed like bright and cheery colors now
seemed drab and pitifully plain to him. Everything about the Pink
Palace was the same, muted rose and pink, for as far as a man could
see.

He closed the straight razor and slipped it into its green velvet
pouch. Picking up a small bottle of bay rum, he splashed a little onto
his hands and rubbed them vigorously into his cheeks and chin. At

least it smelled familiar, not at all like the constant island smells of orchids or soy sauce.

He pulled his collar together and buttoned it, then slipped the four-in-hand knot into position under his chin, pulling the Kelly green-and-red-striped tie into a crisp, sharp line. He then ran a comb through his hair. He had to look good today. He wanted to impress Gwen's parents, even if he couldn't impress her.

His cream-colored suit wasn't his favorite. It looked too much like the one Popov wore every day, and he was tired of even seeing the man, much less being reminded of what he wore. But it would have to do. It was clean and pressed, and it might make a nice statement to Gwen's parents.

He walked over to the bed and put his loafer-clad feet one at a time on the bed, buffing his shoes with a cloth he had packed for just such an occasion. If he couldn't win Gwen's heart, he would at least conquer her mother's heart. Women were like that. There were special bonds between a mother and her daughter. They tended to listen to each other, even if they weren't listening to words.

He stepped over and took one more look in the mirror. It totally escaped him why he should care what Gwen thought of him. He had plenty of glamorous women back in D.C. But he did care. Gwen was different. She was his equal and someone he respected. It was a different feeling for him.

Grabbing the bouquet of carnations he had purchased the night before, he headed out the door, closing it behind him and shaking the knob. Nothing was secure from Naval Intelligence. If they wanted to search his room, they would. This was their island, after all. They had the run of the place. He was the outsider and knew it. His life, or what was left of it, was an open book to those people.

He marched down the hall and took the elevator to the empty hotel lobby. There weren't many tourists loose on the island on Thanksgiving, and just the sight of him was enough to grab the attention of the bellboys in their red coats. Across the lobby, he spotted one of the men who had been his constant tail. He was the Mutt member of the duo. Jeff must have been on a break.

Sam smiled and walked over to him. He tapped the newspaper Mutt had suddenly stuck in his face.

The man lowered the paper, glaring at him with hollow, sleepy eyes.

"Just to save yourself some time," Sam grinned. "I'm going to Gwen Williams's house today for Thanksgiving. I'll be there all day and then return to my room. Thought you might want to know."

Gwen spent the morning in the kitchen helping her mother with dinner. The years spent in Japan hadn't diminished the Williams's taste for a traditional Thanksgiving feast. If anything, it had heightened it. Turkeys could not be found in Japan, and pigeon had never been a good substitute. Gwen stirred the mashed potatoes and watched her mother put together the stuffing. Doris Williams's stuffing was legendary. It contained oysters and sausage, mixed with pecans and pine nuts. The butter gave it adequate moisture. People raved about it, and Gwen wanted to memorize every step.

Scooping fistfuls of the stuffing and cramming them into the large bird, her mother looked over at her. "You go change now and put on something pretty."

Gwen looked at her plain print dress. She put down the spoon and ran her hand over her dress, smoothing it. "This dress will do fine, Mom. It's just us. It's really no big deal."

"No, it will not. Not with a man coming over. I won't have you looking that way. You change and go for a walk to cool off."

"He's just a friend, Mom. He'll never be anything else."

"You don't know that."

"Yes I do, Mother. Sam's a nice man, but that's as far as it goes."

Gwen could see her mother wasn't happy. Doris bit her lower lip. "That is exactly what I said about your father, almost word for word. Now you go change, young lady. Right now."

Gwen didn't have a hard time choosing a dress to wear. After all, she'd come to the islands to work, not entertain. With one or two exceptions, her wardrobe was functional, not fashionable. Fortunately, one of the exceptions hung in the tiny closet of the guest bedroom. The sleeveless, saffron yellow V neck was soft silk and fit her snuggly to the waist. The skirt was gathered with a sheer chiffon overskirt dyed to match and embroidered with hundreds of tiny yellow flowers. Gwen spun in front of the mirror. She didn't get to wear the dress much. It emphasized her long neck and wide shoulders. She laughed, feeling silly but strangely excited. Shoes weren't much of a problem. She hadn't brought any heels to finish the ensemble. A pair of soft leather ballerina-type slippers would have to do. *Besides*, Gwen rationalized, *they're much more suited to walking.*

She stepped out of her room, holding her slippers in her hand, and walked past the kitchen, stopping in front of the door. "Is this all right Mother?" She turned around slowly, forcing a smile.

Her mother continued to stir the gravy, a broad smile forming on her face. "Yes, dear. That looks lovely. Now go for your walk in the park. But be back in an hour." Her smile turned into a grin. "We don't want to leave your friend with your father for too long, now do we?"

The thought gave Gwen some degree of satisfaction. Her father would be Sam's intellectual equal in every way and, unlike her mother, her father wasn't gnawing at the bit in anticipation of grandchildren. If anything, any man who showed any degree of interest in Gwen would have a lot to prove where her father was concerned.

She walked through the living room. "I'm going for a walk, Daddy, as Mother ordered."

He lowered his paper. "That's good. You look lovely."

Gwen glanced down at her dress. "Again, Mother's orders."

He grinned. "Your mother knows best."

"Maybe, but I can't see the purpose of it."

"Perhaps you will." He raised his paper when she stepped out the door.

The park was only two blocks away, and Gwen walked down the street, taking in the sounds of the birds overhead. Minutes later she reached the brick walkway that led under the arch that formed the entrance to the park. Two iron dragons were perched above her head on the redbrick gates.

Out of the corner of her eye, Gwen noticed a man follow her up the brick walkway. No doubt he'd been sent out for the same reason she had been ordered to leave, to get out from underfoot while dinner was being prepared.

She walked through a grove of large banyan trees. Their trunks were huge, with branches that twisted in midair and spread over the walkway. A minute later she came to the redbrick plaza with white concrete benches surrounding a large fountain. She could still see the man behind her. The plaza with its fountain was evidently popular with him too.

She darted down a lesser traveled path, between hibiscus bushes that were in bloom. She picked up her pace, gathering her billowy dress so that she could walk faster. Coming to a fork with three possible paths, she took the one to her right and scampered over stones set in a running stream.

Her heart skipped a beat when she turned slightly and saw that the man had followed her down the lonely path. She began to run up the hill.

S am pulled up outside the Williams house and got out. He yanked at the white convertible top, pulling it to cover the interior but not clamping it in place. That way the top would protect the seats from a sudden shower yet allow him to put it back rather quickly when he left. Reaching in, he pulled out the bouquet of carnations.

As he was knocking at the door, he noticed the array of shoes neatly lined up in rows. Sam scooted his loafers off and left them at the end of the line.

The door opened, and a tall, well-built older man smiled at him and held out his hand. "You must be Sam. I'm Jack Williams, Gwen's father."

Sam stepped in and shook his hand. "Pleased to meet you, Mr. Williams."

Jack looked at the flowers and smiled. "And you brought flowers for Gwen."

Sam shook his head. "No, sir. Actually, these are for your wife."

"My, my, won't she be pleased? You just step into the living room and I'll get her."

Sam walked behind the man into the large living room and waited as instructed. Jack soon returned, with his wife trailing behind him. She stepped toward Sam and extended her hand. "I'm so glad to meet you, Sam. We've heard so much about you. I'm Doris Williams."

Sam shook her hand. "Really? That does surprise me, Mrs. Williams. I would think your daughter doesn't say much about any man." He watched the expression on her face. She tightened her lips. He could tell that he had indeed struck it right. Gwen's father might be suspicious about men, but her mother was worried about Gwen. A man is more independent, and the idea of a single daughter reflecting that choice for a time didn't seem to be all that unusual. Women, however, were more driven by security. There was a nesting instinct, and if Gwen didn't feel it, her mother certainly did.

"He brought you flowers," Jack said.

"Is that so?" She smiled broadly and took the carnations. "They're beautiful."

"It's the least I could do for your kind hospitality, Mrs. Williams. Thanksgiving in a hotel just doesn't seem right. You saved me from that."

Gwen moved quickly through the bushes, leaving the path and searching back down the hill for the running stream. She bounced down the slope, dodging bushes full of thorns but occasionally snagging her dress.

Large thorn bushes were on the other side of the running stream, their layers of green spikes pointed in her direction. Flame red flowers peeked through the spear-shaped leaves like drops of blood.

Gwen removed her slippers, stepping into the stream. The cool water licked around her toes and ankles. She began to move downstream, slowly at first, then picking up her feet and scurrying over the rocks and down into the deeper pools. She held the shirt of her dress as the cool water lapped against her calves. She took several turns in the stream, holding on to the outstretched branches of ferns.

There was a sound behind her. She turned her head sharply. A splashing sound, the noise of someone wading into the water she had just come through. Pushing ahead, she scrambled onto the rocks and began to jump from one stony platform to the next. There was no mistake about it. This was not someone casually following her through the park. This was someone who was determined.

Her heart was beating furiously. Someone had marked her for a target, someone who thought she was easy prey.

Greensword plants were on either side of the stream, their large bulbs bristling with thorns. Gwen stepped out of the water on the hilly side and, using her skirt to protect her hands, spread them apart. She stumbled onto the pathway. Clear. Not a soul in sight.

She put the slippers back on her feet and began to move fast along the side of the hill. She was going to give the man a run if nothing else. He would be breathing hard when he hit the hill.

There was a bend in the path where a large banyan tree was standing. It had one branch continuing up the hill and another going back to the street. If the man was going to try to cut her off, he would go in that direction. The question was, could she get there first?

She picked up her feet, pounding on the path as she ran. She swung around the large tree and ran through what seemed like a forest of tall ferns, brushing them aside as she cut through them, running smack into a man's arms.

She flailed away at his chest with her fists and then backed out of his arms, holding them. It was Sam.

"Hey, sugar. Hold on there."

"Oh, Sam." She fell into his arms, holding him. "It's you."

"Of course it's me. Who were you expecting, King Kong?"

She looked around at the path behind her, panting. "No, someone's been following me since I came into the park."

He grinned. "Then he better be glad he didn't find you. You pack a mean punch."

CHAPTER 40

Sam spent most of the next several days following Popov, making careful notes about who the man talked to and where he went. Since Gwen had been so frightened by the person who had followed her into the park, it had become a personal matter with him, not just a story. He was driving himself now, not taking anything lightly. Story or not, the sooner he got to the bottom of what was happening, the sooner Gwen would feel safe.

Sam knew, however, that she still hadn't taken him into her confidence. She hadn't told him everything she knew. There was the matter of her being Naval Intelligence and him being the grubby reporter who might sell his soul for a byline. It had become a barrier between the two of them. To make matters worse, Sam wasn't quite sure what he wanted. Was he, in fact, trying to use her to get to the front page of newspapers all over the country, or did he care about her? Both might be true. But if Gwen had any place in Sam's future, he knew he couldn't just use her, no matter how good the stuff was that was in her brain. He had to find things out on his own.

Gwen did tell him one thing, but it had taken the scare in the park to do that. She told him where she had gone and the men she had met in her investigation of Aki's murder. Sam had worked hard at convincing her that her stalker could have been connected to the murder and not to Japanese espionage. She was still trying to keep him at arm's length from her Naval Intelligence business. But in point of fact, Sam knew the two things were most likely one and the same.

He would start at the top of the list, men who had known Aki and had also met Gwen. Without knowing it, she may have stepped on toes best left undisturbed. But he hadn't been able to shake the idea that somehow Popov was connected. He was the mastermind behind what went on here. It was Popov's business to know what should be done, not some Japanese attaché. The man had been in his cross hairs for days now, so close and so very obvious.

Gwen had talked with Sam about her meeting with Hiroki. The man seemed to be a perfect fit. He not only had a Japanese ancestry but also had political leanings as well. And he had threatened Aki. He would be the ideal tool for a man like Popov.

Mutt and Jeff had been following him all morning, and Sam had lost interest in seeing just where they were and what they were doing. He didn't care if they saw him talking to this Hiroki fella. It might even be better that way. From the way Gwen painted the man, he might need to have Naval Intelligence keeping track of him, and if Sam could provide the impetus, he was more than delighted to do so.

He walked along the street and stopped occasionally to stare into a window. That was more for Mutt and Jeff's benefit than for anything else. If they thought he didn't care or had lost interest in trying to spot them, they might just wonder what he was up to. navy gumshoes were simple men that way. If he gave them something they had seen before, they were happy. If he surprised them with a curve ball, they just might do something stupid. Sam didn't need anyone doing anything stupid.

The stores in the district had changed over the years, from mom-and-pop five-and-ten-cent stores to pawn shops to Army-Navy surplus stores.

He turned and continued his walk. Sitting on the sidewalk was what appeared to be a harmless barfly. The old man with the pock-marked face held out a tin cup with long, shaky fingers. The cup wobbled slightly as he held it out. His blue eyes searched Sam's as he looked up at him. "Hey, mister," he said. "I know you. I seen you afore."

Sam stopped. "I don't think so, pal. I don't know you."

The man forced his empty cup higher in the air. "Sure you do. I'm your long-lost pappy." A grin spread across his face, showing bright yellow and missing teeth. "You gonna give me a dime?"

Sam reached down and grabbed the man's hand, hauling him to his feet. "I'm going to give you something better than that."

"What's that?" The old man wobbled on his feet, grabbing the lamppost to steady himself.

Sam tugged on the man's sleeve, pulling him toward the door to the Army-Navy supply store. The bell over the door rang as Sam opened it. A man in his mid forties was behind a counter. His brows arched as Sam dragged the old derelict closer to the counter. "You think you can fix this fella up with some clothes and shoes?" Sam asked.

"I don't know. We usually don't do much for old Pete here. We don't wait on his type."

"Well, you're waiting on me. And this ain't exactly Saks Fifth Avenue you're running here. Just find something that fits old Pete."

The man scratched his chin, studying Pete. He went to the stacks and came back with several sets of trousers and two shirts, both khaki in color. It took Pete some time to try on the clothes, but soon he was standing in front of the mirror in a mismatched set of clothes. His shirt was one of the khakis, and the pants were a set of deep green fatigues. He had boots on his feet, white tube socks underneath.

Sam paid the shopkeeper and led Pete back outside, standing him next to the lamppost. "There ya go. Let me see your cup."

Pete held up the tin cup, and Sam fished into his pocket and produced a quarter. He dropped it into the cup. "That ought to do you. You're dressed so nice now, you don't have to ask for dimes. You can ask for quarters."

"Thank you, mister."

"And you don't have to be my father, either. You're somebody's father, and that's good enough for me."

He straightened the man's collar. "If you know what's good for you, you'll use that quarter for food."

Pete nodded.

"See ya around," Sam said. He gave the man a slight salute.

He walked off feeling a little better about his day. It actually felt good to help somebody who couldn't help him for a change. Perhaps it had been his concern over caring about Gwen, giving her attention because of what she could do for him in the way of information. Old Pete could do nothing for him.

Sam walked another block before he came in sight of the Red Lips Bar. The neon sign was going out, and only the upper lip glowed. Even that was flashing. He opened the smoky-glass door, releasing a cloud of cigarette smoke.

The bar stools were dark Naugahyde with chrome legs. Sam walked up to the bar and slid onto one of them. The large Samoan bartender, who was busy at the other end, spotted him and nodded. It gave Sam a chance to give the place a look. The small dance floor was empty; the jukebox had lights and bubbles that percolated up the sides. The bar itself was shiny and black, Formica, Sam guessed. That made it easy to clean, and it was cheap. Beside the register where Sam was seated was a large jar of cigars. At least they would be pure. He doubted this place did much business with tourists, and, from the look of the clientele, all Japanese, he rather doubted it would.

The Samoan stepped over to him. "What'll it be, mister?"

"I'll take a draft beer." He pointed to the jar. "And one of your cigars."

"Help yourself," the man said.

Sam reached for the jar, removed the lid, and took out a large double corona. He bit the end off and spit it on the floor. This was a place that screamed out for people to be impolite, and Sam was happy to oblige. Picking up a match from a tin cup, he raked it on a block of wood that sat next to it. Holding the flame under the tip, he puffed the cigar to life.

The man came back with the beer. "That'll be seventy-five cents for the beer and the cigar."

Sam reached into his pocket and peeled off two one-dollar bills. Laying them on the table, he could see a slight grin cross the man's face. "I'd like some information too. I'm looking to find a man."

"Sure." The Samoan rang up the sale and stuffed the extra bill into his pocket. "I'll help you if I can."

"I'm looking for a guy named Hiroki."

"Hiroki Fujiyama?"

"Yeah. I think that's his name."

The Samoan pointed a thick stubby finger over to a table in the back corner of the room. "He's over at that table. He's facing us right now."

Sam turned around and saw a group of young men. They were smoking and laughing. He got to his feet. "Thanks," he said.

He held the cigar clenched in his teeth and walked though the empty tables in the direction of the man the bartender had pointed out. When he stepped up to the table, he blew out a cloud of smoke. "Any of you named Hiroki?"

The man seated across from him looked up. He was wearing an open-collar black shirt with a string of colored beads around his neck. He seemed to sneer with his upper lip. "We don't do tours. Go see the local boys on the beach."

"I'm not here for a tour. I have a business proposition for a Hiroki Fujiyama."

The other men at the table turned to look at Sam. He continued to grin with confidence, puffing on his cigar.

"Well, that's me," the man said. "So what's the deal? Why do you want me?"

"This isn't something I can discuss here." Sam glanced down at the four other sets of eyes staring at him. "Too many people around."

"You can say anything in front of my friends."

Sam shook his head. "No, you can say anything in front of your friends. I can't. What I have to say is for your ears only."

Hiroki looked around at the gathered men and shrugged his shoulders. Then he got to his feet. "There's a back door and an alley. We can talk back there."

"Sounds perfect."

Sam followed the man past a set of black curtains and down a narrow hall. Hiroki pushed on the bar that sprang open a heavy metal door. The two of them stepped out onto a back porch and then down a set of steps into the alley.

When they got to the bottom step, Sam reached out with his foot and pushed Hiroki headlong into a pile of rubber tires.

The man yelped as he tumbled straight into them. "What the—?"

He didn't have a chance to finish. Sam was on him in a flash. He picked him up and sent a stiff punch into his belly. The blow buckled Hiroki into a pained expression. He doubled over.

"Are you following Gwen Williams?"

"Who's Gwen Williams?" Hiroki had to push hard to croak the words out of his mouth.

Sam hit him a sharp blow with the edge of his hand to the side of his jaw. "You know who she is. She came to see you. Attractive brunette. You followed her into the park."

Hiroki shook his head and put his hand to his aching jaw. "I didn't follow her."

Sam launched another blow into Hiroki's midsection, which caused Hiroki to stumble backward into the brick wall. Sam reached out and grabbed Hiroki's shirt, jabbing his cheek with a fast flurry of several punches.

The blows dropped Hiroki to his knees. He looked up at Sam. "Who are you?"

"Let's just say I'm her protector. Anything happens to her, and I mean anything, she stubs her toe or gets scared by a catfight in the middle of the night, then I'm going to come looking for you."

Hiroki held up his hands. "I didn't do anything to her."

"But you did to her friend Aki Kawa." Sam kicked him in the chest, knocking him to the ground. "You killed her."

Sam reached down and pulled Hiroki up by the shirt. He cocked his arm, preparing to send another blow to the man's face. "You killed her just as sure as you're breathing, which may not be for long."

"No, I didn't kill her. We scared her, but we didn't kill her."

Sam opened his hand and gave the man a slap across the face. "You're lying. You knew she was there. You knew that's where she was going. Nobody knew that but you."

"Yes, they did. I told Mitch, Mitch Krinkle."

Sam reached down and pulled him up by the lapels of his shirt. "You told Krinkle? When?"

"I was at the baseball game. He asked me if I'd seen Aki, and I told him where she was."

Sam heard the back door open. The four men who had been seated around Hiroki came down the stairs. He dropped Hiroki to the cobblestones and turned to face them. Two of them had a knife.

The first man rushed him, and Sam wheeled around and tossed him, knife first, into a pile of crates. When he turned back, he was met by a hard blow from the second man. The man's fist caught Sam square on the chin, sending him back on his heels. But he didn't go down. The attackers fanned out.

"Hey now, what's going on?"

Sam looked up and saw Mutt and Jeff at the entrance to the alley. The two intelligence officers had drawn their revolvers and were walking toward the group surrounding Sam.

The men dragged Hiroki to his feet and back up the stairs. Within minutes Hiroki and his cronies were gone.

The taller of the two agents, the one Sam referred to as Jeff, put his revolver away and asked, "Are you all right?"

"I am now. I never thought I'd live to say this, but I'm glad to see you fellas. What made you come to my rescue like this? It's not your thing to interfere."

The short squatty agent that Sam thought of as Mutt put his gun away and smiled. "Anybody who would buy clothes for a drunk and not just walk past him can't be all bad in our book."

CHAPTER 41

Gwen dashed out the door when she saw Sam's car pull up in front of her house. She stumbled to push her feet into her black pumps on the porch. The white blouse and pleated blue skirt would make her look conservative, but this was going to be a day with the navy. She would have to look the part, especially if she was going to get anyone to listen to her. She clutched her black handbag and a brown leather attaché binder that held the important papers she had to show. They might be the only thing that could save her from disgrace. Time was getting to be an issue, and she knew full well that the clock on the Japanese wall was ticking.

She raced down the walkway. Pulling up a white scarf, she tied it tightly under her chin. If Sam was going to insist on driving with the wind in his face, then she was determined not to let her hair suffer for it.

"Wow, didn't take you long," Sam said.

Gwen opened the door and folded herself into the cramped seat. "I've been watching for you."

Sam grinned. "You're betraying your sex, angel. Don't let it get around that you're ready for a man who comes for you. You're worth the wait. Make 'em do it."

"Just drive," she quipped.

Sam started the engine and threw it into gear. "What's got your tail feathers on fire?"

"Chief Morrow called me this morning. He wants to see me."

"Well, good. Maybe now we're getting somewhere."

Gwen shot him a hard look as he pulled out into the street. Sam had no obligation to read her mind and little or no understanding of just how the navy worked. With the U.S. Navy, no news was good news, and a summons was always bad.

She turned and faced the road, her expression hard as a rock. "Don't count on it. I've never been asked to come to a supervisor's office in order to hear him say 'good work.' It's bad news. I know it."

"You haven't been stepping on people's toes, have you?"

Gwen's mind raced. In many ways she'd always been the perfect employee, just thought of as part of a brainy few who stayed with the books and didn't make waves. Her job had been largely academic, studying the Japanese language and mentality for her bosses in San Francisco. But now she'd gotten personally involved. Aki meant something to her. She was a face, not just a set of books. "In a big way."

"What did you do?"

Gwen turned to look at him. "Brian and I broke into the Naval Intelligence Office. We had to get something from Aki's desk."

"And they saw you?"

She shook her head. "No, we weren't caught, if that's what you mean. But we were seen. The navy takes a while to put two and two together, but they might have a couple of marines who could swear they saw me that night."

Sam steered the car onto the highway that led to Pearl City. "Then let's hope that little midnight excursion of yours doesn't come back to haunt you. I wish you wouldn't do things like that without telling me."

"Now how can I tell you things like that? It's navy business and you're a reporter."

Sam shot her a look and winced. "And that means I don't care? You read me wrong. I've put myself on the line for you here, done far more than I should have, and because I do care. I want to find Aki's killer as bad as you do." He focused on the road and then spoke in his normal tone of voice. "I did talk with this Hiroki fella yesterday."

His face was turned away from her, but she could see that his mind was spinning. "What did you find out? Was he the one who followed me into the park?"

Sam didn't look at her, just continued to drive. It was like he was letting the silence and her curiosity work its way when he couldn't get through to her any other way. "He wasn't exactly the most coopera- tive guy. But he finally had plenty to say."

"And?"

"He denied following you into the park. That didn't surprise me. Few stalkers would admit to such a thing."

"What did surprise you?"

He looked at her. "Quid pro quo, sugar. You tell me what was in Aki's desk, and I'll tell you what I managed to strangle out of Hiroki."

"Look, this is navy business, navy property."

"Fine. Suit yourself." Sam focused on the road, his eyes riveted to the white lines. "And what I found out is the property of the *Washington Post*. I swap mine for yours. It's a fair deal in my book. I can promise you one thing. I won't break the news until I have your say-so."

He looked at her, a slight smile creasing his lips. "You might just want me to, though. There's something about a headline that grabs the War Department's attention. I can scream louder than you can, much louder."

Gwen thought the matter over. She really had nothing to lose by trusting Sam, and she knew he was right. Bold headlines just might be the only way to slap the War Department in the face and get them to pay attention. "All right." Gwen paused for a moment, hesitating one last time. "Aki had a bomb plot designation for Ford Island."

"Battleship row?"

"Yes. It was sent to Tokyo. The location of the American battleships along with the depth of the water and the exact distances from where torpedoes could be launched by planes."

Sam let out a loud whistle. "Man, sugar, that is serious. Surely they can't deny that?"

"They can deny anything they want to. Now what about your news?"

Sam nodded. "It would seem that our man Hiroki was at a company ball game the night Aki was murdered. He happened to tell Mitch Krinkle just where he could find her."

They pulled up outside the gate, and Gwen showed her badge to the marine guard who waved her in. Moments later they were parking out in front of the Naval Intelligence headquarters. Gwen heaved a sigh. Being charged with a security violation would disgrace her parents.

She got out of the car and leaned in to get Sam's attention. "You'd better wait for me here. What Morrow has to tell me shouldn't take long."

Gwen marched across the street, holding her head high. This was a man's world, and every time she went into it she felt a surge of adrenaline. It was more a fight than a fright feeling.

She walked down the long corridor, the smell of ammonia assaulting her nostrils. Not only was the navy clean, but the navy wanted everyone to know how clean it could be. The tile on the floor looked wet. Fresh wax no doubt. She took the steps leading down to the basement, wondering all the way if the marine guard on duty that night had reported the people who had left so late. Brian had been right. The man was responsible to keep people out, not keep them in. But that might not have stopped his curiosity, and he could have reported it. He should have reported it. Gwen wasn't hard to describe, either, and she was one of the few women who actually knew the place.

The guard at the table had her name on his list. He got up and held the door open for her. Moments later, she stood outside Chief Morrow's open door. She knocked lightly.

The man lifted his head from his paperwork and motioned her in. "Close the door," he said.

Gwen shut the door and stepped in front of his desk. He handed her an envelope and continued writing on a pad of paper in front of him.

"What's this?" Gwen asked.

"It's your walking papers, girlie."

Gwen ripped open the envelope and read the orders. They were from her home office in San Francisco ordering her to report on Monday, December 8. She lowered the papers and looked at the top of Morrow's head. He wasn't even giving her the courtesy of paying her any attention. "Are you responsible for this?"

He looked up at her and leaned forward. "No, I'd say you are. They are giving you another week to tie your affairs up here, and it's only because of your boss back in California that we're not bringing you up on charges. All in all, I'd say you were lucky." He grunted slightly, eyeballing her. "Maybe you weren't lucky. Maybe you're just a woman."

Gwen stepped closer to the man's desk. She stuck out her chin. "Yes, I am. But frankly I'd hate to be in your shoes when this thing happens. When the Japanese begin their bombing, people are going to come to you with questions, questions that you're not going to be able to answer. Men will die, and you will be responsible then, like it or not." Her lip quivered. "And you'll have to tell them that a woman warned you and that you didn't listen."

Morrow leaned back in his chair and crossed his arms. "If they ever do attack, it will be in the East Indies or MacArthur in the Philippines. They ain't coming here, missy. The Japanese are already here."

Gwen stopped at the open door and looked back at him. "You know, my friends and I had a couple of shots taken at us the other night. If it was your goons who were trying for us, I'd say they could use a little practice."

Morrow's jaw dropped open.

Gwen stomped out of his office. She had one last chance to be heard, and she was going to give it a good try. Maybe they wouldn't let her in to see Kimmel, the fleet commander, but it wasn't going to be for lack of effort on her part.

She walked out of the building and crossed the street, getting into Sam's car and slamming he door.

"Well?" Sam asked.

Gwen nodded. "Just as I thought. They fired me."

"Fired you?"

"Well, actually, they sent me home. I have to report in a week. To hear the Chief in there tell it, I was lucky not to be brought up on charges. Lucky because I'm a woman."

"That must have gone over good." Sam swallowed. "What now?"

"Drive me to the fleet headquarters. I'm going to take one last shot at Kimmel. If I can't get him to listen, then I'm done with it."

"What about Aki? If we can find her killer, they may just have to listen."

She looked at him. "Are you kidding? Right now her death is a convenience for them, one more person they don't have to listen to. I'm the last one now, and they're getting rid of me."

Sam drove her the few short blocks to the fleet headquarters. She steamed into the building, and her footsteps echoed down the hall in meticulous raps. She had nothing to lose. Maybe Sam was right. Maybe his way was better. But this was her last chance to stop the war before it started and to do it her way.

She stepped into the admiral's outer office. The man's secretary was pecking away at the typewriter. "Is the admiral in?"

The woman looked up from her typewriter, a frustrated look on her face. "Yes, but he can't be bothered now. He has Admiral Picard and General Short in there."

"Perfect," Gwen said. "That's just who I need to see." She stepped over to the door, and the secretary jumped out of her chair to chase her down.

"You can't go in there." She grabbed Gwen's arm. "I've already told you."

"Why not?" She looked back at the woman and peeled her hand off of her arm. "They can't very well fire me twice, now can they?" With that she twisted the doorknob and walked into the admiral's office.

The three men were seated on the leather couch and chair in the corner of the big office, surrounded by two floor-to-ceiling glass-fronted bookcases that contained models of the ships in the harbor and a few that dated back to the Mayflower. It looked somewhat like a little boy's playroom, a place to contain the dreams of manhood. They were smoking cigars and laughing.

Kimmel's secretary followed Gwen into the office, wringing her hands. "I'm sorry, Admiral. I told her you were busy."

Kimmel looked across the room at her. "Miss Williams. Are you still here?"

Gwen nodded and stepped forward. "Yes, Admiral, no thanks to you."

Kimmel got to his feet, followed by the other two men. "Now just what is that supposed to mean?"

"Oh, don't play innocent with me, Admiral. I've been ordered back to San Francisco."

"Then your work is done here."

"Not hardly. You haven't even gotten my report yet and I have something that you need to see."

The man positioned his hands on his hips. Gwen had seen the posture before. It was a look of masculinity and pride. He lifted his chin in another act of defiance. Perhaps it was arrogant condescension. He was allowing her to speak. "Well, what is it?"

Gwen unzipped her leather attaché case and pulled out the papers she had taken from Aki's desk. She handed them over to Kimmel. "These were to be part of a report from one of your intelligence people, a Miss Aki Kawa. They detail the plan of attack by Japanese planes on Ford Island." She noticed that Aki's name drew a response from Brian's father. He stepped over to where Kimmel was standing and looked over Kimmel's shoulder to read along with him.

"Just where did she get this?"

"They were part of a Japanese communication to Tokyo, painstakingly translated by Miss Kawa. It may have cost her her life."

Kimmel looked up at her. "The Honolulu authorities have the man responsible for that, Miss Williams."

"Yes, an innocent man. He was convenient. The Japanese Embassy has a man who was a former ensign in their navy who looks over the fleet every day and then sends messages to Tokyo, detailing changes in our strength here. They also have a willing spy who flashes signals to Japanese submarines from the beach. I've seen the man and watched him do it."

Kimmel handed the papers to Short, who began to study them. Gwen knew he was the general in charge of the army troops on the island. He let the words he was reading sink in and then looked over to Kimmel. "I don't think our danger lies in the direction of the Japanese fleet," Short said. "Our principal danger is from the Japanese already living here."

"If that were true, General," Gwen said, "then the Japanese woman who discovered this would have gotten rid of this document. As it was, she may have died for it."

Short ignored her and continued to talk to Kimmel. "We've taken the precaution of positioning our planes together in the middle of the runways. We don't want to take a chance of local saboteurs."

Kimmel grunted and nodded.

"What if this woman is right?" Picard asked. "What if the Japanese are planning to launch an attack against the fleet?"

"The harbor here is too shallow for their torpedoes. We are too far away for their home fleet to reach us without being spotted."

"Do you have the current position of the Japanese home fleet?" Picard asked.

"Most of them."

"The carriers?" Picard asked.

Kimmel bowed his head slightly. "No, not at the moment. We're searching, and we ought to know shortly."

"You'll find out shortly where they are," Gwen said through clenched teeth.

Kimmel ignored the comment and went on. "They also have diplomats in Washington trying to work out an arrangement with our people there. Do you really think they would be planning an attack here with their people still in Washington? I don't think so."

He looked back to where Gwen was standing. "No, I'm afraid we have an overzealous young woman here with something personal to prove. She's from Japan. If she can find a Japanese hero for us in the person of this dead woman, then maybe it won't look so bad for her people."

Gwen's face went flush with anger. She twisted her fists into tight balls. "You are my people, Admiral, and you were Aki Kawa's people too. I don't think you're going to know who your enemy really is until you see those planes with the red suns flying overhead and dropping bombs on that fleet of yours."

She pointed to the models in the glass case. "They won't be toy bombs, either, and they will kill real men. Your men. Our men."

DECEMBER 4, 1941

CHAPTER 42

T he ball game was on a Thursday night at Kapi'olani Park. Traffic streamed by on Kalakaua Avenue as people were bent on getting home or on finding a place to park for the delights of Waikiki shopping. People strolled down the sidewalk, admiring the beach in the distance and the growing gloom of twilight. The first of the stars had begun to twinkle, winking like faraway street lamps.

Sam wore his jeans, tennis shoes, and a charcoal gray shirt. It made him feel more at home and less like a tourist. Given the fact that the game was between the Krinkle Sugar Company and the

Knights of Columbus, he fit right in. No one was a tourist. It was hard to get used to the fact that this was December and that people were still playing baseball.

The lights over the edge of the baseball diamond switched on, glaring bulbs firing out into the night sky and bathing the green grass and orange crushed rock with a soft amber glow. Palm trees swayed on the edge of the field, dark shapes set against the azure sky. Their black shapes were like the spill of an inkwell over the top of a navy blue sweater.

Sam sat in the second row of a set of wooden bleachers. He leaned forward, his elbows on his knees and his chin on his clenched fists. There was a warmth to the place and time. The giggles of girls as they watched the young men in their uniforms took Sam back to his boyhood days.

Sam saw Hiroki warming up in what served as a bull pen, slamming his pitches into the catcher's mitt of an oversize man who knelt at the other end. No doubt Hiroki was a cagey pitcher, a man who could think and brood about a matter before committing himself. Sam was sure the man still felt the bruises he had dished out several days ago. It would be something to watch out for. Sam was certain Hiroki had friends at the game and, if that were true, that he couldn't count on Mutt and Jeff showing up to rescue him again. For all he knew, they had grown as tired of following him as he had of following Popov.

Hiroki had blurted out Krinkle's name, but he had been under duress. Sam knew he had to keep that fact in mind. Hiroki might have killed Aki himself, and Mitch Krinkle could have seemed like a logical scapegoat. After all, the man was wealthy and white, a perfect target for Hiroki's hatred. He represented everything Hiroki detested about America.

Mitch Krinkle was practicing batting, swinging his bat, and cracking line drives that arched up to the lights and down to the darkness.

With each swing of the bat, feminine gasps were followed by squeals and applause. Krinkle ate it up.

Sam spotted Jerry. Jerry had tried to correct Krinkle that day at the party when the subject of Mitch's whereabouts on the night of Aki's murder had come up, but he hadn't gotten the chance. Krinkle had cut him off. It was doubtful he would say anything tonight either. After all, he was still a member of Mitch Krinkle's adoring fan club.

Jerry was tossing a ball back and forth with another uniformed member of the Krinkle Sugar team. The two of them were laughing and taking turns at fielding ground balls.

Sam slipped out of the bleachers and walked around the backstop in the direction of the two young men. Edging up closer to the field, he watched the game of catch. He stood there for a while behind a waist-high chain-link fence before he finally spoke up. "Hi, Jerry. Remember me?"

Jerry caught the ball, then turned and looked over to where Sam was standing. "Yeah, I remember you. Sam Diamond, the reporter. Right?"

"Right."

He threw the ball back to the other man. "What are you doing here?"

Sam shrugged. "I like baseball, and baseball in December is an oddity to me. You play it year-round?"

Jerry fielded the hard ground ball that had skipped over the ground in his direction. "We've got two leagues, a winter and a summer league."

"You're lucky. Where I come from baseball is just a few months out of the year. You play it in the summer or you don't play."

Jerry threw the ball back. "Yeah, that's too bad." He shrugged his shoulders. "Guess you got to live in paradise."

"Or die in paradise," Sam added.

The remark brought a look from Jerry. It caused him to take his eye off the incoming ground ball, which skidded past him.

"Sorry to distract you. Guess you should keep your mind on the game."

Jerry retreated to pick up the ball, then began slamming it into his glove as he walked back in Sam's direction. He seemed agitated. "Why are you here, Diamond?"

Sam grinned. "To watch a baseball game. Why else would I be here?"

Jerry continued toward Sam, then stopped in front of the fence. "I know better than that. You're still working on that woman's murder, aren't you?"

"What if I am?"

Turning, Jerry threw the ball back to the other man. "Hang on, Hal, I got some business here. I'll just be a second."

"So is this your only game this week?" Sam asked.

"Nah, we got one Sunday morning at nine." He looked up at the lights. "It'll be a daylight game."

"Do you work for the Krinkle Sugar Company?"

Jerry shook his head. "No, I'm studying pre-law at the university. My dad's a lawyer downtown."

"He represent the Krinkles?"

"No way. My dad wouldn't touch them."

"Then why all the fawning over young Mitch?"

"We're buddies, that's all."

"He send you his leftovers when he's through with those women of his?"

Jerry stepped closer. Sam could tell the remark didn't sit well with him. "No, I can find my own dates." He glanced back at Krinkle, then looked Sam in the eye. "Mitch is a collector."

"What do you mean?"

"He collects things from the women he's been involved with."

"What kind of things?"

"Everything. Things they wore: clothes, jewelry, shoes, you name it. It's like he's still got a piece of them in that wardrobe of his. I wouldn't want any part of his collection, and I don't need his hand-me-downs."

Sam smiled. "I'm sure you don't. You're a good-looking guy." He scratched his chin slowly. "Makes me wonder, though, why would you want to protect him from a murder rap? Don't you think that woman deserved to live?"

"Look"—his voice became more animated—"I met her once. She was a nice girl. I hope whoever it was who killed her burns good."

Sam looked off in the distance in the direction of Krinkle. "And what if it's your friend over there?"

Jerry followed Sam's gaze over to where Mitch was now talking to several young women. "If he did it, he should pay. Same as the rest."

"Then why don't you tell me what happened that night? I'd like to hear it from you."

Jerry bowed his head, studying his shoe tops. "I don't know exactly where he was. I know we had a game that night, but Mitch didn't show until the fifth inning. He might have been out with Heidi Campbell. His car was parked here." Lifting his head, he looked into Sam's eyes. "Just because he wasn't here doesn't mean he was killing that woman. Like I said, he might have been out with Heidi."

"Okay, Jerry. I appreciate your honesty. If you hear of anything, anything at all, get in touch with me. I'm staying at the Royal Hawaiian. You might make a lawyer yet."

Sam walked away from the ball field knowing he'd gotten far more than he expected. Mitch Krinkle didn't have an airtight alibi. If he hadn't been with Heidi Campbell, then no one would be able to account for him.

He stopped and looked off at the ocean. The lights of Honolulu were shining on the top of the water, a sea of sparkling crystal. It seemed unreal that there could be trouble brewing for this place. It was so far from the war in Europe but there was trouble, trouble with the Japanese. The problem that kept tumbling through Sam's mind was how someone like Krinkle could be involved with the Japanese. The more Sam thought the matter over, the more Aki's death seemed to be connected to what she knew about Japanese espionage. Surely her murder wasn't just a matter of the throttled passions of a spoiled rich kid.

Sam climbed back into his MG and started the engine. He knew he had to take a look at Krinkle's collection. He would have to see it, and he would have to see it tonight.

He rolled out of the parking lot onto Kalakaua Avenue, shifting through gears and speeding past carloads of cruisers and gawkers. It took him only a short time to make his way to the highway, but there was no need to speed. No matter how anxious he was, he knew he couldn't get there any earlier than ten or eleven. People would still be up. Young Mitch would no doubt stay out till dawn, adding to his collection.

More than two hours later Sam pulled the MG to the top of the hill overlooking the Krinkle estate. He had stopped at a diner on the highway. The place, which looked like an old boxcar, had a plume of smoke coming out a pipe through the roof. Sam hadn't taken his chances with a cooked meal there. Instead, he had ordered a ham-and-cheese sandwich to go, along with a carton of milk.

He sat and watched the lights on the estate as he chewed the soft white bread that surrounded the ham and cheese. He held the sandwich out, eyeballing it with a frown. He didn't much care for white bread. The stuff tasted gummy to him, like dough scraped from the bowl and left to settle in a pan. He much preferred rye bread or something with seeds in it, something where a man could tell he was really getting something and not munching on a soggy piece of cake.

Something about being nervous caused a man to eat. Breaking and entering was not normal for a reporter, although some lived and died by doing just that. Most people felt their privacy was already invaded just by having their name in the paper. Breaking into their home as well went over the top.

Sam thought about the large Samoan who had escorted him off the Krinkle property and the three large dogs. He really didn't know which one would be better to run into. For his money, he picked the Samoan. At least people had a conscience.

He held up the carton and sipped the milk. It was cool and settled in his stomach in a way that reminded him of a late-night raid on his mother's refrigerator. There was something comforting about milk, but it didn't offset his uneasiness about what he knew he had to do.

CHAPTER 43

S am sat and watched the stars for over an hour after he saw the lights go off in the main house. He started the engine. The MG had a purr to it. It wasn't loud, and Sam knew he'd be able to roll up to the house without attracting much attention. The other advantage was that Mitch Krinkle was also driving an MG, a red MG. In the dark they might even appear to be identical. His plan was to roll up to the large palm tree beside the walkway and go in like he was Mitch Krinkle and this was his house.

The MG rolled down the hill. Sam climbed out without opening the door, then looked down at the other half of his sandwich left on the seat. It might come in handy with the Rottweilers roaming about. Stuffing what was left of the sandwich into his shirt, he reached down, opened the glove compartment, and took out the flashlight.

Darkness shadowed the tall stately pillars in front of the Krinkle home. Sam walked toward them but stopped suddenly. A rake had been left out, its teeth pointing up. That could be dangerous. Sam reached down and turned it over. He then glided over the bricks in the walkway and up to the door. He pushed down on the handle, and the door sprung open.

He stepped inside, softly closing the door behind him. A winding staircase split the large hallway down the middle. To the left was a living room; to his right was a formal dining room.

Sam started up the stairs, taking them two at a time. The plush carpet deadened his steps and took him quietly to the landing above. Now was the dilemma. Which room was Mitch's? He certainly didn't want to walk in on the old man and his wife. He figured that given Mitch's tendency to late nights, he would want a room near the end of the hall. Those rooms would offer more privacy, and Mitch and his collection needed privacy. At the end of the hall he could come and go without disturbing his parents.

Sam ambled to the right and looked down the hall. He saw a light under the door of the room at the end. No doubt the parents' room. Turning, he made his way down to the other end of the hall. Sam passed four or five rooms before he came to the one on the end. He opened the door softly.

Stepping inside, he closed the door and switched on his flashlight. It was Mitch's room. A Stanford banner hung on the wall, and deer antlers were arranged in a strange pattern. They were eye level, with ties and shirts hanging from them. The place had a slightly disheveled look to it, with wadded paper overflowing a wastebasket in the corner and trailing a wake of rubbish onto the floor. Evidently the maid hadn't gotten to the room today.

The man had a rack of bats next to the door, and posters of Babe Ruth and Ty Cobb plastered on the wall. A mound of tennis rackets littered the floor next to the bat rack. Sam would have been amused had it not been so pathetic. The place looked like it was lived in by a fifteen-year-old, but in fact it was inhabited by a man who had simply refused to grow up.

Mitch's bed was in the center of the large room, the bedspread had the logo of the New York Yankees on it. Half of one wall contained a large mahogany wardrobe. That would be the place to look.

Sam stepped over to the wardrobe and opened a door. He shined his light inside. Several wicker baskets were on the floor of the wardrobe, and drawers lined the back. Sam picked up the lid of the first basket and sent the beam of light down into it. The basket was filled with women's shoes. None of the shoes would have made up a pair. They were single shoes: red, brown, white, sandals, slippers, and high heels. They must have numbered in the scores. Each shoe no doubt represented a young woman that Mitch Krinkle had long ago forgotten.

He replaced the lid and picked up the one from the second basket. What he saw didn't surprise him. The basket was filled with women's undergarments. It made Sam feel unholy just to look on this part of anyone's life, as if he had eaten a piece of food that had already been chewed and spit out. He felt nauseated.

One at a time he slid open the small drawers. They were lined in green velvet and contained an assortment of jewelry, brooches, necklaces, strands of pearls, and rings. The items all together must have numbered in the hundreds.

He trickled the light over the back wall of the wardrobe, and then he spotted it. A small gold cross was hanging on a peg.

Reaching out, he took it in his hand and then held the light on it. It was Aki's cross, the one Brian had given her. It had to be. It had a black pearl in the middle.

Sam slipped it into his pocket, then turned off the flashlight and closed the wardrobe door. He stood up straight, taking deep breaths. Thinking that Mitch Krinkle was guilty of Aki's murder went against his every instinct. Krinkle couldn't be connected to Japanese espionage. Or could he? The man's motives were more base than that.

He moved across the room and opened the door, slipping into the hall. The house was quiet. When he moved toward the stairs, he could see that the light was out under the door at the other end of the hall. Everything had gone according to plan. He was home free, or almost home free.

Hurrying down the stairs, he opened the front door and stepped outside into the cool air. The breeze had picked up. It was blowing across his face and rippling through the branches on the palm trees. He moved down the stairs and took his first step onto the walkway when he heard a low, menacing growl.

His eyes were drawn to it right away. Not ten yards away was one of the large black Rottweilers, its teeth bared and its eyes shining in the darkness. The brutish dog stepped toward Sam, the growl from its throat growing more intense and deep.

Sam edged his way down the walk, slowly, almost an inch at a time. He was gliding away from the animal, keeping his eyes trained on it.

Suddenly the big dog let out a series of ferocious barks followed by growls. And he lunged in Sam's direction.

Sam knew he had to move fast. There were two more dogs just like this one prowling the Krinkle estate. Sam reached into his shirt and pulled out what remained of his ham-and-cheese sandwich.

He flung it in the animal's direction and began to run down the walkway. When he got to the overturned rake, he stopped and picked it up just in time. He could see the other dogs running full tilt around the house. While the first of the canine sentinels was busy devouring the remains of Sam's sandwich, the other two would have nothing to keep them occupied but the business end of the rake.

He swung the rake, catching the first dog in midair. The animal tumbled to the ground, yelping in pain. A sharp piercing pain sent shivers up and down Sam's left leg. The second dog had seized Sam's calf muscle and was sinking his teeth through the jeans and into Sam's leg.

Sam drove the butt of the rake down into the dog's hard skull. The animal held on tight, shaking his head and refusing to let go. Sam could see that the first dog had finished the sandwich and was now intent on joining its two mates to make Sam the dessert. The dog was taking a few steps down the walkway in Sam's direction. The second dog Sam had clubbed was also coming to its senses. It wouldn't be long before Sam would have all three of them on him. It was doubtful he could survive such an attack.

Then he noticed the lights in the house coming on. For Sam that was almost a greater danger. Chances were that the men who maintained security would come out armed. Dogs were one thing, but the shotguns were quite another.

Sam dragged the dog hanging onto his leg in the direction of his car, swinging the rake in the direction of the first dog on the walkway. The second dog now circled him, snapping at his backside. Sam slashed at him, catching the dog in the side with the prongs of the rake and once again drawing squeals and yelps.

He cranked open the driver's door to the car and eased himself into the seat, the dog on his leg hanging on with all its might. Taking the door with both hands Sam yanked it against the black beast, slamming it repeatedly against the animal's body. He repeated the process, crushing the sharp door into the dog's face. It let go.

Turning on the ignition, Sam rammed it into gear and popped the clutch. The car lurched forward, but not before the first dog leapt over the passenger door and into the seat next to him.

He shifted gears and sped up the hill with the animal snapping at his elbow. Something had to happen with this unwanted passenger, and fast. Sam drew out his flashlight and sparred with the dog's glaring, snapping teeth.

When he reached the top of the hill, he could hear shouts from the house below. Men were yelling, and the two dogs he had left behind were running up the hill, giving chase.

Sam abruptly stopped, opened the door on the driver's side, and dragged himself out. He would have very little time. The two beasts that were coming up the hill wouldn't take long to get there. He closed his door, stepped around to the hood of the car and leaned against his windshield, staring at the snapping barking dog still seated firmly in the passenger seat. "Come on you thing. You want me, you come and get me!"

The sound of Sam's voice was all it took. The animal raised himself up and leapt over the windshield in Sam's direction. Sam dodged as the animal hit the ground. Sam scrambled up the hood of the car, slammed himself into the seat, and threw the car into gear. The tires squealed and spun on the gravel, and Sam swerved in the direction of the dog. Now it was the animal's turn to dodge, and it did, scampering to one side as the MG roared on past him.

Sam's left leg ached, and he could feel the trickle of blood left by the sharp teeth. He shifted gears in excruciating pain, picking up speed as he bounced along the road. He wanted to be out on the open highway and making his way back to Honolulu by the time the men from the Krinkle house found their car keys. It didn't take him long to hit the open road. The wind blowing through his hair felt good. It also felt good to have the first piece of tangible piece of evidence linking Mitch Krinkle to Aki's murder. The only thing that bothered him was that it would never stand up in court. The wounds on Sam's leg would last longer than the trial.

DECEMBER 6, 1941

CHAPTER 44

Saturday was bright sun and cloudless. The late afternoon had turned out to be just as beautiful as the morning. Sam sat at a table near the bar in the beachfront lounge of the Royal Hawaiian. He sloshed a mai tai in his hand. The drink was in a coconut shell with a pink parasol jabbed deep into a string of pineapple wedges and maraschino cherries. He thought of it as a sissy drink, but he had mumbled an agreement when the string-bean bartender with the plastic smile had pushed it on him. Playing with the thing gave him something to do while he waited.

Gwen was going to meet him at the bar. He had called her that morning to say that he had evidence and perhaps the identity of Aki's killer. He had made a special point of telling her that what he had would never see a day in court, but it didn't matter to her. Gwen just wanted to know the truth. Sam wanted that too, but he didn't think he had all of it. Too much was left unexplained.

He had also made a special point of telling Gwen to wear her beach attire and sunglasses. Duskov Popov was due for his afternoon walk on the beach. Sam had the man's routine memorized. If he and Gwen could go together, then chances were they wouldn't be recognized. Popov was used to seeing Sam alone. Today would be different. He was wearing sunglasses, a hat, and his swimsuit. If Gwen tagged along, they would look like any other couple on the beach at Waikiki. In Hawaii it was the single people who attracted attention. Couples were a part of the Hawaiian motif.

He watched as Gwen stepped through the flowered terrace that led to the bar. She was wearing a blue swimsuit and a large straw hat. The sandals on her feet were woven, and Sam leaned forward, drinking in the sight of her legs as they peeked through the flowered sarong she had wrapped around her. The woman was strikingly beautiful in Sam's book, tall and athletic. She would look great on his arm this afternoon, even if it was only pretend.

She caught sight of him and smiled.

Sam got to his feet as Gwen walked over. "Afternoon, sugar. Great to see you." He grinned. "And I mean that."

Gwen looked down at the large bandage on Sam's leg. "What happened to you?"

Sam waited for her to take her seat. He stepped around the table and pushed her chair in. "It's a long story, a matter of three dogs."

"Dogs? Where did you meet up with dogs?"

Sam took his seat. "They're part of the Krinkle family."

"You were there?"

"Yes, I was there and I found this." Sam reached into his shirt pocket and took out the gold cross. He laid it on the table.

Gwen picked it up. "Where did you find this?"

"In Mitch's room. Let's just say it was part of an extensive collection the young man has, souvenirs from his various conquests."

"That's sick." Gwen turned the cross over in her hand. "Why would someone do that?"

"Sickness just about nails it. It would seem the young man needs to relive his exploits. They become part of a trophy case in his mind. Needless to say, I wasn't exactly an invited guest." He took the cross out of Gwen's hand and dangled it in front of her eyes. "But it might be interesting to show it to him. He might just come across with the story if he thought he had to."

"Running a bluff?"

Sam smiled. "Exactly. Hey, you're not such a shy, retiring violet after all. You know poker."

"I know a few poker players."

"I'm sure you do." He dropped the cross back into his pocket.

"So what are we doing here in our beach clothes? Do you plan on taking me swimming?"

"That would be nice, but we're waiting for our double agent to show. I know his every move. Got it down to a science. The man takes an afternoon walk and enjoys the sun when it's not directly overhead. He stops to get a snow cone and then maybe passes the time of day with pretty women in their swimsuits. Most of the time he just waits."

"Waits for what?"

Sam shook his head. "I'm not sure. I figure he's waiting for whatever it is he's been engineering. Maybe he's making contact with another agent. I don't know. What I do know is that Aki didn't die just to satisfy the whims of some sugar heir. There has to be more of a reason than that."

Sam stared off at the white sand beyond the pat were breaking and sending a sheet of salt water "Duskov is involved. He's got his fingers in ever

When the waiter arrived, Gwen ordered a ginger ale a. onded the motion, pushing his liquid toy into the center of the table.

"Are you always like that?" Gwen asked, nodding at his drink.

"Like what?"

"Never wanting what you have, always needing something different."

Sam smiled at her. "Somehow, sugar, I get the feeling that you're talking about more than drinks."

Gwen took off her dark glasses and folded the stems. "Maybe I am. You just seem discontented."

Sam nodded. "I suppose I am. When a man's life doesn't live up to his dreams, it creates that kind of feeling."

"I would think that you have everything. You're trusted enough by your paper to give you all the room you need to bring in a story. Your name is on the front page more often than not. What more could you want?"

"Maybe I want what your parents have. They seem content, and they love each other. I've never felt the kind of love that's based on friendship."

"It's based on more than friendship. They share the same values."

"You mean this Christian thing and their life as missionaries?"

"They believe the same thing. They give to other people. They have the same hope, and it's not a hope that's based on what they alone can produce. It goes much further than that."

Sam leaned forward. "And that's what you're looking for?"

"Yes, I suppose I am."

"And what if it's what I'm looking for too?"

"Sam, you're not really a believer. You're an American, and you may think that makes you a Christian, but it doesn't. Becoming a

Christian is a decision that lasts a lifetime. It has nothing to do with being born in Brooklyn."

"OK, Gwen, you got me. I know when I'm beat."

"Gwen, now is it, not sugar or angel?"

Sam laughed. "See, I do know your name. I like it too. I suppose talking about things like this has a way of drawing the formality out of me. Maybe we can talk about this more later. I'm not a serious reprobate, you know, even if I am college educated and work in the media. You just got to give me a chance."

"OK, we will. I promise."

The waiter served them their ginger ales, and they sat sipping them for a while. Resolving this matter of Aki's death was important. It meant more to Gwen than just saving her job when she got back to San Francisco. Aki had meant something to her.

"There he is."

"Popov?" Gwen turned her head and looked at the beach.

"Yeah, he's the guy in the white shorts and rainbow-colored aloha shirt." Sam got to his feet and dropped a few bills on the table. He pulled Gwen's chair back, and they left the bar and started down the beach. They were a good distance from Popov when they finally made it to the beach, but they had him in sight. "You just pretend we're having a good time, sugar, and that we're in love, OK?"

She looked at him through her dark glasses and slipped her arm into his. "Fine," she smiled. "I'll do my best."

The beach that Saturday afternoon was alive with activity. Men and women were scattered all over the sand, their bodies glistening with oil. Several surfers were riding the waves and posing for pictures. Two hotel employees were holding one rather stocky gentleman on a surfboard, trying to keep him steady as the three of them waited for a wave. The rotund man was having trouble just sitting on the board, and the man's wife further complicated matters by standing on the shore, clapping, and shouting.

"That has always been my impression of marriage," Sam said. "Some poor sap making an idiot out of himself while his wife eggs him on. The trouble with most men is that they'd be willing to do almost anything to impress a woman. It starts with a guy on the jungle gym in the first grade and graduates to something like that out there in the water."

Gwen laughed. "And I suppose the male ego has nothing to do with it?"

"It has everything to do with it. It's just that women find that button to push, and once they do, they keep at it until their fingers get tired."

Once again Gwen laughed. "Men—you're too much. Believe me, if you want to play the male victim here, you're picking on the wrong woman."

Sam grinned. "You're right. I forgot who I'm talking to. Maybe you're just so bright it makes a man automatically feel sorry for himself. Someone with beauty and brains too. It just ain't fair."

They continued to walk, keeping Popov in their sights. The man stopped for a frozen treat at a stand, and Gwen walked out into the water to kill some time so they wouldn't get too close. Out of the corner of his eye, Sam noticed Popov survey the beach crowd. He was obviously looking for anyone who might not belong, anything out of place. But with Gwen playing in the water and him watching her, they fit right in. When Popov resumed his stroll, Gwen retreated back to the beach. "Did I do all right?"

"You were wonderful. Seemed natural."

They watched a policeman walk up to the concession stand and place his order. Popov had moved on ahead. He had been joined by another policeman and had stopped to talk to the man.

Gwen watched the two of them intently. She reached back and pulled on Sam's shirt, drawing him close to her. "Something's not right there."

"Where?"

"Your man Popov and the cop."

"What's wrong? Popov stops to talk to the police all the time. I think it's how he gets his jollies, living outside the law and flirting with danger."

"No, it's the policeman I'm talking about. He has a swagger about him."

"All cops have that way about them, makes them feel important."

"No, it's more than that. I think I know him." She moved closer to get a better look, then lowered her sunglasses to the bridge of her nose. "It is him. That's no policeman. It's Hiroki Fujiyama. Why would he be in a policeman's uniform?"

"Good question. It might be their way of passing information without arousing suspicion. I know I'd never approach Popov while he was talking to a cop."

"What should we do?"

Sam looked back at the stand where the policeman was still talking to the vendor. He walked back and left Gwen standing. "Excuse me, officer. Can I have a moment of your time?"

The policeman looked to be Chinese. "Sure. What's the matter?"

"My girlfriend and I just spotted something that might interest you." He pointed past Gwen to where Hiroki and Popov were still talking. "Do you see that cop over there, the one talking to the man in the white shorts?"

"Yes."

"Well, he's not a policeman. He's someone my girlfriend recognized. I think he works for the Krinkle Sugar people, but he's definitely not a cop."

"Well, let's go find out."

The policeman began taking long strides in the direction of Popov and Hiroki. Gwen fell into place behind Sam, and the three of them closed in on the two figures.

It wasn't until the three of them got within twenty yards that Hiroki spotted them. He pulled on Popov's sleeve and then turned and began to run across the beach. The policeman immediately gave chase, digging up the sand as he ran.

Sam and Gwen walked up to Popov. The man's look of surprise immediately disappeared into a broad smile. "There you are," he said. "I've been looking for you."

"And I'll just bet you're sorry you didn't see me before now."

Popov laughed. "I'm always happy to see you. That way I know where you are."

"And I always know where you are. You've gotten to be pretty predictable. Too bad you don't have your German goons with you here in Hawaii."

Sam looked over to see the policeman tackle Hiroki and then stand him up and start walking him back in their direction. "Of course, I see you have goons with you wherever you go. Not as dependable, maybe, but they're still here to do your dirty work. You figure the policeman's getup will throw people off your meetings, make them more private?"

Popov shrugged and continued to smile. "Makes no difference to me. I'm just an innocent bystander here."

The three of them watched as Hiroki and the policeman walked up to them. Hiroki's hat was missing, and his shirt had been roughed up, but there was no mistaking the man. The policeman pushed Hiroki in Gwen's direction. "You know this man, miss?"

Gwen nodded. "Yes. His name is Hiroki Fujiyama."

"Well, Hiroki," Sam said, "seems like they have you on impersonating an officer and resisting arrest. I can do better than that, though. I think I can put you in jail for murder."

The officer tightened his grip as Hiroki started to struggle.

Sam reached into his pocket and pulled out Aki's cross. He held it out in front of Hiroki's face. "You recognize this? It's a cross that belonged to Aki Kawa. You took it from her when you killed her. We found it where you dropped it."

Sam could see the look of panic register on Hiroki's face. He obviously recognized the cross. "I didn't do that," he blurted out. "I just told Mitch Krinkle where to find her. He killed her."

"Just like you planned, right? She was getting too close to what you two were planning for Pearl Harbor, wasn't she? That's why you baited Mitch Krinkle to go after her. Am I right? And just when is this little party planned for the navy? Is that what you and Popov here were discussing?"

"You don't have to say anything more," Popov interrupted. "They have nothing on you. The charges are minor. Besides, there's nothing they can do about it now. It's too late, much too late."

DECEMBER 7, 1941

CHAPTER 45

S am was up early on Sunday morning. He and Gwen had made an agreement the night before. He would go to Mitch Krinkle's baseball game that morning, and she would go to Pearl Harbor to see Heidi Campbell. If things went well for her there, she might even be able to make it back in time for church. Between the two of them, they hoped to nail Krinkle's hide to the wall. Sam would show him Aki's cross, and Gwen would grill the Campbell girl and try to shake his alibi.

Sam tightened the laces on his tennis shoes. He was still troubled about what they had both found out. Hiroki had used Krinkle's obsession with Aki to do Popov's bidding. Mitch Krinkle had been the weapon of choice, but Popov had pulled the trigger just as sure as the world turned.

He walked over to the mirror and buttoned his white shirt. It irked him that Popov had been so sure of himself. In the man's mind it was too late to do anything about what Sam and Gwen knew was sure to be a Japanese attack. The only question seemed to be when. In Popov's mind, the timing would be soon.

He walked across the room and stepped out onto the balcony. The sky was a bright blue, a perfect Hawaii morning. The water stretched out below, and the beach was deserted except for a few surfers. Diamond Head stood in the background, unmovable and invulnerable. It made the whole island seem safe and secure, far away from even the rumor of war. But Sam knew that was an illusion. If Popov was to be believed, this whole place would soon become the center of the war. America would be in the middle of it, and he had the story. He just couldn't print it, not yet. There were some loose ends to tidy up. Sam would write the story this afternoon and send it off to the paper. Maybe then he could go home. As it was, Gwen was due to take an afternoon flight back to San Francisco. Without her here, Sam hoped the paper would have mercy on him and bring him home.

Sam left the room and took the elevator to the empty lobby. Not even Mutt and Jeff were there. Even they had tired of the chase.

He walked out to the parking lot and started up the MG. Kapi'olani Park wasn't far; it was within walking distance. But the car would give him the opportunity to go to church with Gwen after he was through with Krinkle.

The engine purred as he drove down Kalakaua Avenue. Minutes later he pulled into the parking lot near the baseball field. The place had a fresh look to it. At the far end of the field a man was still cutting the grass. The man had obviously started the project at dawn. A number of cars were already there, including Mitch Krinkle's red MG.

As he got out of the car, he heard a strange sound. A number of explosions echoed in the distance, muffled pops that sounded as if they came from the faraway entrance to Pearl Harbor. For a moment he thought the attack might have started, but then all was calm. Sam was certain the sounds had come from one of the patrolling destroyers, perhaps a series of practice depth-charge runs. No doubt fish had died for the cause of preparedness.

He walked over to the bleachers and took his usual position. The timing had to be right in talking to Krinkle, and Sam figured it might be best before the game and not after. Krinkle would in all likelihood be the hero or imagine himself to be one. He would have the usual crowd of adoring females and select one for special attention. Talking to Sam would be the last thing on his mind.

Hiroki was nowhere in sight. It made Sam smile. Even if they couldn't pin Aki's murder on him, the cop on the beach had heard plenty. The man would be held for questioning and, given Hiroki's tendency toward self-preservation, Krinkle's name was bound to come up. The Krinkle money and name had clout on the island, but Mitch was bound to be subjected to police attention as well as interrogation.

Sam slid off the bench and started his walk around the field. The sunshine poured through the palm trees and a slight breeze rustled the leaves.

He spotted Krinkle in the outfield, playing catch with a teammate. It didn't take long before the man looked over and recognized him. He frowned, caught the ball, and threw it back.

"Good to see you're keeping up your game, Mitch. I hear the prison has a great ball team."

Krinkle caught the ball and snapped his glove closed. He stared at Sam. "What do you mean by that?"

Sam smiled. "I think you know what I mean. That's just where you're going. Maybe they'll have better competition for you in there."

"You're crazy." Krinkle turned and fired the ball back to the other man.

"Not crazy. We have a confession and evidence."

Krinkle waited for the ball's return, allowing it to drop into his mitt in basket fashion, obviously showing off. "You ain't got nothing." He then threw the ball back.

"Oh, don't I?" Sam lifted the cross from his shirt pocket and dangled it in the air. Krinkle turned to look at it. Sam was sure he recognized the thing, even from a distance. The man's face turned white.

"Hey, Mitch, look out!"

Krinkle's teammate had thrown the ball, and Mitch looked up to try and place it. It was too late. It hit him in the chest and bounced to the ground.

"Better watch out, Mitch," Sam roared. "You're going to lose your position in the Oahu State Prison."

Krinkle bent over and picked up the ball, then flung it back to the other man in the outfield. "Just hang on to it, Johnny. I got to talk to this guy for a second."

Turning around, he walked toward Sam in a slow, easy fashion. But Sam could see his tension in every movement. When he reached the point where Sam was standing, he motioned for him to follow. "Come on over to the backstop. I don't have that much time, but I'll answer your questions, even if they are ridiculous."

Sam followed him. "Oh, they're not ridiculous. The cops will be wanting to talk to you, especially after they see what I've got."

Krinkle whirled around. "You ain't got nothing, some little bauble you picked up at the international market for a buck-fifty."

Sam reached back into his pocket and pulled out the cross. He dangled it in front of Krinkle. "I don't think so. We have people who will swear it belonged to Aki Kawa. We have a list of people who know you kept trying to force yourself on the girl. She was killed only a few blocks from here, and you didn't show up for that game until the fifth inning. Even now I have a woman friend of mine over at Pearl Harbor questioning Heidi Campbell. She might have gone along with your story with you standing there and your friends surrounding her, but she won't lie for you to the police." Sam paused to let the words sink in. "Especially when you're locked up in a cell."

Krinkle pointed to the cross. "Where did you get that thing?"

Sam smiled. He could see the fear growing in the man's face. "You know where I got it. I got it out of the wardrobe in your room. It was hanging on a peg."

Krinkle stepped over to a bag of bats. He reached in and pulled one out, then turned back to face Sam. "Give me that thing." He waved the bat. "You took it out of my room."

Sam dropped the cross back into his pocket. "Put that thing down. It won't do you any good."

Krinkle grinned. "It won't do you any good, you mean. I know how to use this."

Sam nodded. "Yes, you used it on Aki that night."

"What if I did? She had it coming, the little tease."

Sam tried to ease the tension. He was determined not to show any fear. "I only feel sad that you were used."

"Used? What do you mean?"

"You were used by Japan."

"That's nonsense."

"Is it? Who told you where to find Aki that night? Your teammate, Hiroki Fujiyama. The only trouble is, he's an agent of Japan. Aki was on to their plans for a Japanese attack. He used you to get rid of her."

Krinkle stepped in his direction, tightening his grip on the bat. "You're lying."

Sam shook his head. "Not hardly. How do you think I found out it was Hiroki that told you where to find Aki?" He let a small smile form over his lips. "I heard it from him, and right now he's telling his story to the police—it's not a story with an ending you're going to enjoy. He's telling all about that note you left for Aki, pretending you were Brian and asking her to meet you on the beach. You see, the story will end with the slamming of iron bars behind you. You're going to jail."

"I didn't leave that note; he did." Krinkle took a swing of the bat in Sam's direction, and Sam jumped back. The man then moved forward, shaking the bat and swinging it. Sam was forced to dodge repeated attempts at his head, spinning around and feinting. He bobbed his head back and forth. He leaned forward after one swing and caught Krinkle with a blow to the ribs.

It staggered Krinkle, who backed up and swung the bat again. This time the bat caught Sam on the arm. Pain shot through him.

Sam stumbled backward, gripping his upper arm. He winced in pain.

"I'm not going to jail," Krinkle roared. He raised the bat and came at Sam.

Quickly Sam threw himself at Krinkle's legs, as if he were diving on the squash court for a well-placed shot.

Krinkle brought the bat down on Sam's back, but Sam's tumbling maneuver shot the man's feet out from under him. Sam scrambled quickly and got on top of him, jamming his knee into Krinkle's wrist.

He raised his fist to deliver a punch when the sound of a low-flying plane overhead stopped him. It was a Japanese Zero. Sam could see the smiling pilot flying the plane as he wagged his wings over the baseball diamond.

Krinkle froze on the ground too and watched the plane buzz by. Soon it was followed by several more. Suddenly waves of planes appeared overhead, flying in formation. The two men had become spectators. Sam was too late. Now the only thing he was worried about was Gwen. She would be right in the path of the attack.

CHAPTER 46

wen walked up to the house near the corner of H and 7th Streets. She had gotten the address from the marine guard. Evidently Heidi Campbell's father was a captain on a minesweeper. The stucco house was painted a drab military green with cream-colored trim. It looked like every other officer's house on base except for the petunias planted in rosewood flower boxes under the front windows.

A rolled-up newspaper was on the sidewalk, and Gwen picked it up. The Campbells must be home. She walked up to the front doorstep and rang the bell. A pair of chimes sounded from inside.

A woman in a pink quilted housecoat and her hair still in bobby pins answered the door. "Can I help you?" she asked.

Gwen fumbled in her purse for her identification badge. She showed it to the woman. "I work for Naval Intelligence. I'd like to see your daughter. Oh, by the way, here's your paper."

Mrs. Campbell took the paper then, looking down at the badge, squinted. "I'm sorry, I don't have my glasses on." She looked up at Gwen with watery brown eyes. "I didn't know any women worked for Naval Intelligence."

Gwen smiled and chuckled slightly. "Well, we are fairly intelligent."

Mrs. Campbell appeared to be confused by the comment. Evidently, Gwen thought, she had little or no sense of humor. Her face was puffy with dark circles running under her eyes. "Which one?"

"Which one what?"

"Which daughter? I have three."

"Heidi."

"May I have the nature of your business with my daughter?"

"I'm afraid that's between me and Heidi, Mrs. Campbell."

The woman blinked and backed up a step. "I'll need to talk to my husband."

"Mrs. Campbell, I'm afraid I don't have much time. I know it's only seven-thirty, and I'm sorry. But I have to get back to town and go to church. If you'll just get Heidi, this shouldn't take more than a minute or two."

In a few minutes, the pink figure emerged from the gloom. A second figure was behind her. Mrs. Campbell pushed the door open, and a sleepy-eyed young woman stepped out from behind her mother. Gwen wouldn't have placed her as over sixteen or seventeen. "This is my daughter, Heidi. You can have a few minutes with her. Won't you come inside?"

Heidi rubbed her eyes with a tiny fist and yawned. She looked almost innocent and vaguely confused, a trait she seemed to share with her mother.

Gwen looked at the mother. It was plain to see the look of distrust written all over her face. The girl looked more than a little sheepish too. It was almost as if she knew her mother would be watching over her shoulder. To make matters worse, Gwen was afraid that since she was there to talk about a claimed rendezvous with Mitch Krinkle she wouldn't be able to get a word out of her. "No thanks, Mrs. Campbell. I think I'd rather speak to Heidi outside. It won't take more than a minute or two."

Gwen knew that asking questions about Mitch Krinkle in front of the mother would be a serious mistake, but she could see the mother's face fall. She frowned but moved aside as Heidi brushed past her and stepped outside. "Don't worry, Mrs. Campbell. Heidi's not in any trouble. She just has some information that could be of help to us. She'll be fine and will be back in shortly."

Gwen steered Heidi down the walkway. "Why don't we take a little walk across the street to the parade ground?"

"What's this all about?" Heidi asked.

Gwen looked at her. She was wearing powder blue shorts and a white short-sleeve shirt. Her tennis shoes were sparkling white. Her wide-eyed look of innocence had disappeared too. This might be more difficult than Gwen first thought. "It's about a friend of yours, Mitch Krinkle."

"What about him?"

"We believe that he is responsible for the death of a Naval Intelligence employee, a young woman named Aki Kawa."

Heidi waved her hand as if to shoo away some pesky fly. "I heard all about that. Mitch was with me that night." Heidi smiled and flipped her hair.

They crossed the street, and Gwen glanced back at the house. The pink figure was still hovering at the screen door. "Is that what you would say in front of your mother and father, that you were with this man all night?" Gwen realized that getting this girl away from her mother's listening ears may have just backfired on her.

The girl glanced. "Yeah, probably."

"Well, you will have to say it, you know, and in open court under oath. Are you prepared to do that?"

They walked onto the parade ground. It was an expansive lawn with a reviewing stand and palm trees lining both sides. A brass cannon and a flagpole stood close to the reviewing stand, and a group of sailors in their dress-white uniforms were preparing to raise the colors. A small band stood behind them. It struck a note, and they began to play the "Star-Spangled Banner."

"Mitch didn't do anything to that woman. I know he didn't. He couldn't have."

"She was killed with a baseball bat. A necklace she was wearing at the time was found in the wardrobe in his room. We think your friend Mitch was a pawn for the Japanese. This woman Aki Kawa was uncovering a planned attack on Pearl Harbor. They were going to sink your father's ship and the others in the fleet. Her death has slowed us down in preventing that. How do you think your father would respond to that?"

Suddenly a low-flying plane buzzed the parade field. Gwen looked up and could see the red sun that marked it as Japanese. It had a long torpedo hanging from its belly, poised for attack. Soon other planes fell into line, all headed for the American battleships anchored at Ford Island.

Heidi froze and looked up at the first wave of planes. The band continued to play the national anthem as a color guard hoisted the flag. It was almost surrealistic, like something out of a fairy tale. Everything seemed to be frozen in time and totally out of place.

Machine gun fire from an overflying plane began to trace divots in the grass in the direction of the band. The sailors in white ran in all directions, scattering like a flock of sheep in the midst of a tornado.

Gwen grabbed hold of the girl and pulled her down to the ground, covering her with her body.

At the end of the parade field a fuel tank exploded, sending up shards of lumber and filling the sky with a ball of flame. A Japanese plane pulled up from where he had dropped the bomb.

"It's too late," Gwen said. "Aki was right."

"I'm sorry," Heidi began to cry. "I wasn't with Mitch the night that woman was killed." She shook her head. "I wasn't with him at all. I don't know where he was. I'm sorry. I should have told that man at the party, the reporter."

Gwen pressed the girl into the ground as more planes flew overhead. "That's not important now. The only thing that's important is getting you home, back across the street. If anything happens to you, I'll never forgive myself."

Brian Picard was running up the ladder that led to the deck of the *Arizona*. He had heard the first explosion and had gotten on top just as three Japanese torpedo planes were skimming the harbor in the direction of his ship. He watched as they released their torpedoes. The cruel fish splashed in the water one by one and, contrary to intelligence reports, did not sink. They skirted the surface of the harbor and then formed a shallow running pattern in the direction of the huge battle wagon.

Brian clung to the ladder as the torpedoes slammed into the side of the ship. Multiple explosions shook him like a rag doll, and he could feel the heat as a ball of fire rose high in the air.

He peeled himself from the ladder and began to run to one of his 50-caliber machine guns. All around him men were running in wild confusion. Overhead the Japanese planes were lazily circling. There was no opposition. They could take their time in lining up further torpedoes, and the dive-bombers hadn't even arrived yet. Brian knew it would be a turkey shoot for them; they were stationary targets with big bull's-eyes painted on them.

Two of the sailors in Brian's command collapsed in front of him, their life preservers ablaze from the ball of fire. Brian jerked a cylinder of fire retardant from a red rack on one of the funnels and stepped over to the screaming men. He pointed the nozzle at them and began to spray a coat of white foam over their backsides. Within moments the flames were extinguished. "Over the sides with you," he yelled.

He moved to the empty gun the men had vacated and strapped himself in. Swinging the weapon around, he began to lay out a pattern of rounds on a plane that was flying parallel to the *Arizona*. It peeled off its attack and climbed for altitude.

Brian's mind raced as he swung the gun around. Aki had been right. They should have listened. He knew they would have too, if she hadn't been Japanese. It seemed all too ironic that he was now trying to kill the Japanese when one of their own had tried to stop them. She was his hero. Her memory made him fight harder. He would be here for her, doing what she had tried to do but couldn't.

DECEMBER 8, 1941

EPILOGUE

W hen Gwen walked out of Admiral Kimmel's office that Monday morning, she wasn't surprised to see Sam sitting in the waiting area. He was nursing a cup of black coffee in a white mug with a blue anchor on it. When he saw her, he smiled. It wasn't exactly a smile. It was more of a smirk. No doubt he was guessing at what her conversation with Kimmel had been about. He got to his feet and put down the cup.

"So, how'd it go, sugar? I got your message you'd be seeing the old man this morning. Just thought I'd come down to help pat your back."

"He's a broken man, Sam. I feel sorry for him."

"He didn't exactly listen when he had the chance."

"Walk with me, Sam." They began to walk down the long corridor. "I think he had too much to listen to, too many messages over too long of a time and, when he needed it most, nothing. If anyone's to blame, it's Washington."

"That's my next stop. I filed my story from the field this morning and have one more to do tomorrow. Then I'm flying back to D.C. to try to put the pieces together, given what I know." He grabbed her arm. "You'll be glad to know that Krinkle's in jail. His old man is trying to bail him out, but this may stick."

"Good."

"The old man, Homer, has been sprung."

"I'm glad to hear that."

"We'll have to see what happens to Hiroki. The Japanese aren't exactly popular right now. As to Popov, the FBI arrested the man this morning." He shrugged his shoulders. "I doubt much will happen to him. The English are working to bail him out. Part of what he does, he does for them."

Gwen dropped her gaze to the floor. "That's so puzzling. Who was he working for here, the Germans or the English? I just don't get it. The English are our friends. Why would they—"

Sam interrupted her. "Friendship stops at the water's edge. They needed us in this war. It's really only speculation as to just whom Popov was working for here. My money's on both of them. I take it you're keeping your job with the navy?"

Gwen nodded. "Yes, and maybe now they'll listen to me. I also managed to get Aki a citation."

Sam shook his head. "You should see that harbor out there. The place is still burning. It's going to take them a while just to put the fires out. If they had listened to her in the first place, none of this would have happened. Those men didn't have to die."

They reached the glass front doors just in time to see Admiral James Picard coming up the stairs. He opened the door and spotted them immediately. They could both see the long, drawn look on his face. He had gotten very little sleep, and it showed.

"I'm glad I ran across you," he said. His shoulders slumped. "Brian's dead. I got word this morning. His mother is in shock, I'm afraid. He went down with the *Arizona* trying to save some of his men. Up until he ran out of ammunition, he was manning one of his own guns." He breathed a deep sigh. "I was on the golf course yesterday morning, and Brian was fighting and dying on his ship. I guess it goes to show you who the real sailor was in the Picard family."

Gwen was silent. She knew the man was heaping enough guilt on himself without anything she might add. It would be something he would carry with him, and she knew it.

He reached out and took Gwen's hand. "I was wrong about this Aki woman too, terribly wrong. She was right all along, and a real hero in my book. It won't be forgotten."

"She loved Brian very much."

He nodded. "I know she did, and Brian loved her. He stuck up for her when I was doing my best to tear her down."

"I hope you won't hate all Japanese, Admiral."

He slowly shook his head. "No, not any more. Just the ones flying those planes with the red meatballs on them." He leaned toward her. "Is there anything I can do for you?"

Gwen shook her head. "No, I'll be all right. I've been reassigned to Pearl Harbor for an indefinite period of time. Admiral Kimmel cleared it just this morning."

"That's good. We're going to need you here."

Gwen nodded. "That's what my home office in San Francisco thought too."

"Well, girl, you hang tight here and give us the benefit of your considerable knowledge. We need you and more like you." He motioned toward the hall. "I'm off to see Kimmel myself. We've got to draw up a defense with what we have left. We can just thank God the *Lexington* and *Enterprise* weren't at Pearl yesterday morning. They're here today, but they're making sail this morning."

They watched Picard walk down the hall in the direction of Kimmel's office. There was still navy pride in the way he walked, but there had been something very different in his eyes. He was a sadder but wiser man.

Gwen and Sam walked out the door and down the steps. The air was filled with the smell of burning oil. It hung like a cloud and left a sooty film on the skin that felt greasy to the touch.

"I'm parked over at the visitors' lot," Sam said. "I didn't know you were staying here in Hawaii."

Gwen nodded. "There's more to be done here now."

Sam had a faint smile on his face. "I think you can count on seeing me again then, maybe soon. The paper wants war correspondents and I think I'm elected."

"Sounds like something up your alley."

He nodded. "I think so. They may have me operating here out of Pearl Harbor for a while. This is where the war is. I have an idea"—his smile brightened—"maybe it's a wild one and off the wall as far as you're concerned."

"What's that?"

He pointed to her. "Well, you're a squash player." He moved his hand, tapping his chest. "And I'm a squash player. We're both unattached. Do you think we could get together and play steady?"

"I don't see why not."

"Great." He turned and started to walk away but then stopped and moved back in her direction. "You know Gwen, actually I'd like to have more than an occasional game of squash with you. I'd like to date you, get to know you. Who knows, you might actually get to like me."

"I already do like you, Sam."

"You do?" His lips arched into a broad grin. "Well, then, you never know where liking is going to go. I could even get to calling you Gwen, real steady-like."

"It'll be something to work on."

ALSO AVAILABLE FROM THE MYSTERIES IN TIME SERIES:

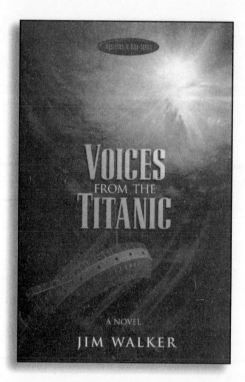